COMES THE WAR WIZARDS' WRATH

The Fabled Quest Chronicles

Book Three

AUSTIN DRAGON

Published by Well-Tailored Books, California

Comes the War Wizards' Wrath
(Fabled Quest Chronicles, Book 3)

978-1-946590-83-1 (paperback)
978-1-946590-01-5 (ebook)

http://www.austindragon.com

Book cover design by Humbert Glaffo

Printed in the United States of America

CONTENTS

Chapter One 2

Chapter Two 42

Chapter Three 60

Chapter Four 68

Chapter Five 74

Chapter Six 96

Chapter Seven 111

Chapter Eight 118

Chapter Nine 132

Chapter Ten 155

Chapter Eleven 158

Chapter Twelve 169

Chapter Thirteen 203

Chapter Fourteen 214

Chapter Fifteen 237

Chapter Sixteen 270

Chapter Seventeen 278

Chapter Eighteen 292

Chapter Nineteen 318

Chapter Twenty 329

FÄE-LAND MAJOR

*The Lands of Elves, Hoofed Fae,
and Goblins*

CHAPTER ONE
Centaur City

"We will return no later than tomorrow," their caravan master had told them.

His dog transformed into some strange muscle-bound flying horse. Traveler took Lady Aylen, Gwyness, and two of the faun warriors with him, all flying away into the night sky. Before they had left, Traveler had the women fetch their personal weapons from their tent. Lady Aylen had her two war tridents, and Gwyness had two long slender war hammers.

No one in the leadership was happy, but there was nothing to be done. They would set out at dawn without their caravan master—the only one in the party, human or fae, who knew the full path through Titan's Trail to Atlantea.

No one would sleep through the night except the giants. The six Antaean warriors settled into their camp after the sun fell and were asleep shortly after as they did every night. When giants were not in battle, they liked to eat and they liked to sleep. For the humans of the camp, they preferred to gossip around their campfires, and the fae sat around them to listen.

Outside the royal tent, Hobbs sat with King Aereth at the campfire. They had dismissed the female half-elves who sat in the women's tent playing fae card games. The females were also unable to sleep.

"We have half the camp telling stories, the other half standing guard, Mr. Hobbs," the king said, as the men drank hot spiced tea—Tyfer's specialty. They had already eaten, though it was a small meal.

"Yes, sire, and none of them will sleep the night."

"What is the mood of the men?"

"Before it was fear, sire, but as the stories get more fanciful and grotesque through the night, that fear will lessen. They will talk their fears away until something reminds them of it again."

"Hopefully nothing will, and we can set out at dawn without incident. I know our master-at-arms is anxious to move on."

"Yes, sire, all the men are. What do you think about the Four Kings still being alive? You have a history with them longer than any of us."

"I do, Mr. Hobbs. My emotions run very dark when it comes to them. We have a quest to fulfill, and we must resist all outside forces in our way, including them."

"Forced ignorance, sire?"

"We have no choice, Mr. Hobbs, unless our caravan sorceress can devise a way to deal with them from afar."

"Oh my goodness." Hobbs had a pained expression on his face, and the king looked too.

At the perimeter were a half dozen darkling sentries. The fae shape-shifters had turned into halfling black minotaurs with wide sparkling human grins.

"Those creatures worry me, sire, but I will have to have faith in Mr. Traveler's faith in them."

"I am beginning to understand their behavior." The king gestured to them, and the black fae ran to the men.

"Yes, king?" one asked in a hoarse voice.

"Outside the circle, is there anyone or thing near us?"

"Oh, yes, king. There are many, many fae watching us closely."

"What fae?" Hobbs asked with concern.

"We are in the land of satyrs and centaurs. There are many, many satyrs and centaurs watching us closely."

Hobbs looked out past the perimeter of the camp. "I did not hear any of the men, including our half-elves, say they noticed anything."

"If our half-elves were night or moon elves, they would. But other fae see them in the distance, hiding in the grass, hiding behind the trees. Shadow satyrs and night centaurs."

"What is a shadow satyr or night centaur?" Hobbs asked.

The darkling burst our laughing. "We lie," one said. "There are no shadows or night in satyrs and centaurs. They are day-walkers like all the fae of these lands."

"Not, night-walkers like you?" King Aereth asked.

"Not like us, king. But, king, there are many, many of them watching us."

"Should we be concerned?" King Aereth asked.

"Will we leave at dawn, king?"

"Yes."

"Then, there is no need for concern, king."

Traveler's dog had flown them out long before the sun had set and landed in a forest clearing. The many fae villages of the Centaurian Fields were a few miles ahead of them at the foot of a series of green hills. His dog transformed from the muscle-bound flying horse creature to a ten-foot faun with the head of an owl. The two fauns found its new form amusing. Traveler led them all with Lady Aylen and Gwyness at his sides.

"We must find lodgings first, then we can set out for Centaur City first thing at dawn," Traveler informed them.

"They will not let us remain in their towns," one of the fauns said.

"Why? Two fauns under the chieftain of Faunus, their faun beast, an elf, and two servants. Why would they not?"

The fauns laughed. "You are crafty, human," the faun replied. "However, your tricks will not work in Centaur City. They will not let any of us in, fae or human."

"We will not need lodging there. We will find out who is in authority, and I will tell them of my sightings, and then we will be gone."

"You make it sound much easier than it will be," the faun said.

"That is why we go tomorrow, rather than today. I am sure it will take us the day to find the right clans."

"Are centaurs dangerous, Mr. Traveler?" Lady Aylen asked.

"Not dangerous. They simply do not like to mix with others, other than hoofed fae—fauns, satyrs, centaurs, and leshy."

"Leshy? The Tree Shepherds you mean, Mr. Traveler?" Gwyness asked.

"Yes."

"These fae villages ahead are fauns only. Where is this Faunus?" Lady Aylen asked.

"Our kingdom is on the other end of the Fields," a faun replied. "Our largest cities are there. Here, small towns are spread far and wide."

"Mr. Traveler, this creature that your dog has taken the form of...?" Gwyness began to ask.

"It is a faun creature that does exist. There are many kinds of hoofed fae and many kinds of faun and satyr-like creatures."

"I still do not know the difference between the two, Mr. Traveler," Lady Aylen said.

"Tomorrow you will."

Traveler's eyes were fixed ahead. They could see fauns standing, waiting for them.

"We will speak with them," one of their fauns said as he took the lead of their group. "We are of the clan of Ammon. I am Zan, and this is Vanus."

"I am Chat of these humble faun towns of Centaurian Fields," one of the approaching fauns said. "We know of your party. Why do you venture off Titan's Trail to our homes."

"We are not here to trouble you," Zan said. "We wish lodgings for the night. Then we move at dawn to Centaur City."

"Why? Why do you go to Centaur City?" another faun asked. He had a stern frown on his face and stared at Traveler then the women.

"We have news of an urgent nature," Zan replied. "We will seek an audience with them."

"Have you seen a group of humans anytime today?" Traveler asked.

They watched him for a moment. More joined, and now almost a dozen of the fauns stared at him. Their appearance was very similar to Zan and Vanus, but they wore no green waist-length robes, instead they were bare chested and hairy.

"You are the only two we have seen in years," one of the fauns finally answered.

"Zan and Vanus can share with you the news. It relates to the stampede of centaurs and the possessed state of the herd of minotaurs who chased them. We simply wish for all of Centaur City to know of our suspicions, then we will return to the Trail."

"That is all?"

"That is all," Traveler responded.

"What of the elf?" the faun asked.

"What of the elf?" Lady Aylen asked with indignance.

"If fauns were in your lands, you would ask the same thing," the faun said.

Traveler touched the princess's forearm to calm her. He turned to the fauns. "This short detour is my doing, no one else's. The centaurs are your allies. Will you help us?"

"Chief Ammon agrees with the human," Zan added.

The receiving party of fauns led them into their general towns. The closer they neared, the larger they could see the population was. Small wooden huts spread across the fields with fauns of all ages, including elderly fauns with whitening hair and children no taller than the fairy sisters in their caravan. At first, they thought there were only men but then noticed female faces peeking at them from within the hut homes.

They were led to two adjoining huts.

"I hope this is not an inconvenience to your villages," Traveler said.

"No inconvenience," Zan answered for the other fauns. "This is our way. We make lodging available to guests. The women will have their own hut. We will sleep in the other."

"What of your faun beast?" Chat asked. "We know it is a shape-shifter."

The dog changed into its grayish wolf-dog form.

"Is this better?" Traveler asked.

"He will be sleeping in your hut, so it matters not to us."

"What is your dog's true form, Mr. Traveler?" Lady Aylen asked.

Traveler turned to her and said, "One that is beyond our comprehension, so let us just say this is his form."

"My people will bring you food," Chat said. "You can stay in you huts to eat."

"Or," Traveler began, "we can join your village for its night meal, and I can pay for your hospitality with a story."

"Story?" Chat asked with a raised eyebrow.

The fauns watched him suspiciously, but they had already noticed the faun children gathering around them with wide eyes.

"It will be about the flying fauns of Zhava I met on my travels through Faë-Land."

"Flying fauns?" faun children asked.

"And since fauns love the sound of the flute, I can tell the tale with the music accompaniment of Zan and Vanus, here."

"How do you know we can play the flute?" Zan asked.

"Fauns can play music. Elves can shoot arrows. Shape-shifters can shift. I can tell stories." He winked at the faun children.

The adult fauns laughed. Chat's face softened, too, then laughed. He pointed at Traveler, "We know about you. The giants in Khury told the fairies, and they told us. You are really a pixy in human's skin. But, we will hear your story."

The faun children applauded.

The women wondered if that is how Traveler endeared himself to so many fae when he first traveled through the magical lands as a boy. Their caravan master literally had every faun in the towns riveted to his storytelling as they sat around a roaring bonfire. Faun children sat closest to him, a few sat on his lap, and one faun-ling was small enough to sit on his shoulder and hold on. All the adult fauns sat around, joined by female fauns wearing grass-woven tops.

Traveler told his great story of the flying fauns of Zhava as meals were served before the setting of the sun and was still telling it long after the moon rose high in the night. Faun children fought to stay awake. All the fauns, including Zan and Vanus, took to their cloven feet to applaud when he was done.

Smiling fauns escorted them to their huts for the night.

"As entertaining as that was, Mr. Traveler, how much of that story was actually true?" Lady Aylen asked.

"I am not sure, princess. I was told all of it was true."

"You were told? But you were the protagonist of the story, Mr. Traveler."

"Yes. I was told that all of it was true."

The fauns laughed.

"Ladies, get your sleep. We leave at dawn. Unfortunately, do not expect as gracious an encounter with the centaurs as we have had with our faun friends here."

Hobbs made his morning rounds through the camp. Most men, by now, got up before dawn, but there were always a few, at bliss within their giant-slippers, that needed help waking up.

"Get up, man!" Hobbs yelled as he turned over one giant-slipper and dumped covers and man onto the ground.

Their weaponsmaster and forge, Mr. Estus, had gotten up even before Mr. Hobbs. He and his men were busy fitting the caravan's giant lizards—two thousand of them—with their new armor.

"Mr. Estus, I can assign some men to assist yours," Hobbs said when he saw him.

"Oh, no, Mr. Hobbs. My men and the lizard minders are all that I need. We will have our reptiles ready to march at set-out time."

"Are they still growing?"

"No, this is their size."

Hobbs stepped back to take in the full view of the particular yellow lizard Estus and his men were strapping new armor on.

"It must be over fifteen feet long, not including the tail."

"Thereabouts, Mr. Hobbs. As long as two large horses. With the tail more than twenty feet."

"Amazing."

"Large enough for a man or two to ride, but that is not their purpose. As Mr. Traveler, told us, they are to be our living wall at our flanks."

"The new armor you're placing on them is…"

Estus smiled. "I have forged them as a woodland fae would. Plenty of crevices, bumps, and buckles. I will have the pech apply fae mud to them, then we will grow our own plant life on them."

"For the swarms?"

"Yes, indeed. Our giant lizards will be even more formidable with our fairy insect swarms."

Both men noticed King Aereth near them, smiling.

"Impressive work, Mr. Estus."

"Thank you, sire."

"Did you get any sleep at all?"

"Some, sire. But this needed completing if we wanted to leave at dawn. I can always take a nap in my pocket-realm if I cannot stay awake on the Trail."

"Hopefully, this will meet with the approval of our two fairies," King Aereth said.

"Oh, it will, sire. I had the Tree Shepherds look over the very first one."

"Well, Mr. Estus, I will leave you to it," Hobbs said. "Sire, I will have the men ready to go soon."

"Oh, very good."

King Aereth noticed the leaders from all the fae parties of the full caravan gathering off to the side. When they were satisfied that the caravan would be starting out, they disappeared back to their camps. He returned to his royal tent again, which was being broken down by some of the men. His guardsman, with his reptile-wolf hybrids and the female half-elves, stood waiting and ready.

"What is that?" The king noticed one of the female half-elves cuddling a small owl-faced creature.

"It is a baby owl griffin, sire. One of the fae parties said I could have it."

"How large will it grow?"

"No larger than this, sire. They are very able guardians."

"I take it there are many types of griffins."

"Yes, sire. Many hybrids."

"Beautiful beasts, the griffin. Though, our caravan does not have especially fond memories of the ones we last encountered because of their masters at the time. But not their fault."

"No, sire. They are loyal to their masters."

"When we set out, I would like to ask you about elves."

The female half-elves looked at each other nervously.

"Oh, do not be concerned. I have read Mr. Traveler's book of elfin protocol and customs, but I had other questions not answered in the book."

"I do not think we would be a good source for you, sire. We are only half-elves, and we were raised by a human."

"But among elves."

"Yes, sire, but we had little contact with them. Our master did, but not us."

"May I ask what the difficulty is with the elves towards you and your colleagues?"

"They hate us, sire."

"That cannot be true."

"It is, sire. Those of like mind consider us lower than humans, and they consider humans lower than insects and goblins."

There was sadness in the king's eyes. "I apologize for causing you any discomfort. I will not trouble you about it further. However, do know that we value your presence within the caravan."

"Thank you, sire. We are honored to be among you and part of this caravan."

◆ ◆ ◆

Hobbs stood tall with pride, gazing out across humans, sprites, giants, fantastical beasts of land and air, crawling trees, and even the pair of fairies—Titan's Caravan. It was beyond anything he could have imagined those months ago in that Hopeshire tavern in Avalonia, in the Lands of Man, when he became the first man Traveler hired to set out on the year-long trek to the legendary kingdom of Atlantea.

They marched in four columns. The outside flanks were the lizards minders and their giant lizards. Both men and reptile, thanks the the efficient work of Estus and his team, were fully armored. The two center columns were made up of not just humans—each equipped with golden and silver fae polearms—but also the pech—the brawny, big-nosed sprite halflings with wild eyebrows, who carried a large spiked dwarvin shields on their arm facing the flank and, in their other hand, any elfin weapon of choice. Also, toward the front of the center columns were the human domestics, servants, and laborers, with their pull carts. One of the crawling trees was at the center, with all the hoofed fae, archers, and servants following. The other two crawling trees were at each end. In the rear, were all the Cut-Throat warriors and their chamroshes, flanked by an Antaean giant each. Mingling through the columns were the roving team of male half-elf fighters.

Pangolin, I-wulf, Hobbs, and King Aereth quickly convened one last time.

"I do hope Mr. Traveler returns," Pangolin said.

"Yes, but we will continue as instructed. He said he would join us today on the Trail," King Aereth said. "We must proceed."

"The giants said it is a straight path," Pangolin said. "The terrain is flat, so we can take comfort in that for now."

"Have you seen the lizards?" I-wulf asked. "They are battle ready."

"Let us hope we do not have any battles," Pangolin said.

The caravan marched.

The formation remained the same. The vanguard leading consisted of Pangolin, Elman the half-elf, four of the giants, and two dozen of the elaphine archer-warriors. Following several yards behind them, at the front of the columns, were King Aereth, with his royal guardsman Nirgund the berserker, and the reptilian fae-hounds, and the female half-elf royal guards. Hobbs walked with young Quillen, followed by the two bodyguards, Tyfer and Oeric. Walking directly behind them were six men carrying the new flags flying high of Titan's Caravan—poles twelve feet high and the white flags featured an iconic representation of the Titan, the Maker of All Mountains, and seven points of light to represent the seven points along Titan's Trail. The Brothers Brimm played harp-like psalteries throughout the main caravan as it marched.

All the other fae parties followed. The drows, the animal men, the fae human berserker warriors, with their pack of owl griffins, the wild woodland elves, carrying red spears twice their size, gnomes wearing purple conical caps, ram-horned gnomoids—spearmen, archers, and axemen. Smaller parties of humanoid animal men followed them: frog men, lizard men, squirrel-like men, fae that looked like raccoons, possums, foxes, rabbits, birds and mice. They came with their own steeds and guard animals: giant crabs minded by the frog men, giant turtles ridden by the possum men, giant porcupines used as guard animals by the raccoon men. Some of the bird men had large jackalopes (rabbits with antlers) as hounds. Other bird men had enfields (animals with the head of a fox, forelegs of an eagle, and the hindquarters and tail of a wolf). There were also giant ducks and cranes and one surly mole-like fae who had a giant carnivorous moose as his companion. Lastly were Ammon and his faun clans.

"When you touch the earth, in the manner I saw, when you defended against the stampedes, nothing can move you?" Pangolin asked the giants.

"Nothing in this world, unless that force could move the very world itself," one of the giants replied.

"You must be the most powerful giants of them all," Pangolin said.

"That distinction belongs to others. There are many races among giants. We like to think of ourselves as the wisest of them all."

"Will we meet other giants along the Trail?"

"It is very likely. It is common among the fae to hire giants."

"Tell us, Pangolin, what is the name of your home and your clan?" another giant asked.

"We humans use other words, but it means the same. I am of my father Fundisa's clan, and my home is Titusland in the empire lands of Gondwana, but I spent half my life in the empire of Laurasia."

"What lies ahead of us?" Pangolin asked.

"We will pass what is called the Ghost City."

"I thought apparitions bedeviled human lands and not yours."

"It is simply its name. There are no ghosts. It is an ancient city of ruins. No one lives there, but creatures have been known to use it as a temporary resting place. We will pass it on the Trail. The main city we march to is the elfin city of Fae'el. It is a wretched place."

"Why is that?" Pangolin asked. "It is an elfin city."

"Not the elves you think of. The real elfin kingdoms you imagine are nowhere near Titan's Trail. This elfin city was built on the Trail to cater to travelers; it is not a real elfin city and there are many more races there than just elves."

"Better or worse than Arion's Spear?"

"The same, only larger and more elves. We will be seeing more elves as we continue on."

"And more sorcerers," Elman added.

"Yes," the giant said. "Many more of those, too, and often not the friendly kind."

"Then to this Titan's Arch?" Pangolin asked.

"Yes, the threshold to the Giant Forest."

"The Great Forest?" Pangolin asked.

"The same thing."

◆◆◆

As King Aereth walked, his mind thought of the three not with them, but there was nothing to do but wait.

"King Aereth."

He turned to see the fae-blood woman nearing him.

"Maiden Ursi, is it?"

"Yes, king, it is."

"May I speak frankly?"

"By all means."

"When Master Traveler returns, can you command him not to leave the caravan again?"

"I could, but it would be pointless."

"Master Traveler is not expendable, king. All of us are, but not him."

"An interesting thing to say."

"But nevertheless true."

"You took a particular interest in this matter of the centaur stampede and the minotaurs. What did Mr. Traveler mean when he said he is tired of all this secrecy among the fae?"

"He knows there are things we cannot speak of. His annoyance is understandable. I believe his choice to be a mistake. The centaurs are not a people to disobey if they tell you to leave matters alone."

"And he will. I have no doubt Mr. Traveler will do as he said and no more. He has done much to prepare our caravan and protect it. He is as eager to get to Atlantea as we are."

"And I do not mean to suggest otherwise. It is simply that we all have our own nature that can sometimes make us dangerous to ourselves."

The king laughed. "Mr. Traveler, dangerous to himself? He is compassionate, but as has already been personally observed, he can be ruthless when it comes to protecting the people of this caravan."

"Yes, that is true. I would simply ask that we all do our best to stay together as a group. We are strongest when we stay together."

"That I could not agree with more. Do you know something that we should, as to the path ahead?"

"Only rumors, king. We will soon enter the lands of the elves."

"I heard you do not like elves."

"My people do not mix with them. But that is not my chief concern. The farther we move along the Trail, the more sorcerers we will encounter."

"Do you fear we will encounter another spell-talker?"

"I fear, king, that we will encounter any number of sorcerers who do not need to be a spell-talker to kill us."

"I agree with that as well. We must listen to Mr. Traveler's edict and stay within the circle."

"Yes, king. We must."

"The clouds are darkening in the distance. Does it rain in these lands? I hope we are not about to experience another 'death rain,' as pleasant as it was to behold live mermaids."

"Mr. Pangolin," Elman called out.

Pangolin turned and stopped in place. He raised his hand for the caravan to stop, but it already had. "What is that?"

Far in the distance was a large black cloud.

"Is that a storm cloud?" he asked. "I have never one move so fast." He looked up at the giants.

They shook their heads. "Mr. Pangolin, that is not a cloud. Look again."

The master-at-arms put his own telescope to his eye and immediately removed it in shock. "That's impossible."

The entire caravan started panicking.

King Aereth's face also grew pale. Hobbs looked at him for instruction. "The pocket, sire?"

Dr'amal, the drow sorceress, appeared near them. "No, we cannot go into the pocket-realm."

"Why?" King Aereth asked.

"The beast may pick up the entire land around it and carry us to its nest. We would emerge into the mouths of dozens of them. They do have their own land. We do not want to be in those lands, king."

"What do we do, then?"

"Get everyone on the ground. Oh no!" the drowess raised her hands and turned the white flags of the caravan to black with a spell. "We must all lie on the ground and remain still. Hopefully, it will leave us be."

King Aereth nodded, and Hobbs ran to the men. The king glanced to the vanguard, which was already prone on the ground. In moments, every human and fae was silently lying on the ground, watching and praying.

From where he lay, Pangolin asked the giants, "My people have heard of the creature, but never did we hear they could grow so large. They are supposed to be large enough to grab an elephant from the earth. That creature can grab an entire city with its claws."

The roc slowly drew nearer from the distance. The mammoth bird creature was so large in the sky that it still looked like a black cloud that was alive. But they could see its beak and talons hanging. Its wings seemed short for its size and, at the moment, glided its mass not directly to them, thankfully, but to pass many miles to the side.

The beast flapped its wings. In less than a minute, the wind that passed over them was like a hurricane. All three of the crawling trees gripped the earth to keep from being blown over. In fact, some of the men's helmets flew off, and some of the carts were blown back before others quickly grabbed them.

"What do we do if it attacks?" Pangolin asked the giants.

"We cannot stop such a creature," one of the elaphines answered, with a wild and frightened look.

"He is correct," Grakdar the giant added. "If it can rip a city from the earth, what can we do? None of our weapons would do any damage to it, and the beast is impervious to most magic."

"Not even magic?" Pangolin asked with surprise.

"No."

The roc glided past them, and everyone held their breath. The flying beast cast an immense shadow but moved past and slowly flew off.

"No!" Dr'amal called out to men who began to stand, including Pangolin. "We are not free yet! Remain on the ground!"

When the roc was a dot in the sky, it turned suddenly, circled, and flew back towards them! Gasps rang out through the caravan.

"Silence!" Dr'amal yelled. "Remain quiet and where you are! The Tree Shepherds and I are casting our spells to confuse its sight. I do not believe it is after us but another quarry. We should be able to escape from this unharmed!"

Pangolin looked at the giants. "If it attacks us, can you stop it?"

"No, Pangolin," another giant said. "As Antaeans, our power with the earth can keep us from being snatched into the sky, but that hardly prevents that fate from befalling any of you. Even if all four of us, here, could strike it with all our might, it would be the same as striking another Antaean in touch with the earth—nothing. There are some giants who could fight it with their bare hands, but we are not one of those giant races."

"Not even a fairy-storm can do anything to that beast," Grakdar said.

Pangolin was angry. "We are trapped under a beast that not even the fairies could defeat. I am not accustomed to hiding from an enemy. All we can do is hide here like children?"

"Yes, Pangolin, that is all there is to do."

"If only Mr. Traveler were here. His dog could at least transform into another roc."

"Yes, a roc could fend off another roc, but Mr. Traveler is not here, and neither is his dog."

Traveler and the others had left the faun villages at dawn as planned. Fauns walked with them for a few miles, and many of the faun children were sad to see Traveler go. With final goodbyes, they waved them on to return to the faun villages as their party continued on.

"Well, Mr. Traveler," Lady Aylen said as they marched. "You are quite the popular one with the faun children."

They walked in the same formation as before. Traveler leading, one of the women on either side, the two fauns following, and the dog in the form of a giant owl-headed faun creature in the rear.

"I am starting to understand your methods, Mr. Traveler. Fae love stories, and you have endless stories from your travels."

"I am simply building good will among people, princess. Faë-Land is no different than the Lands of Man. You can never have too many friends and allies."

Traveler glanced at her but noticed her two war tridents strapped to her back.

"What is it, Mr. Traveler?" she asked.

"Can I see one of your tridents, princess?"

She pulled one of the weapons from her back and handed it to him. He studied it closely.

"I hadn't noticed this before." He looked back at the fauns. "Are you able to see any markings or inscriptions on this weapon?"

"Yes, very faint to the eye," Zan replied.

"I think that is how they did it," Traveler said, "how the fairies knew of you and Maiden Gwyness. They simply saw the markings on your weapon." He handed it back to the princess. "Let me see your weapons," he said to Gwyness.

Gwyness had her dual slim war hammers under her cloak. The inscriptions on her weapons were barely perceptible to the human eye but clear in the silver metal.

Traveler handed it back to Gwyness. "We need to have them translated."

"Can you read them, Mr. Traveler?" Gwyness asked.

"I cannot make out the words on Lady Aylen's, but yours looks to be elfish but a very ancient tongue. Yes, we need to have them translated along the way."

"Another detour, Mr. Traveler?" Lady Aylen asked in an annoyed tone.

"Along the way, princess. And it is for your benefit, not mine. The fairies said you both were of magic."

"Me?" Gwyness asked.

"Yes, you, which does make sense."

"How so?" Lady Aylen asked.

"Princess, why would your people have a human as an attendant with no power at all? If it were just about her amulet, it would be more intelligent to give it to you or have another elf as your attendant."

Gwyness thought for a moment. "Yes, that makes sense."

"However, we can talk more about this later. It is very important for us to complete our task and return to our caravan as quickly as possible."

"I do hope these centaurs appreciate the lengths you are going to on their behalf," Lady Aylen said.

"Whether they do or not is not why I am doing it. I inform them of the danger and we leave immediately. Ladies, I do have to caution you again. Many of the centaurs, and the satyrs, we meet in Centaur City will come across as very...savage. Do not pay any attention to them and show no fear. Lady Aylen, you are an elf. Carry yourself as such. Maiden Gwyness, think of yourself as a warrioress, which I do believe you are, whether you know or accept it yourself. Exude confidence."

"Master Traveler is correct," Zan the faun interjected. "They can smell fear. We do not want them to think we are afraid of them."

The lands of the hoofed fae were of open golden grass fields and pockets of luscious green woods. Long before they saw the city of centaurs, they heard the blowing of ram horns. The fauns told them it was its own language: administrators of the vast city communicating to others about any number of matters, some official, some mundane.

"Centaur City will send its own receiving party," Zan began to say. "Oh, here they are. Our cousins, the satyrs."

"Friendly cousins?" Traveler asked.

"We consider them brutish and overly violent. They consider us aloof and soft. But, yes, we are friendly cousins. The kind who see each other and smile at each other in public but avoid each other whenever possible and curse each other from behind closed doors."

The two fauns removed their green waist-long robes to reveal the brown leather vests they wore underneath. They tied their robes into a sashes and draped it over their shoulders.

"It's best if we look less civilized here," Zan explained.

Ammon's fauns were shorter than an average man, but the satyrs that approached were taller than the average man. They had the same goat horns sprouting above their eyes, pointed ears, legs of a goat, and cloven hooves. They also differed in that their complexion was darker, their eyes were more feral looking, and their build was much thicker. The satyrs' faces were thick with unkempt mustaches and beards. They were all armed with tall spears.

"Ah, our peace-loving cousins visit us," one said.

"Good day, my war-mongering cousin," Zan greeted.

The satyrs laughed.

"Who do you have here, cousin?" the satyr asked.

"This is Traveler, the human male, Gwyness, the human female, and Aylen, the elfess."

"Very good, cousin. You introduce the humans before the elf, so you have not become completely domesticated by the elves and sprites yet. The human female is of interest. The other two you can take with you and return from whence you came."

"I wish an audience with your centaur king," Traveler spoke.

"The human talks. Why, human? He is not expecting any human visitors, nor is any in Centaur City. You are not welcome."

Traveler stepped an inch from the satyrs face. All the satyrs stood tall, bracing their spears.

"I wish an audience with the centaur king. It is for your benefit and the centaur people, not mine or any other human, elf, or sprite. Do you wish me to convey my news that may be related the minotaur fiend-possession or not? Both the fauns and the elves told me not to make this trip. I was the one who did not heed them. I am happy to do so now, keep the information to myself, and be gone. If satyrs or centaurs are killed, it will be on your head."

The satyr glared at him then looked at his comrades.

"You are a brave human. We know who you are. The human who cuts elves in half and travels with a shape-shifter, who I see can take the form of owl fauns too."

"Owl satyrs," Zan corrected.

The satyrs laughed again. "Follow us, human. Have you been here before?"

"I have," Traveler replied.

"Then I need not tell you how to behave."

The satyrs led them over the ridge. There stood Centaur City. The main city was a walled encampment encircling a series of towers. A bustling market covered every inch around the wall. There was nothing remarkable about the structure itself, other than its enormous size and vastness—and the people.

The satyr welcoming party led them to the city, but an even larger party approached them—a party that included several giant satyrs, which were even more hulking in form, some ten to twelve feet tall. Unlike the other satyrs, they had fanged teeth and their eyes had a look of much more animalistic wildness. Other satyrs bore spears; the super satyrs carried battle axes.

Lady Aylen noticed that there were other faun creatures. She saw both owl fauns and eagle fauns in the distance watching them. They were all of different species, with the colors of brown, whites, greens, and gold.

They saw their first centaur of Centaur City—one with large bull horns sprouting from his head. Otherwise, it was as Lady Aylen and Gwyness had seen before—a race of fae with the upper body of a human and the lower body and legs of a horse.

"What manner of centaur is he?" Lady Aylen asked in a whisper.

"I am a cyprean," the centaur answered aloud. "Typical for an elf. I know every species of your race, but you know not of my race."

"She meant no disrespect," Traveler said to him. "She was raised in the lands of humans. They do not know there are many kinds of centaurs, only the ones that look most human, from their stories."

"You have been here?" the cyprean centaur asked.

"Yes, I have, years ago."

"What do you want?" the cyprean centaur asked.

"To speak with your king on a matter of extreme importance to all centaurs and satyrs."

"What would that be?"

"The minotaur ghoul attack on your centaur people."

"Minotaur ghouls says the human," the centaurs yelled to the growing crowds of satyrs and centaurs. There were howls of laughter.

"What is funny?" Traveler asked.

"Ghoul is a human term. There are no such creatures in our magical lands. The minotaurs were rabid is all, diseased."

"Why are you lying?"

Every satyr and centaur quieted. The cyprean centaur trotted to him and almost pushed him over. The owl-faun "dog" jumped to Traveler's side and started to grow in height. In moments it was some fifteen feet tall as its clawed hands grew more menacing.

"Calm your animal," the cyprean said.

Traveler put a hand on his animal; it stopped growing.

"Maybe I should go now. I came here to inform you of danger, but if you repeat things that are lies, then there is no point. I know what the state of the minotaurs was because I was there. We all were. We fought them. I sliced more than one of them to pieces, and each piece continued to move on its own. That is not disease! That is a fiend! To use the fae term. If my animal had not turned to a phoenix and burnt the minotaur fiends to dust, we would still be fighting them, or their pieces. Do you know who else was there? Who is Hycor?"

"Hycor? He was there?"

"He and his centaur warriors."

"Where is Hycor?" the cyprean asked. Multiple voices rang out in the crowd that the centaur was not present.

"Is this true?" the cyprean centaur asked the fauns.

"It is true," Zan replied. "We fired arrows into the minotaurs, too, and the beasts continued their charge. It was as the human said. Hycor spoke directly to our own faun chief, Ammon."

"Spoke to you? You spoke to Hycor directly?"

"Yes," Zan answered.

The cyprean frowned. "Follow me!"

They followed the cyprean centaur with other centaurs and satyrs towards the city. As they passed, angry centaurs and satyrs glared at them. Lady Aylen and Gwyness noticed that some of the centaurs were not horse-like, but some were smaller and deer-like.

"Is it me, or is it you and Gwyness?" Lady Aylen asked.

"All three of us, princess," Traveler answered. "They view our presence as an intrusion."

At the entrance gates stood different centaurs. They were eight foot tall, with golden armor, helmets, longbows—that clearly could also be used as spears to impale—and arrows in the quivers on their backs. The centaurs were part hippogriff—forelegs of a giant eagle and hind half of a horse.

"Who are they?" a hippogriff centaur asked.

"The humans, elf, and fauns have information for our king," the cyprean centaur said.

There was a commotion behind them, and everyone turned to see a large party of six-foot centaurs galloping towards the main entrance. There were cyprean bull centaurs, stag centaurs with large antlers sprouting from their heads, and many more standard centaurs.

They surrounded Traveler and his party.

"Who are these trespassers?" the lead stag centaur asked.

Traveler ignored him and looked at the hippogriff centaurs. "Will I be allowed to speak with your king or not? Obviously, our presence is upsetting the city."

"Yes it is!"

The voice came from above them all at the top of the wall. Only Lady Aylen could see the male centaur clearly with others around him, including a few female centaurs. They disappeared, and the sound of hooves running down cobble steps and the flapping of wings echoed down.

The centaur king appeared from the main entrance of the city. He was a winged centaur! He was unlike any of the other centaurs of the city. His facial hair was well-groomed. His helmet was also a crown. His upper torso was clothed with white leather. He carried a gold shield in one hand and three spears in his other. Flanking him on one side was a unicorn centauress with dark features but a single ivory-like horn pointing upwards from her forehead. The other centauress was a hippogriff centaur. All around them were centaurs with bows at the ready with an arrow each.

"We are visited by human and elfin agents," the centaur king said. "If it were not for the fauns, and our alliance with the fauns, you would have been shot down in a rain of arrows the moment your feet touched the territory of Centaur City."

"So it is King Pegataur," Traveler said.

The centauresses looked at him with surprise.

"He is an agent," the hippogriff centauress said. "Kill them now."

Pegataur smiled. "No," he said to her with a smile. "I remember your smell, too, human. There is much more of you to smell now that you have grown. All the more reason for you to say what you wish to say so you can be gone from our lands."

"King Pegataur, there is no need to treat us like this," Zan spoke.

"Silence!" the centaur king's voice echoed throughout the entire city. "You, faun, will speak when spoken to," he said in a normal tone. "I tolerate you because of our alliance but no more. Again, human, speak your words and go."

Traveler sighed. "Yesterday, the day after the minotaur attack on your people, my party came across a group of humans. There were seventeen of them in all. I spoke to them, but their behavior was strange. They acknowledged my movements, mimicked me, as they moved past on foot. It was clear they did not understand my words but only pretended to. I believe strongly they were lycanthropes. I do not know what kind. They were headed in this direction. In light of the minotaur attack, I thought it essential for your city to be informed."

"Why? You are not centaur or satyr, faun or any other kind of hoofed fae."

"I said what I came to say."

"Yes, you did, human."

"I did not like you when you weren't the king of Centaur City. I do not like you now. But since you feel the same about humans, nothing is lost on either of us."

"Yes, that is true, human. Is there any other acts of kindness you wish to unburden your human soul of?"

"No."

"Good. Then you can leave our lands. I hear you guide a caravan through the Trail. Maybe you should return to them as soon as you can. They could use the services of your shape-shifter."

"Why?" Traveler asked. "What has happened?"

"Return and see for yourself."

Traveler's expression was more of a sneer. He turned from the them. "We leave," he said to his party.

The caravan master led them through the crowds of satyrs and centaurs grudgingly making a path for them.

"You were right, princess," Traveler huffed. "You were all right. I should never have done this."

"No, Mr. Traveler," Lady Aylen said, "you were right. Their behavior was atrocious, but you did exactly what you set out to do.

They know, and I have no doubt they will make use of the information."

"But why are they acting this way, Mr. Traveler?" Gwyness asked. "You came to help them."

"It is not simply because we are humans and elves. It is because we lead a human caravan through the magical lands, which they view as an affront to all the fae empires. Whether Kings' Caravan, ours, or any other human caravan. Also, from my memory of King Pegataur, he has personal loathing for any fae that ally with humans, or any fae alliances at all."

"Nothing like the stories of the centaurs we grew up with," Lady Aylen said.

"I remember him so clearly because, when I first saw him, I never knew there were flying centaurs. I was not unlike our own Mr. Quillen. I ran to him and wanted to know all about his kind. As astonishing a form as he was on the outside, he was, and is, a more horrible and evil-minded beast on the inside. I would not be surprised if he became king by killing any and all rivals."

"Do not judge all centaurs by those of Centaur City," Vanus the faun said. "Pegataur and the centaurs and satyrs of this city are far more war-like and suspicious, and inhospitable than the average. It is what becomes of a people that has been at war with one race or another for endless ages."

"But with whom?" Lady Aylen asked.

"Other centaur kingdoms," the faun answered, "and other satyr kingdoms."

It stood on the ground like an ancient Titan. The mammoth bird no longer looked like a giant black cloud but a giant mountain that occasionally moved. The beast was not looking at the caravan under its magic dome but without it, they would be seen.

By now more than a few parties begged to go into a pocket-realm. It was Dr'amal who insisted that such a move would mean nothing. They could not remain there. The flying beast had to go.

"I know what to do," the drowess told them.

She stood from the ground as all watched from their prone positions. The drowess raised her hands in the air as she closed her eyes. A giant ghostly indigo flower appeared in the sky directly above the creature and floated with the winds. The roc saw it, watched it, then flew after it. The magic flower moved ahead of it fast enough so as to not be caught. Another gust blew over them from the flapping of the roc's wings. They watched as both became smaller in the distance, specks, then disappeared.

The men of the caravan rose to their feet and applauded. Dr'amal sighed as her fellow drows approached her, and her father hugged her from the side.

The bullfrog watched from in the tall grass. It waddled around to turn its body. Traveler ran up and grabbed its legs in mid-jump. He held it above his head to look into the frog's eyes.

"You are going nowhere," he said to it and lowered his arm.

"Traveler is here!" one of the men in the camp yelled.

Traveler walked to the caravan with the bullfrog hanging in his hand.

"Mr. Traveler," Hobbs greeted with a big smile.

"Mr. Traveler, where are the others?" the king asked.

"There, sire," Traveler said, pointing with his other hand.

The same flying, giant, horselike creature landed with Lady Aylen, Gwyness, and the two fauns. The other fauns ran to their two comrades. The female half-elves ran to the women.

"We had to wait until you moved the roc on," Traveler said. "I was wondering when you would."

Lady Aylen walked directly to Traveler, greeted by the men along the way. Gwyness and the female half-elves followed. "You found our frog friend, Mr. Traveler?"

"I did, princess."

"How was your brief journey?" the king asked them.

"Sire, I did what I had to, but knowing what I know now, I would not repeat the act. We should get ready to march on."

Hobbs nodded. "Very good, sir." The steward ran off to get the men ready.

"Mr. Traveler," Pangolin neared him with the giants. "Successful trip?"

"I was telling the king here that I would not do it again if I had to do over. We will march as long as we can before dark."

"Good. What about that creature?"

"The roc will not return, but as you can see from its size, it cannot sneak up on anything. It will move on to the Great Forest and its own home region."

"Are we not headed to this Great Forest?" Nirgund asked.

"We are, but it's doubtful we will ever see it again. I wish I could say we would not see any other creature to replace it."

"What of your bullfrog, Mr. Traveler?" the king asked.

Traveler looked at the amphibian in his hand again. "I will restrain it until I know what or who it is."

The caravan was whole again. They marched on as if Traveler and the others had never been gone and the party had never encountered the roc. The caravan master glanced back, and his eyes connected with Dr'amal.

She moved from walking behind Hobbs and his guards up next to Traveler.

"You summoned," she said.

"I know what your problem is," Traveler said.

"Problem?"

"You have no imagination."

She laughed. "My imagination is good."

"The spell you cast to draw away the roc you should have thought of hours ago."

"I drew it away. No one was harmed or killed within the caravan."

"Dr'amal, we will soon be in the elfin lands. They have sorcerers and sorceresses too. Do you believe you are of the level to do battle with them?"

"Yes."

"Even if we do not confront any there, which is unlikely, beyond the elfin lands, we certainly will. You know this."

"All fae do."

"I do not know what exercises drow spell-casters go through. I am only familiar with some of what elfin ones do. You need to increase your skill, and from what I observe, your problem is a lack of imagination."

Her father, Dr'as, had, as all elves can do, appeared beside them both. He looked at his daughter and then at Traveler. "My daughter is young and new to the ways of magic. But she is powerful."

"She has the potential to be powerful. She is not so now. Mr. Dr'as, I am going to say this to you but not as a caravan master. Your decision will in no way affect your status in the caravan. When sorcerers battle, one of them dies."

"We know that, Mr. Traveler."

"You see your daughter with the eyes of a father. I believe that clouds your judgment. I have seen powerful sorcerers at work and so have you. Your daughter is not ready. Maybe in fifty years, which is still young, she will be, but not now. And the remaining months of this journey is not long enough for her to become powerful."

"Are you saying, Mr. Traveler, that you wish to replace me as the caravan's sorceress?" Dr'amal asked angrily.

"I am saying that you never were its sorceress. You can be angry at me. Drows are quick to anger, and your anger is far sharper than any elf's. But I am no longer willing to take any more chances."

"Your mood has been far darker since your return from Centaur City," Dr'as said.

"We are here for a quest to Atlantea, but there is too much going on around us. With that comes danger. We need to be ready. Every last one of us. Every man and woman, human and fae, must be able in their role for the sake of the caravan, whether I am here or the dog.

"Dr'as, we have dealt with a spell-taker, elfin assassins, and a spell that could have killed every last fae within the caravan, including all the drows. How has your daughter helped in any of those situations? I still have not heard anything of her seeker-spell."

"It revealed nothing," Dr'amal said.

"Or you are not powerful enough for it to work or inventive enough to make it work."

"I am sorry I did not act more swiftly with the roc."

"Dr'amal, you need to think of this carefully. If you find my words harsh, how will you react when we come across our first elfin party, which as you know, will have at least one sorcerer? The most dangerous leg of our journey through the Trail is ahead of us, not behind us."

"Yes, Mr. Traveler. We hear your words."

"Dr'amal, please do remain at the front, but we must find a solution."

"Yes," the drowess said, casting her gaze to the ground.

The caravan marched silently without incident for the rest of the day. All along the way, the men kept one eye on the sky and another on the horizon for the monstrous roc, but it never reappeared. Both the noon meal and breaks were shortened to make up ground. They also marched until just before nightfall, a couple of hours longer than normal. Towards the end, the brownies and the darklings emerged from their pocket-realms to join the march.

Hobbs did not join the leadership but instead saw to the night duties and took Quillen with him. Pangolin also saw to extra security for the night, speaking to the Cut-Throats, brownies, and darklings. In fact, all were busy at work except the royals and Gwyness.

"I feel that we are being left out of the important work of the night," King Aereth said, sitting at the campfire with the women. "Lady Aylen, you and the maiden must tell me about your visit to Centaur City."

"It was an awful place, sire," Gwyness said.

"We saw centaurs that we did not know even existed—part hippogriff, part unicorn, part stag with massive antlers, and the king was a flying centaur. But, Gwyness is correct. They were a disrespectful, ungrateful, suspicious, hateful people. I would gladly deal with the väki or our darklings rather than those centaurs."

"My that is a very damning pronouncement, indeed," the king said. "None of them welcomed Mr. Traveler's information?"

"None, sire," Lady Aylen said. "What's more is that the centaurs were lying to each other about what occurred. The centaurs at the city did not know we witnessed the events directly. It was all very strange. Their behavior was atrocious. Even our fauns were embarrassed by them."

The three of them noticed Traveler returning to his tent, his dog following.

"Is there anything we can do, Mr. Traveler?" the king asked.

Traveler stopped at their campfire and thought for a moment. "How are you progressing with the book of elfin protocols and customs, sire?"

"Quite well. It is a large volume of information, and I skimmed it all first. Now I focus on each section in depth."

"Good, sire."

Traveler said something in another language.

Lady Aylen hesitated. Her eyes looked from side to side. "I will not have any nightmares tonight, Mr. Traveler."

"Good, so you are at least getting to the level where you can understand elfish."

King Aereth stood from his stool at the same moment the dog barked. They all looked out past the circle and could see riders moving fast to the caravan, with torches. However, the riders were on horses that made no sound at all. The riders were not on horses at all but felines. Traveler pulled his sword from his back and moved to the perimeter.

It did not take the visitors long to reach them. Traveler, with sword in hand, waited with his dog. Pangolin and his Cut-Throats stood with him. Most of the men, including most of the fae, stood ready for battle. The visitors were centaurs but not any the non-fae humans had ever seen.

"We look for the human called Traveler," one of the centaurs said.

The fae was a cat centaur—instead of a horse below the waist, he and his comrades had the bodies of large spotted cats. There were a dozen of them in all. Some held the torches, others carried long spears. They all wore helmets, but their cat-like ears were apparent.

"I did not expect to see centaurs again on our travels. I am Traveler."

"We are not the centaurs of the Centaurian Fields. We are from the lands of Chiron near the Centaurian Forests."

"Yes, what brings you and your men to Titan's Caravan?"

"We heard that you and a party were in Centaur City."

"We were. How did you hear that?"

"We have our ways to monitor the goings-on in these lands."

"I see."

"May we speak with you?"

"We are speaking now."

"We need to know what you told the centaur king."

"You know of my visit there but not what I said in the full view of every centaur and satyr of the city?"

"We were told, but we need to confirm it. The matters are very serious, especially if it concerns a traveling party of mute humans."

Traveler's face flashed concern. "I do not believe they are humans at all. They may be lycanthropes."

"We heard of the incident with the rabid minotaurs."

"The minotaurs were not afflicted with disease. They were undead...they were fiends."

The faces of the cat centaurs grew fearful. "How do you know that?" one asked.

"We were there. We fought the beasts."

The cat centaurs looked as if they were in a panic and about to run.

"Have you seen those humans?" The cat centaurs weren't listening. "Have you seen them?" Traveler yelled.

"Yes, there were rumors of them in one of the centaur regions."

A look of anger came over Traveler. "That's why King Pegataur was unconcerned. He knew they weren't in his lands but yours."

"We have no way of dealing with this."

"Do you not have sorcerers?"

"We have none. If we could get word to our larger cousins, the lion and tiger centaurs who are allied with us, their winged lion centaurs are sorcerers. But to get there in time..."

"Do you know where these humans are now?"

"We know where they were last seen."

"Are there any burial grounds nearby?" Traveler asked.

The centaurs looked at each other in panic. Everyone in the caravan exchanged looks of dismay.

"Yes. They were seen near our burial grounds. A few days ago, we too were faced with attacking minotaurs, but we killed them. They were rabid."

"Did you bury them in those grounds?" Traveler asked.

"Yes. That is common practice."

"After the humans were seen?"

"Yes, days ago. The minotaurs were buried only last night. We have no means to deal with this. Our people live in the centaur forests. We have little to no contact with outsiders. We know nothing of this."

Traveler pointed at Gwyness. "Get your weapons. You and I are going." He looked at the cat centaurs. "We will help you. I realize now that I went to the wrong centaurs."

Gwyness did not protest. She turned to go to her tent.

Traveler looked into the crowd of the caravan and saw the ram-horned faun, Ammon. "Have you been listening?"

"I have," the faun leader said, standing quietly.

"Is Pegataur capable of this kind of evil indifference?"

"He is."

Zan and Vanus stepped forward. "What do you intend to do?"

Traveler looked at the leadership. "The dog and I will get the cat centaurs to their lands as quickly as possible. I will take Gwyness."

"Should I go, Mr. Traveler?" Lady Aylen asked.

"No."

"We will go," Zan said.

"Yes, I will take both of you and Hobbs. Where are you?"

"Here, sir." The steward ran to them.

"Gwyness and I will stay at the burial grounds with most of the cat centaurs. Hobbs, I will send the dog with you, the other cat centaurs, and our two fauns. The fauns know both the lion-centaur and tiger-centaur clans."

"We do," Ammon confirmed. "My daughter will go too. As a faun healer and spell-caster she is well-known by the centaurs of Chiron." The fauness also stepped forward.

"This time there are no objections, Mr. Traveler," King Aereth said.

Gwyness returned with her two slender war hammers. Traveler walked out of the camp with the dog. Gwyness, Hobbs, and the fauns followed. Traveler gestured to the lion centaurs.

The dog ran off into the night then stopped. Everyone watched as it transformed into a roc. Not as large as the monstrous one that stalked them earlier in the day but large enough for all of them to climb onto its back. When it flew into the air, the men had to hold all the tents and supplies and stand their ground to keep from being blown away.

◆◆◆

The full moon had reached its apex in the night sky. Gwyness watched it with a pressing feeling of dread. Her back against a tree, she sat quietly. The moonlight illuminated a wide open field around them. There was nothing that she could see—as a human—to indicate that it was a fae burial ground, but she was told that it was.

The dog had dropped her, Traveler, and most of the cat centaurs off first. Then the dog transformed to a smaller roc beast to fly off with Hobbs, the fauns, and two of the cat centaurs. An hour later, the dog, in the form of a giant eagle, flew back. It landed, changed to its usual form, and joined its master near the edge of the tree line. That had been a few hours ago. Both man and animal stared out over the open field, lying on their bellies, stiff like a pair of statues. They had barely moved an inch in all the time that had passed.

Stationed around them were the cat centaurs. Gwyness wished it were not dark so she could get a better view of them. Cat centaurs. She always thought of cats as more aggressive, but these centaurs were more like the deer-like fae of their own caravan—a nervous people. They sat quietly amongst themselves under a few trees—the ten original cat centaurs and dozens more that had been waiting for their arrival. All were merely shadows around her.

Gwyness noticed that the cat centaurs had taken comfort in the fact that Traveler, the dog, and she had joined them, especially Mr. Traveler, who took charge from the moment they landed. Also the cat centaurs seemed to have more faith in her abilities than she did. She occasionally squeezed her dual war hammers in her hands. Other times she ran her hand along one of them to feel the indentations of symbols etched on them. What did they mean? It was a question she had wanted to know the answer to all her life.

She felt a warmness on her chest from her amulet. There was an ever-so-faint glow, then it increased. She looked out and could see Traveler, from his post, lying on the ground, looking back at her.

They all heard it. A noise. The main reason Gwyness did not believe the area was a burial ground was because it was a field as lush as any. There was no barren or undisturbed dirt anywhere. But now, she saw a clawed hand push its way up from the soil and grass. The hand waited, trembling, then descended back into the earth.

The minotaur shot up from the ground so suddenly that Gwyness could hear the cat centaurs behind her gasp. The creature stood on the ground, looking in their exact direction. She could not see its eyes, its front was in shadow, but it stood there without movement. Her senses screamed, and she noticed something on either side of her. Cat centaurs had crept up, crawling along the ground to be at her sides.

An unnerving yell! The minotaur held its head tilted up to the moon, and it yelled out again.

Gwyness had to cover her amulet under her clothes with her hand. The glow had intensified. She did not want the undead beast to see her. At her sides, the cat centaurs aimed their bows. She looked, and Traveler had gotten up on one knee, his sword in hand. The dog, too, was readying itself.

Another minotaur burst through the soil then a third then more. They did the same—stood there, lifted their heads up, and bayed at the moon. More minotaurs jumped through the soil from their graves.

Gwyness battled within herself—the fear. The minotaurs kept coming from beneath the earth. The new ones, however, were not yelling. They all turned and faced where the living waited under the trees in the shadows.

They all yelled! Gwyness jumped to her feet. The minotaurs charged.

The cat centaurs' volley of arrows struck every minotaur multiple times before they could even run a few strides. Their aim was precise: cripple and impale the undead creatures through their skulls. In mere moments, they had done just that. The field was littered with minotaur body parts. But, none of the minotaurs were "dead." The parts writhed around on the ground. The creatures continued their yelling.

Gwyness watched Traveler slowly walk backwards to her. He kept his sword ready and his eyes focused on the undead minotaurs.

"What is wrong, Mr. Traveler?"

"Your amulet grows brighter," he said.

A minotaur burst through the ground in front of them. Traveler severed its outstretched clawed arms at the very moment the dog grabbed the minotaur's cloven feet with a tentacled arm. The dog pulled it away from them all and threw it back into the open field.

More attacking minotaurs burst through the earth.

"No!" Gwyness yelled as she instinctively struck with her war hammer.

She hit a minotaur ghoul that had popped through the soil not more than two feet from them. When her silver blade penetrated the creatures skull it cried out louder than all the others. Then collapsed. It moved no more.

"Move back!" Traveler directed the cat centaurs. "These creatures have crafty intelligence. They are tunneling under the ground to us. We only need to keep them here on the burial grounds until the others arrive."

The cat centaur archers fired a blizzard of arrows as more minotaurs appeared from the ground. Traveler watched Gwyness's amulet closely to know when other undead neared them.

"Move behind Maiden Gwyness! Keep moving back!"

The cat centaurs were frightened but continued to fire their arrows as Traveler directed their path backwards. Some of the minotaurs attempted to run away, but centaur arrows, no matter the species, like elves, never missed their mark. The creatures were cut down whether they were two yards or a mile away.

The sun appeared in the sky. That was what everyone had originally thought it was. However, it was a magical sphere that floated to the center of the burial grounds and landed. Every piece of fallen minotaur ghoul and every full beast still crawling through the soil or waiting to attack, rose into the air and was absorbed into the magical sphere. Then the soil and grass of the burial grounds began to rain— upwards.

Traveler, Gwyness, and the cat centaurs, now more than a hundred in number, had to run back as the area rained up to the sky. A portal opened up near them.

"Hobbs!" Gwyness called out.

The steward stepped out of the portal with the two fauns and fauness healer. As soon as they joined them, new centaurs followed after them: an army of armored lion centaurs, tiger centaurs, and panther centaurs. Flying out of the portal was a winged lion centaur, whose eyes glowed with magic. He landed in front of Traveler and Gwyness. The cat centaurs gathered around.

"You are the one called Traveler?" the winged lion centaur asked.

"I am."

"I am Nemek the Sorcerer. Your noble deed is done. You, your human, Hobbs, your necro-seer, and the fauns can return to your caravan on Titan's Trail. We will cleanse these lands of these fiends and restore it to its state before it was cursed."

"Thank you, Nemek. We will depart immediately."

The centaurs watched the dog take the form of a smaller roc. In a short time, it was in the air with Traveler and his party on its back, flying across the moonlit sky.

CHAPTER TWO

A Most Dangerous Predator

The caravan passed from the golden grass of the Centaurian Fields to dirt paths weaving through wooded forests.

"We have officially left the lands of the centaurs, satyrs, and fauns," Traveler said aloud to the front columns.

"The lands of the elves then, Mr. Traveler?" the king asked.

"Yes, sire. We will be there in a few days."

The King Aereth smiled as he looked at the princess. "We have traveled a long way, Lady Aylen."

"Sometimes, I felt we would never get here, sire. Now it is like a dream."

Behind the royals and Gwyness strode their dragon-horses. The beasts were comfortable spending more time outside their pocket-realm sanctuary. A few fenodyree followed nearby.

When Traveler, Gwyness, Hobbs, and the fauns had returned the previous night, all there was to do was sleep for a few hours before rising again. Most of the caravan had seen the feline centaurs and were eager to hear from Hobbs and Gwyness about the others they had encountered.

The musicians pranced through the caravan playing their flutes. The men were happy. Plenty of different conversations ensued, but they all had learned, especially after the terrifying encounter with the roc, to keep an eye out at all times.

"Mr. Hobbs?" a grinning Quillen asked, walking alongside their steward.

"Yes, Mr. Quillen."

"I know you said to wait til tonight, but can I not get an account of last night at the lunch meal, sir?"

"Lad, I barely got two hours of sleep."

"While the details are still fresh in your mind, sir."

"Mr. Quillen, the details will be fresh in my mind for my entire life."

"I heard they were cat centaurs and you went to their city!"

"Cat centaurs, yes. And lion centaurs, golden-brown fur; tiger centaurs, the hair on their human half matched in the same style of black and orange; black panther centaurs. I saw white panther centaurs in the city, leopard centaurs, both spotted and striped. Oh yes, the one winged lion centaur."

"Their sorcerer."

"Mr. Quillen, if you already know the details from the fae, why ask me?"

"No, Mr. Hobbs, I want to get your version."

"He's a curious one," Tyfer said with a laugh. Both guards, Oeric and he, walked behind them.

"Too curious," Hobbs responded. "Have you ever seen these other species of centaurs?" he asked the guards.

"Oh yes, Mr. Hobbs," Oeric answered. "There are other kinds too."

"Other kinds?" Quillen asked. "What others?"

"Oh, lizard centaurs."

"Lizards!"

"There are the centaurs of the sea too."

Quillen was smiling even more. "What others?"

"I never saw them, but I hear there are scorpion centaurs. Oh, and even dark insect centaurs too."

"Insect? What kind would those be?"

"They are not called insect centaurs," Dr'amal the sorceress interjected. She followed the men with Ursi. "They have other names. They are gigantic humanoids with the lower body of a giant spider."

"Spider centaurs?" Quillen called out with a look of fear.

Dr'amal laughed. "That is not what they are called. And they are not considered centaurs, more goblin or demon, if anything."

The front of the caravan listened to the young Quillen speaking with Hobbs.

"Our young chronicler of fae races and fantastic beasts will give himself nightmares," King Aereth remarked.

"And the rest of too, sire," Lady Aylen said, as she let her kirin catch up so she could stroke its blue fur and scales.

"Mr. Traveler, your mission last night was a success," the king said.

Traveler glanced back at him. "It was, sire."

"You did the right and noble thing."

"I feel so, sire. Very different from my mood after the visit to Centaur City."

"Why such a stark difference between these centaurs, Mr. Traveler?" Lady Aylen asked.

"The centaurs of Centaur City are savage warriors. The centaurs of Chiron are scholars, teachers, builders, and spell-casters. But they both share a distrust of outsiders unless invited or accompanied by one of their allies. Hobbs got a rare privilege to be able to visit their city as a human."

The wooded lands they traveled through were unremarkable and indistinguishable from any in the Lands of Man. They moved down the dusty dirt path, barely large enough for their columns. The lumbering stride of the four giants of the vanguard kicked up especially large clouds of dirt. Traveler increased the distance between the front and the vanguard so those closest to the front of the columns wouldn't be eating and breathing dirt the entire march.

"We will be off these loose dirt paths by tomorrow," Traveler told them.

First they saw the giants of the vanguard stop, then they saw Pangolin with his arm raised, stopping the entire the caravan. Traveler and the dog quickly moved to them.

On the path ahead of the vanguard was a small party of centaurs in golden armor. Their lead centaur approached.

"Master Traveler, is it?"

"Yes," their caravan master answered.

"I am Dorolus of Chiron."

The royals and Gwyness had also joined the vanguard. The centaur saw King Aereth and Lady Aylen and nodded to greet them.

"Good day, Dorolus. How can we be of service?" Traveler asked.

"No, sir, you have already been of great service to our people. I am here on behalf of our centaur king. He was most moved by your assistance in our time of crisis. We see you continue your journey to Atlantea."

"We do," Traveler answered.

"I hear you have been to the fabled city before. It is very much like Chiron. Though, I will confess its libraries are far more vast and beautiful than our own. No small feat to accomplish in this world.

"Our king has been there before, as have some of our greatest sorcerers. The king would like to aid in your journey."

The centaur motioned to another centaur who extended a hand with a scroll. The lead centaur handed it Traveler.

"As the caravan's guide, it may be of value. To all those whom it may concern, allies of the kingdom of Chiron, Titan's Caravan travels under the banner of the Chiron and the Centaur King Lyongriff."

Traveler smiled as he opened the scroll.

"Do you speak hippocentauri?"

"Some," Traveler replied as he rolled the scroll again then handed it to the king.

"Please do thank your king," Aereth said.

"I shall, king." He nodded to them all. "Good journey."

The centaurs galloped away and disappeared into the woods in a cloud of dust.

"Well," Lady Aylen began, "Mr. Traveler, we are now under the banner of another fae race."

The four giants laughed. Grakdar walked over to Traveler and patted his back, which meant that he almost knocked the caravan master over.

"Good job, human," the giant said. "If kindness leads to this, keep it up. We will be be under the banner of all the lands of fae before we reach Atlantea. I see big rewards and big treasures awaiting us. Giants like big."

They found a defensible, elevated hill to rest, and the noon meals were served among the men. The lizard minders created a ring around the main caravan and sat in small camps facing the perimeter to keep watch. The three crawling trees stretched out to provide even more security. All the fae parties following set up their own adjacent circles lining up behind them.

The mood was upbeat, and the lively topic of conversation was of the Chironian centaurs and the Caravan now being under the proxy banner of their centaur king. Everyone was eager for the night to hear from Hobbs about his visit to Chiron.

"Mr. Hobbs it seems that you will be holding court tonight," Traveler said as he ate. He sat on his stool with the royals, Gwyness, and the steward.

"I am not looking forward to it, sir. I prefer not to be the center of things."

"But you are, Mr. Hobbs," Lady Aylen said, drinking from a cup.

The dog ate his chunks of food from the ground, lying on his belly, content. The camp of Nirgund, with his alphyn reptilian hounds sprawled out all around, and the female half-elves were nearby; on the other side was Quillen and Hobbs's guardsmen, Tyfer and Oeric. One of the female half-elves kept an eye on the fledgling owl-griffin still no bigger than a small dog. As a nocturnal beast, it should have been sleeping, but its curiosity of things kept it up. Ursi, the fae-blood, always ate alone, quiet and seemingly disinterested in the conversations around her.

"Mr. Traveler, I wanted to ask you about something you had said days ago," Lady Aylen said. "That you have been endeavoring these past months to prepare us for the leg of the journey that begins in the land of elves."

"Yes, princess. Many more elves, sorcerers, and sorceresses, many more beasts. Then there is the Great Forest."

"Which is its proper name: the Great Forest or the Giant Forest?" she asked.

"Both are correct. Different races use either name."

"Is there a specific danger that we will encounter with the elves, Mr. Traveler?" the king asked.

"It cannot be any more different than what we have already encountered with the fairies or the centaurs," Lady Aylen added.

"Well, sire, the elves are very similar to us with their kings and queens, knights and kingdoms. It is why knowledge of their protocols and customs will be so important. It is why I had Mr. Estus fashion you a comfortable crown for you to wear always, and the princess as well. Status, nobility, royalty, blood of one's race or people are very important to them. We are thankful to have the princess, because we can say we are also under the banner of a elfin royal."

"What if I were not here, Mr. Traveler?" Lady Aylen asked.

"We would have had to part with a very hefty sum and pay an elf from Fae-Wick or Arion's Spear to play that role and accompany us on the journey. It is what all caravans do, and the loyalty of such elves for hire is not always guaranteed."

"No different than with humans, as I found out the hard way," Lady Aylen said with bitterness.

"That is all behind us, princess. We must all focus on what lies ahead."

"But that past, Mr. Traveler, also includes what I would now term our archenemies."

"It does, indeed, princess, but there is nothing we can do about them. We simply must add their names to the list of all the other dangers we will face. What is on my mind of late is being to able to read the inscriptions on your weapon and Maiden Gwyness's."

"What have you come up with, Mr. Traveler?" Gwyness asked.

"It is not on the map, but I vaguely remember a city of magic practitioners."

Traveler stopped drinking from his cup for a moment. The drowess appeared. She had her head cloaked, as all the drows did during the day.

"Dr'amal, is there something you wish to add?"

She took a knee near him and spoke in almost a whisper, but they could hear her clearly. "The city you speak of is called Druid Keep."

A smirk came over Traveler's face. "Like Last Keep."

"Yes, the hidden fae city in your human lands. It, too, is hidden but from fae who are unaware. Why do you seek it?"

"I want to have some elfin inscriptions translated, maybe understand the history behind them."

"You would be able to find those who could fulfill those tasks. However, the city does not only have wizards and sorceresses. It also has warlocks and hag witches."

"Mr. Traveler, please tell me that we will not be making another detour," the king said.

"No, need, king," Dr'amal said. "It is near the Trail."

"Too bad you could not fulfill this task for us," Lady Aylen said to her.

Dr'amal smiled. "Sorry to disappoint you, but my people have no knowledge of the ancient inscriptions. I doubt that many do, but Druid Keep would be the very place you would find those few. I will notify you when we are close. It is after the Dead City and before we reach Fae'el."

"Thank you, Dr'amal. I will leave it to you," Traveler said. "Mr. Hobbs, I think we should get the men ready to move."

"Yes, sir," Hobbs said as he stood.

The dragon-horses refused to leave their pocket-realm when Traveler checked on them. He told their new masters that it was not unusual for the beasts, who had their own minds and moods.

"Mr. Traveler, can the kirins foretell the future?" Lady Aylen asked as the caravan continued down the long dirt path.

"Some have said they do, princess," Traveler answered, "but kirins have diverse species, all with their own specific magical abilities. Do not read anything more into their desire to remain in their pocket. Sometimes they are simply in a bad mood. You will get used to it."

Gwyness walked up closer to their caravan master. "Mr. Traveler, why did you give me the kirin you did?"

"He chose you, Maiden Gwyness."

"I do not believe that, Mr. Traveler. Why did you give him to me?"

"I thought him well suited for you."

"I suspect more than that, Mr. Traveler."

"Maiden Gwyness, in the magical lands where it is from, it is often chosen as a companion for their mystics."

"What do these mystics do?"

"They fight beings and beasts that should not walk the earth. As I said, it is well suited for you."

"That centaur at the burial grounds...he called me a...necro-seer. What is that?"

"Maiden, you do not need me to tell you. You can figure out from the construction of the words its full meaning. Was he not correct? You were the only who was able to 'kill' one of the undead beasts until the master centaur sorcerers arrived. Not me or my dog, you."

"Gwyness? You did not tell me you were attacked," Lady Aylen said.

"We were attacked, and Maiden Gwyness killed one with one blow from her magical weapon. She did not hesitate. It was pure instinct."

"I cannot say I am happy about this conversation that I instigated," Gwyness said. "A seer sees. That is all. Seers do not need weapons."

"Seers in Faë-Land can because some those seers not only see the evil. They are able to hunt and kill it. However, I agree with Maiden Gwyness. This is not the time for this conversation. We can speak in private. And speak when we know more."

"If this hidden city is also inhabited by warlocks and witches..." King Aereth began.

"We will definitely not go in there alone, sire. By no means."

♦ ♦ ♦

"I know we will discuss the journey tomorrow tonight, Mr. Traveler, but what is this Dead City?" Lady Aylen asked. "Why would the fae leave an empty city standing?"

"The city is but ruins, princess."

"But you say it's used as a base of what we call marauders and robbers in our lands."

"Yes, and creatures moving through the lands."

"Such a structure should be completely razed to the ground, then."

"It is a reminder of the ancient kingdoms, princess. That is why it has been left to the elements to be removed from the lands, however many eons it takes."

"I guess they are people so long-lived that time is not as important as it is to us humans," Lady Aylen said.

The king looked at her and grinned.

"Sire, I'm still a human at heart. Mr. Traveler even said so. Is that not right, Mr. Traveler?"

Traveler suddenly bolted away from the front of the columns. Not only did he startle them but then the vanguard as he ran past them.

"Mr. Traveler!" Pangolin called out after him.

At the front of the columns, Gwyness asked, "Where's the dog?"

The royals were still looking out after Traveler. Lady Aylen said, "I don't know. It was there before, but I did not see when it left. It must be with Mr. Traveler."

Pangolin did not stop the advance of his vanguard, but they cautiously moved forward. He glanced back at King Aereth to give him the signal to do the same.

"Mr. Elman, do you see him?" Pangolin asked.

"Yes, sir," their half-elf tracker replied. "He is standing in the middle of the road, with his back to us."

"What is he doing?"

"Nothing. He is just standing there."

"Is the dog with him?" one of the giants asked.

"I do not see the dog, only Mr. Traveler."

"Why would he run out ahead of the vanguard like that?" Pangolin asked, annoyed.

They soon reached Traveler. It was as Elman had said: their caravan master was standing motionless, with his back to them. This time Pangolin gave the signal to the king to stop the caravan, but the vanguard slowly moved forward.

Pangolin took even greater strides to move out ahead of the half-elf, giants, and elaphine archer-warriors. As he neared Traveler, he was about to call out to him but stopped.

He saw Traveler slightly raise his right hand at his side, signaling him to stop his approach. Pangolin slowly stepped to the side, and as he moved around to view what was ahead of Traveler's body, he saw there was something else in the road in front of him.

It was a giant creature that blended almost perfectly into road and the surroundings of the land. At first, he thought it was some kind of giant bat. He stepped closer. He could hear it eating, chewing. He stepped closer. It sat on the ground under the cover of its own dark bat wings. Pangolin could now make out that the creature had an almost-human head. The more he stared, he realized why he could not initially make out the lower half of its face. The creature's human head had a massive mouth filled with sharp teeth. Sadly, he saw that it had in its clutches the body of something—human, elf—he did not know. The creature was slowly eating its prey.

Then it stopped eating. It took notice of Traveler, Pangolin, and the caravan behind them but did not care. Pangolin knew why Traveler had ran out in front. Had he seen the abomination, the vanguard would have attacked. Traveler did not want that. The caravan master was trying to get the creature to remove itself from their path, take its "food," and go without incident. It watched them with squinted, dark eyes.

Pangolin slowly reached for his axe-mace on his back as a precaution. He had it in hand and braced himself. All he wanted to do was look back and signal the men, but he dared not take his gaze off the creature.

The manticore jumped at Traveler so fast that by the time Pangolin yelled "No!" it bounced off of some kind of invisible barrier, flew past, and knocked the master-at-arms on his back. The creature flew past with a speed and fury none of the humans thought possible.

Traveler ran as fast as he could, back to the caravan as they heard gasps and yells. Pangolin picked himself up from the ground. His earthen magical armor had saved his life, because the creature did claw at his body in its flight. The vanguard was already running into the caravan for battle. The fae archers of the vanguard fired their arrows at it and so did the fae archers within the caravan. Pech threw spears at it, and one of the crawling trees struck at it, while another crawling tree created a barrier of branches. The creature screamed as it tried to get at the men flapping its bat wings and hovering in the air.

Magical daggers embedded themselves in the creatures back, and it flew at the source of the attacks. Dr'amal dove for the ground as she panicked. A giant war hammer hit the creature center mass. It screamed, and flew away from the caravan at tremendous speed, disappearing into the nearby woods.

One of the giants picked up his war hammer from the ground, joined by his five comrades. The giants gripped their weapons, waiting for another attack.

"There!" someone yelled.

The creature came out from the trees, flying very close to the ground, and came to the road, where Traveler stood across from it. It retrieved the half-eaten corpse with its triple row of teeth and flew off.

"Shields!" Traveler yelled. Other fae did the same.

The manticore flew across one of side of the caravan, as it swallowed the corpse in its mouth whole, and fired spines from its tail. The deadly projectiles embedded themselves in more than one of the shields of the men. Everyone quickly moved in closer to each other with their shields or hid behind someone who had one.

Quillen had stood in the exact same spot from the time he beheld the creature. There was no joy in his face from its sight. He stood petrified, unable to move, sweating and breathing heavy. Traveler grabbed him and pushed him to the ground, out of the danger of the creature's projectiles.

"Where did it go?" someone asked.

The creature appeared like a blur on the other side firing more spine projectiles at them, hitting shields and striking some of their animals, which screamed out. They were following its trajectory, but it disappeared again.

A white horse ran out of the caravan in sheer terror. It ran along the dirt path alone.

"Where did that horse come from?" Gwyness asked Aylen.

The manticore flew past them all like a devilish whirlwind, smacking them with a fierce gust as it chased after the animal. The horse stopped and turned its head as its ballooned out. It transformed into a beast that looked similar to a buffalo: small horns, matted hair hanging into its eyes, its much larger head bobbed close to the ground. Its eyes! The creature the dog transformed into stared with its red eyes at the manticore.

The manticore screamed with great intensity as its entire body began to lose color. It shot straight up into the sky and flew higher and higher then was gone.

Many of the men were starting to get sick; the buffalo-creature turned its head. Slowly it transformed back into the dog. The dog stood there, vigorously shaking its head. When it stopped, the dog ran into the caravan in search of its master.

All of Titan's Caravan was now in the pocket-realm. Traveler stood at the entrance with Pangolin, I-wulf, and Nirgund. The view was of the clouds, and they were in the hands of the fairy sisters. Traveler had Wildglow, with her sister, move the entrance of their pocket-realm far off the Trail, so if the manticore did return, it could not pick up their scent.

"We will wait in here for a day," Traveler told the men.

"How did you protect yourself?" Pangolin asked.

"I wore a magical necklace that surrounded me in an invisible barrier, same magic as our circle but smaller and less powerful. It is all I needed."

"How did you know it was there?" Pangolin asked.

"A voice told me."

"A voice?"

"One of the fairies."

Pangolin realized, "The fairies could have used their swarms to protect us."

Traveler shook his head. "Fairies are terrified of manticores."

"We're terrified of manticores, Mr. Traveler," I-wulf said.

"If the fairies hadn't warned us, what would have happened?" Pangolin asked.

"It could have been very bad. As you saw, they can also fire poison darts. We were very lucky this time. Manticores are very devious. The fairies will spread the word that one was sighted, but the creatures know how to evade human and fae alike until it's too late."

"Do we have to worry, Mr. Traveler?" Nirgund asked.

"Yes. We may lose it easy enough, but the creatures are intelligent and will know where to find us if it has a mind to."

"Can they be killed?" Pangolin asked.

"Yes, but the price may be heavy losses among our own. That is why I was trying to get it to move on. It had already captured its meal. It did not need us."

"Who was the man? Was it a man or an elf?" I-wulf asked.

"No way to know."

"What was the beast your dog changed to?" Pangolin asked.

"It's called a catoblepas. A beast from magical lands outside of Faë-Land. A beast it would not know or be prepared for."

"A beast that can turn a living thing into stone with its gaze."

"Yes, my dog and I can be devious too. A white horse running alone is a temptation even it could not resist."

"There's another creature that can do that?" I-wulf asked, shaking his head. "How many such creatures exist? I thought it was just gorgons and basilisks."

"This one, too, but its effect takes time. The dog could have turned into other creatures far more powerful, but it would take far more time than we had, and I did not want to take the chance of harming any of the men. More importantly, one should not touch the manticore. Its foul body often carries with it disease that the most learned healers cannot always defeat. So, either the manticore fell back to the earth dead, or it escaped. We will act as if it escaped."

The view of the entrance changed to lush green lands. The fairies flew through the entrance barrier.

"We are safe!" Wildglow said, hovering in front of Traveler.

"Good. Go see if you can help the Tree Shepherds. The creature shot poison darts at the trees too."

"We don't want to see those monsters again—ever!"

"Neither do we."

The fairies flew away. The men looked out across the busy camps. Men were seated or stood conversing. Some smoked pipes around the campfires. They had been lucky—no one was killed.

Traveler approached the Cut-Throats. "Mr. I-wulf, now that you and your Cut-Throats have had days to walk among the fae parties in the rear, you have the authority to enlist who you see fit to protect that part of the caravan. The tactics in these lands are no different than our own: attack or destroy the rear as a diversion before reinforcements from the front can arrive. You have the added burden of not only protecting the main party's rear but watching the very rear of the caravan. Do not allow enemies to exploit any weaknesses we may have."

"Yes, Mr. Traveler. I think the drows could be of benefit, and the fauns if we could get them to talk to us lowly humans," I-wulf said.

"That should not be an issue anymore after the Centaurian Fields."

"Yes. Titan's Caravan is under the banner of their allies after all. The centaurs of Chiron. And there is that fae who looks like a mole, with the huge moose that eats meat. I need to enlist him too."

"Good," Traveler said to I-wulf. "Mr. Nirgund, Mr. Estus will be rejoining us now that his lizard-armor-fitting days are behind him. He will march right next to you. At least that is the plan for now."

Nirgund smiled. "Very good. It will be good to have him back at the front with us."

"He is anxious for it. He also has many fae weapons to test, which I am sure you won't mind helping with."

"Absolutely, no burden to me at all."

"Also, keep the king safe. As an identified royal, he will be targeted."

"By whom?" Pangolin asked.

"Elves, goblins, whomever."

"He can count on me," Nirgund said.

"Mr. Pangolin, when I confronted the manticore, I realized that we did not have a nonverbal signal agreed upon by us."

"Too bad we cannot talk in each other minds when needed, like the half-elves."

"Yes, but we can figure out something, as warriors have done in our lands for ages."

Pangolin nodded. "Are you expecting additional trouble—besides encountering another manticore?"

"No, if we encounter another manticore, it will be this same one from today. But I was thinking of another pending doom. We may have to do battle with a war-pack of gnolls along the Trail. If it should happen, it is essential we engage them and kill as many of them as we can before they reach the caravan. We were lucky with this single manticore. If the caravan has to do battle with an army of gnolls, we will not be."

"Here comes Mr. Quillen," I-wulf said.

The lad ran to the men, but it was obvious he wanted to speak with Traveler.

"Yes, Mr. Quillen?" Traveler asked.

"Sir, I wanted to apologize for my...cowardly behavior."

"Cowardly?"

"I froze."

"Mr. Quillen, why are you apologizing for natural behavior? Brave men in battle are not without fear. They fight through it. Fear is the emotion that keeps us alive to the next day. People without fear often do not live too long," Traveler told him. "However, the next time you are gripped by that emotion, be sure to take a position behind a shield or on the ground. Fear is one thing, but stupidity is another."

"Listen well," Pangolin said to the boy.

"Who will chronicle our adventures with words and drawings if you get yourself eaten?"

Quillen grinned. "Yes, Mr. Traveler."

59

CHAPTER THREE

Frog-Dor

Hobbs sat with dozens of the men, blankets spread out on the ground, creating new protecting-charm necklaces. They also used the time for exchanging gossip while they were hard at work.

"Hello, Mr. Hobbs," Gresham greeted. Hobbs looked up.

"Ah, Mr. Gresham. Any injuries to report?"

"We were most fortunate. Mr. Estus is not happy. He has more metalwork to do, repairing the shields, but it could have been worse."

"Any of the animals died?"

"Fortunately, no, and the ones that were hit are already back on their feet. Our fae parties did not require my services. They have their own. Mr. Hobbs, can I be of any assistance?"

"Yes, Mr. Gresham, if you wish. I never turn down an extra pair of hands."

"How often do our charms need to be changed?"

"Mr. Traveler says they can last months, but he prefers to change them ever month. That keeps the magic more potent."

"Do we need them in the elfin lands?"

"'It is better to be safe than bewitched,' he said."

"Yes, that I would agree with."

Gresham rolled up his sleeves and knelt to help them assemble the charm necklaces of herbs, crystals, and newly added roots.

"Six thousand of these, Mr. Hobbs?"

"There abouts."

"At least we do not have to outfit lizards, too, with them."

Traveler stood in front of his tent. He, too, had much work to do, studying the maps and plotting their course, but today his duties also required quieting nerves.

"If we return to the Trail, the manticore could be lying in wait for us," one of bird men said to him.

"There is no stopping those beasts," a raccoon man said. "They could kill us all."

"Titan's Trail is vast," Traveler began. "It is a trail far more vast than any of this world. Not even a roc could find our exact location. Also, we are far from alone on the trail. There are many parties and many caravans besides us. We do have to watch for the creature, but we have to watch for any creature or sorcerer."

"We are not as strong as the other fae," one of the possum men said. "Our animals are not for fighting."

"But you are a fighter when the need arises. We are a caravan. Parties coming together for mutual safety. Correct?"

The animal men nodded.

"I know you are concerned about being near the end of the caravan. You fear being the party most likely to be attacked."

"Yes," more than one of the animal men said.

"I have already spoken to the leader of the Cut-Throats. We will be extra vigilant. But you can also help each other. We march in four columns at the front. Your parties should do the same. Instead of your single or two columns, march in four or more. Make yourselves look as dangerous as possible. And your giant turtles and crabs should be on your flanks, not following behind you."

The animal men nodded again.

"Will we take on more parties ahead?" a fox man asked.

"Yes, but they will most likely be elves."

"Make sure they are good elves," a bird man said.

"They will be."

The animal men were satisfied. They nodded and left him to return to their camps.

"You are quite good at allaying fears, Mr. Traveler," King Aereth said, standing at the entrance of his own tent with a book in hand.

"I know how they feel, sire. I was in their place when I first came to the magical lands. The caravan master we had was secretive and aloof. He only increased the fear and tension within our caravan. Fearful men on a journey such as this can become dead men."

"So true. You do believe this creature survived."

"I had once thought that I had killed the Four Kings, because no other could have survived. I was wrong. I will not make such a mistake again, sire. If I cannot see the body, then they are alive."

"The manticore is alive."

"That it my assumption, sire. Sadly, some poor soul or souls will encounter it. We must ensure that it is not us."

Traveler noticed her nearby. "Dr'amal," he called out.

The drowess stepped closer. "I am sorry to interrupt you, and you, king."

"Quite all right," King Aereth said.

"May I speak with you?" she asked Traveler.

"Yes."

Traveler stepped into his tent already lit with torches. His map table was set up in the center. All he had to do was spread out his maps.

"Yes?" Traveler asked when sat at his table.

"Your dog is not here."

"He is resting."

"Whenever he transforms to larger animals, or those with a special malevolence, he needs extra time to recover."

"Yes."

"I came to tell you that I cast another spell, a seeking spell."

"To do what?"

"To warn us of any beings of incredible magical power near us. It probably would have done nothing to warn us against those who cast the death-sleep spell against our fae, but what would it hurt to try?"

"What did you find?"

"There is a such a being near us."

Traveler stood from his stool. "Where?"

"Within the camp."

A look of realization came over the caravan master's face. "Hobbs!"

In a moment, the steward appeared at the tent's entrance.

"Yes, sir."

"Where is that frog?"

"You have a quick mind, Master Traveler," Dr'amal said to Traveler. "I locked it away in a cage. It's in one of the pocket-realms."

Traveler bolted from the tent, with both of them following.

"Which one?" Traveler asked.

"One of the small ones. I don't think we used it yet. We were going to use it for extra supplies."

Hobbs picked up a bag from one of the pull-carts. He opened it wide as he lifted it. The magic entrance stuck to the air so the steward could widen it more. They all walked inside.

Hobbs's mouth dropped open.

In the center of the tent was a single cage in the dark, but there was not a frog inside but a man, cramped, naked and crying.

"Quick," Travel said as he ran to the cage. "Can you break the cage apart?" he asked Dr'amal.

She threw two magical daggers at the cage, and the sides fell away. Traveler gently pulled the man from the cage. Hobbs ran from the pocket and soon appeared with a large blanket to cover the man.

They tried to lift him to his feet, but the man's face was in anguish.

"His legs must be cramped," Traveler said. "Find Mr. Gresham. We must transport him to the healing tent."

"Yes, sir," Hobbs said and was gone.

Dr'amal knelt down and watched him. The man kept his head lowered and tucked in, touching his chest, cowering and shivering from under the blanket.

"He has been cursed," she said.

◆ ◆ ◆

Hobbs returned with Gresham. Their new healer collected a few men to help transport the man to his healing tent. Hobbs had also returned with a torch in hand. They were now able to see the man more clearly. He truly was the most pitiful soul they had ever seen. His unkempt shoulder-length hair hung down across his face. His sad eyes were red from crying. The man was in deep agony, unable to fully extend his legs.

As Gresham and his men took the man away, Traveler left the pocket-realm with Dr'amal.

"Dr'amal, when we reach this Druid Keep, do you plan on accompanying us?"

The drowess hesitated. "I had not planned to. The city is known to have elves who my people are at war with, elfin sorcerers and sorceresses."

"And?" Traveler asked.

"If you wish me to, I will. I know you are vexed with me, but we joined your caravan so that we could travel unnoticed. That is what I wish. Once we get to the Great Forest and beyond, we will be more at ease. We act as we do because we also do not wish to attract unwanted attention to the caravan."

"Dr'amal, everyone knows we travel through the Trail. I am certain every elfin party, village, and kingdom knows of our approach. Do you doubt that?"

"No, you are correct. But they do not know everyone in your caravan yet. It is best to keep it that way."

"You do know we intend to take on elfin caravans."

"Why? The elves do not need us to get to Atlantea. And we already have your Lady Aylen."

"Yes, but she will always be more human than elf. We need elves in the caravan for many reasons. Your people better prepare themselves for such an inevitability. I do not want another confrontation as before between drows and elves."

When night fell, Traveler decided to have the caravan remain in the pocket-realm to the relief of all. Hobbs had gathered the leadership for their ritual night meal and took his seat to smoke his pipe. He normally only did so in the morning, but he and his men had worked nonstop to get the new charms done and distributed to all the men before day's end.

"Mr. Hobbs, you look like you need a very long sleep," Lady Aylen said.

Hobbs puffed on his pipe and said, "And I will, princess."

Gresham appeared at the camp.

"Mr. Gresham, pull up a seat at the fire," King Aereth said.

"Thank you, sire." The healer did so.

Meals were served. Everyone took a hearty plate of food and utensils, and once settled, they were served their drinks. The warriors such Pangolin, I-wulf, and Nirgund had never used utensils before joining the caravan but had accepted the domestication that came with being part of the leadership.

"How is our guest?" Traveler finally asked.

Gresham set his plate down. "His name is Frog-Dor, or that is what he says his name is. I have no experience with this, spells and curses and such. By day he is a frog. By night he is in his true human form. Well, I believe he is human. It is very difficult for him to speak. It's as if he fears that he will be struck or beaten at any time. Never have I seen a man so broken."

"Did he save us?" Estus asked. "That night of the death-sleep."

"He did. I fear he believes we were punishing him when we captured him and put him in the cage."

"Oh no," Hobbs said with distress. "And we kept him in the dark."

"Yes."

"Sir, in the morning, I will apologize to him," Hobbs said to Traveler.

"In the morning, he will be in his frog form again."

"If I could suggest," Gresham said, "we should leave him be in the healing tent so he can get comfortable and feel safe. I am sure that with some time, he will fully confide in us."

"Did he get some food?" Gwyness asked.

"Yes, mistress, I saw to it myself. I created a space for him in the corner of the tent away from the door for him to rest. He has a mat and blanket. The torches seem to scare him, but candles seem to soothe him."

"Good. Mr. Hobbs, you should find a place for him during the day."

"Sir, I can see to that," Gresham said to Traveler. "He is under my care."

Traveler nodded. "Good, then, we will leave you to it."

"But is he a wizard?" Pangolin asked.

"He is, but since he has been following us for quite some time, and after his apparent intervention on our behalf in the death-sleep spell-attack, we can safely say he is here to both watch us and protect us when he can."

"Protect us, Mr. Traveler?" Lady Aylen asked.

"Watch for whom?" Pangolin asked.

"We have forces out there trying to harm us and others trying to help us," Traveler said. "The evil ones we know."

"The Four Kings," King Aereth said.

"The others we do not know, but it does not matter. They will reveal themselves when they wish. Or we will wait for this Frog-Dor to tell us."

"Why could this not be a simple caravan quest, as it was intended?" Lady Aylen asked.

"Simple," Traveler said and laughed. "Says the human princess who became an elf."

Others in the leadership began to chuckle.

"Well, thank you for that, Mr. Traveler. Why not tell us more about the Dead City?" the princess directed.

CHAPTER FOUR

The Dead City

At dawn the caravan set out with Traveler marching with the vanguard. After a couple of hours on the Trail, the caravan master peered through his pocket telescope.

"Can you see it, Mr. Elman?" he asked.

The half-elf nodded. "Yes, I started to see it some minutes ago."

"To have Mr. Elman's sight and the hearing of our archer-warriors here," Pangolin said.

"And the strength of an Antaean!" one of the giants added. The other three giants laughed.

Pangolin looked through his small telescope too. "Ruins. How long have they been on the Trail?"

"Many millennia," Traveler replied. "Do we know how long the Dead City has been there?" he asked the giants.

"Probably as far back as the war," one of the giants answered.

"Which one?" Traveler asked.

"Fairies and giants against the elves and sprites."

"Who won?" Pangolin asked.

"Depends on who you ask," Traveler said.

"We did!" one of the giants said.

Traveler glanced at him with a smirk. "Mr. Pangolin, that means neither one did. It was a stalemate. But it was so long ago, Mr. Pangolin, you cannot draw any real conclusions from that war to today. Other than many use it as a source of enmity."

"Why do you say that, Master Traveler?" one of the giants asked.

"Have not the giants warred against the fairies and the elves despise sprites?"

The giants grunted. Elman and the elaphanies did the laughing this time.

"You know too much, human," a giant said.

"We can see it clearly now," Elman said, pointing.

Gresham liked to march in the center of the main caravan, among both human and fae. He could easily look ahead to the front or the vanguard farther on, and he could easily look behind to see the rear. He also liked that he had the giant lizards on the flanks.

Today, he had taken upon himself another duty. In a nearby cart being pulled by one of the pech was the lime-green bullfrog. He had created a nest of blankets for him and plenty of places for him to hide, but the frog jumped to the front of the cart. Quietly and calmly, the frog looked ahead as the caravan moved along the trail.

The vanguard saw two towers, looming shadows at first then more detailed as they neared: ancient gray towers, a crumbling wall encircling another building, all in varying states of decay.

"Reminds me of the Stone Forest," Pangolin noted.

The Dead City did look like petrified white rock. They scanned it carefully for any sign of life. The city was on their left, and the dirt path along the Trail wound the other way. None of them liked that because, as the caravan passed, the city would be at their left flank and then to their rear for miles.

"One of the parties approaches," one the deerlike elaphines said.

The vanguard looked to see the fae-human mercenaries moving to them with their owl griffins hopping around them.

"I will go," Traveler said and left Pangolin to keep the vanguard moving forward.

◆◆◆

"Are you leaving us?" Traveler asked as he neared the one hundred fifty or so mercenaries and their dozens of owl griffins.

"Not at all, Mr. Traveler," one of the fae human mercs said; a scar ran down one side of his face. "We intend on exploring the Dead City for a bit. We will catch up with you at the night camp."

"There is nothing here," Traveler said to him.

"What do you mean, Mr. Traveler?"

"Treasure."

"Then, Mr. Traveler, we will make sure. Our animals here have an uncanny ability to sniff out precious metals and gems. We'll let them run about and see if there is anything to sniff out."

"You are treasure hunters too."

"Nothing wrong with an extra occupation or two, Mr. Traveler. Especially, if it can line one's pocket with coin."

"I cannot make you abandon your detour, me particularly, who has been on my fair share of them on this journey."

"Good of you to realize that, Mr. Traveler."

"Be careful. The Dead City is nothing but decaying ruins, but it does not mean it is free of danger."

"We can handle any robbers or the like," another merc said to him.

"Again, be careful."

Traveler returned to the vanguard.

"They are leaving the caravan?" Pangolin asked.

"Treasure hunters."

"What treasure can possibly be in there?"

"None, but stories abound in fae towns and cities along the Trail. And there always seems to be those who simply want to take a look for themselves. No one ever finds any treasure, despite the stories. But people never learn and sometimes do find other things not of their liking."

"Fools. Will they rejoin us?"

"They said at the night camp."

"As long as they know no one will wait for them. I notice no fae are joining them. Giving humans a bad name."

"That they are, Pangolin," a giant said, and the four giants laughed.

I-wulf the Wicked was his name. All berserker warriors gave themselves "war" names. Nirgund, before he traded it all to become the king's guardsman, was Nirgund the Mad. I-wulf enjoyed being the new leader of the Cut-Throats. He especially loved having their own pack of chamroshes to fight at their sides in battle. Often, he found himself admiring the fae griffin hounds.

Not all the Cut-Throats were berserkers, with the magical battle fury within their souls, which they could tap into to fight longer, fiercer, and with greater strength than any normal man. But all his Cut-Throat warriors were gifted warriors. He reckoned that four hundred of them were better than four thousand regular warriors.

He had spoken to the fae parties that followed in the caravan. The new rearmost configuration was the humanoid mole fae with his giant moose beast in the center, the frog men with their giant land crabs on one side and the raccoon men with their giant porcupines on the other. With some bird men and their enfields and other bird men with their jackalopes, he was satisfied that would be more than a match for any adversary thinking the rear of the caravan was its weak spot.

"I-wulf," he heard one of the Cut-Throats say.

He looked back while he walked. Then he walked out from the columns to stop. The Cut-Throats had noticed that the enfield beasts were reacting to something behind the caravan. He could see nothing. The Dead City was still visible in the distance, but there was little tree and plant life around it to conceal any attackers.

I-wulf threw himself back, instinctively lifting his small forearm shield. He barely deflected the fast-moving spear. Cut-Throats immediately jumped to his defense and surrounded him with full-body shields. Other Cut-Throats drew weapons. Their chamroshes started cawing, ready for battle.

"Fachans!" they heard animal men cry out.

The fae may had seen the attacking creatures before, but none of the humans had. Many of the Cut-Throats were slow to attack, including I-wulf, because they did not believe what they were seeing. The first creature that had thrown the spear hopped in strides of a dozen feet in the air and a dozen feet forward. The seven-foot humanoid looked like a human cut in half. However, its physical form was natural to their race—a single eye in the center of its forehead, a large and flat nose, a large mouth filled with jagged teeth and a single arm protruding from the center of its chest. It moved on a single muscled leg with large throbbing veins. The first one reached them unarmed and was quickly dealt with by the men with their own spears and arrows, cutting it down before it could leap again.

Dozens more of the creatures followed—also clothed in animal skins that covered their hairy, weather-chapped skin. They attacked with multi-chained flail clubs, snapping at the caravan and keeping both chamroshes and men at bay. So wild and effective was their attack, the creatures blocked every spear and arrow shot at them, all the while leaping forward.

I-wulf knew this was his chance to show his leadership. There was no Pangolin, Nirgund, or Mr. Traveler. He was the leader of the Cut-Throats.

"Men! Why do Cut-Throats not use flail-clubs?" he yelled.

The creatures attacked again, but this time Cut-Throats grabbed at the chains. They screamed out as their hands were severely cut. But other Cut-Throats had gloves, and while they grabbed at the attack chains, others hurled every weapon they had on their body at the beasts—daggers, axes, swords, war hammers. One fachan after another was cut down. A shower of arrows rained over their heads and cut down more; both elaphines and drows fired in unison. The remaining fachans hopped away to escape faster than any human though possible.

Gresham had already arrived, looking at the men's hand wounds.

"Men with wounds, go with Mr. Gresham and have them attended to. Men without weapons, go pull them out of those one-legged human hoppers and grab all the rest. Take the flail-clubs too. Mr. Estus might be able to melt them down to use to make proper weapons."

I-wulf noticed a grinning Pangolin in the crowd. He smiled too. Pangolin pretended to clap.

"Mr. Quillen, get away from those bodies!" I-wulf yelled at the lad as soon as he saw him. "How many times must we tell you that one day your curiosity for things to put in your bestiary book will get you killed? Go away from them! They might snatch you with one of their single arms. Wouldn't that give you something to put in your book?"

CHAPTER FIVE

Druid Keep

Clouds blotted out the moon from the sky so completely the darkness was especially stark. Everyone expected the fae-human mercenaries to return to camp that night, but neither they nor their owl griffins were seen. Traveler walked through the camp while the men slept and the brownies went about their nightly chores.

He reached the healing tent. Gresham sat at his desk near the entrance, writing in his journal by candlelight.

"Mr. Gresham. Another Quillen in the making?"

Gresham chuckled as he stood. "Please, no, sir. Merely my own account of the journey and my thoughts."

"You are up late."

"I expected you to show up tonight. Do you think we will see our human mercenaries again?"

"I cannot imagine they were defeated by the fachans. More likely the fachans ran off, or the other possibility is they chased the fachans off. Owl griffins can be a terror regardless of their size."

Traveler had been looking around the tent. In the far corner was another table, but blankets were draped over it. On the ground nearby was a large candle. Gresham gestured him on, and Traveler neared the table. He knelt down and could see the man, Frog-Dor, coiled up underneath. His frightened eyes fixed on Traveler's.

"You are called Frog-Dor?"

The man calmed his trembling. "Yes."

"Why were you following us?"

"I was commanded to do so."

"By friend or foe?"

"Friend."

"A known friend or unknown?"

"Unknown."

"Mr. Gresham told me that you did indeed rouse Mr. Estus who roused the rest of the camp. How did you breach the barrier of his pocket-realm?"

"Physically, I did not. I sent an image of myself into the small-realm."

"By night? Are you not in human form by night?"

"If I work magic, I...return to that form for all of the remaining night."

"Where are the ones who sent you? Are they ahead?"

"Yes, but I cannot say more. I have already said too much."

"Are you in communication with those who sent you?"

"No more. My magic connection was lost when I was captured. But they know what has transpired."

"Are we in any danger from these unknown friends?"

"No. They are true friends."

Traveler nodded, satisfied. "I will let you stay, and Mr. Gresham will continue to look after you. No one will bother you in either form. However, when we meet those who sent you, they best be a friend rather than foe."

"They are friend. I swear."

"Then I leave you to rest for the night."

Traveler stood. "Good night, Mr. Gresham."

"Thank you, sir."

"Get some sleep too," Traveler said as he exited.

"I will, sir."

As Traveler approached his tent, he saw the drowess waiting for him at the entrance. She had a brooding look, standing in her flowing purple robe with the ground torches casting shadows on her dark-bluish face.

"You do know why other fae often refer to you as demons," he said, stopping in front of her.

"My people stopped caring about what other fae thought of us a long time ago."

"Is he dangerous?" he asked her. "Since he has such incredible magical power."

"He is cursed, so it is trapped within him. No, he is not dangerous to us. My spell senses no malevolence within him. Do you not agree?"

"I do, but he serves another. He will remain, and our healer will care for him."

"Yes. Better to keep him under our eyes than to have him stalking us from afar."

"What is it this time, Dr'amal?"

"Tomorrow night we will be there."

"At Druid Keep?"

"Yes."

"It is a moving city, isn't it?"

She smiled.

"Will you be joining us?"

"I do not think it would be best."

"Why?"

"I cannot take the chance that I will be seen and my people known to be among your caravan. It would be bad for you and bad for us."

"We are supposed to walk into a city of spell-casters without one of our own?"

"Take a group of the other fae with you. Their collective magic will suffice. Druid Keep is not a hostile city. They are eager to accept outsiders for trade."

"If you say, but this arrangement is not agreeable to me."

"My father thought that we should find another caravan, but I talked him out of it."

"Why?"

"Where would we find such a situation again? A human-led caravan of human and fae. Under the banners of giants and centaurs, under the protection of fairies and sprites. An elfin princess at the lead. We are in the land of elves, and elves we are not allied with."

"Dr'amal, if we obtain the information that we need at Druid Keep tomorrow night, then you will have earned your keep since you and your people have joined us. However, the fact remains that we venture into the lands of elves without a proper sorcerer or sorceress."

"What of the frog?"

"What of him? He is in no state physically or otherwise to help any of us. You said so yourself: he is cursed. Dr'amal, you and your drows have put us in a precarious situation. But it is my fault. I had thought any sorcerer or sorceress who could maneuver the wizard's puzzle-box test would be what we needed."

"Do not lose hope in me yet, Master Traveler. I may surprise you."

"Dr'amal, this caravan cannot rely on surprises. We need reliable abilities."

"Drows are very emotional beings. We do our best work when angry."

"I do not like the sound of that, Dr'amal. Spell-casters who feed off their own anger or fear, or others, can become warped and twisted in their soul."

"Not I. Not drows."

"Tell me when we near this Druid Keep. I will assemble a group tomorrow. Good night, Dr'amal."

Traveler left her by the entrance as he entered his tent and closed the flap.

The morning marked the third day the caravan was without the fae-human mercenary party. The gossip among the men was that it wasn't the fachan one-legged creatures that killed them but something worse, and the fachans were driven out of Dead City, like the centaur stampede, by that something. Without knowing the truth, there was nothing for Hobbs to say to calm nerves as he made his rounds though the men.

The land became more barren as they traveled. Rather than simply a dirty, dusty path, all the surrounding lands had become flat and barren. On either side in the distance were ridged mountains. There was an uneasy stillness to it all, but at least nothing could sneak up on them. However, it also meant there was no place to hide or use for defense.

On the march, the Tree Shepherds and the crawling trees stayed in their pocket. They emerged whenever the caravan stopped to provide extra—and welcome—security, with the three crawling trees stretching their branches out and above all the men. The chamroshes and alphyns especially liked to play in the trees.

The fairy sisters finally emerged from the same pocket-realm too. They had shaken their fear of the manticore and believed the caravan was beyond it. Out they came and so did their swarms—millions of magic butterflies resting on the armor of the giant fae lizards. The fairies had plenty of animals to play with to amuse themselves, appearing as large fireflies in the day.

After a two-day absence, the dog returned. He walked alongside them in his gray wolf-dog form, looking alert and content.

"How many days to this Fae'el city, Mr. Traveler?" Lady Aylen asked.

"If we have no delays, we should be there in seven days, princess."

"Is all the land as dreary as this?"

"The land will get worse before it gets better, princess. This path intersects another called Wurmroad."

"Oh my," Lady Aylen said. "What is the story behind a road with such a name? Please do not tell us that real wurms live beneath it."

"No, princess. But it is the path often used by dark fae, especially goblins."

"Goblins, Mr. Traveler," King Aereth said. "Will we encounter any of them here?"

"It is highly likely that we will, sire."

"So we will be delayed," Lady Aylen said with annoyance.

"We may encounter them, but that does not mean we will do battle with them. They are as anxious to move to their destination as we. Titan's Caravan is commanded by humans, not any of their elfin adversaries. If we see a small party or full caravan, we will let them pass, whether they are moving east or west, then continue on the Trail north."

"We will not have any trouble?" the king asked incredulously.

"No, sire. We should have none."

"Good," Lady Aylen said. "I prefer positive news. But what if they see me?"

"They will ignore you, princess."

"Good."

"Will Lady Aylen be able to do that invisibility too like other elves, Mr. Traveler?" Gwyness asked.

"You would like that wouldn't you, Mr. Traveler?" Lady Aylen asked. The women laughed.

"Lady Aylen is a water elf. If she learns how to do the trick, she will be able to become invisible within bodies of water or even in the rain."

Night had fallen, and the caravan had stopped for camp. As the quartering party set up the tents for the royals, women, and Traveler, their caravan master disappeared into the camp. The royals and Gwyness waited for him.

"This is the most untenable situation. We enter a secret magic city, but our caravan's supposed sorceress will not accompany us," Lady Aylen said with a huff.

"I don't want to go," Gwyness said.

"It will be fine, Maiden Gwyness," the king said. "It must be done."

"Here comes Mr. Traveler, our able caravan master and more."

Gwyness almost screamed. "What are they?"

Traveler approached with the youngest of the Tree Shepherds. Little Root walked with his large wooden staff, curved at the top, and the two fairy sisters buzzed around him in the form of fireflies. But that is not what frightened Gwyness, and the royals watched with apprehension. Their caravan master also walked with five black humanoids with the heads of locusts. With their large antenna swaying from their heads and jiggling as they walked, the darklings smiled at them with white teeth in their human mouths.

Gwyness stepped back. "We are going to the city with them, Mr. Traveler?"

The darklings laughed.

"Maiden Gwyness, how many times must I tell you that if you don't mind them, they will not bother you. Besides, focus your mind on where we are going. It is a city of both light and dark, sorcerers and warlocks, sorceresses and witches. Trust me when I say, you will be glad they are with us when we enter those gates."

"Do be careful," King Aereth said. "I cannot say I am comfortable with the prospect of you walking into such a city without the one sorceress our caravan does have."

"Why do we allow these drows to remain?" Lady Aylen asked.

"My displeasure with her is no secret, but their collective value will be realized later on. Sire, we leave you here."

Lady Aylen was reminded of the secret city of Last Keep in the Lands of Man. Druid Keep was also invisible to all but those who knew of its magical existence. Traveler and Little Root led the party. The dog's fur was as jet-black as the five darklings who walked at the rear of the group. Lady Aylen and Gwyness walked directly behind the men. Two fireflies sat perched on top of Little Root's walking staff.

"Do you know of this city, Little Root?" Traveler asked the leshy.

"My people know of it, but we would never venture to it."

"Your people are shape-shifters too. Is that correct, Mr. Little Root?" Lady Aylen asked.

"We are, princess," the Tree Shepherd said and looked back.

"There, Gwyness," Lady Aylen said. "We are surrounded by shape-shifters. What could go wrong?"

"Spiders and snakes, snakes and spiders!" They heard the darklings singing behind them and cackling. Gwyness tried her best to contain her disgust for them and resisted the urge to look back at them.

A single castle stood before them with a larger and taller center tower, smaller ones on either side. An empty moat surrounded the structure, and the open drawbridge rested upon the earth. There was not a soul to be seen, only a few torches inside. As they crossed the drawbridge, the castle looked to be made of black gemstone.

Then, it was as the women thought. Once across the threshold of the open entrance, they passed into another pocket-realm. They were met with an explosion of sights and sounds. Crowds of people filled the streets, humanoids, elves, sprites, a couple of giants in the distance, all going about their business. They heard many different languages and noticed quite a few of the people wore hooded cloaks. They also noticed that most in the city were women.

"May I be of assistance?" A hag stood next to them. One of her eyes was white, as if blinded. She was hunched over in her hooded black cloak and attire. She smiled with an excessively wrinkled face.

"We need a reader of ancient symbols," Traveler said.

"What type of objects?"

"Weapons."

"Created by what hands?"

"That we do not know, but the inscriptions are ancient elvish."

"Ah." A note appeared in her hand, and she reached to give it to him. "Take this and follow its path." Her eyes moved to the fireflies on Little Root's staff. "My, you have two little fairies with you." She smiled again.

Traveler looked up from the note then tossed her a large glittering coin. "There could be more."

She gave him a nod and a smile. Traveler led them away from the hag. She watched them as they moved through the crowds down the street and then around a corner. Shops, taverns, and inns lined the roadway on either side, every one of them busy with patrons.

Gwyness did glance back at the darklings. Their form had changed to the heads of black cats. She smirked; she did not imagine they would keep their hideous insect form within the city. They all smiled wide at her in unison and waved. She huffed as she returned her gaze forward.

As with any town or city, there were more than a few people standing on the roads to take notice of the new visitors to their city.

Traveler and Little Root said nothing, briskly walking through the crowds. Traveler held the note up in front of his face as glowing arrows directed him.

"Mr. Traveler, that was a hag," Lady Aylen said. "Can she be trusted?"

"All she cares about is payment, princess. She can be trusted to tell us what we want for that."

They entered the shop. The women were struck by the coldness of the interior, and how small it was. Staffs, wands, and weapons adorned the walls, each item lit by a single candle. All looked unremarkable and old. At the back, three dark haired women in robes stood behind a counter with a large candle to the side. They appeared to be middle-aged and watched the group as they entered.

Traveler walked up to them. "We were sent here to find the Keep's greatest historian, all-knowing of all the fae races and clans."

"That would be us, kind sir."

"What are your true names, ladies?" Traveler asked.

They smiled. "We are Gana, Gaila, and Gaea."

"No, ladies, you are not who we seek."

"We are not?" one asked. The three women looked at him with confusion.

"But I am willing to pay handsomely for the knowledge to meet with this person."

"Pay, sir. With what, sir? Tell us exactly what coins or gems you have to trade. Druid Keep does not except human coin. "

"We have great gems to trade. I do not wish to haggle, so I will give you my best offer first as we need to be quick and on our way. Introduce us to the one we seek, and we will pay you with three of the largest and most expensive gems we have, from the very vault of my elfin princess's kingdom. They are in my pouch here." Traveler held a pouch in his right hand.

"What are these exquisite gems called, human?"

"Gana, Gaila, and Gaea."

The three women disappeared.

Lady Aylen and Gwyness cried out, startled.

"Where did they go?" Lady Aylen asked.

"Ladies, we must continue our search elsewhere."

He led the party out of the shop. The darklings were beside themselves with laughter. The fairy sisters were also giggling in their firefly forms.

"What happened, Mr. Traveler?" Lady Aylen and Gwyness asked him.

"They tried to rob us," Traveler answered.

"I do not understand."

"If Master Traveler had spoken the names of the gems, they would have disappeared from our possession and the women would have flown away. They were witches," Little Root explained.

"It is a common spell among magic-casters who are also thieves. The method is used against unsuspecting fae and humans every day, I would imagine," Traveler said.

"Where did they go then, Mr. Traveler?" Gwyness asked.

"Wherever they had the spell take the stolen goods. Hopefully, they can all fit comfortably and there is a means for them to escape."

"How do you know these things, Mr. Traveler?" Lady Aylen asked.

"Lady Aylen, I lived in Faë-Land. Everyone who lives here or has lived here knows of these tricks."

"Did you know of this?" the princess asked Little Root.

"I did from the moment the hag appeared before us."

"We did not know," they heard Wildglow's high-pitched voice from one of the fireflies.

"Did you know that soon Mr. Traveler?" Lady Aylen asked.

"Yes."

"Then why did we go to their shop?"

"For the rare chance that we may have been able to get the information we wanted. In cities like these, there is no way to judge between liar and truth-teller. You just have to see. We would have genuinely paid them for the information if they had what we requested."

The women stood to the side as Traveler and Little Root spoke to passersby on the roads for referrals. Most were receptive, and Traveler, especially, found himself engaged in full conversations.

"Where are the fairies?" he asked suddenly.

The women looked around.

"Where were they, Mr. Traveler?" Lady Aylen asked. "Were they not on our Tree Shepherd's staff?"

"No, they were hovering above your heads."

The women looked up. Traveler's face was concerned. He stepped into the middle of the street then ran.

"You there!" He ran in front of a hooded woman.

"Did you see two fairies?"

The woman smiled and shook her head. She continued past but Traveler then ran back to the same woman.

"Tell me where you are from," he directed.

The woman shook her head again without saying a word. She was about to continue on, but he grabbed her shoulder. She slapped it away and bolted. The dog ran into her legs, tripping her. She felt hard to the ground, face-first.

She turned over, her eyes glowing red. Traveler swung his blade and beheaded her.

The women screamed.

"Mr. Traveler, what did you do?" Lady Aylen cried out. She ran to grab his sword arm.

Traveler knelt down and pulled a dagger from the back of his belt and sliced the women's stomach open.

"No!" the women screamed.

The women looked on in shock as her belly opened up and bodies spilled out. Two of the victims were the two fairies.

"Help me!" Traveler commanded.

Traveler took his cloak and wiped the yellowish ooze that coated Sunpetal, the smaller fairy. He handed Little Root the fairy then wiped the ooze from Wildglow. Both of the fairies were semi-conscious.

The other bodies were three halflings that looked like gnomes without their hats, several cats of varying colors and two young women wearing purple hooded cloaks. Gwyness and Lady Aylen attended to the young women; the darklings turned into furry humanoids and wiped the cats clean with their own hands.

"Little Root, you hold onto the fairies," Traveler said and set the other fairy sister in his arms. Foliage grew out of his body to shield them.

The cats awoke and ran away. Then the gnomoids jumped to their feet and scuttled away too. The two young women needed more time to collect their wits. Another party ran to them, men and women, all wearing purple hooded cloaks. The two women stood to embrace them.

"Thank you," the eldest woman of the group said to them.

The party quickly moved away with the two young women.

Lady Aylen and Gwyness looked at what remained of the hag on the ground. Her head stared up at the sky with blank, dead eyes. There was little blood from the head or neck and none from the open chest, only the yellowish ooze. Gwyness turned her head away from the gutted mess but then turned to look again.

"There are no entrails," she said.

"Let us move on," Traveler said.

"What will become of the corpse?" Lady Aylen asked.

"The city will take care of it. When we pass by here again, it will be as if she was never here."

They had not stepped far when an elderly elfess with flowing white hair and wearing in a white robe stood in their path.

"People tell me you are looking for me," she said.

The white elfess led them to a secluded tavern. They saw only one other when they entered—a giant sitting at the door in black clothes, his head concealed by a knight's helmet. His clawed hands rested on a broadsword in his lap.

"Do not mind my guardian," she said. "I keep him around because he is older than I am. A rarity for me these days. Your friends can wait out here, your shape-shifter too. The women and you follow."

The elfess stopped to look at the Tree Shepherd. Her attention focused on the two fairy sisters peeking out from behind the leshy's foliage covered body. "Poor things," she said sadly. "You may be terrified, but remember that in a few days, it will only be a distant memory."

She gestured for Traveler and the women to follow with one hand, but with the other, she pointed at the dog to remain. The white elfess passed through a barrier barely perceivable to the eye. Traveler, Aylen, and Gwyness followed her in.

Little Root carried the fairies in his arms to an empty table at the side. The darklings had turned into black crows and flew up to the perch themselves in nooks all along the top of the wall connecting to the ceiling. The dog—a black dog with all-black eyes—sat at the threshold of the barrier. It gave a low rumbling growl as it watched the white elfess, its master, and the women on the other side.

"Here we can speak undisturbed and from any spying eyes or prying ears," the elfess said.

She slowly walked to a large table in the center. They all looked around. It was a tavern that could serve forty or so comfortably but was empty save for them. Traveler sat directly opposite her at the table; Lady Aylen and Gwyness sat together on one side.

"I would offer you a meal or drink, but this place is closed today. I do not cook anymore, and my servant does not pour drinks with those hands." The white elfess turned her attention to Traveler. "Well?"

"You learned of our inquiry from the city."

"No. I learned of your inquiry from someone called Dr'amal."

"Dr'amal?" Lady Aylen asked.

"Yes. She sent word to me by courier two days ago. Normally, I ignore such things, but her story intrigued me. Not much does these days."

"I doubt you would be moved by any you did not know, even out of boredom. Do you know this Dr'amal?" Traveler asked.

"I know her people."

"What people would that be?"

"I know she and her people are drows."

"What would a high elf know of drows?"

"Drows were high elves before they dabbled in magic they should not have and turned their skin forever blue with that magic. So long ago. When my clan and theirs were one."

"D'Shar before the D'Shar."

"That came much later. Another time and many wars ago." She looked at the women. "What do you have for me to look at?"

Traveler looked at the ladies. Gwyness set her war hammers on the table. Lady Aylen stood and pulled her dual war tridents from her back, set them on the table, too, and sat again.

The elderly elfess's hand was about to touch the tridents, but the war hammers caught her eye. She picked them up, squinting as she drew one close to her eye to examine it thoroughly. She set it back on the table then examined the other.

"The weapons are called the soul-strikers," she said, looking at Gwyness. "You do not know this."

"I am just a human."

"You are not a mere human. Where are your parents?"

"I never knew them."

"Your mother and father were both sorcerers."

"But I cannot do magic."

"Who ever said people of magic must only cast spells?"

The white elfess examined both war tridents then set them back on the table.

"Tell me what you know," she said to Lady Aylen.

"We know nothing really. Both Gwyness and I were taken from our elfin kingdom as infants, the kingdom of Faylen. It was destroyed. I do not know if it was while we there or after we were taken from there. I may be the last surviving member of its royal clan. I remember that somehow in my mind."

"Someone told you," the white elfess said.

Lady Aylen continued, "We were taken to the Lands of Man, to the kingdom of Sirnegate, as infants. We were raised in the royal house. I was raised as the king's daughter and Gwyness as my aid."

"Who brought you to this kingdom of Sirnegate?"

"We had a governess, but she died when we were little children."

"How?"

"I do not know."

"Human?"

"We cannot remember," Lady Aylen said then sighed.

"She was human," the elfess said.

"How could you know that?"

"If she were an elf, you would have remembered. What do you remember?"

"Gwyness remembers more than I do."

"Elves have better memories than humans, so that's another indication that your aid is no mere human."

"Faylen was destroyed by creatures," Gwyness said.

"She also possesses an amulet," Traveler added.

"Show me the amulet," the elfess directed.

Gwyness pulled it up from under her top. The white elfess leaned forward and held it in her delicate hands.

"She is an exorcist," Lady Aylen revealed.

"No," the white elfess said. "Exorcists cast out spirits. They don't kill evil creatures with offensive weapons. She is much more than an exorcist. These are the weapons and amulet of a sin-seer."

"What is a sin-seer?" Lady Aylen asked.

The elfess ignored the princess. "The amulet shines when evil creatures are nearby?"

"Yes, undead creatures."

"Undead?" the white elfess asked.

"Fiends," Traveler interjected.

"I do not know this human word 'undead,' and fiend is inaccurate fae slang, but so few fae know of such creatures. What do you humans call 'undead'?"

"Strigoi, lycanthropes, ghouls, and the like," Traveler answered.

"What are strigoi?" Gwyness asked.

"Blood-suckers," the elfess said.

"Vampires!"

"Strigoi are non-existent in our lands. Our lands are of light. They have no power here, so they do not come. The others are rare but do exist in our lands."

"Gwyness also knows how to kill them," Traveler added.

"I only know what I studied in books."

"Books from your governess?" the elfess asked.

"Yes, it is all that we have from her."

"Gwyness, you have a natural instinct with your weapons," Traveler said to her. "You stopped that minotaur ghoul."

Gwyness sighed, remembering.

The white elfess sat back. "I know of Faylen."

"You know the kingdom?" Lady Aylen asked.

"Yes, I visited it many times."

The women looked at her with surprise.

"Tell us, then," Lady Ayen said.

"The elfin kingdom of Faylen was destroyed. Water elves lived within its walls—river, ocean, sea elves. It was a kingdom of sorcerers, magic-casters—including elementals—mostly women, but I do remember a few men in their ranks. They were a specific and unique kingdom. They trained warrior clerics. Do you have those in your lands?"

"Clerics? Yes," Traveler answered. "Battle clerics, of a fashion."

"Well, elfinkind has them too," she said.

"A fairy queen and recently a winged lion centaur called her a necro-seer," Traveler said.

The white elfess smiled. "Yes, they call them by that name. We called them sin-seers. Another word for them is spectral slayers. It was the only order in all of elfdom that kept the secrets and trained the warrior clerics to fight these...undead as you call them but much more. To fight evil that no others could. Beings who walked and plotted, though their bodies no longer pumped the blood of life within, their hearts remains still and cold, they breathed not. There are many other beings than those you named, not just those created by such dark magic but the necromancers who create them with their dark magic.

These warriors clerics could see them, sense them, and destroy them. No others could."

"So that is what I am?" Gwyness asked.

"That is what you both are. You both can slay these creatures with your weapons. You are the seer with your amulet. The elfin princess is the elemental."

"Elemental?" Lady Aylen asked.

"Do you not control water with magic?"

"She is learning," Traveler said.

"Faylen was a kingdom led by mages, who trained warrior clerics. It was a sacred city. Its people were devout. It is a shame your governess was not able to pass on your history to you. The water elementals of the city used their powers to harness the kingdom's streams of holy water to defend against, fight, and kill evil creatures."

"What happened to Faylen? Why does no one talk about it?" Traveler asked.

"No one knows what happened," she answered. "It was destroyed. The battle was long and fierce, but that is all that is known. Some high elves may know much more, but they stay silent—out of fear, not treachery. If Faylen could be destroyed, then any other kingdom could be. Also, elfdom was involved in many wars and entanglements in this realm and elsewhere. There was no one available who could have truly discovered the fate of Faylen."

"So all the knowledge is lost?" Gwyness asked.

"No," the elfess replied quickly.

"The sylphs have that knowledge, and you know the other."

"The Atlanteans," Lady Aylen answered.

"Your real reason for traveling there."

Gwyness looked at Traveler. "We were not being dishonest."

"Maiden, there is no reason to apologize. I knew treasure was not your or the princess's motivation for going on the journey the very first day I met you both. Treasure was a far distant secondary reason."

"We would not want you to think us dishonest," Lady Aylen said to him.

"May I ask a question?" Traveler asked the white elfess.

"You may, but I may not answer."

"What can you tell me of the human kingdom of Xenhelm?"

"Their Kings' Caravan began the year after the destruction of Faylen." She smiled. "But that is, of course, a mere coincidence."

"Yes. Coincidence," Traveler said suspiciously.

She looked at the women. "I would acquire every book and reference about warrior clerics that you can before you get to Atlantea. It should become your obsession. The sylphs will be reluctant or even refuse to share if they suspect you know nothing. The Atlanteans, I do not know. I have not been there in such a long time. They have not been accommodating to high elves at all since the war with them ages ago. I did fly over their city once as a little girl. I was riding with my mother in our wagon drawn by six of the most prized flying steeds. Beautiful animals; I still miss them."

She looked at Traveler directly. "May I ask you a question?"

"You may, and I will answer," Traveler replied.

"Are you continuing on with your journey, or building an army for warfare?"

"Why would you ask that? We are Titan's Caravan. Atlantea is our destination for the reward of fabled treasure. Nothing will stop us in our journey."

"I remember another who said the same thing. His name was King Oughtred."

Traveler and the women froze. They hid their fear well, but it was there.

"If I intended to harm you, my servant would have done so. I was merely comparing statements. You humans often say one thing and do another."

"Is that any different than elves?" Traveler countered. "Such as elves do not invade the lands of others."

"Do not combine me with the star elves. I live in elfdom and care not for any other empire or realm. You may be continuing on with your journey, but I would build an army, too, if I were you. You may be righteous people. I believe you are. I saw what you did to the hag, saved those fae and animals from certain death. But, there are many who will try to involve you in their affairs."

"The fairy queen told me the same thing," Traveler said.

"If a fairy queen tells you a thing and then an elfin queen tells you the same thing, then it must be true."

"Can you help us, then?" Gwyness asked her. "You saw our city of Faylen. Can you tell us anything more?"

"I could, but it would only serve to distress you. They are dead, but you must carry on." She touched Gwyness's hand. "Do you head for Fae'el?" she asked Traveler.

"Yes. Straight through Wurmroad."

"Wurmroad. That is a vile place. May not be as straight as you hope. But if you make it to Fae'el, I will send my servant to you. He will give you any information I still possess about the Faylen's mages and warrior clerics."

"At Fae'el?" Traveler asked.

"Oh, no. Too many spying eyes and prying ears. Later on your journey on the Titan's Trail."

"Thank you," Lady Aylen said.

"Yes, thank you," Gwyness said.

"What is your name?" Lady Aylen asked.

"I am Queen Mother Anelle of the Celestial Elves of Nimbus. But I am no more than a royal figurehead in name alone. Young ones rule today.

"I would be very careful on your journey, though. The knowledge you possess only puts you in more danger. Also, I know of King Oughtred because his kingdom created his Kings' Caravan under the banner of the celestial elves, not Nimbus but others."

"Why would they do that?" Traveler asked.

"Why would Titan's Caravan be under the banner of the fairies of Chrysa, giants of Antaeus, and the centaurs of Chiron? You can also add the banner of the lost elfin kingdom of Faylen. None do it because they like you, though it seems that many do, strangely enough. You seem to have a prior history with many, including phookas, the evil things, even the benevolent ones. It is all done for the benefit of kingdoms.

"I did not fully trust the Xenhelmians then, but did not stand in the way of my royal house when they gave them their blessings and tacit assistance. So, I help you to make up for the error in judgment of my kingdom and others. I help you, human, because I heard you lived in Atlantea previously. I was told you cared little for its riches, so you would not care now. You cared only for adventure. I can hardly relate, but I hear it is a common sickness among your kind. I gladly help the women, the water elemental and sin-seer, because they will begin again the Faylen warrior clerics for all of elfdom. So continue your journey through Titan's Trail, and watch for my servant."

CHAPTER SIX

Fairy Warrior Party

They exited the empty tavern back into the crowds of the streets. The darklings changed into giant insectoid forms again, following the dog at the rear. Traveler glanced over at Little Root cradling the fairies in his arms. Both sisters were still shaken by their ordeal. Lady Aylen and Gwyness walked beside the Tree Shepherd.

When they crossed the threshold of the magic city, and stepped across the drawbridge, it closed. The women glanced back to see the entrance, moat, and city were all gone.

"They're back!" they heard someone call out as they neared the camp.

They could see King Aereth appear at the perimeter with a torch in hand. The darklings transformed into furry dog-like creatures and ran into the camp to join their other comrades dancing in the form of raven-headed humanoids.

King Aereth saw the faces of Traveler and the women. "Did something happen?"

"We are fine, sire," Lady Aylen answered.

"I will take the little ones to our sanctuary," Little Root said as he passed.

"Thank you," Traveler said to him. He saw Dr'amal and her father, Dr'as, also waiting.

"I think we need to talk," Lady Aylen said.

Hobbs had also appeared, but Traveler sent him back to bed. There was a tent already setup, the opening an entrance to another pocket-realm. Traveler, the royals, Gwyness, and the drows entered. Dr'amal sealed the door.

"Did you get the answers you sought?" the drowess asked Lady Aylen.

"I did," the princess replied.

"Thank you, Dr'amal, for arranging the meeting," Lady Aylen said.

"You are welcome."

"You know high elves."

"We know some. She is one."

"I wish to speak with the king and the women alone," Traveler said. "The words of the elfin queen were both revealing and distressing."

"Yes, of course," Dr'as answered. "We will leave you, but I do wish to speak with you alone too. Maybe tomorrow."

"Yes."

The drows nodded and left the tent. Traveler sealed the entrance after them.

"You did not ask them about King Oughtred," Lady Aylen said.

"King Oughtred?" King Aereth asked.

"Yes, sire. Gwyness and I will tell you the whole story. Mr. Traveler also saved the lives of our two little fairies."

"What happened?"

"A hag tried to run off with them lodged in her stomach," Gwyness said with distress.

"Pardon me?" the king asked, incredulous.

"We will tell you the whole story later, sire," Lady Aylen said.

"Did you find out about your origins?" the king asked.

"Yes, sire," the princess replied. "We did. More than we could have asked. I have to sleep on it to determine if I am happier knowing or not. Is there more, Mr. Traveler?"

"To answer your question, princess, I did not ask the drows about their knowledge of the elfin queen and Oughtred because it does not matter."

"Does not matter? The drows were very hot at any mention of the Xenhelmians but sent us to a person who collaborated with them."

"That is too strong a word, princess. She did freely reveal her involvement with them. You and Maiden Gwyness received the information you needed."

"Is that it, Mr. Traveler?" Gwyness asked.

"Yes, unless you wish to remain here. We will be on our way to Fae'el. All our detours are behind us."

"I get the impression, Mr. Traveler, that you did not believe everything she said," Lady Aylen said.

"Because I didn't. She knew everything about us."

"You said it yourself. Everyone in Faë-Land knows us."

"Perhaps. But I know her people."

"Meaning?" Lady Aylen asked.

"It does not matter. We all must get our sleep and be ready to rise. The road from here to the elfin city of Fae'el is an unfriendly and treacherous one."

"Goblins," King Aereth said. "The other fae in the camp were talking about them."

"Yes, sire. Ladies, you can recount your story to the king later. But when you do, do it here. Also, do not speak aloud about your true origins to anyone."

"Why?" Lady Aylen asked. "Can I not say I am the elfin princess of both Sirnegate and Faylen?"

"You can but no more. We are a simple caravan on the way to Atlantea. There are still months of travel ahead."

The caravan set out under an overcast sky. Some remarked that they hoped it was not a bad omen of rain or ill events ahead. By now the gossip had spread about the hidden city with witches and warlocks within its walls, which added to the caravan's unease.

When they stopped for the noon meal, the sight of the bright-green leaves of the crawling trees was a blessing on lands as dark, gray, and dreary as they traveled. The only thing to be seen were the mountain ridges on either side.

"Mr. Tyfer and Mr. Oeric," Hobbs said, "I will be right back." He got up from his seat, his meal finished. The guardsmen watched him walk off.

Hobbs returned a short time later with a few of the pechs. The two guardsmen stood.

"Gentlemen, Mr. Traveler tells me that as we approach, there will be other opportunities to add to our caravan. Mr. Tyfer and Mr. Oeric, you know these lands and its people better than I, but I wish to add fae to our team when I access newcomers to the caravan."

"But you are a good judge of character," one of the pech said.

"Yes, but I am still human. You may see something we may miss."

"Yes," said another pech, "you humans do have feeble eyesight, are practically deaf, and smell funny."

Hobbs and the fae humans laughed.

"But we will work with you," the pech said.

Traveler ate his meal quickly and then sat off to the side by himself to study his maps. He looked up. Dr'as stood nearby, his head well covered by his hood.

"Yes, Mr. Dr'as."

"I hope my daughter has redeemed herself in your eyes."

"I do not know. Has she?"

"The princess and the human female received the information they needed. Such knowledge is not easy to obtain, especially if you do not know where to go or who to ask that you can trust."

"True. Do you trust the white elfess from Nimbus?"

"I do. My clan has known hers for ages. We have never lifted a hand against the other, even when our races were at war."

"Even if her race aided the Xenhelmians?"

"They did not aid them. They allowed their caravan into the magical lands. But they were hardly the only fae kingdom to do so, and that was before we knew what we know now. Nothing changes in our hate for the Xenhelmians."

"What did you wish to speak to me about?"

"I want my people to be allowed in as part of your main party."

"Why?"

"You know why. Soon the land will be thick with elves. I must keep my people protected."

"Your people are not shy about battles."

"No, we are not, but do you want battles or to move through this wretched region at our quickest pace without delay?"

"Mr. I-wulf and his Cut-Throats have observed your people more than any of us at the front. I will speak with Mr. I-wulf. If he has no objections, Mr. Hobbs will make the arrangements. "

"My people are quiet and have caused no trouble, and we will continue to cause no trouble."

"Where is that fae-blood woman who introduced us?"

"She is…resting."

"Mr. Dr'as, is she hibernating? I do know of her race."

"Yes. She could no longer postpone it. We are to wake her when we reach the Great Forest."

"She allowed you and your people to watch her?"

"She is under your healer's care."

Traveler's eyes narrowed.

"Do not say anything to him. She made him promise not to tell you."

"I will keep it to myself."

"Thank you. I await a visit from Mr. Hobbs then." The drow nodded. "I will leave you to your important task of charting our safe path through the Trail."

Dusk arrived again, and the revelations of the white elfess in Druid Keep still weighed heavily on Gwyness. Any could see it in her face as she moved through the main camp to where Pangolin and the giants camped. The giants were already sleeping, a few were even snoring.

"Mr. Pangolin," Gwyness called out.

Pangolin looked up from where he sat at his fire, set his tea aside, and walked to her.

"Maiden Gwyness."

"I was hoping for advice."

"Yes, maiden. You look troubled."

"The princess and I found out about our origins. Apparently, I am destined to be some kind of warrior against evil."

"But, maiden, we already knew that from your weapons and your use of them."

"Yes, I suppose so."

"And you are not comfortable with that fact?"

"No. I thought maybe I could train with some of your men."

"Who? The Cut-Throats?"

"Yes."

"They are under Mr. I-wulf's command."

"Who would you recommend that I should train with?"

"Maiden Gwyness, I do not believe your issue is with your skills but your nerve. All the training in the world will be of little use if, within yourself, you have not accepted your destiny."

"Destiny? I have always loathed that word. As if one has no choice in the matter."

"You do have choice, maiden. You can choose to accept and embrace it, or you can choose to shun it. When I was young I had to make a similar decision. Follow in the footsteps of my ancestors born with my gift or leave it all behind. I chose my destiny and took the armor and weapon of my forefathers. I would hardly be of use to the world as a farmer because, even as a farmer, I would still be a berserker."

She smiled. "You are a philosopher too."

"Only an observer of people. You doubt yourself when you think. You act when you forget to think, as you did in our time of need when King Oughtred sought to kill us all by stranding us all at the river. You decided on the course and not only saved all of us, but brought our king into the caravan. That was all your doing. You must stop doubting yourself. Mr. Traveler also told me of your attack on the undead minotaur. You did so without hesitation or fear—pure instinct."

"But to face these creatures—."

"Then face them. You have the weapons. Mr. Traveler even found you a magical companion."

"Yes, the black kirin."

"I think, before you start any training, you must get comfortable in your destined role. You must embrace it first, and fully. You can't do so half-heartedly. Those who do, die."

Gwyness sighed. "I am scared."

"All brave people are, maiden."

"Yes."

"Whenever you are ready, I will recommend the Cut-Throats who are best. Your weapons require you to strike with speed. Fighting with dual weapons is an art most do not do well. One hand strikes, while the other counter-strikes or blocks."

"Yes."

"There is no rush. Tell me when you are ready. In the meantime, we have our leadership meeting, and I already see our Mr. Hobbs coming this way to fetch us."

The leadership assembled in the royal tent. I-wulf, Estus, and Nirgund sat together on one side. Lady Aylen and Gwyness sat with the king. Quillen waited with Hobbs at the door until everyone arrived. Gresham strolled in last. Traveler was already seated, with his dog lying on its belly next to him.

"How is your patient, Mr. Gresham?" Traveler asked.

"He is doing well, sir, doing much better each day."

"Good."

Quillen sat on a stool. "Mr. Traveler, why do these sprites have such funny names, these pech?" he asked. "There is Mr. Truestrike and Mr. Longback, Mr. Strikeback, Mr. Pitchhammer and Mr. Battlefuzz is my favorite."

There was chuckles from the group.

"They think our names are funny, too, Mr. Quillen."

"I wonder what are the name of some of the brownies?"

"Ask them and find out," Traveler said to him.

At the tent's entrance, Nirgund's alphyns lay about, keeping watch. The two fairy sisters flew in. Neither fairy had fully recovered from their ordeal, spending all that day within the pocket-realm of the leshies. Wildglow landed and looked around at all of them. Her sister, Sunpetal, was clamped around her waist. Wildglow looked at Traveler with sad eyes then looked around again, nervously.

Traveler stood and walked out of the tent. Everyone watched him. When Traveler returned, Wildglow smiled, and Sunpetal let her sister drop to the ground. Traveler handed what looked like a small green apple to the older sister then another the younger sister. He returned to his stool.

"Let us go over our strategy for when we arrive at Wurmroad," Traveler said to the leadership.

Everyone listened and engaged in conversation, but really, they watched the two fairy sisters. They sat on the ground, first biting into the tiny apples with chipmunk-like teeth then peeling off the green skin. Inside, the fruit looked like oranges coated with honey. The fairy sisters could not be happier. They made a mess as they ate the candy fruit: Wildglow's mouth was covered with the honey as she ate the whole thing. Sunpetal's face, arms, and part of her chest were wet with the honey mess as she nibbled at it.

Wildglow started licking her fingers and hands clean. Sunpetal was obviously full and held the candy fruit in her hands.

Traveler continued talking as he stood up again and took the candy fruit from Sunpetal and wrapped it in a cloth from his tunic pocket. Lady Aylen held in a laugh. In fact, all of them were doing the same or smiling.

"Come over to the water here, and wash your hands and face," he said to them, and both fairies flew up to land on the table where he stood. A bowl of fresh water sat on the top of it. When they did as instructed, Traveler returned to his seat, and the fairies returned to a spot near him and stretched as they yawned. Wildglow curled up and closed her eyes. The smaller Sunpetal did the same near the small of her sister's back on the other side.

"Is there anything else?" Traveler asked the group.

No one answered. They all looked at him, chuckling.

"Then, I'll put these two in their proper sleeping place in the Tree Shepherd's sanctuary realm. We all need our sleep too."

"Then, it will be so, Mr. Traveler," King Aereth said as he stood.

Traveler scooped up the two fairies carefully in each hand. The meeting was adjourned.

Traveler sat at his table studying his magical maps one last time. Dawn was upon them, and the caravan would set out soon.

"Sir." Traveler heard Hobbs's voice from outside his tent.

"Yes, Mr. Hobbs."

Instead Lay Aylen stepped in.

"Princess. You can mimic Mr. Hobbs's voice too?"

She smiled as Hobbs popped into the tent.

"I'll have your tent taken down once you're done, sir."

"Yes." The steward disappeared again. "Princess."

"Mr. Traveler, you summoned me?"

"Yes." He stood from his table.

"Before you start, what are your true thoughts about our encounter with the elfin queen at Druid Keep? I know you have much more to say about it."

"I do, but there is nothing to say. You and Maiden Gwyness learned what you needed. We can thank her for that."

"But?"

"We should not think of anything else but getting to Atlantea."

"You sound as if you do not trust the white elfin queen."

"We can trust anyone we want, princess, as long as they are afar."

"Mr. Traveler, is that what humans call 'talking like an elf'? Saying little but meaning a lot."

He smiled. "You are learning, princess. Before our Mr. Hobbs tears down the tent around us, I believe we should take advantage of your true birthplace. The last princess of the lost elfin kingdom of Faylen. State it loudly and proudly."

"Why the change?"

"I have learned that there is an elfin caravan waiting for us when we arrive at Fae'el, courtesy of our tree friend, Browncrown."

"Oh yes," she said with a smile. "How do you know?"

"Tree people and leshies magically communicate all the time. The Tree Shepherds informed me. You are our elfin royal. No need to have you in the background. Also, your confidence in yourself has returned. I believe you are quite happy with being an elf."

"I am, Mr. Traveler. Your exercises for me, I have to admit, have been most beneficial."

"How is the language learning progressing?"

"Well, though I am not ready to start speaking. When I do, my tongue feels strange."

"Because you are speaking magic."

"Like a spell?"

"Magic language. Magic words. For me, it will always feel strange. For you, the sensation will disappear.

"Going forward I will introduce you as the princess of the human city of Sirnegate and lost elfin kingdom of Faylen."

"Do you want others to know about my existence, Mr. Traveler?"

"I do."

"Is that dangerous?"

"Fae already know, princess. Fairies have already seen the inscription on your tridents and also Maiden Gwyness's weapons. Anyone interested already knows too. You have the female half-elves as your royal guard. Speak with them. Our caravan will be under Faylen's banner and so will they."

"I see. The fairies of Chrysa, giants of Antaeus, the centaurs of Chiron, and the banner of the lost elfin city of Faylen. Not even the Four Kings of Xenhelm traveled under such an impressive array."

◆◆◆

Lady Aylen, followed by all seven of her female half-elf guards, walked to a section of the camp where Mr. Elman and the ten half-elf mercenary team stood waiting.

"Have you heard?" she asked them all.

The half-elves looked at each other.

"Mr. Traveler told me something of this concept of being 'forsaken' by some elfin clans," the princess said. "I will not pretend to understand it all. Though, I do understand it as the cause of your unease at first with the caravan, and with me, as an elf."

"It is a good caravan, m'lady," Elman said.

"And you are a good leader, m'lady," one of the female half-elves said.

"All of you are valued members of the caravan. You will no longer be without a kingdom. As of today, you are honorary citizens of both my kingdoms."

"Both, m'lady?" Elman asked.

"The human kingdom of Sirnegate and the lost elfin city of Faylen. You can be proud to announce to any and all who challenge you. How does that sound?"

She could see their smiles.

"Thank you, m'lady."

"It is settled then," Lady Aylen said.

◆◆◆

Titan's Caravan had hardly begun its march when the vanguard and men in the main party saw it—an approaching fairy storm. Pangolin gave the signal to stop, and Traveler joined him with the dog.

Dozens of human-sized female fairies landed from the swarm in front of them. Their most striking feature was their big bright-crimson humanoid eyes. They had pale almost-transparent skin. Their hair was short, dark, and filled with leaves and thistles, and they had the same forehead antennae and translucent wings as the fairy sisters. The six-foot-tall fairies wore crimson dresses, and they were armed with spiked spears, though they only had two arms rather than the two sets of arms on each side, unlike the previous fairy-storm.

"Why do you block our path?" Traveler asked.

One of the fairies stepped forward. "We wish to join your caravan."

"Why?"

"Why would you not wish fairy warriors to join your caravan?"

"Titan's Caravan already has fairy warriors. We do not need any more."

"What fairy warriors?"

"We have two."

The news surprised the fairies. "You have no fairy warriors," the same fairy challenged.

Wildglow and Sunpetal appeared at the front as fireflies then grew in size. This time the two were of equal size, at two feet, hovering in the air with fluttering insect wings and wearing what looked to be beetle exoskeleton pieces of armor.

The fairies laughed. "They are children."

"We are not children!" Wildglow yelled. "We are fairy warriors!"

The fairies above them in the sky also laughed. Traveler looked at the fairy sisters' faces growing red. He winked at them.

"Titan's Caravan is under the banner of fairies of Chrysa," Traveler said, pulling a parchment from his cloak pocket. "The fairy sisters are acting as their fairy-warrior emissaries with the full command of three swarms."

The fairies in front of them had stunned expressions. The laughter ceased from the fairy-storm.

"Why would the fairy queens of Chrysa empower two fairy children with such a position and give them such a command?"

"Why not ask them?" Traveler said. "You are, after all, part of fairy-dom."

"You will come to regret this decision, human. There is much danger ahead."

"I will come to regret nothing about my decision. You are fairy warriors, and Titan's Caravan is not an army."

"Yes, you are treasure hunters," the fairy warrioress said with contempt.

"If you have such disdain for us, why would you want to join us?"

"We will go to Atlantea on our own, then."

"Then, do so, and trouble us no more."

"You will wish you had real fairy warrioresses at your side ahead."

"If I were you, I would see to it that we do not come across any dangers. If our fairy sisters are injured or killed and their fairy-queen mother were to find out you had knowledge that could have prevented it, I suspect her wrath upon you, all of you, would be quite severe."

"Our mother will kill you!" Wildglow yelled at them.

The fairy warrioress leader studied Traveler. "We came to form an alliance, not make an enemy."

"Then, we will see you in Atlantea. Ensure there are no dark fae ahead that could harm us."

"We know of no dark fae ahead or anywhere else. We are fairies of light."

"The Crimson Thorn fairies know many dark fae, so I will take your words to mean there are none that you know of ahead. Thank you for your offer of an alliance, but we will decline. However, the Trail is long, and we are barely at the halfway mark. Should you need a friendly caravan to follow along with you, you can seek us out again."

The fairy warrioresses looked at each other. They spoke to each other in a language that was faster than the caravan had ever heard. The leader returned her gaze to Traveler.

"We may take you up on the offer. Thank you. Have a safe journey, and take care of our sisters."

"We will," Traveler said.

The fairy warrioresses turned into balls of light that flew up into the center of the fairy-storm. They all rose into the sky. Like millions of fireflies, they dissipated into the clouds.

CHAPTER SEVEN

Wurmroad

Quillen looked at the sun at its apex in the sky. However, when his gaze returned to the surroundings, it made no difference. The land was dreary, alternating between dusty and dirty or muddy and dirty.

They had stopped for the noon meal. He took the time to recall the fairy warriors they had just encountered and sketched their likenesses in his magical book.

"I wonder what Mr. Traveler's dog really looks like in its true form," he said to Hobbs who returned to his spot next to him. The steward sat to smoke a quick pipe.

"Why do you ask?"

"I remember his story when the tree people and nisse visited us."

"Yes, a remarkable story. A shape-shifter not of this world. But he nursed it back to health. Our Mr. Traveler is a true healer to the end."

"So many of these fae are shape-shifters. I was wondering what their true forms really are."

"Does it matter?" Hobbs asked.

"I guess not. How would we ever know? Mr. Hobbs, this is a wretched place we travel across. I cannot wait to have it behind us."

"I agree. So do the men."

"A wurm is a dragon is it not?"

"There are no more dragons, Mr. Quillen. But, yes, a wurm is a reptile creature that still exists in the lands of magic—or so I am told. However, we will not be seeing any on this road, if that is what you're thinking."

"No. No wurms, but we will likely see goblins. Will that be worse though?"

"Mr. Quillen, do not worry yourself. Regardless, you will have more subjects to sketch in your book."

Quillen showed him his rendering of the fairy warriors.

"Oh, very good, Mr. Quillen. That is those fairy warrioresses exactly."

The caravan had only been marching for a short while when Pangolin gave the signal to stop. Traveler joined the vanguard with his dog.

"I see them," Elman said, squinting.

"How many?" Pangolin asked.

"Maybe as many as five hundred."

Traveler looked at Pangolin. "Keep your post here. I will get the Cut-Throats."

The caravan master ran back, past the front of the columns to the rear, with his dog following. Soon, all heard the movement of the caravan's warriors and berserkers and the cawing of their chamroshes. The night before, Traveler had all the Cut-Throats switch to goblin armor. Three hundred of them stood tall with their weapons in hand; the other one hundred managed their individual chamroshes on thick leather leashes. Traveler joined them. Then, the dog began to change into a giant twelve-foot-tall green humanoid creature with thick green fur on its body, clawed lizard hands and feet, and a goblin-like head covered in tusks.

The wait was short. The human men of the caravan for the first time saw a goblin party. Whether it was returning from a battle or going into one, no one knew, but the goblin war party moved in front of them, from west to east. Some of the men might describe them as elfin, not knowing better. Their skin was green, their frame stout and muscular, their noses flat, and their pointy ears were larger. They all wore rust-colored goblin armor and carried goblin shields in one hand and weapons in the other—maces, battle axes, spiked clubs, spiked maces, or war hammers.

Traveler stood with Pangolin and the vanguard over one shoulder and I-wulf and the Cut-Throats over the other. The giant goblin creature "dog" stood with arms folded behind them. The giants glanced back at it and realized that it was now fifteen feet in height and bulkier.

The eyes of everyone in the Titan's caravan was on the passing goblin war party. Every goblin watched them with gnarled frowns and bared fanged teeth. However, the goblins did not stop. They moved past, ignoring the caravan. The goblins were soon specks in the distance.

"Do you think they are heading to battle?" Pangolin asked Traveler.

The caravan master nodded. "I do but not our concern. We should move ahead as quickly as we can. Hopefully, we will not encounter any other war parties."

Quillen was happy to see Dr'amal walking nearby Hobbs and him at the front of the column. Her place was supposed to be near the royals and Gwyness, but she sometimes marched with them. Other times she was not to be seen.

"They look like elves," Quillen said to Hobbs, "only ugly, big, and green."

"You should not say that," the drowess cautioned him. "Never compare an elf to a goblin or the reverse. You might receive a blade in the chest."

"Is it an offense to drows too?" Quillen asked her.

"Yes, but we seldom fight over it. We simply ignore the insult. But it's best you remember this. We will be in the land of elves. You will learn that elves take offense easily at a great many things. Your princess may be an elf, but she is also not."

The caravan's chronicler returned his attention to the front where King Aereth and Lady Aylen walked in front of them. Gwyness and the royal guards followed. The lad looked around as the noise became louder. The sounds were of metal, upon metal but no one could see where they came from.

A magical explosion startled everyone as the large bag to the pocket-realm of their weapons cache—and the väki—on one of the center pull carts blew open. Several green halflings were thrown out of the realm, flying through the air and crashing several yards away. One of the väki stepped out of the bag to their pocket-realm. Most in the caravan had never seen their gnomoid guardians, but another appeared then another. Three of the surly, frowning bearded little men in their charred dark-brown and orange attire grew in size as everyone watched. Some of the caravan had stopped their march; others continued.

"Stand your ground and prepare for battle!" a voice yelled out. It was Traveler's voice.

The fae humans, Tyfer and Oeric, grabbed Hobbs and Quillen.

"Stay close," Tyfer directed as he and Oeric stood with their swords in hand.

"What are those green halflings?" Quillen asked. His eyes widened as the creatures blown out of the väki's pocket-realm ran at the flank. The lizard minders and their giant lizards readied for attack.

"Those are hobgoblins," Tyfer answered.

The creatures were about three feet in height. Their pointy ears were longer and thinner, sprouting from the sides of their heads. Their noses were hooked. Their teeth reminded Quillen of fish—long and sharp—and the hobgoblins had beady little eyes. They were clad in dark clothes—tunics and trousers and curled pointed shoes.

"Dive!" Tyfer yelled.

The guardsmen pushed Hobbs and Quillen to the ground as a blue fireball erupted from one of the creatures hands and fired at them. One of the väki threw a large orange fireball from his own hand, obliterating the blue one. The other two väki hurdled their own fireballs at the hobgoblins.

Everyone in the caravan instinctively knew to get out of the way as hobgoblins and väki battled each other with their magic missiles of fire.

"Traveler!"

The caravan master looked to the vanguard. He did not have the eyesight of Mr. Elman or other fae, but he could see them coming fast.

"I-wulf protect the rear and the other parties!"

The Cut-Throat acknowledged him by raising his battle-axe in the air. His Cut-Throats rallied around him, and the chamroshes were released from their collars.

Traveler drew his magical sword. His dog ran with him, growing larger and fiercer with each step. The new war party that charged were goblins on black war wolves.

King Aereth ran into the caravan to the pechs, who waited for instructions.

"Can we hit them with our heavy weapons?" the king asked.

"No," one of them replied. "They move too fast for your humans to hit them. But—"

"But what?"

"We can throw the projectiles by hand and maybe hit a goblin or two, maybe a wolf too."

"Then do it!"

Nirgund stood next to the king with his alphyns. The reptilian hounds growled, filled with hatred at the sight of goblins.

"Mr. Nirgund, protect the men, not me," the king commanded.

"Yes, sire." The guardsman gripped his sword and charged away. "We attack!" he yelled at his pack of fae hounds. The ran ahead of him.

Already, the pechs were throwing boulders and large metal projectiles at the attacking goblin war party. The caravan's elaphine archer-warriors showered the dozens of goblin riders and their giant dire wolves with elfin arrows. The four giants attacked with their large war hammers, and Pangolin with his axe-mace.

The caravan had formed up in a circle. Their armored giant lizards created a wall, the lizard minders behind them. The men of the heavy weapons teams stood shoulder to shoulder with their tall rectangular shields to protect all the non-fighters of the caravan. Estus and his men created their own inner circle with Dr'as and his drows. The humans were armed with spiked shields and spears; the drows held strange curved throwing axes of a dark elfin metal. In the very center of the caravan, other elaphine and cervid archers fired their own arrow volleys. Near the rear of the caravan, the faun archers unleashed their volley of arrows at the goblins.

A contingent of the main goblin war-party charged the rear of the caravan but were met with a storm of attacking chamroshes by air and berserkers on the ground. The goblins were so outnumbered they retreated as quickly as they appeared. The griffin hounds gave chase but were called back by their human masters.

The väki continued to battle the hobgoblins on the right flank. Three of the väki against dozens of hobgoblins, and growing. The creatures were appearing out of thin air. Their pocket-realm erupted again, and a giant hand emerged to throw several more hobgoblins out directly into the advancing hobgoblins at the flank, knocking them all tumbling to the ground. The giant hand shrank in size as a fourth väki emerged.

The fourth väki joined his comrades, and they all grew steadily larger. One of them sucked in air, and the hobgoblins stopped their advance. The väki were almost twenty feet tall when the one exhaled fire from his mouth. The hobgoblins screamed as they caught fire. The creatures could not run away fast enough and disappeared from sight.

Lady Aylen had stood in her same spot, waiting. She had a trident in each hand. The female half-elves stood behind her with swords drawn and spears ready. Gwyness stood nearby with her war hammers. However, there would be no battle for them. The fairy sisters appeared, hovering in the air, and surrounded the entire caravan in a swarm. They giggled as they watched the fighting.

Pangolin took the lead in the vanguard's attack. The goblin warriors were shocked that none of the blows of their weapons did anything against Pangolin's magic armor. He crushed one after another with his axe-mace; the giants killed the dire wolves with their war hammers. The alphyns attacked one goblin after the next as a pack, knocking them off of their wolves. Elman and Nirgund had little to do; the fae hounds fought so ferociously around them. The elaphines protected them all with a steady barrage of arrows.

The goblin war party had had enough. The survivors fled on foot with the few dire wolves that remained alive. When they were gone in the distance, the entire caravan, human and fae, erupted in cheers.

CHAPTER EIGHT

The Elfin Wizard King

The caravan's weaponsmaster, Mr. Estus, moved through the camp accompanied by a few men. He did so after any battle. While Hobbs was diligent in the caravan operating smoothly, Estus was as fastidious in making sure weapons were well maintained and supplies were always stocked. He insisted on sharp, clean blades and quivers filled with all the arrows they would need in battle.

"Will you ever need use of the heavy weapons?" he asked the pech.

The sprites shook their heads. "We can throw a boulder as far as it if needed," one said.

"You humans can use them. If we are ever attacked by a giant beast of any kind, you can never have too many projectiles fired at an advancing ogre," another said.

"Yes, we dealt with one of those already. No, actually two of them while we were still in the Lands of Man," Estus said.

"Two? Ogres will eat each other if there's more than one in a given territory."

"There were two of them. Both probably sent to us by magical means by the same evil party."

"We heard about that."

"Do fae use catapults?" Estus asked them.

"Most fae can't be bothered. Elves are very much like humans, so they like them in their wars from time to time."

Estus smiled. "Elves and humans. Are you insulting humans or elves? Both probably."

The pech nodded.

◆◆◆

Camp had been set up within the circle, with the three crawling trees spaced out equally from each other in the center and the sentries stationed. At the top of the trees, men and fae peered through telescopes to watch for any other attacking goblin war parties.

"There!" one of the half-elves yelled from the top of one of the crawling trees.

People looked and saw a lone figure on a large dire wolf. After a while, it disappeared back over the ridge.

"It was a scout," Traveler said to the men. "Some will be visible; others not. Simply stay within the circle and maintain a constant vigil of the surroundings."

The men that had gathered around the caravan master nodded.

Traveler walked back to his tent with his dog. The royals and Gwyness sat at a campfire, talking. It was still a few hours until night, but the dreary lands were also colder than any of them had experienced since crossing into Faë-Land months ago.

"Mr. Traveler, neither one of us got to participate in our caravan's battle," Lady Aylen said disappointedly.

"Do not worry yourself, princess," Traveler said as he passed with the dog. "You will have your chance again, on many occasions." He stopped. "We should be very proud of the caravan. Human, sprites, fairies, giants, other fae. All worked together quickly and ably to repel our attackers. More importantly, no life on our side was lost. This was a good day, princess."

She nodded. "Yes, Mr. Traveler, it was."

"I dare say Titan's Caravan is more impressive than the Kings' Caravan ever was."

"Do goblins attack at night, Mr. Traveler?" Gwyness asked.

"They do, Maiden Gwyness, and their hobgoblin cousins are especially fond of night stalking. There are also many dark creatures they employ for their evil deeds."

"Such as?" Gwyness asked.

"The brownies, darklings, and our human night watch will deal with any night attackers. You will be sleeping."

"I see now why you employed those morose väki," Lady Aylen said. "They protect our weapons' pocket-realm."

"Yes. Hobgoblins are very clever in their dark magic. Without the väki as guardians, the creatures would have stolen every single weapon from our hoard or would have corrupted every weapon with some malevolent spell. I have seen it before—make the weapons rust away to dust, make them kill whoever wields them, whatever their minds can conjure up."

"But how could they breach the pocket-realm?" Gwyness asked.

"No pocket-realm is impenetrable. They are of magic, so they can be breached by magic, which is why you need magic to defend them."

"I am sure none of the men will ever say an unkind word about your väki friends again," Lady Aylen said.

Traveler smiled. "*Our* väki friends care not either way. We must be thankful to have them."

"Yes, what about that, Mr. Traveler? These väki can throw fireballs. They *breathe* fire like dragons. Can they all do that?"

"No, ours are väki of fire, or *tulen väki.* Their magical abilities involve fire and heat. There are many kinds of haltijas, or väki: of trees, mountains, water, precious metals or gems, underground. They are the best sprite guardians."

"You have assembled a powerful group, Mr. Traveler," Lady Aylen said. "Is there more to come?"

"Yes, princess. We still have not added our elfin members, present company not to be ignored."

♦♦♦

All six of the Antaean giants were already fast asleep in their camp, but the human warriors were far from tired. The Cut-Throats remained in a celebratory mood. They, more than any other in the caravan, enjoyed battle whenever it was to be had. Pangolin sat with I-wulf and the other warriors at the campfire, happily talking about the encounter with the goblins and their dire-wolf steeds. Nirgund visited with them shortly but spotted their healer and led his alphyns over to him.

"Any of them wounded?" Gresham asked.

"None, Mr. Gresham," Nirgund replied. "They all performed admirably. Not a goblin or giant wolf touched them."

"Good. It was the same with the chamroshes. None of them received any wounds either. We were fortunate."

"No, sir, we were exceptional."

"Well, the steady rain of arrows from our archers did make our easy victory possible."

"I would not disagree. I have been on the receiving end myself in many battles. Poor, poor goblins. Dodging swords, axes, arrows, dagger strikes. What is a goblin to do?"

"And did you see the väki? They can spit fire and throw fireballs from their hands!"

♦♦♦

Traveler sat at his desk, looking at the maps. The magical paper changed again. There was not one goblin war party in the area but several. He watched closely. If they all joined together, that would mean trouble, but instead, most of them moved away. A single party remained about ten miles away, nestled in the hills. If there was a night attack, it would come from them.

"Sir." He heard Hobbs's voice outside his tent.

"Come in or send them in, Mr. Hobbs," Traveler called out.

Dr'as and Dr'amal entered. The two drows approached his table.

"One goblin party remains," Dr'as said, noticing the magical maps.

"Yes, but I am not concerned."

"I wanted to thank you for allowing my people within the main camp," Dr'as said. "We work well with your Cut-Throats."

"Yes. There are no complaints."

"I wish to offer some of my men for the caravan's night watch too. We have always done so alone, but now that our parties are joined, my men can continue. They can perform their duties for the entire camp—sentries or patrols. Your decision."

"Speak with Mr. Pangolin. We are increasing our night watch with the Cut-Throats. You can add your men. We might as well establish a solid routine before we get to the Great Forest."

"Yes, that would be wise," Dr'as said. "How many times have you visited the Giant Forest?"

"Many times. None of them pleasant."

"It is a savage place."

"Mr. Traveler, I was hoping I could convince you to change your mind," the drowess said.

"You are not the sorceress we need."

"I have not been the sorceress the caravan needs, but I can do better. You must understand that we drows are not accustomed to working with others. We are a private race."

"A secretive one."

"No different than most fae. But once we feel comfortable we are capable of doing much more than when we are not."

"We soon cross into the lands of elves. They will have wizards. You know that. I have taken on the responsibility of not just guide and trailmaster but assembler of the people, animals, weapons, and supplies that will keep this caravan safe."

"You have accomplished that superbly," Dr'as said.

"Except for one final piece. We had three sorcerers when we began, King Aereth's sorcerers. The Xenhelmians' treachery took them from us. They have not been replaced."

"All that we ask is for you to not replace them with elfin wizards," Dr'as said.

"Why?"

"Because their loyalty will be in question," Dr'amal replied.

Traveler found her response amusing.

"Yes, you could say the same about us," Dr'as said. "My daughter is far more powerful, and you will see so for yourself. Also, this caravan is not without magic. The väki, the leshy, the fairies, even your Lady Aylen will soon realize her own magical abilities."

"As much as we hate them, the creatures you call darklings are also wizards of a sort. I suggest that the caravan acquires as many magical arrows as it can afford and equip every archer with them. Your sword is magic. Your master-at-arms' armor and weapon is magic. And we must not forget the three dragon-horses," Dr'amal said.

"Yes, the kirins are powerful."

"And our latest guest."

"A man cursed to be a frog by day is hardly an asset."

"I am certain that when he feels comfortable, he will also be far more powerful. His curse is from dawn to dusk. Outside those hours, we should learn what he can do."

"I would prefer to learn who he is in the employ of first."

◆◆◆

There was not a human or fae that did not want to be in a pocket-realm. The night air was freezing, and those men who had not accepted a giant's slipper from Quillen wished they had. Those who had them were bundled up deep within to keep as warm as possible. Even the brownies were dressed for a wintry climate, the lower half of their faces wrapped in scarves, but they were not bothered. They cheerfully moved through the camp, building more campfires and making the ones they had already created larger with a magical snap of their fingers. Tonight they would be spending even more time keeping the heat pits burning for the two thousand fae lizards that were always craving heat.

Most of the men had been preoccupied by a nighttime goblin attack with the full moon above, but the cold had put that out of their minds. Warmth and sleep was all they cared for.

The Cut-Throats, unlucky to be on night watch, kept warm by standing on their feet around large fires and drinking plenty of heated liquids. Their posts were near the perimeter at different key spots. The drows on night watch walked the perimeter in groups of three or four, seemingly unbothered by the cold. They kept their heads covered with their hoods and their spears in their hands in constant motion.

The very outer perimeter of the caravan was the domain of the darklings. To those who observed them in the night, it seemed the phookas conducted their guard duties by running or flying around, chasing each other as whatever animal they transformed into.

A half dozen of them stood quietly at one end of the camp, watching, smiling. They were in the form of humanoid goats with six horns on their heads, eagle-taloned hands, and glowing blue eyes.

Facing them, not far away, were a half dozen other phookas in the same form but with red eyes. The red-eyed phookas stood with a few dozen hobgoblins. No one in the camp saw them in the darkness, not even the drows, but the caravan's darklings could. The stand-off could last all night—the goblins and their phookas would not retreat; the caravan's darklings would never let them breach the caravan's circle.

They all looked up. The moon hung large in the sky, but then a second moon appeared in the distance. It approached, sending the goblins and their phookas scurrying off into the night. The darklings stared at the second moon slowly descending to the ground. By now, drows and brownies stood alongside the darklings. Soon the human night watch joined them and so did Traveler and his dog.

The second moon, several yards across, touched down on the ground nearby. The entire caravan was wide awake and up, including the giants. The light of the magical moon grew steadily then, in a flash, engulfed them all. Night turned into day.

A party of riders on black hippogriffs waited before them at the spot where the magical moon landed. Foremost among them was a tall thin elf with a jeweled band around his forehead. He was elfin royalty, with long dark hair that had white at the ends. The others were elfin knights in black chainmail armor, also wearing black cloaks and silver belts.

The caravan had not had good encounters with any who used hippogriffs as steeds, though that was not the fantastic animals' fault. The beasts remained still and made no sound at all.

"King, you will come with me," Traveler said. "You too, Lady Aylen. Consider this the first of many exchanges with elves you will have on the Trail."

"Is there any danger?" Pangolin asked, standing next to them, with Hobbs, Gwyness and the royal guards looking on.

"No," Traveler replied. "Even hostile elves talk before they fight. Evil ones attack you first and talk later, if ever."

A fenodyree had already appeared, holding the reins of both King Aereth's and Lady Aylen's kirins. In the blink of an eye, Traveler's dog transformed into a gray horse-headed lion beast.

Gwyness noticed her antlered black kirin walking to her. The animal stopped before her, and she stroked its mane.

"I will need to rely on you for strength in the coming days," she said to it. "But you need a name."

As Traveler, King Aereth, and Lady Aylen approached on their mounts, they could see the elfin king's face more clearly. Elves were extremely long-lived, but even in their end days, they had a look of vibrance. The elfin king looked tired and elderly. On the wrist of his right hand was a glowing band of light.

They stopped in front of him and waited. The elfin king studied each of them.

"King Aereth of Helm Earldom. Lady Aylen of?" the elfin king asked.

"Faylen, sire," Lady Aylen answered with confidence.

He shook his head. "Faylen was an elfess, and the name of her clan. The elfin kingdom was Rivermouth. I know this well because she could have been my wife. But that was ages ago."

He sighed heavily then looked at Traveler.

"The one who calls himself Traveler. Your third full trek across our lands: the first as a boy, the second with your other-worldly shape-shifter, the third you lead an impressive fae and human caravan to Atlantea."

Traveler glanced back. There was Frog-Dor in his human form, standing but shaky. Gresham stood next to him.

"Yes, Traveler. Frog-Dor is mine," the elfin king said. "Though I did not expect you to capture him. But it seems that he has been well cared for."

"Who do we have the pleasure of addressing?" King Aereth asked.

"I am the Elfin Wizard King Rael of the kingdom of Griffinheart. It was once a great kingdom."

"Why did it lose its greatness, King Rael?" King Aereth asked.

"Because, King Aereth...I lost my mind," he replied.

"To what do we owe this royal visit?" King Aereth asked.

"I never thought you would make it this far. When your caravan made it out of Fae-Wick, I said to myself: Maybe there is a chance. Maybe they can make it to Atlantea." He looked squarely at Traveler. "You destroyed the entire army of war wizards of the Four Kings. You destroyed his new kingdom in Faë-Land. None of us thought that to be possible."

"There was also an army of battle elves, King Rael," Traveler added.

"Yes. Elves. Wretched elves. But then I am not much different. If you have not surmised it by now, there is much happening in Faë-Land within the shadows. You can say it is the eternal battle between good and evil and all of us in between. You are determined to stay uninvolved, but your very presence in these lands involves you."

"You are the third fae to tell us so, King Rael," Traveler said. "However, our caravan moves to Atlantea regardless."

"As you should. I tasked Frog-Dor to follow and watch over you, help where he could, keep me informed. You struck a near-fatal blow against a power I consider an enemy to all elfinkind and all fae. The least I could do was aid you in return. Maybe, in the future, you might strike the final blow."

"King Rael, should I understand that your purpose is to keep us alive because you hope the Four Kings will attack us again, and we would be forced to kill him for good?"

The elfin wizard smiled. "Yes, that is exactly my motivation. Does that shock you?"

"King, I have had many dealings with elves. Many have not been pleasant."

"I would say much the same thing. You and your shape-shifter companion went to war with an entire race of them. Here you both stand, alive and well. Those you battled do not."

"King Rael, can you enlighten the princess and me?" King Aereth asked. "You and our Mr. Traveler have knowledge that we do not possess."

"I am sure he will fully inform you of that history. I come to you because I want to ensure you get to Atlantea. The gnoll party that the Four Kings sent after you will engage you not at Titan's Arch as you suspect but likely after you depart Fae'el. My knight here will give you a map that will show you the moving invisible realm they hide in. You can bypass them completely and hopefully be well on your way in the Great Forest before they become aware. I will cast a spell to slow them down to help."

"Thank you, King Rael," King Aereth said. "However, it is a guarded thanks since you truly admit you are using us for your own purposes."

"That should not trouble you. We both want the same thing. The death of the Four Kings."

"We want to reach Atlantea, King Rael," Traveler said.

"And you shall."

"King Rael, I cannot say I know the full story of my origins and my lost kingdom. Can you explain more about this Rivermouth?" Lady Aylen asked.

"You know the story. That small piece was not told to you, I suspect deliberately. Rivermouth trained Faë-Land Major's warrior clerics—seers and slayers. Their mage clans go back as far as the birth of fae. Queen Faylen was the mage mother of Rivermouth. The entire kingdom was destroyed, but no one knows how for certain. My advice to you, Lady Aylen, is if you wish to be discrete, say that you are from the lost elfin kingdom of Faylen. If, however, you wish to be more provocative, say you are from the lost elfin kingdom of Rivermouth."

"So, king, the one who gave her the information may not have been trying to be deceptive but could have been trying to protect her?" Traveler asked.

King Rael studied him. "Yes. She could be an ally too, or not."

"Is there any more, King Rael, I should know?" Lady Aylen asked him.

"No. You and your human female are likely all that is left of the Rivermouth warrior clerics. If their clan is to be reborn, it will be by your hands alone."

"It would appear, king, there are many more sightings of undead beings and dark magic in Faë-Land of late," Traveler said.

"Yes, there are."

One of the knights held a parchment in his hand. King Rael waved a finger, and the parchment floated through the air to Traveler's hand. Traveler opened it and quickly looked at it; the royals glanced over it too.

"King, can you tell us how many gnolls are in the war party?" Traveler asked.

"If you encounter them, you will not be able to so easily repel them and cheer like children afterward as you did with that pathetic goblin attack yesterday," the elfin wizard replied.

"We will manage, King Rael. May I ask why you have not personally dealt with the Four Kings? So many wish for their demise but remain in the shadows without lifting a hand."

"I am lifting a hand to help you. That is all I can do. I may be an elfin wizard, but I am not as powerful as I once was. And I am not the only elfin wizard in these lands."

"King Rael, let us speak plainly," Traveler began. "What would happen if you struck a blow against them?"

"Elfdom would erupt in war."

"Civil war?" King Aereth asked.

"Yes. That is what this is about. The Four Kings still retain powerful allies and in Atlantea too."

Surprise flashed in the royals' faces. They looked at Traveler who was unmoved.

"But you knew that already," King Rael said to Traveler.

"I did. In fact, I had a dream where we arrived in Atlantea and King Oughtred himself was standing at the gates."

"What?" Lady Aylen said incredulously.

"Sounds more like a premonition," King Rael said.

"Don't be alarmed, princess. Even if such a thing came to pass, I know something he does not. Remember, we have allies too."

King Rael smiled, nodding. "I have chosen wisely. Yes, you will make it to Atlantea. I am convinced and will not worry about it again."

"What of Frog-Dor, king?" Traveler asked.

"I also came to take him back."

"Why, king? What did he do for you to curse him so?"

The elfin wizard's face turned angry. "What he did is not your concern."

"King Rael, when we first came into the magical lands, I came across a human wizard who apparently met me when I visited as a boy. He had been in charge of a group of half-elves. The attitudes towards their kind in his elfin kingdom have dramatically changed in a dark way. He was dying but used all of his magic to sustain himself until he could find another to take over his role. He found me. He turned them over to me, and they are part of our caravan. Our caravan will move to Atlantea and then move from these lands, probably never to return again. I do not know what he did, but when a wizard of light uses their magic for darkness they shorten their life and lessen their powers. You have seen yourself in the mirror. Release him from his curse and turn him over to the caravan. You will never see him again. Releasing him from his curse frees you as much as it frees him."

King Rael's face turned sad and hung downward. His gaze fixed on the ground as he thought. His eyes teared up.

"Hatred can be such a pernicious emotion. It's been so long that I can barely remember the reason for it all. I ignored all the counsel against my actions. My magic has only brought on madness and misery. I am why my kingdom is no longer great, why all the elfin kingdoms and clans shun us."

The elfin wizard sat up straight on his hippogriff and beckoned. Frog-Dor shuffled forward to them. He could barely stand up straight and was under great pain with every movement of his legs.

"Frog-Dor," King Rael said. "I release you from your curse."

There was no magical light, or grand gesture of the elfin wizard's hands. He spoke the words, and that was it. Frog-Dor struggled to stand still against his body's shaking. Tears streamed down his face.

King Rael turned his attention to Traveler and the royals. "I am glad I had a chance to meet you in person. I have not had the opportunity to meet many new people in many, many years or even set foot outside my castle. Safe journey, Titan's Caravan."

The day disappeared and so did King Rael, his elfin knights, and their hippogriff steeds. Titan's Caravan stood under the full moon of the night.

CHAPTER NINE

The Elfin Questing Knights

The power of the elfin wizard king was not lost on anyone in the caravan. The man called Frog-Dor huddled on the ground, sobbing uncontrollably. Gresham had some men help carry him back to the healing tent.

"We should all get back to sleep. This encounter should not delay our departure at dawn," Traveler told them.

"Then sleep it is," King Aereth said. "We will have much to speak about on the march."

"How far are we from Fae'el, Mr. Traveler?" Lady Aylen asked.

"We will be there the day after tomorrow."

"How dangerous is this city compared to the other two we have visited on the Trail?" Pangolin asked.

"It's the third major city in Faë-Land on the Trail, therefore, far more dangerous. In the land of the fairies, their wizards are as plentiful but have no interest in displaying their magical abilities. Elfin wizards are a different breed, and I have never felt comfortable around them. The elfin wizard King Rael is an ally, but I was not comfortable around him. Sire and princess, both of you will do most of the talking until we get to the Great Forest. Get accustomed to it. And princess, you must familiarize yourself with as much elvish as you can, even if it is to understand what one elf is whispering to another around us."

◆ ◆ ◆

The patch of land known as Wurmroad was behind them, and no one in the Titan's Caravan was sad to see the back of it. The path was still barren of the green and vibrant plant life they had grown accustomed to seeing in the magical lands, but their feet walked on real soil not dust and mud. Soon, both flora and fauna would be returning to their sight.

"The elfin races, broadly, are divided into two categories," Traveler began, walking alongside the royals. Gwyness and the guards walked on one side; Hobbs, Quillen, and Dr'amal on the other. Nearby the three kirins casually followed, with four of the fenodyree behind them. "High elves, who live in grand castles and highly advanced kingdoms. Included are celestial, star, cloud, moon, elemental, and even drows I would group together with high elves."

Dr'amal scoffed. Traveler ignored her. The royals grinned.

"What of water elves?" Lady Aylen asked.

"Yes, I would group them mostly with high elves. Then there are woodland elves, mountain, night, forest, desert, and elves of the underground kingdoms. Those elves live more like what you have seen of the sprites. Large collections of family dwellings, much more connected with their natural surroundings."

"Fairies are matriarchal, sprites are patriarchal, how are elfin societies structured?" Lady Aylen asked.

"Very similar to humans. Many more kings than queens, but either is equal in the eyes of their people. Succession is by blood or marriage."

"I have noticed that despite all the tales we have heard of the nobility of the elfin race, you do not seem to share that belief," King Aereth said to Traveler.

"Sire, pay no attention to my own biases. My encounters with collective elfinkind have not been particularly pleasant, but they had to do more with the specific elves I encountered on the Trail rather than a reflection of the people."

"You also have a more nuanced view of goblins," Lady Aylen pointed out.

"Yes, my encounters with their kind were not as dark as I expected. However, had I been an elf rather than a human, I have no doubt those interactions would not have been pleasant either."

"Are there good goblins, Mr. Traveler?" Lady Aylen asked.

"A better question, princess, which should also be asked of any elf, is: Should I ever lower my guard or turn my back on them? The answer is always, no."

"As always, Mr. Traveler, you give us much to consider," King Aereth said. "I must ask about the new addition to the caravan, this Frog-Dor. Should we have accepted him so freely? Though I disapprove of his curse, we do not know what he did. What if it was evil?"

"Sire, if it were evil, he would have been killed. Also, he would never have been given a job of some importance. I suspect our Frog-Dor was a great wizard himself, and he did something of paramount offense to the elfin wizard king and was punished for it, punished for a very long time. So long that the elfin wizard King Rael may not live much longer."

"What do you think this Frog-Dor did?" Lady Aylen asked.

"If I had to guess, maybe a wife or daughter was involved."

"Are you serious?" Lady Aylen asked.

"If I had to guess, princess. Or he inadvertently caused the death of a loved one. Whatever it was, it does not matter. I am certain whatever it was, was done before any of us were born. He received more than any just punishment a long time ago."

"How strong of a sorcerer is he?" Lady Aylen asked.

Traveler looked to Dr'amal.

"Far more powerful than any other in this caravan," the drowess answered.

"We will let him have the time he needs to recover. This will be the first day of his new life as human during the daylight," Traveler said.

"Is he human?" Lady Aylen asked.

"We will know soon."

"Mr. Traveler, the elfin wizard king also made light of our triumph over the goblin party. The men were quite uplifted by the encounter. Am I to assume they were an unworthy adversary?" King Aereth asked.

"Sire, it is doubtful any future battle encounters will be so…easy."

Pangolin raised his hand in the air to stop the advance of both the vanguard and the full caravan. In the distance, a figure in a dark hooded robe waited on the trail.

"What do you see, Mr. Elman?" their master-at-arms asked.

"A puck. He looks to be alone and unarmed, but they can cast spells."

"A puck?" Pangolin asked.

"A type of sprite. Like a pixy but tall as an average human male and intelligent, also crafty, and…"

"And?"

"They fly."

The puck jumped into the air at that very moment and sailed to them. He floated as high as the giants with a mischievous smile. He abruptly landed in front of Pangolin, Elman, and the elaphine archer-warriors.

The sprite had a slightly hunched-over posture. His arms were skinny and moved as if they had no bones. His calculating eyes were large under bushy eyebrows. His nose was long, and large ears were outlined from under his hood.

"My name is Scratch. I seek the one called Traveler."

"I am Traveler." The caravan master had reached them with his dog.

"Ah, very good. King Browncrown made contact with the parties I represent."

"Who would they be, specifically?" Traveler asked.

"My elfin parties await you."

"I expected to meet them in Fae'el, not along the Trail from Wurmroad."

"This is precisely where we must meet you. We must conclude our business before reaching Fae'el."

"Why is that?" Traveler asked.

The puck smiled. "You truly do not know. The Kings' Caravan is no more."

"We know that."

"No, not the Four Kings. There were over one hundred fifty thousand men and beasts who were their Caravan. The Four Kings left one day, months ago, and never returned. The King's Caravan has been scattered throughout the elfin lands, and is no more. But Titan's Caravan remains."

"What are you not telling us?" Traveler asked.

The puck cackled. "I leave it to others to explain. I am only the messenger, a mere emissary sent to prepare you for their arrival. I will signal them now."

The puck raised his hand, and a magical dove flew out of the sleeves of his robe into the air. It was then that something swayed around from behind his back. Pangolin's eyes narrowed as he realized what it was. The sprite had a slender prehensile tail on his backside.

Titan's Caravan's royal welcoming party moved ahead of the vanguard. Traveler rode on his giant gray wolf-dog, King Aereth on his golden fur and scaled kirin, Lady Aylen on her kirin with its lucent-blue fur and scales, and Gwyness on her black kirin with antlers.

Scratch the puck walked and floated beside them, his eyes fixed on the kirin steeds.

"I have never seen such magical steeds before," he said. "Beautiful they are. How do they taste?"

The royals shot him shocked expressions. Gwyness was unamused.

"He is not being serious," Traveler said.

"It would seem pucks are no different than your darklings. Eager to provoke," Gwyness said.

The puck cackled. "The human maiden is correct, of course."

When they came over the ridge, they stopped. It was a vast valley larger than any they had seen in the Lands of Man. The area closest to them was of the same barren land, but as it stretched away it regained the green life of flora, and they could see camps of humanoids and beasts. Beyond them were mountains, and beyond them they saw the heads of massive statues in the distance. Their path was clearly marked through the valley to the distant statues.

The beasts of the parties below were horses (or what looked to be horses), unicorns, flying horses, flying wolves, large birds, and large mammals that looked like ferrets. The beasts that drew everyone's attention were larger than elephants—lionlike creatures with bodies covered in rock-like turtle shells with spikes. They had six clawed legs and long ridged snakelike tails, each ending in a spiked ball.

"They are called tarasques," Traveler told them.

"The beasts are the superior equivalent to our own armored giant lizards," King Aereth said.

"We have two thousand of ours, and tarasques do not fight as a pack. We have the advantage, sire, though the beasts' effectiveness in battle cannot be underestimated."

"I will lead you to my masters," Scratch said. "They have seen us and ride to us."

The puck led the way, his tail swaying back and forth.

More than one elfin rider approached. The first was a lean, tall elf. Both his armor and skin had a green tint. His green eyes had an especially brilliant quality. His dark hair was tied back to dangle behind his pointy ears. The rowdy animal he rode had the head of a plumed hawk and the body of a large spotted leopard.

Two other elfin riders followed, riding in tandem. The elf on the left wore a gray hooded robe. His eyes were clear, like a human albino, but his hair was black. Of note was the unusual white staff in his right hand, carved at the tip to look like the head of a unicorn. His steed was a white unicorn, but besides the single ivory horn, it had smaller horns above each eye. The other brown-eyed elf had a dark tan and rode a falcon-headed brown griffin. This elf wore a robe of brown feathers and gloves. His forearms were covered with thick leather.

All three elves wore bands around their foreheads to symbolize they were royalty of some kind.

King Aereth nodded. "Greetings from Titan's Caravan."

The three elfin leaders nodded back.

"I am King Aereth of the human kingdom of Helm Earldom. This is Lady Aylen of the human kingdom of Sirnegate—"

"A human kingdom with an elfin princess?" the gray-hooded elf asked.

"And the lost elfin kingdom of Faylen," King Aereth continued.

"It must be lost indeed if we have never heard of it," the green-armored elf said.

"Beside her is her aid, Maiden Gwyness. To my side is Traveler, our guide and trail master."

"Yes, we have heard of him," the tan elf said.

"I am Druil, wizard of the high-elf kingdom of Magica," said the elf in the gray hooded robe. "My comrades-in-arms are Taylon of the desert-elf kingdom of Falconbright and Galadaer of the woodland-elf kingdom of Bravehowl.

"You can thank King Browncrown of the Tree People for contacting us and having us await your arrival. We doubted we would ever see you, despite the Tree King's high praise for your caravan and your caravan master. But then we began receiving word of your caravan. What fae banners do you currently ride under?"

"Titan's Caravan carries the banners of the fairies of Chrysa, the giants of Antaeus, the centaurs of Chiron, and the elfin kingdom of Faylen," King Aereth replied.

"And look at the beautiful steeds they ride," Scratch said from where he stood nearby. "Too bad they are not for eating." The puck cackled.

"Pay no attention to him," Druil said. "We are elfin questing knights riding for the honor and glory of our monarchs. Three elfin kings and one human king."

"Please, not four kings again," Lady Aylen said. "Four is an unlucky number for us when it comes to kings. Say, four kings and a princess, or five royals would be even better."

"The Four Kings," said Galadaer.

"They do not know," Scratch said.

Traveler, the royals, and Gwyness watched the elfin kings. The elves studied them closely, then their eyes looked past them to their caravan.

"We apologize," Druil said. "It is simply that we cannot believe our eyes. In all my years, I have never seen a human-led caravan such as this. You are not a war party, but you could obviously hold your own in any battle. Humans, giants, sprites, fairies, Tree Shepherds. I have seen leshies many times, but never a Tree Shepherd, or more than one, with my own eyes. Hoofed fae and half-elves, fae beasts, shape-shifters. Humans are not known for impressing anyone in Faë-Land Major."

"Then I am pleased that you have been surprised," King Aereth said.

"You are clearly not the average human, to reach this far. Of all those in your caravan, two are of special interest to us."

"Who would they be?" King Aereth asked Druil.

"Your caravan master and the water elf. Your human apparently does know the way to Atlantea. Your water elf's lost kingdom that no one has heard of is unimpressive, but her sub-race is of value."

"Why is that?" Lady Aylen asked.

"There are rumors that water elf clans have already gained entry to Atlantea as we speak. So any caravan with its own water elf would have a distinct advantage. But your caravan has many advantages already."

"May I ask if your Titan's Caravan has the necessary tribute to gain entry to Atlantea?" Galadaer asked. "They will talk to you, but without it, they will not let you in."

"Yes, we know the formalities of the kingdom of Atlantea," King Aereth said. "You must pay for entry into their walls, which encompass their vast lands. Lands which contain their treasures. Their people have no interest in digging for treasure, but they are happy to allow others to do so for a payment. Before we entered Faë-Land, we were three separate caravans, each with their own tributes. I traveled with two other colleagues, both rulers of allied kingdoms in our region. We are called the Kings Elder. They returned to the Lands of Man, but I retained their tributes as well, on their behalf. I remained and joined the princess and Mr. Traveler. We are now one. Also, our caravan master has lived in Atlantea."

"Yes, we heard that rumor," Taylon said. He looked at Traveler and asked, "Is that true? Have you walked the great caverns of their treasure troves?"

"I have."

"And you took nothing for yourself when you were there?"

Traveler reached into his cloak and pulled out a bright-green gem. The longer he held it in the sun, the brighter it got.

"I did. However, since most of my party I traveled with did not make it, I lost any real interest in such riches."

"Then why do you return?"

"I was an inexperienced healer's assistant then. I am the caravan master this time. The adventure will be on my own terms. I do it for the adventure, sense of accomplishment, and on behalf of the many poor souls who have died on the Trail."

"There have been many deaths, and there will be many more," Druil said. "Browncrown said you did not have that wild lust for treasure that has doomed so many others—human, elf, and more. What caused your other Kings Elder to return to the Lands of Man?" the elf asked King Aereth.

"The Four Kings, of course, or their allies making war against our kingdoms to draw us back to our lands. They returned with most of our seasoned fighters and principally our chief sorcerers."

"Have you acquired new sorcerers?" Druil asked.

"We have acquired one," King Aereth answered.

"Then there is something we can offer your Titan's Caravan. My kingdom of Magica is a city of wizards. On this journey, my party includes conjurers, illusionists, seers, magic slingers, and spellbinders. Many more than three."

"Excellent," King Aereth said with a grin.

"Taylon's desert elves are falconers. Elf and falcon fight as one. Galadaer's party manages our beasts—tarasques, the giant shell-armored lion beasts; the ichneumons, the giant weasel-like beasts able to wrestle and kill beasts ten times their size. All our royal unicorns and flying steeds will return to our kingdoms. "

"Do you know of kilmoulis?" Taylon asked.

"I know of their race," Traveler answered. He looked at the royals. "They are sprites with huge noses that take up most of their face. Most fae dislike them immensely and call them lazy, which they are. However, they possess an ability of smell beyond that of any fae race or animal."

"Yes." Taylon nodded. "They can be of value in the Great Forest, and they stay to themselves, so no one should be especially bothered."

"Kings, we appreciate this conversation," Traveler said, "but what we are more interested in is why you are so nervous, why you are meeting us here rather than at the gates of Fae'el, and what has happened that your puck has already hinted about?"

"Caravan wars," Druil answered.

Hobbs had the men set up camp near the elfin questing knights. The caravan had reached the lush green of the valley. The elfin knights had their standards high throughout their camp—the image of a heraldic dragon with pointy ears. Hobbs made sure to have their Titan's Caravan flags also prominently displayed at the front of the camp.

"A meeting, Mr. Hobbs?" one of the pech asked as the steward walked past.

"Yes, Mr. Battlefuzz."

The pech roared with laughter. "How, human, did you remember my name? There are five hundred of us, and I am sure, to your human eyes, we all look alike."

"Mr. Battlefuzz, you do all look alike."

The pech laughed again. "Yes, we do!"

"I remember you, sir, because you have absolutely the funniest name of them all. And you are one of the few who actually initiates conversation with us humans. I would guess you are the leader."

"Flattering, but we pech don't have leaders. We pick amongst ourselves to do what is needed."

"Well, regardless, I do endeavor to learn the name of every human and fae in this caravan before we reach Atlantea."

"That would be quite an achievement."

"What were you saying about our meeting? Are you asking to join us?"

"Please, no. You humans should be quite content now. You have found a fae race who are as fond of useless gatherings as much as you. You humans and elves will be able to have endless meetings to talk about who knows what."

"All races have their particular peculiarities."

"Very true, Mr. Hobbs."

◆ ◆ ◆

At a larger tent, the three elfin-knight leaders impatiently waited for the night meeting as everything was set, and both food and drink were brought in before all the leadership had arrived.

Galadaer stepped over to the female half-elves who also waited. One of them petted the tiny owl griffin in her arms.

"How fortunate you half-elves must be? Nowhere else in Faë-Land would forsaken be allowed to serve a true blood."

The female half-elves glared at him but said nothing.

"What is this forsaken concept?" Lady Aylen appeared.

Galadaer turned to her. "Is your sense of elfin noble pride also lost like your kingdom?"

"Let me be clear with you. Do not disrespect my guardswomen."

"Guardswomen?" He laughed. "A female half-elf is as useless as a female human in battle. That little owl griffin would be a better protector for you."

"You can throw whatever insults at me because I do not care. I, and my royal guards, will be at the front. You and yours will be at the rear—where you belong."

Galadaer laughed. "Good."

"Did I pass your infantile test?"

"You did, princess. My clan, in truth, has no qualms with half-elves. However, there are those in Fae'el that are more radical in their beliefs. I had to be sure. You are a caravan that is neither led by those with treasure lust nor goaded into foolish action by mere words."

"Are you more comfortable in your decision to join Titan's Caravan?"

Galadaer nodded. "Our Elfin Questing Knights are. We have to be certain because, once we cross into the Great Forest, there is no turning back. We must all be certain about each other."

It was dusk and Hobbs neared the perimeter where a group of brownies waited. Hobbs had his two guards, Tyfer and Oeric, and two pech with him, Mr. Battlefuzz and Mr. Truestrike. Beyond the circle was a party of black-clad elves sitting on large owl griffins. One of them dismounted and walked to them.

"He is with us," a voice said. Hobbs and those at the perimeter turned to see the high-elf wizard, Druil, walking to the circle. He greeted the new elf in black who had snow-white hair to his shoulders. "This is Staric. His party is also with our Elfin Questing Knights."

"What manner of elves are you?" Hobbs asked.

The snow-white-haired elf smiled. "We are moon elves."

"It is nice to meet you. I have never seen a moon elf before."

"I have never seen a human before."

Staric looked at Druil. "We are joining them?"

"We are," Druil answered. "It is as Browncrown said."

"Then we can depart soon."

◆◆◆

Quillen was in Nirvana as he stood to one side of the large tent. Pangolin entered with I-wulf; both men personally oversaw to the increasing perimeter security for the night. King Aereth, Lady Aylen, and Gwyness waited quietly with two of the elfin- knight leaders: the desert elf, Taylon, and the woodland elf, Galadaer. Druil, the high-elf wizard had left and not returned yet. Gresham and Estus stood nearby, quietly. Traveler had not arrived yet with his dog.

Hobbs appeared with Druil and a new elf clad in black, with flowing snow-white hair. Quillen smiled to himself. He would have much to draw and write in his magic book of fae races tonight. The steward quickly walked around to ensure no one wanted anything additional to drink. Most wanted nothing. They were all anxious to get started.

Traveler finally appeared, followed by his wolf-dog.

"Sorry I am late," Traveler said aloud. "There is an approaching party about twenty miles behind us. We are trying to determine who they are."

"I can answer that," the elf with snow-white hair said.

"This is Staric of the moon-elf kingdom of Nightshade. He is the other elfin leader of our Elfin Questing Knights."

"So you do represent four kings, four elfin kings. I have to agree with Lady Aylen. Four has not been a lucky number for us," Traveler said.

"Then my news should be of interest," Staric said. "The party that approaches are a group of mountain, forest, and desert elves."

"Not desert elves," Taylon interjected. "They are not our race. They are savage elves."

"If you know them, why did you not allow them to join you?" Traveler asked.

"None of us knew when, or if, you would arrive," Druil answered. "They decided to collect supplies and go on minor excursions. They told us when they passed here next, if we were ready, they would join us but if not, they would proceed without us."

"They are hunters," Staric said. "Monster hunters."

A dismissive look came over Traveler's face.

Galadaer laughed. "I like you even more, human." He looked at Druil and Taylon. "Even the human is of the same mind about this party as I am. We should let them move on without us. We are questing knights, not base hunters of beasts who display the bones on walls as ornaments."

Traveler looked at Staric. "What do the moon elves say?"

Staric raised a single eyebrow. "We do not care either way. However, this is the season of caravans in our lands. Not all of them are for the noble pursuits of securing alliances with the kingdom of Atlantea for prestige and trade. There are caravans that travel to the lands of the dwarves and other realms for the same purposes. Many are no more than hunting parties—heading to the Great Forest alone, the Nether-Lands, and elsewhere. Let them hunt their beasts there rather than have those beasts at my kingdom's door."

"As long as their hunting does not distract us from our noble pursuits," Traveler said. "Or endanger our caravan in any way."

"Agreed," Staric said.

"To balance my praise of our possible human caravan master, I have a severe critique. You have drows in this camp," Galadaer said.

"Yes," Traveler said. "We told you already. We lost our sorcerers, and we needed others. Their sorceress was recommended by another fae. To get their sorceress, we took in their entire party."

"What fae recommended them?" Druil asked.

"A fae-blood," Traveler replied.

The four elfin-knight leaders looked at each other.

"They are here," Galadaer said.

"What is the significance of that?" Traveler asked. "There are two different parties of fae-bloods in the caravan."

"Do you know what clans?" Druil asked.

"Bear and wolf."

Druil nodded. "We have encountered cat, chameleon, and hawk on our journey."

"I still do not see the significance."

"The fae-blood kingdoms are on the rise," Staric said. "They used to be as prominent as elves, but forsook all that for obscurity from all the other fae races, even from other clans. Their group appearance is significant to us because they are a people of great magic. Some of that magic is immune to the magic of our own wizards." He looked at his elfin colleagues. "There is no more to discuss. This Titan's Caravan is more than anything we could have imagined or prayed for."

"Yes," Druil said. The others nodded.

"We should discuss the marching formation," Galadaer said.

"Yes," Traveler answered. "My thoughts were to have your party as the very last because of your tarasques."

"Yes, they are ferocious beasts and do not take kindly to sneak attacks," Galadaer said.

"Ahead of you should be Taylon and his desert-elf falconers. Druil and his group would lead your elfin questing knights."

"Would you not wish for any of my wizards to walk with your vanguard or at the front of your column?" Druil asked.

"Of course, but the likeliest point of attacks is the rear of the caravan. That needs to be protected more. And from consulting my maps, I am concerned with the number of goblin and troll sightings.

They love to attack the rear of a moving caravan first, so they should be met with our most formidable magical defenses."

"Will we stop in Fae'el?" Druil asked. "Do we need to stop in Fae'el?"

"What are these caravan wars you mentioned?" King Aereth asked.

"It is complete chaos," Galadaer replied. "With the Kings' Caravan no more, everyone is trying to get to Atlantea as quickly as they can—elves, dwarves, nymphs, elementals, but also dark fae and races of goblins that none have ever seen. It is a race, but we have the advantage. No one else is ready."

"But you said wars," King Aereth said.

"The remnants of the Kings' Caravan were scattered through the lands because they were attacked and many were killed by other caravans," Taylon answered. "When we arrive at Fae'el, many will insist they join with us—or they will—try to kill us so we cannot continue onward."

"Is there not a way to bypass Fae'el?" Lady Aylen asked. "We do not need to stop. Mr. Traveler made sure we secured all our food, water, and supplies to carry us through the entire Great Forest."

"No, princess, there is no other way," Traveler said with a sigh. "The mountains allow only one path—forward. And Fae'el sits right on that path. It is why the city was constructed where it stands."

"Why can't any of our wizards use a spell to teleport us to the Great Forest?" Lady Aylen asked. "King Oughtred used such a spell, against our will, to send us long distances. We should be able to use such a spell for our purposes now."

"Is that how the Xenhelmians attempted to dispose of you?" Druil asked.

"It was his most direct way to destroy us," Lady Aylen answered. "Dumped us at the side of a raging river to await the appearance of pirates in a ship of bones. I always wondered why he did not just land us all in the river."

"Maybe his spell attempted to, and that was the closest he could manage," Druil said. "The pirates were simply to ensure all were dead and gone, or he meant for them to capture survivors for other purposes."

"Since he is alive, I will be sure to ask him the next time we meet," Traveler said, "before I kill him, or he beats me to it."

Traveler's wolf-dog, sitting in the corner, growled.

"Yes, your shape-shifter we heard of too," Druil said.

"We must accept the eventuality that the only way to get beyond Titan's Arch to the Great Forest is to kill our way through any opposing caravans," Staric said.

"Is that the real reason you elfin knights waited for us?" Pangolin asked.

The elfin-knight leaders chuckled.

"Why yes, human," Druil answered.

Hobbs led the four elfin leaders from the tent. Everyone else began to file out too.

"We will have dinner shortly at the royal tents," Hobbs called out.

Traveler gestured for the royals, the warrior leads, and Estus to remain behind. Dr'amal appeared and closed the entrance of the tent.

"Where did she come from?" Lady Aylen asked.

Traveler handed King Aereth a leather-bound book. "Sire, do you remember the boy king of Ironwood?"

"Yes, of course."

"He gave me this book. It was the account his mother, the queen of Ironwood, made of the interactions between his father, the king, with King Oughtred. I ignored the book all this time. We had other concerns, but you may review it thoroughly as we march on."

"You still believe he killed my son?" the king asked him.

"I do, sire, but you were there. I was not. However, since he is alive and there is a gnoll war party waiting for us somewhere, it is best to have more information about him, not less."

King Aereth took the book. "I will see what I can glean from her observations."

"Mr. Pangolin, I want you and the vanguard to prepare for an all-out battle once we reach Fae'el."

"Do you really believe other caravans would attempt to stop us only because we are prepared for the trek and they are not?"

"Our two fairies were scouting ahead," Traveler revealed. "What they told me today is disturbing. There isn't a handful of caravans ahead. There are hundreds of them."

"Hundreds?" Lady Aylen asked.

"If anything our elfin knights underestimated the danger." Traveler looked to I-wulf. "Mr. I-wulf, you and your Cut-Throats will need to do the same. Prepare for battle. Mr. Estus, as our weaponsmaster, ensure that they all have weapons of fae metal only."

"I may have a few surprise weapons for the men too," Estus said, "and my own."

"Mr. Traveler, are you suggesting we may not be able to pass beyond Fae'el?" King Aereth asked.

"Sire, as of now, Titan's Trail is blockaded by all these caravans camped around Fae'el with great magic. My chief task in the next few days is to figure out how we can get through. Our caravan was under nine thousand strong before the elfin questing knights. We are now a caravan of over twenty-two thousand, and that does not include all our animals. Not the one hundred fifty thousand colossal numbers of the Kings' Caravan, but we are not a tiny caravan that can simply slip past them all in the night."

"Is there no way we can?" Lady Aylen asked.

"Why do we have to remain a few days?" Pangolin asked.

"We must allow that other party to catch up and assess them, but the real reason is I have to study my maps and devise a plan for us. Even if what we faced ahead at Fae'el did not exist, we would be doing the very thing we are doing now. There is another danger that none of you are aware of but I know the elfin leaders will discuss later."

Quillen sat immediately next to the four elfin leaders. His bowl of food was full but he ate without taking his eyes off of them as they talked. Adjacent to the royal tents, everyone sat around twin campfires when Traveler and the others, who had remained behind in the meeting tent, appeared. They joined the elfin-knight leaders.

"You have phookas too," Galadaer the woodland elf said. He looked at Traveler, who gave a piece of his food to his dog. "How does a human know phookas?"

"Phookas are goblins," Druil said to Quillen.

"Goblins!" Quillin sat up straight then looked over his shoulder.

Five of the darklings, in the form of shadow-like elves with glowing white smiles, danced at the perimeter. "Spiders and snakes, snakes and spiders!"

"They are not goblins, Mr. Quillen," Traveler said. "Do not take Mr. Druil seriously." Traveler looked at the elfin wizard. "And that title is not meant as an insult. In the Lands of Man, we address our knights as 'sir,' but it is not the same custom for elves. However, I do not think they could pronounce any of the many elvish titles you use."

"Do you all use this 'mister' title?" Druil asked.

"Except for the king, princess, and women."

"Then 'mister' it is for us in Titan's Caravan," Druil said. "Actually, I am not a knight. I am the wizard leader of my kingdom's knights. Only Mr. Staric here was born a knight. Taylon and Galadaer accepted this roles to become royal knights in their kingdoms."

"We thank you for inviting us to your nighttime meal," Staric said.

"We are glad that you accepted," King Aereth said.

"Shall we talk about what awaits us at Fae'el or that other thing?" Staric asked.

"Other thing?" Lady Aylen asked. "The other thing, of course."

The elves laughed. She looked at Traveler.

"Well, Mr. Traveler?" Lady Aylen asked.

"Princess, our new elfin colleagues are probably more nervous about what awaits us in the Great Forest than what awaits us in Fae'el. At least the dangers in Fae'el are known."

"You know of the disappearances?" Staric asked.

"When I traveled through as boy, we had heard the rumors," Traveler said, "but we were preoccupied with other dangers. So much so that we forgot all about them. I had forgotten them myself until a few days ago."

"What disappearances?" Lady Aylen asked.

"The great mystery of the Great Forest," Galadaer replied. "The disappearances of parties and whole grand caravans attempting to cross the Great Forest, never to be seen or heard from again. No trace of them ever to be found."

"Is it because of the Four Kings?" King Aereth asked.

"No," Druil began. "The mystery of the Great Forest existed long before the kingdom of the Xenhelmians were born. Those who have disappeared include my own father."

"I am so sorry," Lady Aylen said.

"No need to apologize. It was a long time ago. It devastated my family and our very kingdom. How could such a thing happen to a wizard as powerful as my father? Him, an elfin caravan of tens of thousands, including wizards, knights, and noble animals. Nothing. No trace. Every spell cast to reveal what happened to them failed."

Lady Aylen and Gwyness looked at each other nervously. The princess looked at Traveler.

"We are going into the Great Forest where these disappearances occurred," Lady Aylen said.

"Yes, princess, but remember that the Great Forest is filled with giant animals and more evil beasts than our Mr. Quillen could sketch into his magic book if he had an entire lifetime."

"But what does it mean, Mr. Traveler," Gwyness asked. "If powerful wizards could be made to disappear, what will we do?"

"Mr. Druil already used the correct word: mystery. It is a mystery his people have been unable to solve, nor has any other elfin kingdom. Many have tried."

"But what are the theories as to what is happening?" Lady Aylen asked.

"I am not sure you want to know," Staric said. "Some of those theories are worse than the unknown."

"They say the Spirit of the Great Forest kills trespassers," Galadaer said.

"Some say a lost Titan hides in the Great Forest underground and feeds from time to time," Taylon the desert elf said.

"Others have said a creature similar to a gorgon or basilisk roams the Forest, and anything it sees turns to dust rather than stone."

"I must say I am as unsettled as the princess," King Aereth said. "Could any of these theories be true?"

"Any of them could be true," Druil said. "The question is how to confirm it."

"The objective is to not have to confirm anything but safely move through the Forest to the oceans," Traveler said.

"Hear! Hear!" Pangolin said. "We journey to get to the riches of Atlantea, not solve ancient mysteries in giant forests."

"We agree completely," Druil said.

"I mean no disrespect to your late father," Pangolin said.

"Of course. Again, it was a long time ago now," Druil said. "However, some thought must be given to this mystery. Not to solve but to survive."

"That is what we will do," Traveler said. "For my part, I will consult with all to come up with my own theories. We are a caravan of elves, fairies, sprites, leshies, fauns, brownies, pech, gnomes, drows, and even the phookas."

"You believe that all the information that we know separately may reveal this mystery of the Great Forest when put together?" Druil asked.

"It is the hope," Traveler said.

"Mr. Traveler, that is not very reassuring," Lady Aylen said. "We will be there soon."

"Princess, we must still get past Fae'el, hopefully without having to fight a war for the next days, weeks, or months. Once we get to the Great Forest, there will be much to keep us occupied. I would not concern myself at all with this mystery of the Great Forest."

"But it is a serious danger, even if it is unknown," King Aereth said.

"Yes, sire, but whatever that danger is, it is so powerful that it can make entire caravans, including those with powerful wizards disappear from the world without a trace. I suspect it happens so fast, the act is so overwhelming, the death so complete, that neither you, nor I, nor anyone here would have any time to think about it. We must avoid it completely, whatever that 'it' is."

CHAPTER TEN

The Ground Shakers

With night upon the caravan, everyone was asleep except for the night watch. The brownies of the main camp did what they did every night: lit the torches, made sure all the campfires burned bright and, ensured all the men were tucked in their beds, and the camp was orderly. Then they sat in small groups throughout for meal and conversation, keeping a watchful eye over everyone.

The darklings were giddy at the fact that the numbers of the caravan had swollen so large. There were twenty-five hundred high elves with their white war unicorns, three thousand desert elves with their falcon griffins, five thousand woodland elves with their leopard axexs, and three thousand moon elves with their large owl griffins. That meant plenty of new elves and beasts to spy upon. The darklings spent most of the night, in addition to their guard duties, transforming into variations of all the new griffin beasts and axexs.

The drows and Cut-Throat guards remained serious in their duties—Cut-Throats at their posts, drows on constant patrol. The moon was bright in the sky, but dark clouds blocked it from time to time. Under cover of the crawling trees within the magical dome protection of the circle the caravan had every reason to feel safe.

It was only a few minutes past midnight when the earth began to quake so violently that every human and fae was wrenched from their sleep; the animals began to panic. Drow patrols screamed out warnings in their language. A thundering yell from high above echoed throughout the caravan. The quaking intensified, and the land began to break up. Many could see giant shadows almost on top of the caravan. People yelled out.

A shadowy figure more than twenty feet tall yelled as it slammed into the magic dome of the circle and fell back, crashing to the ground. The earth buckled, and men throughout the caravan were knocked off their feet. Animals began to stampede—giant lizards, alphyns, chamroshes, and the animals of the animal-like humanoids and animal men. All the torches and campfires were blown out.

"Get the fires lit!" a voice yelled out.

Väki spilled out of their pocket-realm with their hands raised magically engulfed in flame to be torches for the camp.

"No!"

Who cried out no one knew, but the second after they did, a much larger figure landed with its full body weight on the magic dome of the circle. The wave of energy knocked everyone, including the väki, off their feet, and many crashed into the magic barrier itself. The caravan was in total darkness again. The dome would have collapsed on all of them if not for the support of the crawling trees. However, the force of the figure's landing almost made the three trees' branches slam to the ground.

Traveler flew through the air on a shadowy creature, with a glowing bag. Up he flew on the back of the black flying beast as he threw a handful of magical balls of light at the gigantic figure. They crossed through the circle and exploded on the giant's body. Like when they encountered the elfin wizard king, night turned into day.

The nearly fifty-foot second troll screamed as its eyes widened in terror. There were three other giant but smaller trolls charging. They, too, stopped in their tracks. The fourth troll, who had fallen, was back on its feet. The trolls tried to shield themselves from the sunlight erupting from the magic spheres. Traveler threw more at them. The bodies of the trolls petrified. Before the sunlight was gone and night returned, the trolls had turned to stone.

CHAPTER ELEVEN

Hunters

No one could sleep after the attack. The camp looked as if a hurricane had blasted through it. The brownies hurriedly set new campfires and set up new torches. The men and other fae restored some semblance of order under Hobbs's supervision. The most immediate task was to calm all the animals.

All two thousand of the giant lizards had attempted to run, run in any direction, in the chaos. Lizard minders had to find their lizard, calm the panicked giant animal, and then coax them back to their place. The pech helped by remaking the fire pits that the giant lizards would sleep over. The lizards would not rest, either, but maybe it would help soothe the animals.

Nirgund had to take his thirteen reptile hounds, the alphyns, into a pocket-realm—the beasts were so frightened. The Cut-Throats had to do the same when they finally were able to grab hold of their chamroshes. The griffin hounds took quite a bit of time to relax and get into their own pocket-realm to be calmed.

"How are your trees?" Traveler asked Mossberry.

"Our trees will recover," the Tree Shepherd answered.

"How are the fairies?"

"They are under Little Root's care. We might not see them for a day or two."

The Tree Shepherds used their magic to restore the crawling trees to health. Traveler moved to the hoofed fae, where Gresham attended them. The larger elaphine archer-warriors looked worn but fine. All of them had large cups of water and were drinking freely. The cervids were less well. The medium-sized hoofed fae were all lying prone on the ground, awake but resting. The smaller halfling rusines were in the worst state. They were all comatose. Gresham attended to them, covering them with blankets with the help of some men. In the night attack, the rusines tried to stampede away in sheer terror, despite not being able to see where they were running. If the magic of the circle had not been strengthened by the Tree Shepherds, the rusines would have crossed the circle and still been running away in the night. Instead, they crashed into the barrier, as did the animals.

"I will stay with them, sir," Gresham said to Traveler.

Traveler nodded and moved on. Pangolin and the giants had taken on guard duty. Their master-at-arms stayed in the center of the camp keeping his eyes roving. The giants walked the perimeter on patrol. The drows kept guard positions with their throwing blades at the ready.

With the main caravan in good hands, Traveler moved on to the fauns and other fae parties.

"How are your men, Ammon?" Traveler asked the ram-headed faun leader.

"We stood our ground."

"Good."

Hax, the lion-like humanoid, waited with his fae berserkers.

"Mr. Traveler, that was an interesting night we would not like to repeat."

"I agree completely, Mr. Hax."

"Titan's Caravan does everything bigger than all others. Four trolls at once. Troll hunting parties are so rare in these lands, it's nearly impossible. Trolls, like their daylight cousins, ogres, prefer not to share with even their own kind."

"Someone must have told them that there was more than enough eating for all."

"Yes, that must have been what it was. Too bad they did not tell them that you also kept a bag of sunlight."

"Yes, too bad—for the trolls."

The gnomes had been shaken but remained in good spirits. The original woodland elves that were part of their caravan were also fine. Unlike the woodland elves of the elfin questing knights, they were rustic merchants only. Traveler made a note to himself to talk more with their leader along the Trail.

The humanoid animal men had a more difficult time than all others with their animals.

"How are you? Were any of your animals injured?" Traveler asked.

"We had quite the chore to recover all of our jackalopes," one of the bird men said.

"We recovered all our enfields," another bird man said.

"Our giant crabs were not injured," one of the frog men said.

"Neither were our giant turtles," one of the possum men said.

"Our giant porcupines were not injured, but they will not move," a raccoon man said.

"We can provide a wagon if needed, so you can transport them," Traveler said.

"Yes, that would be welcome."

"Your giants birds? The ducks and the crane?"

"They are not wounded, only frightened," a fox man said.

Traveler looked at the mole-man fae. "Your moose?"

"He slept through it all."

Traveler smiled. He looked over at the lizard men, squirrel men, and the mice men. "All fine?"

They all nodded.

"Good."

"When will we leave?" a lizard man asked.

"When we are all recovered and organized, we will march on," Traveler answered. "I would guess a full day of rest. Do you agree?"

The humanoid animal men all nodded.

"Good."

Scratch the puck stood before him, appearing from nowhere.

"Are you waiting for me?" Traveler asked.

"My masters are expecting you."

"I am ensuring all is well within the caravan."

"Oh yes. My masters are well. The trolls made quite the noise but were not at our camps. I will take you to them."

Pangolin had assigned all the male half-elves to the royal guard. King Aereth, Lady Aylen, and Gwyness sat at a campfire in front of their tents. The female half-elves sat at another fire. The male half-elves sat around a third.

With the coming dawn, the petrified trolls became more visible. Everyone in the caravan looked at the troll "statues" no matter what they were doing.

Traveler appeared, walking to them with his dog following. He stopped at the campfire with the female half-elves.

"Keep your pet close," he said to the one with the tiny owl griffin in her hands. "If he gets near the larger owl griffins, they might eat him."

"They would not do that. Would they?"

"They would."

Traveler walked past them for his tent. He abruptly came back out.

"Forgot something, Mr. Traveler?" Lady Aylen asked with a smile.

"I did, princess."

◆ ◆ ◆

All could clearly see the four trolls of stone towering above the caravan. Three were twenty feet tall, and the largest one that almost crushed their circle dome was fifty feet tall. The baldish humanoids had large noses and ears. Their eyes and mouths were wide in agony. Their arms were longer than average, their legs a bit shorter, and both hands and feet were oversized. They looked hairy and were without clothing.

"The creatures look so unremarkable despite their size," Lady Aylen said. "But if they had gotten a hand on one of the men or any of our animals, they would be at the bottom of their bellies."

"Creatures who do their hunting in the dark of night," King Aereth added.

"Mr. Traveler did say that there have been many sightings of them on his maps," Gwyness said.

"These four won't be among them anymore," Lady Aylen said.

"What is the tallest a troll can be?" Gwyness asked the female half-elves.

"The smaller ones, maiden, are their normal size. The tallest one, is extremely rare," one answered.

"I heard of one sighted that was nearly one hundred feet tall," Elman added. "Farther north though."

"You mean in the Great Forest, where we are going?" Lady Aylen asked.

Elman did not answer.

◆ ◆ ◆

Traveler reached the healing tent and peeked in, knowing Gresham was still with the deerlike fae.

"Hello," Traveler called out as he entered.

Near the entrance was a table with a lit candle. In the far corner was another table with blankets draped over it, and a large candle on the ground nearby. Traveler could see someone sitting behind it.

"Your curse is lifted. There is no reason for you to be in this tent away from everyone anymore."

A head popped up from behind the covered table. Frog-Dor struggled to his feet and ran to Traveler with bow legs. The man threw his arms around Traveler's shoulders, crying.

"Thank you," Frog-Dor said.

The man was again overcome by emotion.

"Sit down properly before you fall over," Traveler said.

Frog-Dog dropped to the ground. Traveler grabbed a stool from the side of the tent.

"Mr. Gresham will work with you to help strengthen your legs again."

Frog-Dor sat on the stool uncomfortably, sniffling.

"It will take time, but you will walk normally again. I have no doubt of it."

"Thank you. Thank you for saving me."

Dr'amal stood, staring at the troll "statutes." With so many elves officially part of the caravan, she kept the hood on her head and her arms covered.

Traveler saw her as he returned to the royals and Gwyness. "Should we leave the trolls where they stand?" he asked.

"As a reminder of what happens to those who challenge Titan's Caravan?" Lady Aylen asked.

Traveler and King Aereth laughed.

"I say leave them," Lady Aylen said. "Give the caravan something to speak of for the day."

"I agree," Traveler said.

He walked to their drowess. She turned to look at him. "I heard what you all said."

"Were you planning to throw a magical dagger at them?"

"I was. I was studying whether I could destroy all four with a single throw."

"That is the talk I want to hear. We will be in Fae'el tomorrow."

"You do not truly believe they will let us pass."

"Why not? We are Titan's Caravan."

She smiled. "I do not believe in fables, and neither does Fae'el."

"Not yet."

Traveler made another round through the caravan with his dog as the noon meal was served. Gresham had remained with the hoofed fae all day. Traveler was happy to see the rusines seated, alert, and eating normally. A couple of times the fairy sisters had flown out of the pocket-realm to look around. The second time, they flew right up to the stone faces of the dead trolls before quickly disappearing.

The caravan master joined Pangolin and Elman at the rear perimeter. Both of them ate from plates, standing up.

"How far away are they?" Traveler asked.

"Only a couple of miles away," Elman replied. "They're eating their meal too."

The welcoming committee of Traveler on his giant wolf-dog and the royals and Gwyness on their kirins were joined by Druil the high-elf on his war unicorn, Taylon the desert elf on his falcon griffin, and Galadaer the woodland elf on his large leopard axex.

The party of fae and animals approached them on foot. It was led by a kind of fae they had never seen before. He looked like an elf but had a large, brawny, wide frame and was very tall. Elves had tall sleek bodies; his was bulky like that of a dwarf, but dwarves were halflings. He had dark hair and wore dark-brown leather attire, a sword on his belt—a belt made of skull fragments—had a quiver of arrows on his back, and his walking staff had an axe blade near the ground.

At his side was a seven-foot man of metal, a golem, with a war hammer in each of his hands. The iron man had an expressionless face, fashioned to look as if it wore a helmet, but the eyes were empty. On its back was a giant crossbow.

The party itself was made up of mountain elves in dark-brown leather attire with long bows and long axes strapped over their backs, forest elves in dark-green attire, all with longbows and full quivers on their back; and the other sub-race was called wild or savage elves, cousins to the desert elves, who had light brown hair, bigger pointed ears sprouting from the sides of their heads, but fanged teeth and clawed nails on their hands. They were tall, muscular, and their eyes had the look of a wild animal. In their hands were multiple javelins, and their belts were lined with darts and knives.

All around were their animal steeds. The beasts looked like muscular horses but with wolf-like paws rather than hooves, and they growled with the teeth of a carnivore.

"You have found them!" the brawny elf-like fae leader exclaimed.

"We have, Bragg," Druil said from his steed.

"What lies have you told them?" he asked with a smile. "I am Bragg Emberstone of the mountain-elf kingdom of the Labyrinth Mountain. I travel with the forest and desert elfin warriors and trackers of a dozen other kingdoms."

"They are not desert elves," Taylon said angrily.

The wild elves stepped closer. "Why do you insult us, cousin?"

Traveler had a slight smile on his face, looking at Bragg. "Sir, are you a...dwelf?"

Bragg chuckled. "Yes, human. My people are dwelfs. All the strengths of both elves and dwarves but none of the weaknesses."

"I never thought I would see your kind, even though you are as plentiful as both elves and dwarves."

"There are many fae who choose not to be seen by outsiders. My race is no different, but I am the exception. I crave adventure above all else."

"Why do you call yourself a mountain elf then?"

"I said I was of the mountain elfin kingdom of Labyrinth Mountain, not that I was a mountain elf. My colleagues here are the mountain elves. They have simply hired my services, so I work on their kingdom's behalf. I wish my kingdom were more forward-thinking like elves, but they are worse than dwarves. They wish to neither be seen nor heard. I think my race is the epitome of beautiful perfection. It should be seen and seen often."

"I am happy to meet my first dwelf, then," Traveler said. "I will not hold any of your future activities against your race."

The dwelf laughed. "Then my race thanks you. They are as judgmental of my actions as your elfin questing knights," Bragg said. "Human, I heard that you killed seven elves with only a dagger."

"I did."

"And your steed is a shape-shifter." The dwelf smiled as he stared at it. The dog growled. "He does not like me yet. Oh, I have a companion too. My golem companion is Glog. He is not very talkative, which I prefer. Our animals are Diomedian Mares, both steed and attack beast in one."

Traveler introduced King Aereth, Lady Aylen, and Gwyness.

"The steeds you have. They are...kirins."

Traveler smiled. "Yes."

"From the fabled lands of the Celestial Empires," Bragg remarked.

"Yes," Traveler said.

"Here we all are. To behold a caravan led by humans, comprised of both human and fae, capable of getting to Atlantea above all others.

That the Kings' Caravan, after decades, is no more. I heard that was also by your hand."

"They should not have tried to kill us," Traveler said.

Bragg laughed. "As those trolls found out. To think that the human actually called himself King Oughtred the All-Knowing. So much for that myth." The dwelf laughed louder, and his men joined in.

"Bragg, get on with it," Druil said. "Maybe you should go on ahead without us."

"Oh, do a group of fae human barbarians belong to you?" he asked Traveler. "We came across them near the Dead City."

The humans looked at each other. "Where are they?" King Aereth asked.

"We have them," Bragg replied.

"What happened to them?" Lady Aylen asked.

"They ran into an unfriendly beast while foolishly looking for treasure. You humans can do the most foolish things sometimes. The manticore got about a dozen of them."

"Manticore?" the royals asked.

"Manticores are very particular hunters," Bragg said. "They lock in on a food source and will stay with it forever. Seems that Titan's Caravan is that food source. But fortunately for you, I specialize in hunting manticores. They used to frequent the lands around my kingdom, but I killed them. Then I did the same for others. Then I decided I'd hunt other beasts.

"So, my party will join your caravan, and I will kill your manticore whenever it shows again. You will get my party to Atlantea, and while we pass through the Great Forest, leave us to hunt an occasional beast or two. Seems to be a fair arrangement to me. What do you say?"

"How many men do you have?" Traveler asked.

"I wish we were a bit smaller, but five hundred of us. For a true hunting party, even in the Great Forest, smaller is better."

"What about your Diomedian Mares? They like to eat other animals, including people."

Bragg laughed. "We will keep a firm hand on our animals and away from everyone else."

"Your party will be the rear guard, and your Mares are never to be left unattended. The first time they are will be the last time."

"That is fair."

"The men from the Dead City?"

Bragg gestured to one of the forest elves. The elf wore a cap, which he took from his head and threw to the ground nearby. The hat grew and became the opening to a pocket-realm. Inside they could see men asleep on mats everywhere.

"I did my best to restore the ones I could," the forest elf wizard said. "Some did not make it. Their wounds were too severe, and manticore wounds are not the easiest to heal."

"There were about one hundred fifty of them."

"There are eighty-six of them resting."

"Our healer will see to them," Traveler said.

"We have the others' bodies for you to bury or burn as your customs command. The others are with the manticore," the forest elf wizard said.

"Against my better judgment, you are accepted by the caravan."

"I knew the words of my elfin-knight colleagues would not endear you to us," Bragg said.

"Why should you care? If you can kill our stalking manticore, that is endearment enough. In the meantime, prepare your party for battle. We arrive at Fae'el tomorrow."

"Yes," Bragg said without enthusiasm. "Though, I would rather hunt manticores."

CHAPTER TWELVE

The Elfin City of Fae'el

Pangolin and Estus quietly waited in one of the smaller pocket-realms within one of the caravan's tents. Night was only a few hours away, but both men had much to do for the next day's march to Fae'el. Traveler entered and closed the flap of the entrance. A single magic torch hung in the air a few feet from them.

"Gentlemen," Traveler greeted.

"Mr. Traveler, I normally take to fellow warriors, whether they are human or fae, but my instincts tell me that this Bragg may be no good," Pangolin said. "Is he really a manticore hunter, as he claims?"

"Your instincts may be correct. We do not know. However, he truly is a real manticore hunter—a very good one I am told. I'd rather have him watching for a manticore than the vanguard."

Pangolin nodded grudgingly.

"He did return our men," Estus said.

"Those men went off on their own when they were told not to," Pangolin challenged. "They should be thankful that they were not all killed."

"They were still returned to us. They did not have to do that or even rescue them to begin with," Estus said.

"If they are unable to do their duties, they may need to remain in Fae'el," Pangolin said.

"We can discuss them later," Traveler interjected. "I have convened this meeting for a specific and secret task. Pick someone from your teams, someone inconspicuous, who is trustworthy and dependable. There are specific weapons and supplies we must secure. The caravan is being watched by many eyes, so these agents will move out under the cover of darkness and see to these tasks unobserved and unimpeded."

"We should not have done it," said one of the fae human mercenaries, a man with a scar down one side of his face.

The healing tent had been expanded into three large ones to attend to the fae human mercenaries attacked at the ruins of the Dead City. One tent had the physically wounded, recovering on cots. Another tent was a general area for men to sit and talk. The third was the working healing tent for procedures and to administer medicines. There, Gresham changed the bandages on the man's leg. The man lay on a cot; Gresham sat on an adjacent stool as he worked.

"No point in fretting about it now," Gresham said.

"Men were killed."

"You knew the risks."

"But did we? We saw those one-legged hopping cyclops creatures. Some of us laughed, but one of the creatures killed the man next to me with a flail club. Chains caught him in the neck. He bled to death there. We attacked the creatures with everything we had and they hopped away. We thought they panicked and ran, but they weren't running from us."

"You don't have to talk about it," Gresham said to the man.

"We should have known something was terribly wrong. All our little owl griffins flew away as fast as their wings could manage. They have never done that before. They are little, but they're as fierce as any griffin. Not this time."

"The medicine I treated your leg with will help it heal nicely as long as you keep off of it."

The man still spoke, but he had a faraway look in his eyes. "You hear about them. Fae tell you that they are so rare. We didn't even have time to cry out. It flew at us so fast there was no time. It killed...I don't know how many. We ran, but we all knew there was no escape. It could kill any and all of us no matter what we did."

"You did escape though. You are here. Most of your men are here."

"One of the men the creature swallowed whole. I never saw something like that before. I thought it was a story, a tall-tale, but it did it right in front of my eyes. Eating men whole and slashing others apart, as it flew by like a gale force wind. There was nothing to do but run and hide."

"You escaped. You are here safe in the caravan."

"But are we safe? It is still out there. It's the same one we came across before, after the Centaurian Fields. It could be watching us right now."

"Then let it watch. Since you were last here, we added more parties to the caravan—elves, elfin knights, and...a fae manticore hunter."

The man looked at him.

The tallest of the three crawling trees always stood in the center of the camp. The deerlike fae who used it as their base camp were always watching—it was their nature. As Pangolin approached, he could see their silhouettes, both antlered and without horns, all watching him.

"Strag," the berserker master-at-arms called out.

The tall elaphine leader stood. Pangolin was always impressed by the look of these fae with their huge antlers sprouting from their skulls. As was also in their nature, if you spoke with one, you spoke with many. Strag moved to Pangolin with other elaphine and their slightly smaller cousins, the cervids.

"Yes, Pangolin."

"I am sorry to disturb you, but we will be in Fae'el tomorrow."

"Yes."

"Your archer-warriors are all exceptional, but who would you say are your most-experienced, most-gifted archers?"

The elaphine leader thought for a moment. "Aron and Eren. They are twin brothers."

"The elves will have their best with them. I want our best with me when we encounter them."

"Yes, I will have them join your vanguard. However, with the elves, it is not only their skill with the bow that makes them so formidable. It is the magical arrows they use."

"Are your arrows not magical?"

"Not like theirs."

"Then I will speak with Mr. Estus, and you and your men will have magical arrows."

The caravan marched promptly at dawn. Pangolin led the vanguard with all six of the Antaean giants. The male half-elf warriors joined the front of the columns with Traveler, the royals, Gwyness, and six flag bearers holding high their twelve-foot standards of the Titan's Caravan. Everyone was on foot, but the three kirins had come out of their pocket-realm and walked behind their masters. Traveler, every so often, glanced back towards the rear. Titan's Caravan was now over twenty thousand strong.

"It is magnificent to see how far we have come, Mr. Traveler," the king said with a smile. "We have achieved far beyond what any of the Kings Elders' could have imagined those months ago in Hopeshire."

"Yes, sire. I am also pleased but more pleased with the fact that capable people such as ourselves found each other."

"Yes, indeed," Lady Aylen said.

"What is it, Mr. Quillen?" Traveler asked. He could see the lad holding his magic book, looking for a chance to speak up.

"Can I show you something, sir?" Quillen asked as he moved to Traveler's side.

"Do not bother Mr. Traveler with your scribblings," Hobbs said.

"It is okay, Mr. Hobbs. We remember when we were young. The young mind cannot hold onto too many things before it forgets."

"I am not elderly, Mr. Traveler," Quillen said with a laugh.

"What is it?"

Quillen opened his book to a rendering of the hawk-headed beast with the body of a large spotted leopard of Galadaer the woodland elf.

"That's an axex," Traveler said.

"What, sir?"

"Pronounced A-Z-E-X. They were popular in the Lands of Man before the griffins. They have different species like most animals—different large feline bodies. That is a leopard axex. They are swift runners."

Quillen showed him another page. Traveler took the book from his hands.

"This is a tarasque. A giant armored turtle beast with a lion's head."

"Six legs," Quillen said.

"Some have scorpion tails, others forked tails. I heard some have tails ending in the head of a snake, but I think that is a fairy tale."

Quillen laughed.

Traveler turned the page. "Falcon griffins, owl griffins, the larger regular griffins we know of are also called hawk or eagle griffins, depending on the region of Faë-Land.

"Ichneumons. The giant weasel-like beasts despise any snake creature and can kill a wurm many times its size. They are impervious to fire attacks."

"Diomedian Mares are man-eating horses with wolf feet rather than hooves."

"Man-eating horses?" Lady Aylen asked rhetorically.

"Do griffins and hippogriffs like to eat them, sir?" Quillen asked.

"Well, no, Mr. Quillen. Diomedian Mares are not horses."

"We should have had them back in our lands, sir."

"No, we should not have. They are aggressive and carnivorous. They would eat every man, woman, child, dog, cat, pig, cow, horse, chicken, rooster, fox, and wild bird they could find."

Quillen laughed.

"Where are the unicorns, Mr. Quillen?" Traveler asked.

"Unicorns, sir? Unicorns are so...common."

"Mr. Quillen," Lady Aylen called out playfully. "Hold your tongue."

The approach to the Elfin City of Fae'el had the eerie repeat feel of when the caravan arrived at Arion's Spear. The city was not as wide as Arion's Spear, but the golden elfin kingdom stretched from the ground to hundreds of feet into the sky. One-hundred-foot statues stood on each side of the city's entrance—one was an elfin king with his sword raised in the air; the other was of an elfin queen with a long bow raised high. Both were garbed in ornate royal draping.

Both kingdom and colossal statues could be seen from the day before. Neither was what commanded the attention of the caravan—it was the camps that surrounded the city on the Trail. It was exactly as the elfin questing knights had said—a sea of different camps, under seemingly hundreds of different flags. Titan's Trail cut a single opening in the mountain range ahead, but they faced a complete blockade.

"What do you see, Mr. Elman?" Pangolin asked.

"Elfin royals, knights, other warriors, riders. I see high elves, woodland elves, mountain elves, forest elves, desert, underground or cave elves. Lots of steeds and animals, some I have never seen before. And they have giants too."

Pangolin heard the giants grunt amongst themselves, and when he glanced back at them, the giants were gripping their huge war hammers. The berserker master-at-arms returned his gaze ahead and stopped in his tracks. Lumbering towards them was a blackened giant figure with six arms, each with a double battle-axe.

"Antaeans!" the twelve-foot giant yelled.

"What is that?" Pangolin asked the giants.

"Our enemy. The Gegenees. Do not call on the archers. If there is to be a battle, we will deal with it ourselves," the Antaean giant Grakdar said as he and his five comrades moved ahead of the vanguard.

Elman looked at Pangolin. "It begins already," the half-elf said.

"If the giants fight, ensure no one else joins in on the six-armed giant's side," Pangolin said to the elaphine archer-warriors.

The Gegenees laughed loudly. Clad in black painted armor and a spiked helmet, he watched them closely with pale eyes. "The weakest of all the giant races. So the human caravan has found six dogs to lead it."

The Antaeans swallowed their pride and kept their anger at bay. It took all their effort, but they did not charge or raise their hammers.

"And soft too. Well trained by their human masters."

The Gegenees was quickly joined by elves on armored winged horses. The elves stared at the Antaeans then they looked at Pangolin and the elaphines.

"This is the caravan we have heard so many rumors of," said one elf. "There is nothing impressive about what I see."

The elf was knocked off his steed and crashed hard to the ground. The Gegenees and the other elves looked at him with shock. All the noise in the watching camps ceased.

Traveler approached them with his dog at his side. The caravan master had his unsheathed sword in hand. The fallen elf got back to his feet, and Traveler walked right up to the elf.

"What kingdom are you with?" Traveler asked the high elf. "Before you answer, think very carefully. At this moment, nothing has happened. It is merely a human and elf talking. However, it could become so much more. We encountered some elves from the kingdom of Raindark who disrespected us, and now their kingdom is exiled from the lands of the fairies and all their heirs to the throne lie dead. I once came across another royal who disrespected me. My dog transformed into a five-hundred-foot-tall beast, picked up their entire castle, and threw the royal house and their entire people into a volcano in the Nether-Lands. Do what you will, but remember there will be a response."

The men stared at each for the longest time.

"We only came out to greet your caravan," the elf finally said, ending with a smirk.

"Then Traveler of the Titan's Caravan greets you."

"I am Fenian of the wind-elfin kingdom of Spirit Thunder. We have been expecting you. Our king and queen wish to speak with you."

"For what purpose?"

"The Kings' Caravan is no more. There must be a replacement."

"Must there?"

"There must. You have a caravan. My king has consolidated all elfin clans under our kingdom to create our own. A human caravan and an elfin caravan."

"We are not a human caravan," Traveler corrected. "The caravan that was human was the Xenhelmians, the Kings' Caravan, and as you said, they are no more. Titan's Caravan is an alliance of different empires of the Lands of Man, and different kingdoms of fae to create a greater caravan. The races of humans and elves are but two of many represented in our caravan."

Traveler smiled. Fenian did not.

"I will return to my king," Fenian said. "We can arrange a meeting and meal."

"We will happily await your invitation."

Fenian nodded and effortlessly jumped back on his steed.

"I have never been knocked from my mount by any wizard before," the wind-elf said. "You must show me that trick. But your ploy accomplished its objective. We will withdraw."

Traveler did not answer. Fenian led the other elfin riders back into the crowds, followed by the Gegenees giant running after them.

"You see what Genenees giants excel at," Graktar said. "Running away. Real giants cannot run, but they are the only race of giants that can do it so well."

Traveler sat on the ground in the chief's tent—the chief of the caravan's three hundred woodland elves that had joined them at Titan's Step. A large fire burned in the center, encircled by rocks. Traveler was their guest, with his dog lying on its belly next to him and a dozen of the elves sitting around the fire in a circle.

As he was their guest, an elf would hand him a large bowl of food, Traveler would take a portion for his plate and pass it to the seated elf next to him, then for the next bowl, he would help himself and pass the other way. It was the custom of many rustic and nomadic fae peoples that Traveler had encountered.

"We should have done this sooner, Master Traveler," the woodland elf chief said to him.

"Yes, chief. I felt it rude to have a meal with woodland elves who just joined the caravan but not to have done so with those who have been with us already. I notice that though you are the same race, your clans are quite different."

Chief Ethor smiled. "Some woodland elves wish they were high elves and live in large cities. We are content to live in nature as our ancestors did—simply. We may be both woodland elves, but we share little in common nowadays."

"What do you think of our new elves joining the caravan?" Traveler asked.

"We were a great caravan before them. There is no change to that with them. We stay away from the matters of cities. We truly have no interest. But you are wise to add as many elfin clans to the caravan as you have."

"It would seem unlikely that your people would wish to travel all the way to Atlantea."

"Most see Atlantea as a fabled kingdom of untold riches, but that is not its true value. It is a gateway to other realms and other peoples. If the city dwellers build their alliances with them, rustic people should too."

Traveler nodded. "You are very wise, Chief Ethor. We should have talked a long time ago."

"Master Traveler, we can talk any time you wish, but we are not like the city elves. City elves and humans, you both are fond of your endless meetings."

Traveler laughed. "So I should not send Mr. Hobbs to gather you up for our nightly leadership meetings."

"That would be a no."

◆◆◆

Traveler entered the king's tent with his dog. At the entrance were the royal guards of Nirgund, the female half-elves, and the reptile-hound alphyns. Inside, their royals and Gwyness were seated around a table. Pangolin paced on the other side.

"Ah, Mr. Traveler, how was your lunch?" King Aereth asked.

"Very productive, sire," Traveler answered. "The rustic woodland elves may be quiet and unobtrusive, but they are very knowledgeable and observant. We should seek their counsel often on our journey, if even to get a different perspective from the other elves."

Hobbs entered the tent and immediately noticed Traveler. Pangolin walked to the steward. "The lizards seem extremely agitated," Hobbs said to both of them.

"Invisible elves?" Pangolin asked Traveler.

"It could be sprites or fairies too," he answered.

"Are we not beyond the lands of the fairies?" King Aereth asked.

"We are, sire, but they travel to the lands of the elves as often as elves travel to their lands. And sprites are everywhere. We already know we are always being watched by others, so if our giant lizards are seeing them, it means fae are wanting to get a closer look at us."

"I wish your pixy dust worked on these invisible intruders," Pangolin said.

Traveler smiled. "Sorry, Mr. Pangolin, the usefulness of our pixy dust is behind us. We should not be concerned. We are in our circle. They are outside it. We need to keep it that way."

"Mr. Traveler, can we talk about this impending invitation to meet with the wind elf monarchs?" Lady Aylen asked. "Is is wise? Every one of our encounters within a fae city on the Trail has not been a good one."

Hobbs swallowed hard.

"I am sorry, Mr. Hobbs, to remind you of your attack."

"No need to be sorry, princess. I am alive and well."

"Yes, you are, and we mean to keep it that way. The caravan relies on you," Lady Aylen said. "Mr. Traveler?"

"I completely agree with the princess," Pangolin said.

"I agree, too, but we will be accepting the invitation."

"Why, Mr. Traveler?" Lady Aylen asked.

"We all feel there is great danger involved," King Aereth said.

"We are gathering information, sire." Traveler looked at them all. "Do we not wish to bypass all this and continue our journey on Titan's Trail?"

"Yes, Mr. Traveler. That is the point of not wanting to accept this invitation or set one foot in Fae'el."

"If we want to continue our journey, we have to meet with the wind elves. We need to know everything there is to know. Not because we have any intention of involving ourselves in any of this chaos. We merely need them to think that we are helpless to resist their plotting."

"Mr. Traveler, are you hinting that you may have devised a way to get beyond Fae'el and all these elfin caravans?" King Aereth asked.

"Sire, I need you and the princess, especially, to act as if you never asked me that question. We are playing a deadly game when we meet these wind elf royals."

Pangolin grinned. "That is a game to be enthusiastically played, then."

"What are wind elves?" Lady Aylen asked Traveler. "There is such a race?"

"Wind elves are high elves who are also wind elementals."

"I do not like the sound of that, Mr. Traveler. Does that mean they can send a magical windstorm at us?"

"Yes, princess, among many other things, but we need not worry. We have a water elemental."

Lady Aylen laughed. "Water elemental, indeed. All I can do is make water from glasses float in the air. No, Mr. Traveler, I would remain worried."

"I have complete confidence in your abilities, princess."

"That makes one of us."

◆◆◆

Night had arrived when the puck Scratch appeared at the main camp's circle, wearing his dark robe with the hood on his head and his tail swaying back and forth from behind. The men summoned Hobbs.

"Mr. Scratch," Hobbs greeted.

"Pucks require no titles, but I thank you for it nevertheless."

"How can I help?"

"It begins. The royals of Spirit Thunder have requested the representatives of Titan's Caravan as their honored guests."

"Will you or your masters be joining us?"

The puck stifled an outburst of laughter and said, "No."

◆◆◆

A halfling in a black robe led them to the city's gates. King Aereth followed at the lead, dressed in silver attire with a cloak and his Helm Earldom crown. Lady Aylen walked on his left, wearing her Sirnegate crown and dressed in cloaked blue attire. Traveler walked on the king's right, in dark clothes and a hooded cloak, his dog to his side.

Behind them marched Pangolin in the center, Dr'amal wearing her hood and dark-purple attire, on one side, and Gwyness in black on the other. The fifty-foot entrance loomed over them, and now they could see that the entrance of the slim city wall was indeed a pocket-realm to a far vaster inside, as Traveler had told them. They could also see the detail of the elfin statues on either side of the entrance.

Gwyness leaned forward to Traveler. "The statue's toe moved."

Traveler only turned his head slightly and nodded.

Following all of them were the female half-elf royal guards, the male half-elves save Mr. Elman, and a contingent of the Cut-Throats. Two of the Antaean giants, Grakdar and Barg, were the rear guard.

The guards at the entrance were Fenian and two dozen other wind elves in black. He held up a hand to stop their advancement. "No weapons are allowed in Fae'el," the elf said.

"That is an unusual request," King Aereth said. "The weapons of our party are ceremonial. Why would they not be allowed?"

Fenian smiled. "Of course, you are correct. Disregard my comment."

One of the wind elves pointed. Fenian walked to Dr'amal. The drowess stared ahead, not making eye contact with him. The wind elf then stepped to study the half-elves. Fenian returned to his place before King Aereth.

"You have a drow amongst you. Their race is an enemy of mine."

"They are part of our caravan, as are other elves such as yourself."

"Yes, so true. Their kingdoms obviously have no sense of honor. You also have Forsaken with you."

"I am not familiar with that term," King Aereth said.

"The half-elves. Elves are a race of true blood. It is such that makes our magic great, and our people the dominant of all of Faë-Land."

"There would be fairies, sprites, and many other fae who would strongly, some violently, disagree with you," Traveler said.

"The envious ones."

"What is your point?" Lady Aylen asked. "The half-elves are my royal guards. Do not call them forsaken, because they are not. The drow is also none of your concern. If any or all of them are an offense to you high wind elves, we can return to our camp and your royals can dine without us."

"That would not be their wish, Lady Aylen. Disregard my comments."

"You are an elf of many comments to disregard."

The elf looked at their party again. "Do you not have a dog?" Fenian asked.

"Are companion animals allowed in the king's court?" Traveler asked.

"No, they are not."

"I thought so. I sent my dog back to our camp."

The elf smiled and turned away. King Aereth and Lady Aylen looked at Traveler suspiciously.

The Tree Shepherds had commanded the three main crawling trees to create a net above the circle to cover and protect the main party. All four Tree Shepherds stood at the base of the trees in the center of the camp. The crawling trees had increased in size, and their branches looked more like elongated fingers to the eye. All other joining parties created a second adjoining circle.

Both Hobbs and Estus were left in command. Through a telescope, Hobbs watched the entrance of Fae'el. From that distance, all he could see was the outline of the two giant statues and a faint glow of light from within the city's walls. Estus, clad in new armor, stood with him.

"Do you wish you accompanied them?" Estus asked.

"I would have liked to have seen another fae city, but no, I am happy to have remained behind."

"We are the masters of the camp for the night, Mr. Hobbs."

"That is only a good thing if nothing happens."

A group of Cut-Throats waited nearby, with their chamroshes sleeping at their feet. Most of the day fae, like the giants, were asleep. The darklings had taken the form of cat-headed monkeys and were crawling around the net of the crawling trees, chasing each other, and occasionally cackling.

But it was when the brownies appeared with hatchets in their hands that both Hobbs and Estus were alarmed.

"Is something the matter?" Hobbs asked one of the brownies.

"No." The brownie was uncharacteristically abrupt.

"Brownies have been with the caravan for a good while now, and we have never seen any of you carry a weapon."

"Brownies can fight too."

"I do not doubt it. Will you be fighting tonight?"

"Maybe."

"Maybe?" Estus asked. "Against what?"

"Someone approaches," the brownie said.

Hobbs and Estus returned their attention to the perimeter. A group of riders neared them, but so did a giant carrying something large on his shoulder.

"Is someone there?" an elf asked from a winged horse, both in armor.

The branches of the crawling trees pulled back. "I am Hobbs, the steward of Titan's Caravan." He stepped forward; Estus and the Cut-Throats remained close. "How may I help you?"

"We heard the former Kings' Caravan were enemies of the Titan's Caravan."

"Yes."

"Fae'el, or the kingdom of Spirit Thunder, has a gift for you."

The giant of nearly fifteen feet was a cyclops, and it dropped the weight in its hands to the ground. They immediately recognized the colors of its kingdom—orange and white. The wagon was filled with bodies—bodies of Xenhelmians.

Hobbs gasped as he recognized one of the corpses.

"What is it?" Estus asked.

"I know that man," Hobbs replied.

"Yes, who is it?"

"He was that swordsman named Bilfreth. The caravan's original master-at-arms."

"Yes, the one that Mr. Pangolin replaced. Looks like Bilfreth paid dearly for his ill-advised decision to join the Four Kings."

"They all did."

◆◆◆

The sky was dark outside Fae'el, but inside the city was bright as day with glowing balls hovering in the sky of the inner pocket-realm. The streets looked to be paved with white luminescent metal, but they had a firm rather than slippery texture as they walked. The halfling led them through two receiving columns of black-clad elves facing each other. Crowds of elves watched them pass, whispering amongst themselves in other languages and dialects. They wound through the street to a floating white castle, where a full brigade of more elfin warriors in black sat upon armored winged horses. The flag on the towers of the main castle were that of moving storm clouds. As they neared, a hooded elf appeared at the entrance of the castle, and stairs magically appeared, connecting the ground to the main level, two stories above.

"What is the term? Sacrificial lamb. I feel that is what we are, Mr. Traveler. I hope your gamble bears fruit," Lady Aylen whispered.

"Princess, the gamble is not about me. You and the king are the ones on center stage tonight. I am but a mere commoner to them. Oh, and remember elfin ears can hear whispers too."

"What?" Lady Aylen instinctively put her hand on her mouth.

"Mr. Traveler, do elves have the titles of duke or count or earl?" King Aereth asked.

"No, sire. Those are human titles. Kings, queens, princes, princesses and lords. Those are the titles of elfin royalty. Why do you ask?"

"Only curious."

The elfin wizard in a dark hooded robe had jeweled rings on each of his fingers. "King Aereth," he greeted. "I am Genus and I welcome your Titan's Caravan to Fae'el. Follow me."

Into the large, long corridor they followed. The elfin wizard pushed with his hand, and the doors to an inner chamber opened. They were overwhelmed by joyous music.

They entered the throne room. Genus turned to them and gestured for them to halt. He moved ahead on a golden carpet to the elfin king and queen in white attire, sitting on their large, golden thrones surrounded by royals, nobles, knights, warriors, and attendants—all also dressed in white. Other elves in elegant dress of many colors waited in the audience around the elfin royals, standing on either side of the golden carpet, watching them.

Young elfin girls appeared out of the air and encircled them. The females floated in the air as they greeted them with flowered necklaces made of multicolored petals.

"Welcome," one of them said to King Aereth and Lady Aylen.

A very tall elf in a regal one-piece black outfit appeared and approached them with a stern face. He nodded and said, "I am Rodgal, steward to the Royal House of Spirit Thunder. As royals, King Aereth and Lady Aylen, you will be announced and sit in the company of our king and queen. Your servants will remain here and will be attended to by my staff."

"Mr. Traveler, our caravan master, is also a royal," King Aereth said quickly.

"Oh, I was not aware. Forgive my oversight, King Aereth. Does he have a title he wishes to be addressed as?"

King Aereth looked at Traveler with a wicked grin.

"Be careful, sire," Traveler whispered with his own grin.

"Lord Traveler would suffice," the king said to Rodgal.

"Thank you, King Aereth. He will be so announced."

The elfin steward turned and walked down the golden carpet. Lady Aylen held in her laughter.

Traveler looked back at Gwyness and Pangolin. "Not one word of this to anyone in the camp."

"Yes, lord," Pangolin said with a grin.

The grin vanished from their master-at-arms's face. From one side of the throne room, a party of six-armed giants entered in their black armor. From the other side came a larger party of elves in golden clothing.

Angel-winged fae halflings in white descended from above and blew horns to silence the room.

"I announce our guests for the night. King Aereth, human king of Helm Earldom in the Lands of Man," Rodgal called out and gestured.

King Aereth moved down the golden carpet. He observed the crowds on either side as they passed. The elves smiled, but not all their eyes were friendly. He moved to where Rodgal gestured and stood in the middle. He could see the king and queen better. Both elves seemed to glow. He had dark hair to his shoulders; she had golden hair to her waist. The thrones they sat upon were of golden metal.

"Lady Aylen, elfin princess of the human kingdom of Sirnegate," Rodgal announced.

The princess joined King Aereth to one side. The wind elf royals watched her with particular interest.

"And finally, Lord Traveler, the caravan master of Titan's Caravan."

Traveler joined the royals.

"Thank you, Rodgal," the wind elf king said. "I am King Zephyr of the wind elf kingdom of Spirit Thunder. My wife and queen is Gale. We are honored to have you join us tonight for dinner. Let us move to the dinner hall."

Rodgal led the three of them one way around the thrones. Those not in white followed. The king and queen appeared from another entrance, followed by their royals, knights, guards, and attendants in white.

The dining hall looked as if it were out in the open woods. There was the royal table—long and rectangular. Both king and queen sat next to each other at the head. King Aereth was seated on the side of the table closest to the king, Traveler next to him; Lady Aylen was seated on the other side to be closest to the queen. All the others in white were seated at the table around them.

There were many tables in the dining room: those for the elves in golden clothes, another for the Gegenees, all the other elves, and the table where they placed Pangolin, Gwyness, and the others.

Rodgal had food served immediately. The servers were not elves. They looked like sprites, both male and female, with big, bright eyes.

◆◆◆

Pangolin, Gwyness, and Dr'amal were seated at their own table with the half-elves, and Cut-Throats. A larger table was brought in by stocky sprites for the two Antaean giants, Grakdar and Barg, to sit alone.

Pangolin and Gwyness noticed that Dr'amal seemed strangely distant from them all. She sat quietly staring ahead with a blank look. Their food servers appeared. Not dignified sprites with large eyes in silver attire, but the same stocky sprites in brown attire. They had large heads, brutish arms, slightly hunched, and thinning dark hair. Their facial features were also larger: noses, mouths, and ears.

"I have not seen your fae race before," Pangolin said to one of the servers. "What is your kind's name."

"We are grunts. Servants of the kingdom of Spirit Thunder."

"Good to meet you."

The grunts served the food and drinks.

"Seated at these outer tables, I feel as if we are the outcasts," Gwyness said.

"I am proud to be a commoner," Pangolin said.

"Are you, Mr. Pangolin?"

He had a smirk on his face. "Whatever do you mean, maiden?"

"Oh, thank you for your recommendations. My training is progressing with the Cut-Throats."

"Confidence, maiden. Your challenge is lack of confidence."

"Yes. Sometimes I feel afraid."

"Afraid?"

"Afraid of what I will become or...what I truly am."

"You are becoming nothing but what you already are. And there is no evil in you, if that is your concern. Remember, your princess can sense evil."

Gwyness brightened. "Yes. You are correct, Mr. Pangolin. Look at our two giants. They are like two children exiled to the corner for misbehaving."

Castle guards had cordoned off all the streets from Fae'el's main gate entrance, but all establishments remained open for business. Whether day or night, commerce on the merchant streets would never cease, which was no different than any other city, human or fae, on the Trail.

In one tavern three wizardly hooded figures sat in front of mugs of ale, though none of them had taken a drink and not one of them spoke. It was one of the larger drinking taverns on the merchant street. Small tables were near the entrance for solo patrons, larger tables near the center and rear for larger groups. The place was filled with elves, sprites, and a wide variety of animal-like fae.

The three figures had been at their seats all day, silent and motionless at a medium-sized round table in the center. Patrons and passersby noticed that their forms beneath the table were not visible. Their hands were pale and long, and their feet were lizard-like. Some mused whether the wizards were dark fae, but none sensed any dark magic radiating from them.

What elves and other fae also observed was the shadiest of the city's merchant class entered the establishment, sat near them for a while, ordered a drink or two, then left. A high elf, always dressed in white, as bright as his soul was black, sat near the wizards now. He too drank his spritely ale bubbling from the cup. He knew he was being watched by many eyes, and smirked to himself. His movements were not as natural. He touched the side of his chest, feeling for something underneath. Satisfied, he rose from his chair.

He froze with an expression of shock. A half dozen wind elves stepped into the tavern and immediately walked to his side.

"Why are you here, merchant?" the wind-elf leader asked.

"Good evening, good elf. Simply washing down a few drinks after a good, honest—and profitable—day's work. I am actually on my way back to my shop."

"You never leave your shop."

"I obviously do."

"You only leave your shop to do business, often of the more dubious kind."

"I choose not to take offense at your insinuation. I am a Fae'el citizen of good standing. You and your wind elves are guests of our great city."

"We are much more than that."

"I am sorry. Your king and queen are paying guests. As much as I would enjoy the conversation, I have a shop to run."

The wind elf held back the high-elf merchant.

"Is there anything else, good elf?"

"No."

"Then have a good night."

The high elf walked past them and out of the tavern into the street as the door swung closed. The wind elves turned their attention to the three seated wizardly men and approached their table.

"You there," the wind elf said.

The hooded men neither moved nor answered.

"Did you hear me?"

"Are we obligated to speak to strangers in this city?" one of them finally replied in a strange voice with a deep bass.

"You are obligated to answer the knights of Spirit Thunder."

"But this is Fae'el, not Spirit Thunder."

"The Fae'el king and queen have given full authority to Spirit Thunder's king and queen and all of their knights."

"Since we cannot sit in peace we will leave."

The three figures rose from their seats.

"Many merchants have been observed entering this tavern since you all took your post here. Merchants who sell many illegal objects of magic. There is an embargo of all caravan supplies by order of Fae'el until the new elfin caravan departs for Titan's Trail. Have you been illegally trying to circumvent the order of the Fae'el royals?"

"We have been legally trying to sit in peace in a simple tavern. We shall leave."

"We would be in our rights to detain you and question you until we are satisfied."

"Since you have offered no proof of crimes against the laws of Fae'el, we would be in our rights to turn you into dirt worms, wind elf, and crush you under our feet."

"Wind elves are not frail by any means."

"Then use your wind magic against ours. Everyone in this dwelling and beyond would be killed, but at least we would both have the satisfaction of knowing who possesses the greater magic."

Everyone in the tavern stood to their feet, nervously moving away from both parties. The wind elves looked at the crowds then back at the hooded figures.

"Maybe next time. Our king and queen are entertaining guests themselves. If not for that, we would be of a different disposition."

"Of course. A likely excuse, wind elf."

The three hooded figures brushed past them. The wind elves still could not see their faces with their elfin eyes. The wizardly men left the tavern.

♦♦♦

Everyone at the king and queen's table enjoyed their meal, but no one spoke. The royals ate slowly; no one would speak until they did.

"Aereth," King Zephyr began. "It is a strong wind-elf name."

King Aereth smiled. "Thank you, king."

"Oh, my congratulations too."

"Congratulations?" King Aereth asked.

"You have come a long way. Assembled a worthy caravan for the journey ahead to Atlantea. Many wagered that a human-led caravan with no alliances in the magical lands could accomplish such a feat, but you did."

"Thank you, king."

"I heard you had a few unfortunate encounters with the Xenhelmians. When you return to your camp, you will find a gift waiting."

"Gift, king?"

"Yes. You will be pleased."

"Then, I thank you again."

"A human kingdom with an elfin princess?" Queen Gale asked Lady Aylen.

"Yes, queen. I was taken there as an infant."

"Oh, so you are returning to your lands?"

"Yes, in a way I am."

"What is the name of your original elfin kingdom?"

"Faylen."

The queen looked at her husband. "We do not know of that kingdom. But water elves have many more cities than us land and sky elves combined."

"You have a very curious caravan," King Zephyr said to King Aereth. "You carry how many fae banners presently?"

"The fairies of Chrysa, the giants of Antaeus, and the centaurs of Chiron."

"And this elfin city of Faylen," Queen Gale added.

"Yes, queen."

"We have attempted to do the same," King Zephyr said. "Our elfin caravan is an alliance of the mountain elves of Bravebow, the elves in golden dress; the giants of Gegenees; and the dwarves of Iron Hooves. Soon other elfin kingdoms will join. I am sure you have heard other water elfin kingdoms have already arrived at Atlantea."

"We heard so."

"The water elves are attempting to shut out all other elfin kingdoms. It is already offensive to many in elfinkind that the alliance of celestial, star, cloud, and night elves have attempted to do so in the past and retain a presence in the fabled kingdom." The wind-elf king's face expressed a visible hatred as he spoke of the other elfin races. "That is the reason for the sense of urgency among us all. The Kings' Caravan may be dead, but we must establish a new caravan of Titan's Trail to replace it."

"How do you find our elfin dishes, Lady Aylen?" Queen Gale asked.

"Queen, the food is the most delicious I have ever tasted."

"The secret is our elfin spices."

"I wish we had some in our caravan."

"Then you shall. I will have Rodgal see to it and send you a healthy supply for your entire caravan and its journey. We have more than we could ever use."

"Thank you, queen."

"Maybe you, King Aereth, and Lady Aylen can tell us of your kingdoms. Neither the queen nor I have ever been to the Lands of Man. All we have heard are stories. We have encountered very few humans in our lives," King Zephyr said.

"I would be happy to," King Aereth said. "Hopefully, we can hear an account of your kingdom of Spirit Thunder."

"Of course."

The entire table listened intently to King Aereth's colorful description of Helm Earldom and his people as everyone enjoyed food, drink, and music played unobtrusively in the background. He could not help but speak of his colleague kings of the neighboring cities of Strongbridge and Eastmoor. It was clear he missed them and his lands.

After a while, the princess had her turn. Lady Aylen was not comfortable in her account of Sirnegate, but as she continued to speak, her descriptions got bolder, her presentation livelier, and she managed to elicit more than a few laughs with her stories of life as a princess.

◆◆◆

Hobbs and Estus had been summoned to the perimeter of the caravan again. They were accompanied by armed brownies, and several darklings were waiting. The darklings were in the form of humanoid goat beings, and they pointed to three figures in hooded robes.

"I know who they are," Estus said. "Let them pass."

"Mr. Estus?" Hobbs asked.

"Let them in, and I will attend to them."

The three figures were allowed into the circle, and Estus led them to one of the tents. All four of them entered, and the flaps were closed. Hobbs and the brownies looked at each other.

A single standing torch burned in the center of the tent. One of the hooded figures clapped his hands and a purple fire engulfed them and disappeared. The center figure turned into Elman, the second to Tyfer, and the third into a grinning Quillen. The humans were fine, but Elman shook his head vigorously and touched his forehead.

"I may be a half-elf, but my elfin half did not like this drow spell at all."

"It did what it was supposed to. Did you get it?" Estus asked.

"We did, Mr. Estus," Quillen said, pulling a pouch from his cloak pocket. "We were lucky."

"Mr. Tyfer, thank you so much for doing this," Estus said. "I know your apprehension about entering fae cities."

"It was fine, sir. I was happy to help the caravan." He too pulled out a pouch from his cloak pocket.

Quillen put his pouch in Estus's hand. "All the items from the list Mr. Traveler gave us—herbs, roots, powders, seeds, mushrooms, leaves, anti-poisons. Why was the moly herb so expensive?"

"The moly herb is used to protect from magic," Elman answered and put his pouch in Estus's hand. "Mr. Traveler wanted magical arrows. We have enough to equip an army from here to Atlantea and back. Be careful when you open the pocket-realm. It is a vast supply."

Estus smiled. "My men and I will happily organize it all, no matter how vast." He looked to Tyfer.

Hobbs's chief guardsman handed Estus his pouch.

"How did you fare, Mr. Tyfer?"

"Food, water, and plenty of ambrosia for our animals and giants. We will never have to stop at another city or town."

Estus smiled as he weighed the pouches in his hands. "I so love the magic of these pocket-realms."

"What does this mean, Mr. Estus?" Quillen asked. "Are we about to leave soon?"

"That, Mr. Quillen, you will have to wait for our caravan master to inform us of. Out we go so Mr. Hobbs and the others do not think you murdered me or something else sinister."

◆◆◆

Lady Aylen continued with her tales.

"Lord Traveler," King Zephyr interrupted her. "What are your thoughts on the matter?"

"Which matter, king?" Traveler asked.

"The only matter there is in this room and in this city. Should your caravan and our caravan join as one?"

"Clearly, king, once you have all of your parties assembled, we can discuss it in depth. Does it make sense for us to join forces? Or does it make sense to travel as separate parties? I personally do not think it is a big issue. Whether together or separate, both our caravans are impressive and capable and will have no problems successfully reaching Atlantea."

"You are that confident?"

"I am, king."

"I believe you underestimate the dangers ahead. There are dark forces that will try to prevent any from reaching Atlantea. The Kings' Caravan may be no more, but their allies remain."

"Do you know what became of these Four Kings?" Queen Gale asked Traveler.

"No, queen, not exactly."

"Do you know what became of their second city of Xenhelm here in Faë-Land?" she asked. "The power of the sun blotted it from the earth. Its land still burns to this day."

"Queen, you both know what transpired. They tried to kill us more than once but failed. I failed in my attempt against the Four Kings. However, I did not fail in regard to their armies and their new city in the magical lands. If we ever see them again, we will see to it that they never get another chance to kill us or any other. They are not only an enemy of humankind but to all elfinkind and all of faekind. Separate from that, the journey to Atlantea is our only focus."

King Zephyr set his goblet on the table. "Our caravan has its own wizards led by our wizard master, Genus. Our Black Walkers are the most accomplished fighters in all of Faë-Land. The golden archers of Bravebow are also the best in these lands. You have six Antaean giants. Our caravan has dozens of Gegenees giants."

"King, who are the others who will be joining your caravan?" King Aereth asked.

King Zephyr hesitated in his answer. "Other fae, but I cannot reveal their identities, at least for now."

"I apologize for the intrusion."

The wind-elf king returned his attention to Traveler. "I must press the issue since you are the one in true command of your caravan and not the human king or water elf."

Traveler set his own cup on the table and gave his full attention as King Zephyr continued.

"The dark forces I speak of will be here shortly. Unfortunately the kingdom of Atlantea does not recognize the differences among fae. In their eyes, an elf or an evil goblin are the same. The goblin kingdoms also have their own caravans, hastily assembled and ill-equipped, but they advance to the Trail even now. The consequences of such caravans reaching Atlantea and being accepted would be catastrophic to all of Faë-Land. Your caravan and ours must join forces."

"But only ours is ready to go now, king."

The king and queen wind elves watched him with cold smiles.

"Ours will be ready in no more than a day or two," the wind-elf king finally said.

"Who would be in charge of this combined caravan?" Traveler asked.

"We also know the way to Atlantea," Queen Gale said.

"Your usefulness as guide would not be needed, and our warriors are far more formidable than your caravan's," King Zephyr said. "The kingdom of an elfin king and queen is of higher standing than a human king, elfin princess of a human city, and a supposed human royal. It is not disrespect but the protocol of royal status that dictates who commands."

"King Zephyr, you speak correctly," King Aereth said. "We are in elfin lands, and we respectfully observe its courtesies, customs, and the laws that maintain the order of things."

"We are happy to hear you say that, King Aereth," Queen Gale said.

"I am royal too. It would be the same if Atlantea were in the Lands of Man and people traveled from these lands there."

"I doubt it. If the situation were reversed, our land would have descended upon yours and taken what we wanted. You humans would be in no position to stop us," King Zephyr said. "Do not believe otherwise."

"That is a strange thing to say, king," Traveler said, "since I have observed for the past twenty years a human king descend upon your lands with caravans of one hundred thousand or more strong, crossing to and from Atlantea without your kingdom or any other stopping them."

"I explained the reason for that offense."

"The celestial, star, cloud, and night elves?"

"Yes, but I am not interested in whether you understand the complexities of our realm or not. Your caravan will fall in under our command, and when all our forces are assembled, we will advance to Atlantea."

"My caravan will have to deliberate on the matter," King Aereth challenged respectfully.

"This is not a negotiation. This is a courtesy to you. You have nothing to negotiate with. Our forces are superior. Our magic is far superior. And we do not require the services of a human guide. We do not need your caravan. Negotiate? I am an elfin king and my wife and I have ruled since before the parents of your grandparents were born. It is pure insolence. Your royalty means nothing to us. You are commoners. You are humans, even your elf here. She has the smell of a human, like your half-elves.

"Accept our terms now, or remain here and return to your own lands. No human-led caravan will be allowed to travel to Atlantea again. You have reached Fae'el, an admirable accomplishment, but you will go no further."

King Aereth and Lady Aylen looked at the wind-elf king and queen with disgust. Traveler's gaze was at his plate in front of him, his hands folded on his lap.

He looked up. "For someone who has been alive before the parents of our grandparents were born, you elves still do not know how to talk to humans. We survived the Kings' Caravan and will survive Spirit Thunder's. The reverse is also true, king. We do not need your caravan to get to Atlantea. We will leave tomorrow morning and your caravan can catch up when you are ready and able."

"Our wizard master can transport our entire caravan to Atlantea in a day," Queen Gale said angrily.

"Oh, then if that is in fact true, your caravan will get to Atlantea first, and we will catch up when we are able."

"Rodgal!" the wind-elf queen yelled.

The elfin steward promptly appeared and escorted Traveler, King Aereth, Lady Aylen, and their party from the table, then from the dining hall. Outside, he turned them all over to Fenian the elf and his men. The Titan's Caravan delegation was led from the city of Fae'el. The magic steps disappeared the moment the last person's foot touched the ground. Then the very main gate entrance vanished from the wall.

◆ ◆ ◆

"I had to use every ounce of magic to protect us within their dining hall," Dr'amal revealed. She could not hide her nervousness, and all of them felt they would be attacked at any moment up until they crossed the circle into their camp.

The large meeting tent was filled with the leadership: the elfin leaders Druil, the high-elf wizard; Taylon, the desert-elf falconer; Galadaer, the woodland-elf knight; Staric, the moon elf; Bragg, the dwelf, and his elfin comrades; Dr'amal, and her father Dr'as. Outside, the royal guards stood at the entrance, but they were as curious about the conversation within as all the men and fae standing in the camp. Rumors had already circulated, and fear grew that they might soon be at battle with the wind elves and the six-armed giants.

"Hobbs, did anyone touch those bodies?" Traveler asked Hobbs.

"We did as you instructed, sir. No one left the circle."

"And we were all successful," Estus said.

"Good." Traveler shot a look at a smiling Quillen. "And the supplies?" Traveler asked Hobbs.

"When did the supplies of these elfin spices arrive?" Lady Aylen asked Hobbs.

"Right before you arrived, princess. And, sir, no one left the circle for the supplies either."

"Burn the bodies and the supplies, Hobbs," Traveler instructed. "Have the brownies do it."

"Yes, sir." The steward left the tent.

"This wind-elf king and queen did not even allow us the time to pretend to be their allies and decide on a strategy. Mr. Traveler, how will we leave this valley now?" King Aereth asked.

"They are wind elves," Dr'amal said. "They can magically control the air to attack us. They also have many wizards. If there is a battle coming, it will be of magic, and they will win."

"We will wait here in the circle," Traveler said.

"Wait?" King Aereth asked.

"Wait for what, Mr. Traveler?" Lady Aylen asked.

"Wait until these others King Zephyr and Queen Gale are waiting for arrive," Traveler answered.

"Why should we wait?" Pangolin asked.

"I am about to say something, but I do not want any of you to panic."

"Oh no, Mr. Traveler, not another shock," Lady Aylen said.

"I thought it best, after the incident in Fae-Wick, for us to know exactly who all the fae allies of the Four Kings, the Xenhelmians, were. We almost lost our Mr. Pangolin in Fae-Wick, and we almost lost Mr. Hobbs in Arion's Spear. None of our fae would talk, including our drows here."

"The drows did so not to hide anything," Dr'as said. "It is because powerful kingdoms are involved. Theye have eyes and ears everywhere. We may be here with the caravan, but our kingdoms are not. Why bring trouble to them?"

"There are fae within our caravan who are not bound by such pledges of secrecy."

"The common woodlanders," Galadaer, the woodland elf said.

"Yes, and confirmed by others."

"Oh no," King Aereth realized.

"Yes, sire. They were playing deceptive games too. These wind elves were—are—allied with the Four Kings. But I did not need to confer with others to know they were allied against us. They set up this blockade for us. Also, since they are wind elves, I believe they sent those trolls after us. Despite their insulting insistence tonight at dinner that Titan's Caravan fall in under their caravan, they do not want our caravan to join. They want our caravan to disappear. The two things that they said that were true is they hate the alliance of the celestial and sky elves, and they hate humans, more than they hate goblins and other dark fae.

"We may not be in the lands of the fairies anymore but their network is vast, and I sent our two fairies on a mission on our behalf. They sought out the celestial elf that Lady Aylen, Gwyness and I met with in Druid City, who is also not bound by royal secrecy. She is not afraid of other powerful fae kingdoms. She is one of those kingdoms. What we needed to know is precisely who the wind elves of Spirit Thunder are waiting for, who are their allies, besides the six-armed giants.

"Finally, there is one other matter. We also need to know which elves and drows in this tent and our caravan are also allied with the wind elves and the Xenhelmians."

The sound of a feather falling to the ground could have been heard in the tent.

Bragg the dwelf burst out laughing. "I like these human meetings!"

CHAPTER THIRTEEN

Dark Fae

Dawn in the lands of fairies was bright and bold, with rainbow skies of birds and butterflies. The air was warm and often magically erased any troubles from the day before. In the lands of the sprites, it was the same; maybe the skies were not as colorful. Dawn in the lands of elves was much more like those in the Lands of Man, or as some fairies and sprites would say, despite the beauty, "plain." Titan's Caravan was camped in the lands of the elves, but the area of Fae'el was different. Traveler noted that it was as if they were in the lands of goblins; other fae agreed.

The half-elf leader, Elman, was convinced there was a nearby darkness, and he was not the only fae to believe so the next day. His eyes scanned the distance. All three of the crawling trees were as high as the facade wall of Fae'el, one hundred feet in the air. At the top of the center one, with the hoofed fae camped at its base, elaphine archer-warriors were doing the same—he surveyed the lands from his new aerial post. Elman noticed that even with their cloven feet, the elaphines could scale up as fast as any tree mammal or reptile. At the top of the other crawling trees at both ends were the other male half-elves. He watched from the very top of the crawling tree until they came.

Elman did not use ocular instruments like humans. His eyes were gifted with magical eyesight greater than most elfin races. He saw not one caravan approaching Fae'el but two.

◆◆◆

Hobbs entered the leadership tent, where Traveler sat at a large table with the royals. Their caravan master studied the maps; the royals were impatient.

"Sir," Hobbs began, "the elfin parties do want to speak with you."

"I am sure they do but not now, Hobbs. The allies of the other parties will soon be here. We must be ready."

"Why do we not know who they are yet?" Lady Aylen asked.

"They are invisible, princess, but the magical maps know they are coming. We need to see them with our own eyes to know who. Hobbs, is there any activity from Fae'el?"

"Nothing yet, sir. Mr. Pangolin and the Cut-Throats are watching closely."

"Tell the elves we will speak soon, but we must get past this coming crisis first."

Hobbs nodded and left the tent.

"It is almost noon," Lady Aylen said. "This waiting is infuriating."

"Mr. Traveler, I noticed that these wind elves engage in the same method as Xenhelm. King Oughtred and Xenhelm took over the kingdom of Ironwood for his purposes in our lands. This king and queen of Spirit Thunder seem to have done the same with Fae'el."

"You are correct, sire. If King Oughtred used Ironwood for a weapons vault, for what purposes do the wind elves use Fae'el. I wonder."

"What do you plan to do about the elfin parties, Mr. Traveler?" Lady Aylen asked. "I do not believe they are in league with the wind elves. They would have joined them if they were."

"True, princess. But we must be sure, and they must be sure they wish to side with us. That is what it will come down to."

Elman, the half-elf, burst into the tent. "They are here!"

Traveler stood from his table. "What do you see?"

"Two different parties approaching. One from the south and another from the west. They use magic to obscure a clear view, but they near."

"Mr. Traveler, where is your dog?" King Aereth asked. "We haven't seen him since last night."

"He is here, sire. Mr. Elman, we must know exactly who they are."

Elman nodded and rushed out of the tent. Pangolin entered the tent with I-wulf.

"Mr. Elman told us," Traveler said to Pangolin.

"The Fae'el doors opened. The wind elves and their six-armed giants came out."

"Sire, you and your pech heavy-weapons teams should get ready," Traveler said.

"Yes, we should, Mr. Traveler," King Aereth said.

The king ran out of the tent. Nirgund stood outside the tent and followed the king with the alphyn hounds as the king passed.

"Lady Aylen, have your weapons ready, and stand at the front with Mr. Pangolin's men. There should be at least one elf visible."

Elman returned to the tent.

"Mr. Elman, what do you have?" Traveler asked.

"The party to our south are fairies—dark fairies and lunatishee. Do you know them?"

"Yes," Traveler replied.

"The other is actually two groups: One is a war party of goblins. The other are dark sprites."

"Which party are the wind elves waiting for?" Lady Aylen asked.

"Let us go and see," Traveler said to all.

Human and fae took positions along the perimeter. In the distance, shadowy figures approached from two different fronts. Traveler looked on, the royals next to him.

"Mr. Traveler, have you come up with a way for us to leave all this to get back on the Trail and our journey?"

"I have, sire."

King Aereth smiled. "Then I will see to my duties and allow you to continue with yours."

The king had dozens of pech, with their big forearms, and men waiting near the caravan's catapults.

Lady Aylen and Gwyness joined Pangolin and the Cut-Throats with their anxious chamroshes at the front. The female half-elves stood behind the princess, and dozens of elaphine archer-warriors took positions behind the Cut-Throats. All six of the Antaean giants stood behind them all. Lizard minders and the caravan's giant lizards in armor were positioned at the threshold of the entire circle. Teams of men with crossbows as their primary weapons and swords as their secondary stood with them.

From the road to Fae'el, both King Zephyr and Queen Gale rode to them mounted on large winged horses surrounded by elfin knight riders in white and elfin archers in black, both groups on armored winged horses. The elves in golden attire with their large long bows stood to one side. An elf with golden hair sat on his own winged steed. With him were another elfin king and queen—likely the true rulers of Fae'el—on dark unicorns and an army of elfin warriors, both archers and lancers. Dozens and dozens of the six-armed Gegenees giants in black spilled out of the city, an axe, sword, mace, or morning star in each hand. Floating above the wind-elf king and queen was their master wizard Genus, in his silver hooded robe. The elf landed, then three other elves appeared on either side.

Titan's Caravan stood ready. The fae berserkers under the lionoid Hax stood with Ethor and his rustic woodland elves. Both were well-armed—the fae berserkers with their blade weapons, the elves with their bows and arrows. The gnomes, horned gnomoids, and humanoid animal men stood quietly in the center of the camp. The humanoid animals kept their own animals—giant animals, jackalopes, and enfields—close and calm. The center crawling tree had all four Tree Shepherds in its branches, and all the other hoofed fae readied their own bows and arrows.

Traveler could see that Dr'as of the drows was eager to speak with him. Dr'amal appeared at his side, but all conversations would have to wait. On the other side, the other elfin parties and the puck, Scratch, waited. Only Bragg the dwelf had an eager smile on his face.

From the south along the Trail came the dark fairies. Flying vertically in the air were humanoid female fae with large eyes, flapping mothlike or translucent fly-like wings. They had large woolly antennae sprouting from the tops of their heads. Some had pointy elf-like ears. Others had no visible ears at all. They wore a variety of colored frocks made of different fabrics under armor that were like insect exoskeletons or shells of snails or turtles. All carried pointed razor-edged spears.

On their flanks were strange sprites. Ugly, old-looking halfling sprites with large child-like heads. Wearing earth-toned clothes and pointed-tipped shoes, they pranced towards Titan's Caravan with grins on their faces.

"Hobbs," Traveler said.

"Yes, sir."

"Find the brownies in their pocket and tell them that the dark fairies have spriggans with them."

The steward nodded, and ran back into the camp.

Marching behind them were a type of fairy that, other than Traveler, the humans had never seen—the lunatishee. They were wingless fairies covered in sharp thorns over their entire bodies. The other fairies were tall and slender; these fairies were no taller than gnomes, and they looked more like devilish males than fairies.

Swarms of black flies and large dragon flies encircled both parties. They continued on to the waiting wind- and high-elf parties. The humans heard many of the sprites in Titan's Caravan gasp when King Zephyr and Queen Gale greeted the dark fairy leaders.

"What is happening, Mr. Traveler? Who are those fairies and the creatures with them?" Lady Aylen asked.

"Both groups are fairies. The flying ones are dark fairies and the thorned ground halflings are called lunatishee. If that fairy-storm we encountered at Arion's Spear were here, they would immediately attack those fairies."

"Is such an elf-fairy alliance common?" King Aereth asked.

"Not between high elves and dark fairies, sire."

"Why are they called dark fairies, Mr. Traveler?" Gwyness asked. "I would not be able to differentiate them from any other fairies we have seen."

"Maiden Gwyness, in Faë-Land dark has to do with magic and not visible appearance. These fairies use dark magic. That is why the sprites in our caravan are shocked. High elves do not associate with those who use dark magic—at least, it is forbidden."

"And the other approaching group are goblins. Are we about to see them battle the goblins?" Lady Aylen asked aloud.

"Princess, you are making the same assumptions that our caravan's elves have made. I believe we are about to see something that no one else has ever seen before, or not for many eons."

◆◆◆

The goblin party from the west marched to Fae'el. The goblins were of another clan. Their dark rust-colored armor was spiked on the chestplates and on the back. Otherwise, their physical appearance was the same as they had seen before—green skin, stout and muscular frame, big noses, and pointy ears. They were heavily armed with spiked maces, battle axes, and spiked war hammers.

Following in packs were tiny hobgoblins with smiles of razor-sharp teeth, beady eyes, green attire, and pointed green caps. Every hobgoblin led a giant black dire wolf.

The humans of Titan's Caravan saw a type of goblin and dire wolf they had never seen before. The black dire wolf was twice the size of others, and had long horns like a bull. Its goblin royal rider had more refined facial features, and his nose was not bulbous and large like other goblins but like a human or elf.

Their rear guard were hundreds of dark sprites that included bugganes, dark sprite shape-shifters that appeared as a large humanoids with thick black hair, sharp tusks on the sides of their mouths, and glowing eyes; boggarts that looked like ugly hairy humanoids with arms so long they dragged along the ground; and bugbears that appeared as ten-foot black bears with humanoid noses and faces, and blank white eyes.

Even Quillen, who relished the sight of new fae, was scared. Titan's Caravan watched the goblin party stop, and then the goblin royal galloped to the dark fairies and wind elves on his dire-wolf creature.

Both King Aereth and Lady Aylen noticed Traveler's hand reach under his cloak to his belt. The goblin dismounted, walked forward, and shook the hand of King Zephyr then Queen Gale.

There was an explosion of outrage from both drows and elves within the caravan.

Druil, the high-elf wizard, Taylon, the desert elf, Galadaer the woodland elf, and Staric, the moon elf, joined the front with all of their elfin questing knights. Dr'as led the drows to join them, but Dr'amal held them back. A smiling Bragg casually strolled to the front, but the dwelf was more amused by the anger and shock of the elves and drows than the apparent alliance of the high elves and goblins.

"This is an abomination!" Druil yelled. He shot an angry look at Traveler. "Do you still believe we are in league with the wind elves?"

"It is evident that you are not. What will you do?" Traveler asked.

"What will we do? High elves allying with goblins. Even drows would not do this. No elf would. This is an affront to elfinkind. As the master wizard of Magica, I must answer this heresy. I must restore the honor of all high elves." He looked at his comrades. "Are you with me?"

"Falconbright stands with you," Taylon said.

"As does Bravehowl," Galadaer said.

"Bragg?" Druil asked.

"I am a dwelf, Druil. My race does not involve itself in conflicts of elves or goblins."

"We shall remember that," Druil said contemptuously.

"Please do. As we remember the age when the sky was black with flying reptiles of fire ravaging all of elfinkind and it was my race and the dwarves that answered the call, while elves hid underground like rats."

"That is a lie!"

Traveler stood between the fae. "Druil, what are you and your men about to do?"

"We, Mr. Traveler, are about to go into battle to destroy the wind elves and their unholy alliance of evil."

"What do the drows say?" Druil turned to address Dr'as.

The drow leader hesitated.

"Mr. Druil," Traveler began. "You must all decide on your next action carefully. Titan's Caravan will not go to war. We are a caravan not an army. However, we will fight to the death to protect any of its humans or fae, but our objective is to get out of this valley and continue our journey onto Atlantea. Any who go to war with the wind elves, dark fairies, and goblins, even if victorious, will not leave these lands on the Trail. You must decide carefully."

"What would you have us do?" Galadaer asked.

"If I were you? The question is a clear one: What is more important? Elfinkind or Atlantea?"

The Elfin Questing Knight leaders looked at each other. Traveler knew they were conversing with each other in each other's minds. Even Lady Aylen could almost perceive of it, though she could not hear their words.

"Nothing is more important than elfinkind," Druil said for them. "I am a high elf, and no high elf, no matter their blood or status, must be allowed to sully the honor of our race."

"I have sympathy for your blight, Druil. I would do as you are in your place. However, my answer is Atlantea," Bragg the dwelf said.

"Atlantea," Dr'as said. "I agree with the dwelf. You must not make the same mistake that we drows made ages ago when we ignored the users of dark magic within our ranks. Drow honor still suffers to this day."

"It is settled, then," Traveler said. "Our last task as a caravan together will be to decimate their numbers so that the elfin questing knights can remain and be victorious. However, we cannot engage them with their fairies. And princess, since we will battle wind elves, it is time for you to realize your full power as a water elemental."

"And how do I do that, Mr. Traveler?" she asked.

"Our drow sorceress will help you," Traveler replied.

"Mr. Traveler and I spoke earlier. I will use a simple spell for you to 'know' how to use your elemental magic," Dr'amal said.

"We will attack when our other two parties arrive," Traveler added.

"Other two parties?" Druil and Lady Aylen asked at the same time.

"I sent out our two fairies to summon the Crimson Thorn fairies. They are the mortal enemy of lunatishee, and when they see the other dark fairies, it will be a terrifying spectacle to behold two fairy-storms battle a third. That will leave the wind elves and goblins to us."

"So it is war again with those in league with the Four Kings," King Aereth said.

"They want to stop us here in their lands, sire, where their magic is strongest. Once we pass beyond Titan's Arch, with the vastness of the Great Forest and the oceans we must cross to Atlantea, they know the odds of finding us again on the Trail are remote, even on the most fortunate of days. We have gotten this far. We may one day in the future simply show up at the entrance of Atlantea, especially when we are guided by a human who has lived in its city."

"This is not really about us, Mr. Traveler, is it?" King Aereth asked.

"No, sire. For the Xenhelmians, yes, but for these wind elves and their allies, it is about keeping any others from reaching the legendary kingdom before them. Humans are the only race the Atlanteans will always give an audience to, no other."

"Mr. Druil was correct then. Caravan wars are inevitable. No way to avoid them," the king said as he sighed deeply.

"We fight them here, sire. We must be free of them to get to Titan's Arch. Remember, there is another inevitable war party we may or may not face."

"The gnolls," King Aereth said.

"Yes."

"Will your dog be joining us in the battle, Mr. Traveler?" Lady Aylen asked.

"He will, but this battle is ours not his. He has another purpose. This will be our first true battle in Faë-Land. I said we are a caravan not an army. Today, however, we must be the most ruthless force these wind elves and their dark-fae allies have ever battled. We must take advantage of their arrogance and ensure that this will be their last battle not ours."

"Titan's Army," Pangolin said.

Traveler nodded. "Yes. Today that is what we are. Titan's Army. The fae are fond of legendary stories. We will give them one."

CHAPTER FOURTEEN

Caravan Wars

Traveler emerged from his tent, clad in elfin armor with a slight orange tint. His magic sword was in his right hand, but he had another sheathed sword on his back. Waiting was their weaponsmaster, Estus, who inspected the fit more like a mother would do with a younger child.

"I have worn elfin armor before, Mr. Estus."

"Of course you have, sir. All us weaponsmasters fuss over anything from our armory. Here's one more item." Estus clamped a band around each one of the forearm sections of Traveler's armor. "Now, it is complete."

"Thank you, Mr. Estus. Now, General, get your army ready."

Estus grinned. "Yes, sir." As the weaponsmaster walked off, Traveler turned his attention to the fifteen waiting fae-blood mercenaries dressed in black and identical to humans, except for their wolf-like eyes.

"I expected to see you in your place with the animal men," Traveler said to them.

"We have simply stayed away from circumstances that do not interest us," their leader said.

"Does this battle interest you?"

"We do not care about elves or most goblins, but the goblin royal is a high goblin. They may consider themselves as fair as elves, but their hearts are blacker than night."

"You are not friends, then?"

"Their race is a mortal enemy of our people. We will be very active in this battle if they attack the caravan."

"Goblins ride dire wolves."

The fae-blood smiled. "The goblins will soon wish they did not."

"Do not get yourselves killed."

"We intend to be at Atlantea with you."

"Good. Then, let us get this battle over with."

Traveler joined the berserker war leaders. Pangolin always wore his magical earthen armor and helmet but now had the same bands around his forearms. So did the Cut-Throats still quickly checking every piece of their goblin armor and weapons a final time.

"It is real this time," Traveler said somberly to the men.

Pangolin nodded.

"Yes, sir," I-wulf acknowledged.

Traveler addressed them all. "Berserker humans have the magic within them for strength and endurance, but even so, direct hand-to-hand combat should always be a last resort. You must resist the urge to charge onto the battlefield. The elfin archers never miss targets, and the goblins have dark fae with them that are true shape-shifters. Think of the circle as the wall of our castle and we are under siege. Your men must ensure the wall is not breached, no matter the cost. If any of them do, they could kill hundreds of us in the blink of an eye. For our part, this battle will be fought with arrows and magic. The elfin questing knights will do the direct combat on the battlefield."

"When will the fairies arrive?" Pangolin asked.

"Soon but not before the battle begins."

"I hope our wizards are better than theirs," I-wulf said.

"We are equally matched," Traveler said.

"But we have surprises," I-wulf said, smiling.

"Mr. I-wulf, this is the land of magic. They will have surprises too," Traveler said. The Cut-Throat leader's smile disappeared.

The caravan's catapults were lined up to face Fae'el. All the humans, in their elfin armor, stood beside them. A large boulder sat in the bucket of each, ready for launch. All around them were pech, each with their own pull cart filled with large rocks.

King Aereth stood in front of their formation, Nirgund and his alphyns at his side. The king called out to the heavy-weapons teams.

"Men, it will not be long. For us humans, the task is simple: launch your payloads at the center of our attackers as we have practiced for so long. We do not need to hit them. We only need to keep them off balance. Our pech allies have the task of hitting them with their incredible strength and aim. For both groups, once we start we do not stop until the battle is over."

"King, you should take care," a pech said. "They know you command these teams. Elfin or goblin archers will try to put an arrow in your heart or through your head. We have the protection of the circle, but it's magic, and so are their arrows. The circle and your armor are not invincible."

"We do our jobs. We let others in the caravan do theirs, which is to make sure our circle is not breached," King Aereth said with confidence.

"And, sire, my task is to see to it that no arrow hits either one of our hearts or heads," his royal guard, Nirgund, said. "Is that not right, lads?"

His pack of reptilian hounds yelped.

◆ ◆ ◆

Gwyness stared at her war hammers in her hands.

"How are you doing, Maiden Gwyness?"

Gwyness glanced at a calm Hobbs, also in elfin armor. The caravan's steward's ability to reassure, inspire, and motivate was always exceptional. "I have never fought in a real battle before."

"Maiden, neither have I, not directly. We will do no less than our best."

She nodded and managed a smile.

"Is that not right, Mr. Quillen?" Hobbs asked.

Quillen stood quietly near them. "Yes, Mr. Hobbs." The fear of what was to come was clear in the lad's face. Something caught his eye and he perked up. "The lizards," he said. "They see something."

Others in the camp also began noticing the growing agitation of the perimeter's giant, twenty-foot fae lizards in dwarvin armor. The teams of lizard minders, two men to each reptile, moved to calm the growing frenzy among the beasts. Both human and fae readied themselves for whatever was invisibly moving to the circle.

◆ ◆ ◆

The giant lizards startled the caravan when they leapt up in the air and others whipped their tails at something in front of them. Lizard minders were knocked off their feet. The lizards snapped with their mouths and swatted with their forelegs at things no one else could see, even the fae.

The center crawling tree of Titan's Caravan grew in height and width; the leaves of its branches enlarged to become as big as full shields. Its branches covered the full caravan. A second crawling tree became like a snake and wound itself along the ground and around the entire perimeter, including all the fae parties. The third crawling tree shrank in size, taking the form of a spider-like creature made of branches and stood on its many legs next to the four Tree Shepherds, who held their staffs in hand.

The first wave of invisible attackers came into view—spriggans appeared, floating in the air all around the dome of the circle like a swarm. The large childlike headed halflings had twisted smiles on their faces, their arms raised. One by one the bodies of the giant lizards convulsed, and whatever their color—blue, yellow, green, or orange— the reptiles' skin slowly lost its vibrance and took on a grayish tone. From the second crawling tree encircling the perimeter like a snake, thorns burst out and sprayed the spriggans. The dark fae screamed in pain as they flew back and away then disappeared.

A magical doorway opened to the west of the caravan, and from it, goblin warrior riders armed with blades or bludgeoning weapons charged on their giant dire wolves. The sky turned black as arrows rained down on the caravan, appearing out of thin air. Goblin archers came out of invisibility, forming up behind their goblin rider brethren in column after column. It was a goblin war party of thousands.

Within the caravan, Strag, the elaphine, gave the signal. Elaphine archer-warriors fired their arrows at the goblins. Like elves, they could fire multiple arrows in the time a human archer could fire one. The twin brothers fired their volley last.

The goblin archers raised an arm in the air, and magic shields appeared in front of their bodies. The shower of elaphine arrows was deflected. Then came the arrows of the twin archers. Aron and Eren hit the center of the goblin archers—lightning arrows. The magical explosion blasted screaming goblin archers, their weapons, and their shields everywhere. All the goblin archers lay scattered on the ground. None moved.

The elaphine archer-warriors had no time to react. From where the main enemy army gathered in front of Fae'el, elfin winged arrows from the Bravebow party ripped through the circle and struck down many elaphines; other elaphines dove to the ground for cover. The winged arrows magically circled back after their original targets but were snatched from the air by vines sprouting from the staff of one of the Tree Shepherds. The wall created by one of the crawling trees rose to block more incoming Bravebow arrows, which struck, penetrating into its bark armor. The tree screamed.

The four Tree Shepherds grimaced in pain, as they were magically connected to all of the crawling trees. Mossberry extended his tree staff, and vines shot out to pull the elfin winged arrows from the crawling tree. The vines crushed the arrows to sand.

The caravan's new volley filled the sky. Large boulders from the catapults and smaller ones thrown from the pech sailed to the Bravebow archers. More arrows shot out of the caravan but from the faun archers under Ammon and the caravan's woodland elves under Ethor. Drows under Dr'as joined in, throwing their magical daggers called two-blades, each end a curved blade. Aron, the elaphine archer, jumped up from behind the tree wall and fired more lightning arrows.

Traveler watched—everyone watched—the air thick with projectiles and arrows arcing down to their targets in front of Fae'el. But the volley crashed into an invisible wall. The enemy army had its own magic barrier.

The caravan's giant lizards lay helpless on their backs, unconscious, their skin gray.

"Do what you can to protect your animals!" Hobbs said to them. "Spread the word to all the lizard minders!"

The men complied as the two-man teams braced—one man to defend with a shield, the other with sword or halberd. Brownies flew out of the caravan's pocket-realms and began to drag the magically sickened lizards in and away from the danger.

"We lost all our lizards!" Quillen said, exasperated.

"Mr. Quillen, go with the brownies and take charge. Ensure the lizards are safe in the pocket."

"I'll go with him, Mr. Hobbs," Oeric said.

"Okay," Hobbs said to his second guardsman then looked at his main guardsman, Tyfer. "What were those creatures, Mr. Tyfer? What did they do?"

"Dark sprites called spriggans, Mr. Hobbs. They can do all manner of dark deeds. They can blight crops and wildlife and make animals sick with disease. They can also cause whirlwinds. We cannot let them into the circle."

Thousands of goblin dire wolf riders reached the perimeter. They could not breach the caravan's circle but slashed at the barrier with their weapons. The goblin riders even took to jumping their dire wolves on the magic dome so that their beasts could claw at it. From within the circle, human and fae of the caravan stood fast in the face of the yelling goblins and the war-howls of their dire wolves.

At Fae'el, both King Zephyr and Queen Gale sat on their large winged horses, with smiles, surrounded by elfin white knight riders and elfin archers in black on their armored winged horses. Formations of the golden-clad elfin archers of Bravebow fired their endless volleys of arrows at the caravan, overseen by their prince on his winged steed. The Fae'el elfin king and queen on dark unicorns and their army of elfin warriors of archers and lancers watched the battle quietly from the side of the wind-elf king and queen. The master wizard Genus, in his silver hooded robe, stood quietly on the other side of the wind-elf royals with his six other wizards. The dozens of six-armed, black-armor Gegenees giants followed with swords, axes, and spears in their hands, flanked by dozens of their two-headed giant wolves. Behind the wind-elf royals sat the single goblin king on his giant bull-horned, black dire wolf.

The wingless thorn fairies, the lunatishee, stood before them all but then disappeared from sight. The winged dark fairies, in their exoskeleton and shell armor, rose into the air with their razor-edged spears and also disappeared.

Then a magical doorway appeared near the ground in their place. New wind elves in black marched out, walking on cushions of air, and threw their aerial javelins. They watched as the magic dome of Titan's Caravan became more visible with every volley of their javelin attacks, as did its growing cracks.

"The wind elves!" Traveler yelled to Pangolin and the Cut-Throats.

Pangolin gave the signal, with his axe-mace raised. The berserker master-at-arms ran across the circle with their Cut-Throats and their war-flock of chamroshes.

Traveler looked back at Strag. The caravan master did not even have to say a word. The hoofed fae leader commanded his party, and they fired their arrows at the new wind elves.

"The wind-elf warriors are Wind Slicers," Ethol, the woodland elf, called out to Traveler. The elf's words echoed in his mind rather than his ears. "None of our arrows will hit them."

None of the arrows did hit the wind elves, who waved the projectiles away with a simple hand movement no matter how fast they came at them. Then they focused their attacks on Pangolin and his force. Chamroshes were blown back into the magical dome of the circle first, then every single Cut-Throat was knocked back, too, sending them crashing into their own fae animals. Pangolin's magical armor made him immune to their wind weapons, but now he charged them alone.

It appeared from nowhere. A shadow descended from the sky. Pangolin looked up to see a giant golden winged battering ram hit the very top of Titan's Caravan circle dome, colliding from miles above. Sections of their magical protection cracked. Gusts of wind blew in and turned into more black-clad wind elves on armored winged warhorses. The magic battering ram fell to the ground and disappeared.

"It's collapsing!" Both human and fae yelled the same words.

The six Antaean giants dropped their war hammers to the ground. They reached out their arms and pressed their palms against the magical barrier. The giants glowed yellow with magic from within, the light beaming from their eye sockets, ear canals, and mouths; their size increased. A ghostly form took shape behind them, a composite of each of the giants, its size many times theirs. The form drew in its shoulders, lowered its head, chin to its chest, and held up the circle dome with its back and pushed out with its palms and forearms.

Wind elves raised their wind swords to attack, but their magic weapons dissipated to nothingness the moment they crossed into the circle. The elves were enraged and clenched their fists to fight barehanded.

"Fire!" King Aereth yelled at the distracted heavy weapons teams as he raised his own sword to block an attacking wind elf before him.

The band that Estus fitted on the king's forearm, along with all the human fighters, created a small magical shield, but the wind elf used his fist to hit King Aereth so hard that the king's sword arm gave way. The king was hit on his own forehead and fell back. Nirgund struck with his halberd, but the wind elf easily blocked it and laughed.

"Weak humans!" The wind elf suddenly braced himself.

Appearing from nowhere too, King Aereth's kirin kicked the wind elf with its powerful hind legs. The wind elf sailed back through the circle, crashing to the ground dead. The magical beast had no wings but galloped on the air. It let out a roar, and all the winged warhorses that had flown in through the breach of the circle turned in panic and flew away into the distance, with their riders or without.

The wind elves that remained had to face Traveler.

"I am a weak human," Traveler said. "Shall we engage in a simple battle of swords."

"We will take your own sword and kill you with it," one wind elf snarled.

Three of the elves ran at him. Traveler's sword sliced through one elf's arm, landing a blow to the chest. The caravan master turned to catch the landing fist of another wind elf. Nirgund, consumed by his berserker rage, engaged another wind elf. The alphyns viciously attacked the elf fighting Nirgund as a pack, seizing on the elf's throat and legs. Traveler killed the second elf with a quick blow of his sword. Nirgund and his alphyns killed the third.

The golden kirin landed on the ground next to King Aereth. The king patted the beast's fur and scales.

"Mr. Nirgund, the kirin will protect the king. Protect this breach until the Tree Shepherds can repair the circle."

They all looked up at the magical ghost form of the Antaean giants; its size continued growing, now more than fifty feet.

Their attention was diverted. "There it flies," King Aereth said as they watched one particular projectile fly above their heads to the wind elves advancing on foot.

◆◆◆

The human catapults continued to launch their payloads into the air over a charging Pangolin. The master-at-arms reached the wind elves. He swung his magical axe-mace and cut apart stunned wind elves. He swung again and knocked another into several more with such force that half of the advancing wind elves fell to the ground. The projectiles of the caravan landed, among them a magic pouch strapped to a rock, and a doorway opened.

Taylon and his thousands of desert elves in their brown-feathered armor flew out, riding their falcon griffins, a flock of their falcons all around them. The desert elves overwhelmed the wind elves. Pangolin fought with the desert elves at his side.

Within the caravan, the female half-elf guards and male half-elves fought with Gwyness against other wind elves who had entered through other breaches of the circle. Every magic wind weapon the wind elves bore also disappeared as soon as they entered the circle, but the wind elves did not retreat. Half-elves fired magical arrows from their crossbows. The wind elves were fast but not fast enough to dodge the arrows. Gwyness struck with her dual war hammers and was smacked away by the wind elf. Gwyness's black kirin appeared and butted the wind elf. The blow knocked the elf out of the circle and far away into the sky. The kirin stood at Gwyness's side.

"Hobbs," Gwyness said. "Are you injured?"

Their steward touched his armor. A wind elf had punched the chest of his armor, and he felt winded, but he was uninjured.

"You and your half-elf guardswomen are far more capable fighters than I."

The half-elves pointed into the camp. "More of them," one of the female half-elves said and fired an arrow.

She hit a wind elf in the back, but he ripped the arrow out and kept fighting. More wind elves fought the animal men and their animals. The wind elves struck with bare hands against enfields attacking from the air and jackalopes attacking from the ground; the elves were winning. Then the Diomedian Mares galloped in and attacked.

The wind elves were finally retreating when a net covered them and they fell to the ground. Bragg appeared with his metal golem, Glog. "Remove them from my sight," Bragg said.

The golem dragged the net of trapped wind elves out of the circle. Then the automaton picked up the net and used its body to fling them all into the distance, knocking aside any other goblin, dark fae, or wind-elf attackers in its path.

The cracks of the circle closed. Within the camp, wind elves that could not escape were cut down by fae archers, drow two-blades or overwhelming numbers of Titan's Caravan fighters.

At the entrance to the pocket-realm housing the sick giant lizards and half of the lizard minders, several wind elves appeared with desperate looks of rage. The moment they stepped across, there were screams. Some of the men ran out, including Quillen.

"What's wrong?" one of the male half-elves asked as he reached the entrance. "Where are the wind elves?"

"A bear killed them," Quillen said.

"What bear?"

Ursi, the fae-blood, stepped out of the pocket-realm. Her eyes were drowsy, but her hands were claw-like and bloody.

The heavy weapons teams fired more projectiles then giant arrows from giant crossbows. The arrows hit their marks: the giant male and female elfin statues at the entrance of Fae'el. *The one-hundred-foot statues yelled!*

Everyone, on both sides, even animals, froze for a moment and watched the giant statues collapse to the ground and blood spill out. The statues were in fact giant white trolls—magically able to be in sunlight. One of the Fae'el wizards cried out. His body shook violently, then he turned to stone.

Traveler killed more wind elves he engaged that breached the circle. The alphyns killed one winged warhorse; another flew away, escaping. Nirgund helped King Aereth to his feet.

The bodies of the two white trolls decomposed to dust before everyone's eyes. The wind-elf king was enraged. "Attack now!" King Zephyr yelled.

The desert elves had defeated one war party of wind elves, but a new one, far larger, flew out from the gates of Fae'el. The advancing enemy army were white wind elves, goblin dire-wolf riders, six-armed Gegenees giants, and dozens of two-headed giant wolves (orthuruses).

Taylon raised his sword to lead the charge as caravan elf and elaphine arrows shot forth, accompanied by drow two-blades. The white wind elves engaged their air magic. Several conjured vortexes to grab boulders and arrows from the air and send them back the way they came—suddenly, the projectiles exploded to dust, surprising the wind elves. Only the drows' magic blades and a single lightning arrow continued on towards the enemy army. But Genus, their wizard master, instantly conjured a giant shield in front of the elfin royals and warriors. The drow blades and the lightning arrow exploded.

King Zephyr rose in the air with his arms raised, and the air above Fae'el darkened. A cyclone began to take form.

Genus raised his own hands to cast another spell. His mouth dropped open in shock as his chest was impaled by a tail. Scratch the puck came out of invisibility before him, cackling. An enraged Genus yelled, and Scratch caught on fire. The puck flew away as he shrank into nothingness.

King Zephyr watched his master wizard drop to a knee, clutching his chest. The wind-elf king clenched his teeth and made the cyclone larger in size above Fae'el.

"I will kill them all with one blow!" Genus yelled, sputtering blood.

Zephyr looked down at his wizard. "Genus, rise to your feet. You are master wizard of the Kingdom of Spirit Thunder! Are you no greater than a lowly puck? You and all of our wizards will—"

Zephyr's eyes widened as he saw it.

Several of the caravan's *tulen väki* ran from the circle and jumped over the crawling tree wall, growing in size with each step. Their eyes blazed with fire as they threw fireballs at the wizards.

Genus yelled as he and all the Spirit Thunder elfin wizards were engulfed in flames. Scratch the puck's cackling echoed through the air, and most of the elves grabbed their ears in agony, including King Zephyr.

"Enough!"

He commanded his gigantic cyclone to advance on Titan's Caravan, but then saw a shadow from the corner of his eye. He looked up too late to act. The tidal wave of water appeared in front of them and crashed down. All of the elves of Fae'el, Bravebow, and Spirit Thunder were swept back into the city.

The goblin riders and Genegees giants stopped their charge to watch their elfin allies and their winged horses washed away. The giant väki stepped forward, and they thrust the gates of the city closed with one giant fireball from the hands of four of the guardian sprites.

Lady Aylen stood at the base of where the tidal wave had appeared, Dr'amal's hand on her shoulder. The princess breathed heavily and bent down to rest the palms of her hands on her knees and compose herself.

More arrows and boulders were already in the air from Titan's Caravan. Goblins and dire wolves were hit multiple times by arrows or crushed or knocked to the ground by boulders. The goblins fled.

One of the Gegenees yelled, "Fight on!" The giants resumed their charge with their orthurus beasts.

Gegenees giants were magically plucked from the ground and thrown into the sky. Druil the high elf walked to them. His fellow high elves on their white war unicorns charged. Staric and his moon elves, mounted on their owl griffins fired their magic arrows at the two-headed orthuruses, cutting them all down.

Galadaer and his woodland elves on their leopard-axex steeds also charged with their vicious weasel-like ichneumons at their side. Like the Cut-Throats and their chamrosh griffin-like hounds, the woodland-elfin knights and their ichneumons fought as a unit. The elves easily matched the attack of the giants' multiple arms with their superior elfin speed. The ichneumons attacked and killed their orthuruses and then attacked the Gegenees' legs.

An even larger army of goblin riders came out of another doorway that opened on the ground. They were met by the fae-blood men. The fae-blood wolf clan ran from the circle, eyes glowing blue. Then the eyes of every dire wolf ridden by a goblin glowed blue. The fae-blood men did not transform into wolves, but they appeared as two images in one—a running human on two legs and a running wolf on all fours. Every enchanted dire wolf followed the fae-bloods moving as fast as the wind, with their goblin riders screaming helplessly to control their mounts. The goblin army was led away towards the mountains in the distance.

There was no respite for Titan's Caravan. More dark sprites came. Hobgoblins fell from the sky, armed with daggers and hatchets, trying to cut their way into the circle dome. They expected to see the goblin army, but it was gone. The largest crawling tree was using all its power to repair the breaches and strengthen the circle. The tree that encircled the caravan in a snake-like form had been seriously wounded but kept its shape. However, the hobgoblins were no match for the remaining crawling tree that appeared as a fast-moving spider. The tree shot vines from its mass, stabbing at the hobgoblins in every direction. The dark spritelings hopped away and disappeared as quickly as they could.

The caravan heard new armies moving quickly to them— spriggans, bugganes, boggarts, and bugbears. Druil, from his place near the battle with the six-armed giants, yelled another spell. The elfin questing knights' tarasque beasts appeared in front of the attacking dark sprites. The long-armed boggarts and bugbears ran away as the giant shell-armored lion beasts snapped at them. The bugganes shape-shifted into gazelle-legged wolves and stampeded away.

The new spriggans gathered together into a pack, creating their own violent gusts of winds to lift one of the tarasques off the ground. They were showered with elfin arrows and drow two-blades. Yelling, they ran away then disappeared.

The Gegenees that survived, threw down their weapons. They grabbed the corpses of their fellow giants and their two-headed war wolves and dragged them eastward.

Traveler, Pangolin, the elfin questing knights—all the victors—surveyed the area.

Gwyness ran to Lady Aylen, who was still disoriented. "You did it, m'lady!"

"We did it," I-wulf said cheerfully.

"We are not done with battle," Pangolin said to him. "Where are those dark fairies?"

◆ ◆ ◆

The swarm of black flies reappeared all around Titan's Caravan, but it was far larger than before. The dark fairies reappeared, floating in the air with their shiny large eyes, moth or translucent fly-like wings flapping. Both armored and armed with their pointed razor-edged spears, they hung above the caravan.

The circle of the caravan had been restored, and the Antaean giants had let their magical projection dissipate. The giants returned to their normal sizes, however, the four Tree Shepherds increased in size and their staffs turned to pointed razor-edged spears similar to the dark fae. An eruption of laughter rang out from the dark fairies as the sky blackened.

Traveler watched them, unconcerned, and his lack of fear was noticed by every human and fae who could see him. Everyone expected the dog shape-shifter to appear in some hideous form to save them, but instead they heard:

"You are forbidden to be in these lands!" the high-pitched voice of Wildglow said. The fairy appeared with her sister, Sunpetal, hovering above the caravan.

Both fairy sisters were in their own insect exoskeleton armor.

"Go back to your hive, children!" one of the dark fairies yelled.

"No!" Wildglow yelled.

"No!" the voices of many, many others echoed through the air.

Pale, six-foot-tall female fairies began to appear everywhere. The caravan had seen these fairies before, with their almost-transparent skin, their short dark hair filled with leaves and thistles, their humanoid eyes, translucent wings, and forehead antennae. Dressed in crimson dresses, they were armed with red-tipped spiked spears.

"We are the fairies of Crimson Thorn. You are forbidden from these lands!"

Swarms of fireflies and multi-colored butterflies began to thicken the air.

"Retreat or die by our hands!" the Crimson Thorn fairies said.

"We do not fear you!" shouted the dark fairies.

"For every one of yours, you will face millions of ours. Darkness can never defeat the light, but shall we play again? Let the dark fairies make war on all of fairydom and all of its queens!"

"We will kill you!" Wildglow yelled.

The dark fairies disappeared, taking all their insect swarms with them.

Traveler stood before the Crimson Thorn fairies. "Thank your queen on behalf of Titan's Caravan."

"Yes, and me too!" Wildglow added. "And my sister too!"

The Crimson Thorn fairies laughed at the fairy child.

"You are welcome, human. You as well, fairy warrioress, Wildglow and Sunpetal," a crimson fairy said.

The fairy sisters giggled, floating next to Traveler.

"What of the lunatishee that had joined the dark fairies?" he asked.

"They fled as fast as they could back to their dark domains when they saw us. You won't see them again," the crimson fairy said.

"Good."

"Do you still intend to continue your journey?" another crimson fairy asked.

"Nothing will stop us," Traveler replied.

"But a good deal may delay you," she said. "Not good when you humans live for such a short time."

"Have a safe journey, Titan's Caravan," the Crimson Thorn fairies said. "Whenever that journey may be."

The Crimson Thorn fairies rose in the air as they turned into balls of light. As they had done before, like millions of fireflies, they disappeared into the clouds.

Traveler had taken off his main elfin armor and emerged from his tent into the chaos swirling within Titan's Caravan. However, Hobbs calmly waited.

"What is the news from our healer, Mr. Hobbs?" Traveler asked.

"Mr. Gresham's healing tent is quite busy, but thankfully no one was killed or needed the services of your Caladrius bird."

"Thankfully, indeed, but much more than that. Had the wind elves known their magic wind weapons would evaporate within our circle, our casualties would have been severe. Elves have superior strength and speed and can easily kill with their bare hands. They were caught unprepared. As supposed nobles, they are bred to view killing with their hands as beneath their dignity. That notion defeated them more than anything."

"Do not leave the circle," Hobbs said.

"Indeed."

"Mr. Gresham did say many men are badly wounded, some seriously. They will not be participating in any battles for a long while."

"The lizards?"

"The Tree Shepherds are attending to them. They will need much rest but will recover."

"Mr. Hobbs." One of the caravan's lads appeared at the entrance.

"Yes, lad."

"Oh, Mr. Traveler," the boy said. "The elves are here for you, sir."

"Thank you. I will be there."

The boy disappeared, and Traveler returned his attention to the steward.

"Mr. Hobbs, get yourself out of that armor and carry on. How is Lady Aylen?"

"She is sleeping. She appears—"

"She will be fine. She never used her elemental ability before, not truly. To use it with that kind of power is both a strain and unsettling. It is one thing to get accustomed to being a magical being. It will take a much longer time to get accustomed to using such magic when you have never done so before. We will talk later."

"Yes, sir."

Traveler walked alone to the perimeter where the elves waited— Druil, the high-elf wizard, Taylon, the desert elf, Galadaer, the woodland elf, Ethor, the leader of the rustic woodland elves, and Staric, the moon elf. Bragg the dwelf also accompanied them.

"Ah, a meeting," Traveler said.

Bragg laughed.

"Were any in the caravan killed?" Druil asked.

"No, we were very fortunate."

"Yes, it was if the gods themselves protected your caravan, especially the humans. Mr. Traveler, besides the drowess, does your caravan have another sorceress or sorcerer we have not seen?"

"No," Traveler replied, intentionally unbelievable. The elves smiled.

"Where is your shape-shifter?" Staric asked.

"He is sleeping," Traveler replied.

The elves laughed.

"What happens now?" Traveler asked. "My men told me that you have seized Fae'el."

"Fae'el is under the protection of the kingdoms of Magica, Falconbright, Bravehowl, and Nightshade. King Zephyr and Queen Gale of the wind elves of Spirit Thunder, King Hir and Queen Aldena of the city, High Prince Azimor of Bravebow, and their goblin king ally, Zem, are all under arrest and will face an elfin tribunal."

"Our kingdoms will send delegations here to attend, and all of elfinkind will do the same," Taylon said. "We will not blacken the sky with our numbers like the fairies, but it will be equally substantial."

"These lands are thick with elves," Traveler said.

"Yes. Tell me, did you really believe any of the questing knights would be in league with the Xenhelmians?"

"No, of course not. I trust Browncrown's judgment implicitly."

"As do we."

"I was merely judging for myself how you, as noble knights, would act after being accused of something so ignoble. You reacted nobly."

"We are a noble lot," Druil said with a grin.

"Are you still planning on continuing with the journey?" Staric asked.

"Absolutely."

"We are foregoing the journey for the coming tribunal. These royals will pay for their crimes against elfinkind, and the goblins will know that no elves will ally with them against other elves ever again," Taylon said. "The dark fairies will also pay a heavy price."

"You and your caravan will have to give statements to the tribunal," Druil said.

"How long will the tribunal take to reach its ultimate decision?" Traveler asked.

"Nearly every elfin kingdom will be represented. It could take many months."

"Celestial, star, night and cloud elves too? And the water elf kingdoms?"

"That I do not know about."

"Drows?"

"Nor that."

Traveler looked at Ethor. "What will your clan do? Will you continue with us when we finally can move on or remain here?"

"We will continue with your caravan."

"Good."

"You should take in the kilmoulis," Taylon said. "Your people should get used to their ugly appearance and habits if you are determined to continue your journey."

"Yes, I agree with you that they could be valuable on the Trail."

"I know you are disappointed about this new delay," Druil said, "but your caravan performed bravely and admirably. We all survived to live another great day."

"We humans especially like living our days," Traveler said with a smile.

"I am sure that you do," Druil said.

"When will your elfin kingdoms begin arriving?"

"Tomorrow at dawn," Druil answered.

"Then I will spend the rest of today telling the men and preparing them. We have come a long way and most will not be happy with sitting here for many months, as beautiful as elfin lands are," Traveler said facetiously. "I will take my leave, then."

"We will see you at dawn, Master Traveler," Druil said. "Maybe even your dog too."

A smiling Traveler turned to a waiting King Aereth, Pangolin, Estus, and I-wulf at the caravan master's tent.

"What do you think?" Staric asked when the human was out of earshot.

"By tomorrow dawn, Titan's Caravan will be gone," Druil said.

"Impossible. How?" Taylon asked.

"A human who can lead a ground caravan of humans and fae—fight and kill elves in street fights with mere daggers. Look at the fae animals he acquired for their caravan, the fae allies he has secured. Do any of us know how to find a Tree Shepherd? We have lived in Faë-Land all our lives, and I don't. Any of us know about the giant's Erymanthian Games? This human is craftier than an imp or pixy. He knows a way out of this valley even if we do not. I am certain of it," Druil mused.

"It was unusual for King Browncrown of the tree people to speak so highly of a human, even if he could tell good stories," Galadaer said. "There must be more."

"He has been through the Trail before," Taylon added.

"He has been through the Trail many times before," Druil said.

"If you are so sure they will leave and make it to Atlantea, why not act?" Taylon asked. "We were supposed to be our kingdom's Questing Knights."

"Ethor would gladly carry our banners and present our kingdom's proclamations to the Atlantean royals," Galadaer said.

"I can be part pixy imp too," Druil said. "Ethor will have all our banners and a contingent of questing knights to join his men."

"Very wise," Staric said.

"Our kings would punish us all if we set off with them. We have our own noble duties to perform in this coming high tribunal to both cleanse and restore the names of elfinkind in the face of the gross treachery that we have beheld. For us, the journey to Atlantea will have to be another time. However, our kings would severely reprimand us if we did not, at the very least, anticipate their move and have our own questing knights represented among them." Druil watched the human caravan master and the humans disappear into their tent.

Elfin guards were posted around Fae'el's walls, and riders patrolled its lands to watch for returning goblins or other dark fae. But it was also to keep an eye on Titan's Caravan throughout the night.

Dawn arrived. Titan's Caravan was gone.

CHAPTER FIFTEEN

Below

When the men walked through the magical doorway of one of the caravan's tents before dusk the previous day, they smiled. It was the same pocket-realm where they had camped in their ordeal in the Dark Forest. The same sunny environment of blue skies and vast green fields with a warm breeze, waterfalls spilling into a river, and an adjoining lake.

With most of the elfin questing knights gone, the caravan was less than half its size, but nearly ten thousand was still a very large party. The tallest of the crawling trees was the center of the camp, and all parties, both new and old, had set up in a spiral around it.

Hobbs shared the leadership tent with representatives from the smaller party of the elfin questing knights that remained: one hundred fifty high elves with unicorn swords, one hundred fifty desert elf falconers, one hundred fifty woodland elves in green armor, with leopard-axex steeds, and one hundred fifty moon elves.

"Curious that your masters would insist on you remaining with us," Hobbs said to the four representatives.

"They suspected that Titan's Caravan might not remain another day. Our masters were forbidden from carrying on with the journey or even sending a large party, but a small group from each would be overlooked," a high elf said.

"Is this journey that important to your kingdoms?"

"It is," the high elf replied.

"Even if our kings do not realize the fact now, they would, and it would be too late," a moon elf said.

"Mr. Traveler welcomes you, so I welcome you. He said from the beginning that we would need elves within our ranks to reach Atlantea. Six hundred Elfin Questing Knights to join the three hundred rustic woodland elves already with the caravan."

"Titan's Caravan now journeys forward under the elfin banners of Magica, Bravehowl, Nightshade, and Falconbright," the desert elf said.

"Amazing," Hobbs said in reflection.

"It is indeed," the high elf added. "I would say many would be impressed by the sight of us, but once we pass Titan's Arch, we will have passed beyond fae civilization. The beasts within the Great Forest are not concerned with such things."

"No civilization at all?"

"We have heard many rumors, but we are fortunate to have a guide in your Mr. Traveler, who has been through the Great Forest at least once before."

"Yes, he will ensure we all know what to expect. There is much for us to do before we can set out. My plan is to have you set up camp with our rustic woodland elves and also march with them."

"That is acceptable," the high elf said. "It has already been decided. Ethor is an elfin king, so we will defer to his general command."

"I understand. Mr. Traveler does, however, want your moon elves to shore up our night watch."

The moon elf nodded.

"Then I leave the Elfin Questing Knights to it. As knights, discipline and routine are second nature. Ethor of the rustic woodland elves will inform you of the day duties, which includes training and tending to your own animals. Night watch begins at dusk."

"What other races are on the night watch?" the moon elf asked.

"The darklings—"

"Darklings?"

"Phookas?"

The elves laughed. "Darklings, indeed," the moon elf said. "The dark shape-shifters. They must be very fond of the name."

"Mr. Traveler calls them that."

"Yes. What others?"

"Drows, humans, and brownies."

"Yes, elves are fond of brownies. Not sure what I think of the other two yet."

Hobbs smiled, then them from the tent.

For most of the caravan, it was relaxation and gossip. Their battle with wind elves, goblins, and other dark fae would be all the men talked about until they reached Atlantea. Every telling of the story became more epic and more exaggerated, but that was what men did. This time, however, the conversations among the few women and all of the fae were no less grandiose.

But some did have to work.

Quillen watched near the lake where the brownies had carried all the lizards to recover. The lizard minders attended to them and were joined by fauns and some of the animal men, both of whom had gifted animal healers. The caravan's giant lizards were freed from the dark magic disease of the spriggans, but it would be days before the brightness of their skin and fullness of their energy returned. The lizards did not go into the water, but all of them flicked its surface with their tongues.

"What are they doing?" Quillen asked.

Tyfer and Oeric had traded in their armor and weapons for aprons and spoons. They were on cooking duty. The two men had taken charge of the caravan's cooking staff, which was not as hectic as days before with the decrease in their numbers, but punctuality had to be maintained.

"Mr. Quillen," Tyfer began, "you are supposed to be doing your inventory for Mr. Hobbs."

"But what are the lizards doing?"

"They are drinking, lad," Oeric answered. "Have you never seen how a cat drinks its water or milk? Very similar with these lizards. The more they drink, the sooner they will be normal. Spriggan disease magic can kill animals as readily as plant life."

"Mr. Quillen!" Tyfer said.

The lad looked at him, grinning. "I'm going."

"You have not even started."

"I have." Quillen was distracted again. "Where do you suppose we are, Mr. Tyfer?"

"Why ask? We are safe to allow our wounded and sick recover. We are secluded to rest and prepare for our journey in peace. What does it matter where we are?"

"It has to do with Mr. Traveler's dog. I wonder what beast it turned into to carry us away in the pocket."

"Oh, hello, Mr. Hobbs," Tyfer said looking past Quillen.

The lad almost shrieked as he ran. Only when he turned to see there was no one behind him did he laugh.

"Next time he will be there, Mr. Quillen," Tyfer said as he added more seasoning to one of the boiling pots of broth.

"Full of life, the lad," Oeric said. "I barely remember it in myself."

"We do remember it well in ourselves. We are not old and dead yet."

♦♦♦

Traveler appeared at the women's tent, where all seven of the female half-elf guardsmen sat on either side of the entrance. He noticed that one of them had more than one tiny owl griffins the size of small puppies playing around her legs.

"Did you not have only one of the animals?" Traveler asked her.

"I had the one, sir, but when the fae human mercenaries returned after their ordeal, one of them had more. The animals were hiding in a satchel, and the mercenary is still wounded and recovering in the healing tent."

"So you have the good fortune to care for them all."

"I do, sir."

"They seem to take to you more than the others."

"I like them, sir."

"I suspect it has more to do with your elfin heritage. They are in much better hands with you than the mercenaries. How is Lady Aylen? Is she feeling better?"

"She is still weak, sir."

Traveler entered the tent and saw the princess lying prone on her trussing bed. She was not asleep; her eyes were wide open as she stared at the top of the tent. Gwyness sat at a small table in the center of the tent, reading. She closed the book and stood when she saw Traveler.

Traveler walked over to Lady Aylen's side. "Princess," he said. "What is this I hear that you refuse to let our healer see to your needs?"

Lady Aylen did not look at him as she made a disapproving sound. "Healer? Our Mr. Gresham is not a bad man, but if I were a man wounded in battle my spirits would not be lifted, knowing his talents, or lack thereof, awaited me."

"Princess, my are we in a negative mood today."

"She is not herself, Mr. Traveler," Gwyness said. "She chased our royal guards out of the tent and tried to do the same with me, but I know to ignore her."

"Princess, why are you acting this way?" Traveler asked.

"I should never have done what I did," she replied. "The moment I crashed that giant wave of water down on them I felt...that I did something wrong within myself. I cannot explain it."

Traveler held her hand. "I know exactly what you mean."

She looked at him, and her eyes teared up.

"I need you to prevent your mind from thinking what you want to think about. Maybe it was too soon for you to use your elemental powers. We need to return you to your state of mind before Dr'amal helped you use them."

"How?"

Traveler gave her a hesitant look. "Please do not laugh at me, princess."

Lady Aylen did laugh. "Vapors again, Mr. Traveler."

"I told you not to laugh at me."

"Yes, Mr. Traveler. Concoct your vapors. Where is your dog? He has to join me."

"He is here."

She noticed the furry scarf around his neck. A single eye opened up.

"There you are!"

Traveler returned to his own tent to get his supplies and a large black pot. The female half-elves helped by filling the pot with water, setting it up under a high flame in the center of the women's tent. Traveler added his medicines, and soon the tent was filled with bluish vapors.

"Mr. Traveler, you did not tell me what your vapors today will do to me," Lady Aylen said.

"They will temporarily numb all your senses."

"I am feeling drowsy too."

"That too."

"As long as I do not turn into a frog."

"No chance of that, princess. When you wake, you will be back to who you were before you used your magical powers."

"Good." Lady Aylen had closed her eyes and was already fast asleep.

◆◆◆

Traveler added more medicine to the boiling water, stirred it with a large wooden spoon, and moved to the exit of the tent. Gwyness followed him.

"What was wrong with her, Mr. Traveler?" Gwyness asked when they were outside the tent. "She was disturbed."

"She was given an ability, and she could not handle it. She is not ready."

"The magic of a water elemental."

"Yes, and she will be very powerful one day."

"But why should that disturb her the way it did?"

"Every droplet of water within her range of senses she was able to control."

"Yes."

"Most living things, their bodies, are mostly water."

"What are you saying, Mr. Traveler?"

"Exactly what you think I am. She summoned the water from the river in one of our pocket-realms to create a water cyclone and send it crashing down on our enemy. That's what elementals can do—manipulate the water of streams, rivers, lakes, oceans, and seas, rain falling from the sky. Our väki are fire elementals and manipulate fire to their wishes. The wind elves are air elementals. Earth elementals can manipulate the ground beneath our feet—hills, mountains—some even the stone of buildings and castles. However, certain dark water elementals, or the most powerful of benevolent ones, can summon the water from the body to harm or even kill us."

"Does she know this?"

"No one has to tell her. She can sense all the water around her—in every cup or plate of food, coursing through our bodies, hanging in the air. That is why she is so disturbed. The vapors will deaden all those senses so she can go back to a state when she could not sense that. She will not be able to use her water-elemental magic for some time until she is ready. She is missing the years of discipline and control she would have been taught as an infant if she were raised as an elfin elemental. To learn it as an adult, all in such a short period of time, when one is already set in their ways, is extremely difficult. She may never be ready."

"Sometimes I feel we should never have left these lands back then."

"No, maiden, you and the princess had to leave. Remember that an entire kingdom was destroyed. Had you not been taken away, you would have undoubtedly joined them in death."

Gwyness saw flashes of hazy images in her mind. She felt a terrifying fear.

"Maiden Gwyness, you have visitors," Traveler said.

She looked to see her black kirin next to her. She patted its side, feeling its fur and scales then rubbed its forehead. She no longer feared its sharp antlers. With it was Lady Aylen's kirin—lucent blue, like a unicorn and a catfish in one.

In one of the pocket-realms within the main one that Titan's Caravan rested and prepared in was a vast plain of golden grass with a small castle in the center, encircled by silvery water. The castle housed a magical furnace and smithy. It was the base of their weaponsmaster and forge, Mr. Estus.

King Aereth entered the castle with his kirin of golden fur and scales. Estus had sent most of his men to the main realm to rest with the camp but kept about a hundred to help him finish his day's task.

"Mr. Estus," the king said as soon as he saw him. "I have never been to your domain."

"Then I will give you the grand tour, sire." Estus wiped the soot and dust from his arms. He wore a thick dark leather smock to protect his clothes.

As with most magical buildings in Faë-Land, they were larger inside than they appeared from the outside. It was the same with the small castle, but inside was room after room, and level after level. Estus's men worked on the weapons that the men had used in battle, ensuring they were not damaged and polishing them to look like new. "Each weapon is painted with a clear concoction created by Mr. Traveler to make them resistant to magical attacks," Estus told him as they walked.

"The caravan performed admirably in battle," King Aereth said. The golden kirin followed them both.

"Yes, everyone did. If only our enemies knew we were fighting to appear weaker than we actually were. I still do not know how every magical weapon that crossed the circle disappeared," Estus said.

"We must have more than one powerful sorcerer or sorceress in our midst."

"Here is something you will be interested in, sire."

Estus led them into a large hall filled with empty standing suits of armor.

"How many are here, Mr. Estus?"

"An army of ten thousand, sire."

"Is this for the men?"

"No, sire. Mr. Traveler has had my men and me working on this ever since learning of the gnoll war party we may encounter. These are not empty suits of armor. They are armor golems."

King Aereth looked at the weaponsmaster with an expression that was both questioning and pleasantly surprised.

"Yes, sire. The suits of armor will move and attack that army or any other when given life. It will be our own army. All that remains is for my men to arm them."

"The...what is his race called...dwelf? Mr. Bragg has his own golem."

"Yes, it's made of dwarfin steel. These are made of the toughest elfin steel."

"And I thought you called me to show me new projectiles for our heavy weapons teams."

"I have that too, sire. But I thought you would find our new army of interest."

"Who will be their general?"

"I will, sire. I always wanted to be a general, and I may soon have my chance. As for your new projectiles, we are in the lands of magic, so we will no longer be using simple rocks or metal projectiles. We will take a page from the wind elves. Our projectiles will use elemental magic."

"Lead on, Mr. Estus. I cannot wait to see what you have created for us."

In another pocket-realm, where the brownies had carried the sick giant lizards during the caravan attack, it was quiet and seemingly empty. Its magical fields were awash in new life, with plants of rainbow colors sprouting from the ground and the sky filled with floating water-lily-type flowers, only the breeze was their river. Here the four Tree Shepherds stood in a circle, eyes closed and arms outstretched. Before them was a crawling tree and, on either side, another. Their soul tree glowed, and rays of green light poured into the other magically damaged trees. As all four crawling trees slowly grew in size, their roots flailed around.

The sky flashed with lightning, but there was no sound of thunder. It began to rain, and with it, the appearance of air lilies multiplied. Both Tree Shepherds and crawling trees continued to grow is size.

In the distance were many underground caverns, their small entrances covered over by thick grass. In one, with a thick blanket made of grass, dirt, and leaves was the fae-blood, Ursi, back in deep hibernation.

In a much larger healing tent, Gresham moved through rows of cots with a few lads following closely. The cots had elaphines, some cervids, and some brownies, who had gotten sick from the dark magic on the giant lizards. A section of the healing tent had many of the fae human mercenaries, still recovering from their manticore wounds.

Gresham had grown comfortable in the fact that when it came to healing magical wounds, he knew very little, but he was as eager to learn as the lads who wanted to know everything there was to being a healer.

"How are you doing?" he stopped to ask one of the elaphine archer-warriors, who very much hated lying prone on a cot.

"When can I leave?" the hoofed fae asked him.

"You look very uncomfortable. You will not recover if you are not at rest. I will move you to the corner of the tent and your fellow fae too. I have observed that you prefer—sitting together as a group. Would that be suitable?"

The fae nodded. With his size and the antlers on his head, his body was not made for a human cot. Gresham and one of the lads helped him up. The elaphine was still weak and part of his shoulder bandaged.

They moved him to the side of the healing tent and let him sit down on the ground where he wanted.

"When was the last time you drank some water?" Gresham asked.

"You human healers think consuming water is the cure for everything."

"Yes, we do, because water does help cure most everything."

The elaphine looked funny, shaking his head side to side with his large antlers.

"Give me your water and move away from me, or I'll butt you."

The young lads laughed.

Gresham said, "You heard him, lads. He wants plenty of water. Then we move his comrades to join him, and hopefully that will make him a better resident of the healing tent."

Gresham noticed Pangolin at the entrance. "Lads, I will leave you to it."

The master-at-arms berserker looked around the healing tent as Gresham joined him.

"Mr. Gresham, how are your patients?"

"All are well, Mr. Pangolin. I view it as the Fates themselves smiling upon our caravan."

"That and superior defenses and one or more sorcerers of our own. As long as we have no dead to bury, that is my only concern. We have yet to cross into the most dangerous part of Titan's Trail."

"Is it called the Giant Forest or Great Forest?"

"The names are the same. It is a forest populated by giant animals and beasts of great and evil magical power. If you have heard the elves speak about the region, it is a sobering conversation. Flying over the forest is dangerous but doable. Walking through it from one end to another is something even they fear."

"But we are Titan's Caravan, Mr. Pangolin. We are uniquely assembled to achieve our goal."

"How are you doing, Mr. Gresham? Are you becoming what is needed to be the caravan's chief healer?"

"I am learning everything I can from not only Mr. Traveler but the many fae healers that are also within the caravan."

"Good."

"I suspect Mr. Traveler will have to be more warrior than guide shortly. I do not want him distracted by falling back to being a healer again. He has a deep sense of duty to the men and a deeply compassionate streak at his core."

"It is what makes him such an accomplished caravan master."

"So true."

All four of the Antaean giants were fast asleep. Fae had told Pangolin they would sleep straight through at least three days and then wake and spend two days eating. Pangolin rejoined the male half-elves waiting in his camp. The Cut-Throats were especially boisterous, telling of their "fabled" exploits in their caravan war.

"What lies are you telling your men?" Pangolin asked I-wulf.

"Mr. Pangolin, they are called tall tales, I'll have you know."

"Those wind elves were formidable," Pangolin remarked.

"Wind weapons. I did not know one could make a weapon out of the wind, but I was hit by one and, if not for my elfin armor, would have been cut in half. I am sure of it," I-wulf said.

"There are many kinds of magical weapons we could face. We need to know how to defend and defeat every one of them."

"What do you propose? We have magic armor and magical weapons."

"You have armor and weapons forged by magical means. Elfin steel is of magic but is not magic."

"You believe some of our men should wield magic weapons."

"Yes, and we need to think of it in those terms. What weapon could defeat a wind sword? What weapon do we use against a fire lance? What do we use against a manticore or whatever foul beast we may encounter?"

"Do we know what beasts we will encounter in this Great Forest?" I-wulf asked. Both he and Pangolin turned to the half-elves.

"We have never been there," Mr. Elman said. "But the rumors are not good. Mostly it is animals of tremendous size: mammals, birds, insects. Everything there makes our own giants look like dwarves by comparison. Not all of them are predatory, but all of them are dangerous."

"What of the dark creatures in the forest?" I-wulf asked.

"I wish I could say that I knew what creatures we might encounter, but I do not," Elman answered. "We could still meet dark fairies or fae in there, too, especially closest to the border. The beasts of the forest do not differentiate between light fae and dark fae. They will attack and eat either."

"We could have to battle goblins in there as well," Pangolin said.

"Yes," Elman replied. "Goblins have far more allies than just hobgoblins."

"Why do you bring that up?" Pangolin asked.

"These are not the lands of the goblins, but we have come across more than one party since we entered the elfin lands. There must be many more parties than we have seen. Whenever goblins are in elfin lands, they bring their evil allies and animals with them."

"Sounds to me, Mr. Pangolin, like we should be drilling the men and our animals for future battles," I-wulf said.

"I would say so," Pangolin said. He looked at the male half-elves. "Have you spoken to Mr. Estus? If the hoofed fae have lightning arrows, why not you?"

"What of those winged arrows those other evil elves used?" I-wulf asked. "They burrowed right through our magical barrier. You need those too."

Elman smiled. "Mr. Estus gave us many new arrows."

"Did he?" Pangolin asked.

"He did."

◆◆◆

Within another pocket-realm it was always dusk. A black mountain with a cavernous interior held the caravan's vault of armor and weapons, encircled by a wall of black, volcanic rock. It was the domain of the väki. They protected every part of the mountain stronghold, both exterior and the vault. Estus was the only human who visited frequently, sometimes with his men to help with tasks. Traveler was the only other man the väki allowed to pass.

The caravan master approached the outer entrance guarded by dozens of väki. The gruff halflings watched him as he waited. Another group appeared from the interior.

"Was there any damage?" Traveler asked the väki leader.

"No damage," he answered. "The hobgoblins did not get into the vault."

"But they did get into the pocket-realm."

"That is nothing. That is what hobgoblins, imps, pixies, and gremlins do. They get into things. That is why we are here. They got no farther than the castle wall and were immediately thrown out or burned out."

"Could they have left anything behind?"

"We know our job. You do yours. We will do ours."

Traveler knew he shouldn't have asked the question. He had a slight smirk on his face. "Oh, and thank you."

The väki leader's eyes narrowed. "Thank you?"

"For joining the attack against the caravan. Your fire magic and the princess's water magic destroyed the wind magic of our elfin king adversary."

The väki leader grunted. "He could have used his air elemental magic to breach this small-realm and steal the weapons. That is why we intervened. We did not trust him. When väki are hired as guardians, we guard against any threats, even potential ones."

"And I still thank you."

The väki grunted in unison. "You humans use too many useless words. 'Thank you?' We did our task."

"We humans like our useless words. Oh, one more thing before I leave you to your work."

"What is that?"

"Thank you."

The väki leader threw up his hands in a huff and stormed away. The other väki closed the thick doors of the mountain wall entrance as Traveler laughed.

In the main pocket-realm, the fairy sisters flew through the sunny sky, giggling and chasing any one of the three swarms of butterflies that moved as dense clouds. Strag and the other hoofed fae—elaphines, cervids, and rusines—ran as a pack through the vast green fields. It was a rare opportunity for them to safely exercise as a group. They would run for hours through the fields and along the river and near the waterfalls. All the giant lizards rested along the river, with their lizard minders in small camps next to them. The men were talkative and in good spirits, as were all in the caravan.

Traveler saw no chamroshes or alphyns as he surveyed the camp, so he guessed that the Cut-Throats and Nirgund were doing their own training within their own pocket-realm. The three kirins rested near the royal tent, with their fenodyree attendants nearby. King Aereth and Hobbs were gathered at a fire in front of it. At the front of his adjacent tent were Dr'amal, Dr'as, and a few other drows, waiting at a fire.

He continued to his tent then noticed the fifteen fae-blood men waiting for him.

"I looked for you earlier, but you were resting," Traveler said to them.

"Yes, we are like your animal companion. When we use our powers extensively, we need to rest for a time afterward," said their leader.

"How far away did you lead the goblin war party?"

"The land turns treacherous not too far away. We led them to a cliff to pitch their goblin masters over it."

"If they only knew your clan can mesmerize their dire wolves better than they can."

"We wanted you to know about their goblin king."

"Yes?"

"His name is Zem. No goblin royal of his stature would enter the land of elves with such a small force."

"That was small?"

"When goblins enter the lands of others, they use small scouting parties then larger war parties, but neither is their main party. There is always a larger caravan or army somewhere."

"We already have to keep an eye out for a gnoll war pack. We will keep an eye out for any possible goblin army. But would that be wise for them to remain in these lands? Even now there are many elfin armies around Fae'el with more arriving."

"Yes, but high goblins are wizards of special power when it comes to the enchanting and summoning of beasts."

"The giant trolls at the entrance of Fae'el were under an illusion spell to make them appear as statues," said another, "and to be immune to the sunlight."

"The elves have Zem now," Traveler said.

"He is one, but he will have traveled with others of his kind."

"We have you, the Elfin Questing Knights, the drows, and more."

"We are not being critical of Titan's Caravan. We only want you to be aware. These high goblins are fond of attacking with dark beasts that both human and fae may be unfamiliar with. They are wizards who revel in transmuting magic."

"They can attempt to change our humans and fae into whatever dark animal they wish, but they will fail."

"They are also allies with other rare dark fae," said another fae-blood.

"Your clan is especially well-informed about these high goblins."

"We should be. We have fought them for a long time. They have invaded our lands many a time."

"We will rest here for a time. I will consult the maps and, with a bit of good fortune, we can get to the Great Forest without any outside of our caravan laying eyes upon us."

"But there is Titan's Arch," said the leader.

"There is that. But we will be well prepared."

"Titan's Arch is infested with harpies."

"We will be well prepared," Traveler repeated. "If we do encounter these goblins or any of their allies on the Trail, I will expect you to provide all the information the leadership needs to defend against them."

"Yes."

"Good."

The fae-bloods left him to return to their camp. He could feel the anger from the fae-bloods about the goblins. They had remained quiet and inconspicuous since joining the caravan until the sight of the goblins. Now they were eager to lead the charge against the dark fae.

The drows sat patiently near the tent for their turn to speak with the caravan master. Traveler knew they would not speak outside the tent. He moved to the entrance of his tent.

"Mr. Traveler," King Aereth greeted.

"You are in especially good spirits, sire."

"I met with Mr. Estus."

"Ah, that is why."

The drows stood when Traveler passed into his tent. Hobbs came in after him.

"Should we have our nightly meeting, sir?" Hobbs asked.

"Yes, Mr. Hobbs. Have everyone attend."

"Very good, sir."

Hobbs left the tent, and the drows entered.

"Will the drows be attending our leadership meeting?" Traveler playfully asked.

"We will," Dr'as replied, "since the elves will attend."

"Good. What do you want to talk to me about before the meeting?"

"Do you know where this gnoll war pack is?" Dr'amal asked.

"I believe I do."

"How?"

"Partly, the kilmoulis. Their smelling senses are without equal in Faë-Land."

"They are lazy creatures and disgusting, eating by stuffing food up their noses," Dr'as said.

"They are not here because of how they eat. We have them as part of our defense."

"What is the other part?" Dr'as asked.

"The elfin wizard king we encountered gave me a magic map. It shows a moving pocket-realm they hide in."

"How many does it show?" Dr'amal asked.

"That it doesn't show, but we both know that any gnoll war party would be vast. None of the humans here have ever seen these beasts in action."

"Most of the fae here have never seen them in action," Dr'amal said.

"What do you intend to do?" Dr'as asked.

"Nothing, for the moment."

"We cannot have that war pack after us within the Great Forest," Dr'as said. "They are exceptional hunters in that kind of environment. If we were a small party, we might have been able to stay out of their grasp, but not with our numbers."

"I agree completely. What do you suggest?"

"We need to move them off our scent," Dr'amal said.

"Have you ever seen a gnoll war-party attack?" Dr'as asked.

Traveler looked at him directly. "I have."

"The men outside are all happy that we defeated caravans of wind elves, goblins, and assorted dark fae, but you and I both know, Mr. Traveler, that our caravan has not yet had a real battle," Dr'as said. "We have our first battle, and we will be burying bodies. If the gnolls find us, we will have that real battle."

"You are not telling me anything I do not know, Dr'as. Again, what do you suggest?"

"Assemble a small party, and go find them first," Dr'amal said.

"Are you volunteering?" he asked the drowess.

"I am. We have done this before."

"Then I agree."

"That was a quick response. I did not think you would see it our way," Dr'as said.

"Not your way? It is what is best for the caravan. The Great Forest is a vast expanse of danger. We do not want the gnolls on our path in there. Gnolls are not dumb like orcs. They are stronger and much more cunning."

"That they are," Dr'amal said, "and the larger the pack, the stronger and more cunning they are."

"Hobbs is assembling the leadership meeting. I want to make one more visit before then. Once we discuss our normal business, we can discuss the gnolls."

"Who else will go with us?" Dr'amal asked. "Will your dog be ready?"

"He will remain sleeping."

"Do you plan to take any of the elves?" she asked.

"Yes, woodland elves are the best trackers."

"That dwelf would disagree."

"Mr. Bragg may, but he is by no means nimble on his feet. Mr. Elman's elfin half is woodland elf. I wish he were an accomplished archer. We need a few drows with your two-blades, you, Dr'amal as our sorceress, a few desert-elf falconers, and our main group."

"Main group?" Dr'as asked.

"The darklings, of course."

"You cannot be serious. Phookas are goblins."

"They are not goblins any more than drows are evil elves. This is exactly the type of mission they excel at."

"Phookas are creatures—" Dr'as began.

"That is the team. There is nothing more to discuss. What is best for the caravan is the only consideration here. We shall lead the gnolls away from Titan's Trail."

Traveler moved to the busy healing tents. Gresham was in full command of things and attending to his patients. Their healer did not see Traveler as he passed by with his dog. Behind the healing tents was a single smaller tent, and when Traveler reached it, he peered in.

"Please do not get up on my account," Traveler said as he stepped in.

Inside, the man called Frog-Dor sat alone, a book on his lap. He had tried to get to his feet, but his legs were in metal braces made by Estus. Frog-Dor had a single candle nearby and more books around him.

"How are you?" Traveler asked.

Aside from his legs, Frog-Dor looked stronger, and mentally he seemed in better spirits. He wore clean clothes, and his hair was groomed and parted. However, he still fought a nervousness in the presence of others. "I...I am well," he replied.

Traveler sat down on the ground in front of him. "Your magic was exceptional. Men's lives were spared in the attack. They would thank you personally if they knew their magical protection was your doing, so I thank you on their behalf."

Frog-Dor never made eye contact for too long. His eyes wandered to the ground. He did not know how to respond.

"Your magic made every magical weapon of the wind elves disappear once they crossed into the circle."

"I could have done more," Frog-Dor managed to say.

"You did enough. A caravan must always be the sum of its members. If only one or a few have to shoulder the burden of its defense, then it is not a strong caravan but a weak one, which will soon be lost. I have seen it before."

"It is a good caravan."

"When your legs have healed, you do not need to stay here in your tent alone. Whenever you are comfortable, you can join in with the men."

"Yes. Thank you."

"I will leave you, then." Traveler stood.

"The Xenhelmians—"

Traveler stopped mid-stride. "You know of the Xenhelmians? King Oughtred. The Four Kings."

"The Kings' Caravan."

"Yes."

"King Oughtred the All-Knowing. I heard him refer to himself as that."

"You heard him? You met him?"

"I was in a room where he visited. There were elves there. I was cursed at the time. They paid no attention me in a green room of flora. My former master sent me there to watch them. He hates the Xenhelmians."

"Yes, he does."

"I heard your men speak of the previous encounters with the Xenhelmians."

"Yes."

"You thought you had killed him. You did kill his armies."

"I did, with my dog."

"The Xenhelmians were like most human kingdoms. They sought out the best practitioners of magic they could find. Humans use the words interchangeably—sorcerer, wizard, mage."

"Humans think of a sorcerer and sorceress as a practitioner of benevolent magic, witch and warlock as users of dark magic, and wizard is a more neutral term. Mage is an archaic term to us. Spell-caster is the more modern term, especially among youth. Are you not human?"

Frog-Dor struggled to remember something. "I...I cannot remember. I have been in Faë-Land so long. Maybe, I will remember one day now that I am free of my curse." His eyes teared up again.

"Yes, you are free and must learn to re-embrace life again."

"I believe that is what led to my curse to begin with."

"That is all in the past. What are you trying to tell me about the Xenhelmians?"

"Their shadow has followed you from the time you entered Faë-Land and will follow us till Atlantea."

"That I know."

"You did kill the war wizard army, but their leaders survived. They are the ones responsible for the spell-talker, the death-sleep, the rest."

"How do you know this?"

"I can see the traces of their dark magic."

"Where are they?"

"I am not sure, but I believe they expected the elves and goblins to defeat us."

"They did not know about you."

"Yes, or that the elfess could use her elemental powers."

"Then, what will they do now?"

"I sense they ready another army for us."

"The gnoll war-party?"

Frog-Dor looked up at him with fear. "Yes, but their numbers are far larger than you know."

"Our plan is to lead them astray from the caravan so that we will not face them."

"There are too many. We cannot escape their wrath."

"What about our wrath?"

"They grow desperate. You have defeated them at every turn. I heard their thoughts. They said...no one has gotten this far before. They must destroy us or they will be destroyed."

"By whom?"

"Oughtred."

"Do you know where he is?"

"He has not yet succeeded in retrieving his son from the creatures of the Far Nether-Lands, but he speaks to the war wizards."

"Will he succeed in retrieving his son?"

"I believe he will."

"How long will it take for them to reach us when they do?"

"The Xenhelmians use portal magic to travel. They can walk through a doorway to us at any time."

Traveler looked around. "Then, the circle must be fortified."

"Their portal cannot breach the circle. But they fear us greatly. They attempted to kill you all before you joined together. Now you are one."

"Can King Oughtred see the future?" Traveler asked directly.

Frog-Dor strained in his reflection.

"He can see things, but they can still be changed."

"What do you advise?"

Frog-Dor sat quietly. Traveler realized that the man himself was a seer too. "I do not know," Frog-Dor said. "The Xenhelmians have powerful allies."

"I know that. Who?"

"Elves, elementals, goblins."

"Why would elementals ally themselves with elves who conspire with goblins?"

"I do not know."

"Frog-Dor, this is a very important question. Were the Xenhelmians responsible for the destruction of Rivermouth and the Faylen kingdom?"

Frog-Dor shook his head. "I do not know that answer. But that is not the important question. The important question is how long have the Four Kings been dead?"

Traveler was caught off guard. "I did not tell the other this, but I was assured the Four Kings were dead because I asked a magic charm in my possession to verify it. My own instincts said they lived but I listened to the charm. Others said otherwise. It all makes sense now."

"You asked a magic telling-box, 'Are the Four Kings dead?' The box answered, 'Yes.' But you did not realize that they were dead long before your attack upon them."

"I now have my answer as to how the Xenhelmians could form an alliance with elfin kingdoms who would never ally with humans."

"They are more than human."

"Yes, and it also explains why elementals would ally with them."

"Does this help you?"

"Greatly."

"You must use the information wisely. We are powerful but not so powerful as to defeat them when they come."

"We need to get to the Great Forest. Can you see these war wizards and where they are?"

"Oughtred commanded them to stop us before we reach the Great Forest. There is more. The goblin."

"What goblin?"

"Their goblin king ally escaped from Fae'el; he is called Zem. Elves helped him escape. The goblin king is known as the Beast Lord. There is fighting at Fae'el."

"Where is this goblin king Zem?"

"I do not see him. I only have a slight feeling of him. He is not near, but he can reappear at any time."

"Goblins never appear alone, and neither do goblin kings."

"This goblin king is also a wizard of great power."

"Goblins can mesmerize malevolent beasts, as fairies, sprites and some elves can mesmerize benevolent ones. I have encountered goblins known as beast lords before. They are a type of evil wizard, and they can control the minds and actions of not just one beast but many."

"You do know."

"Why are the Xenhelmians so determined to stop us from getting to Atlantea?"

"If this caravan passes through Atlantea's gates, then all their power and their alliance ends." Frog-Dor looked at him with a strange smile. "You have said it before. Atlanteans prefer humans to fae."

Traveler watched him and wondered if Frog-Dor was trying to make a joke.

Frog-Dor's smile disappeared, and his gaze returned to the ground.

"It will take me some time to learn how to interact with people again. I do not remember how. Mr. Gresham said he would help me."

"So will Mr. Hobbs and anyone else who can."

"You rescued me from my curse, Mr. Traveler. There isn't anything I would not do to repay that debt. The curse not only made me into a frog during the light of day, it prevented me from killing myself. I wanted to so much, for so long."

"It is all behind you."

"That is why I am not scared. I am free. I am happy."

Traveler had seen it before in many men. To suffer horrors broke some men irreparably. Hopefully, Frog-Dor would be made whole again in body and mind. However, it would be a slow process.

"Frog-Dor, you must get well fast, or as well as you need to be for this. We are days away from the Great Forest, and I want you ready when we cross into it."

"Yes, I will be."

"Titan's Arch is extremely dangerous, as any elf will tell you, but I have devised a strategy for us to pass without incident."

"Yes."

"Rest yourself, then. You have time until we reach the Great Forest and its wild and savage territory, when we leave civilization behind. Be ready. Not simply to protect the caravan, but to fight if need be."

Frog-Dor's eyes were sad as he gazed down to the ground. "Yes," he finally said.

"Keep this conversation between us."

Frog-Dor nodded.

◆ ◆ ◆

Quillen stood at the entrance of the leadership tent. Everyone waited for Traveler, but Quillen was not watching for him. He stared at the fae that were new to the caravan: the sixteen kilmoulis, with their huge noses covering most of their faces. The fae slowly marched single file to the water.

"Are you going to add our lazy additions to your magical book, lad?" Estus asked, standing beside him.

"I will eventually."

"Mr. Traveler was speaking with them earlier."

"He was?"

"Yes, our fae with the noses for heads will be part of our defenses."

"Why? What do they do?"

"The elves brought them along, so they must be able to do what they say. Smell a living thing from leagues away."

Traveler and the dog arrived. They entered the full tent of leadership, the drows, Dr'as and Dr'amal, Ethor the elf, and Bragg the dwelf.

"All are here, sir," Hobbs told the caravan master.

"Thank you, Mr. Hobbs," Traveler said. He glanced at Lady Aylen, who still appeared weak.

"I already tried, Mr. Traveler," Gwyness said to him. "She will not sit."

"Princess, there is no shame in taking a seat when you are not well."

"I will manage."

"Then I will be quick about our gathering."

"Mr. Traveler, we are in this wonderful pocket-realm, but where are we?" Pangolin asked.

"Mr. Pangolin, we are in a tunnel many miles under the earth and many miles from Fae'el. We are about half the distance between Fae'el and Titan's Arch."

"Did your dog dig the tunnels?" Pangolin asked.

"He did. We needed an escape, and we needed a place to rest. The soil of this region was once a volcanic mountain, many eons ago. It was destroyed in a war between elves, dwarves, and goblins. The mountain fragments are part of the ground and prevent detection from above."

"May I ask how we were able to escape without detection by the Fae'el elves?" Dr'as asked.

"The man named Frog-Dor. He cast the spell to nullify the wind weapons of the wind elves. He created an illusion of our camp so that all who watched us would not know as we departed through our secret tunnel. My dog dug the tunnel then erased any trace so none could follow."

"Will our new sorcerer help further?" Dr'as asked.

"He will. So will all our magic practitioners of the caravan, which includes you."

"I did not know our Antaeans had magical abilities," Pangolin said.

"Yes, it was a group spell. Many fae can do the same and use their collective magic for defensive purposes or fighting."

"This war between those fae you mentioned, Mr. Traveler. Who was warring against whom?" I-wulf asked.

"They were battling each other. It was long before this region was permanently settled by the elves."

"A lot of wars, these fae," I-wulf said.

"Yes, as many as us humans." Traveler looked at Hobbs. "Mr. Hobbs, the kilmoulis. I spoke with them earlier today, and they will be under your charge. If they pick up the scent of anything of note, they will either seek you out or me."

"Yes, sir."

"Their appearance is off-putting, I know, but they are harmless and always try to be friendly. The elves were wise to include them. Our caravan will be able to hear, see, or smell any beast long before it is in striking distance."

"I would not put much confidence in our big-nosed, pot-bellied sprites," Bragg said. "Not all beasts allow their scent to be carried by the wind. Without that, the kilmoulis are useless."

"Everything helps, Mr. Bragg. When our caravan left the Mirage Plains, we left all human civilization behind. When we enter the Great Forest, our caravan will be beyond all fae civilization for many months. Even if those big-nosed, pot-bellied sprites' smelling ability can steer us away from one attack, it will be well worth it."

"Agreed," Bragg said.

"That brings us to the matter of supplies," Traveler said.

"We are well stocked, are we not, Mr. Traveler?" King Aereth asked.

"We were, sire."

"Were?"

"We need more water. Lady Aylen's water attack used far more of it than we could spare. Lady Aylen, it was not your fault. You had never used your water summoning magical abilities before. You inadvertently summoned water from more than just the pocket-realm you and Dr'amal were in."

"I am so sorry," Lady Aylen said.

"I should have known," Dr'amal said. "It was my fault."

"It was no one's fault. None of us could have known what her power would be, because she never used it before. Your spell did as it was supposed to. It amplified her latent water-elemental magic. However, that is the past. We will simply acquire more water, much more."

"More than the amount of water lost?" Pangolin asked.

"Yes. There are several watering holes along the Trail. Some are large. Some are hidden. However, I want us to avoid all of them. It is where we could be ambushed by beasts or anything else that could be tracking us."

"You are expecting other parties?" Ethor asked.

"Goblins."

"Mr. Traveler, isn't this Great Forest so large that we will be lost to any who follow?" Gwyness asked.

"Yes, maiden," Traveler said, "but not lost to any party or beast waiting for us at a watering hole, a point on the Trail we may pass, or a ravine where we might set up night camp."

"What are our next steps, Mr. Traveler?" Lady Aylen asked. "When do we set out again? And please, do not say, when I am recovered. If I must, I can rest in one of the pocket-realms or a wagon pulled by one of the pech."

"As much as I would like to say that we should not move one step until every man and woman is fully recovered, we must move forward as quickly as possible. We must reach Titan's Arch then cross into the Forest."

"Why quickly?" Lady Aylen asked.

"What happens at Titan's Arch?" Pangolin asked.

"At Titan's Arch, we get to do battle with harpies!" Bragg the dwelf said with a smile.

"Mr. Pangolin, you will take a party of half-elves and elves to obtain our water. One of our animal men, the mole man—"

"The one with the giant carnivorous moose?" Pangolin asked.

"Yes. He knows how to find the water."

"Water? Water where, Mr. Traveler?" King Aereth asked.

"There's an underground river not too far away, sire." Traveler looked at their master-at-arms. "Mr. Pangolin, I will leave the mission in your capable hands. Replenish all the water we lost, and then double it."

"Oh, no," Lady Aylen said. "Where are you and the dog off to now, Mr. Traveler?"

"Not just us," Traveler replied. "Mr. Elman, Dr'amal, three drow blade-throwers, three desert-elf falconers, and—"

"Mr. Traveler, please reconsider," Dr'amal said.

"The darklings."

"Darklings?" Gwyness asked. "You mean those black shape-shifters?"

"Where are you taking everyone, Mr. Traveler?" King Aereth asked.

"Gnolls, sire."

Everyone in the tent got quiet.

"They are nearby?" Bragg asked.

"Yes, and we need to make sure that the caravan does not meet them in battle."

"How will you do that?" Pangolin asked.

"We are going to make them chase us," Traveler said.

"Chase you?" Lady Aylen asked.

"Is that not extremely dangerous?" King Aereth asked.

"It is, sire, but it is what has to be done. In this tent, only a few of us have had the 'pleasure' of seeing a gnoll war pack with our own eyes. However, none of us in this caravan has seen a war pack of this size."

"How large?" Ethor asked.

"I believe the pack numbers in the hundreds of thousands."

The humans saw the fae in the tent gasp.

"How bad is that?" Pangolin asked.

"A war pack that size—" Bragg shook his head. "Even if they couldn't get past our circle, they could pin us down fighting for months...or years."

"Years?" Pangolin asked with disbelief.

"They never stop fighting," Dr'as said to him. "Never. They create settlements on the battlefield, and while one group sleeps, the other fights, then they reverse places. They never stop fighting until they kill their prey or they are killed, every last one."

"How can I lead a party for water when you face this danger?" Pangolin asked Traveler.

"Mr. Pangolin, your party will get our water. Our party will move this danger away from the Trail and us. Elfin armies will deal with the gnolls for us. But when they do we must be long gone. If not, either the gnolls or the elfin armies or both will keep us from ever leaving the lands of Fae'el, and our journey to Atlantea will be at an end. I am sure that all would agree that we have come too far for that to be allowed."

"Hear! Hear!" Lady Aylen and others said in unison.

CHAPTER SIXTEEN

Gnolls!

"Water is life!"

Pangolin was only a small boy when his great grandmother spoke the words to him. Dehydrated and near-delirium, he had attempted to cross the desert of their region with a single water skin. He needed ten times that, and if he had not been found by his kingdom's warriors, his life and body would have been claimed by the sand.

Titan's Caravan was unique in every way. The journey they traveled was a distance longer than the most ambitious treks. They did not have horses and livestock. No, they had two thousand giant lizards, more than fifteen feet in length, and a wide assortment of fantastic beasts. More than that, they had six giants that literally drank more in a day than six thousand men. Titan's Caravan could not survive without water, so that was a mission he was glad to lead.

When they left in the middle of the night, Pangolin could not imagine what their path would be. His party was only three: the youngest of the Tree Shepherds, Little Root, and the one surly, mole-looking humanoid fae, who was upset that he had to leave his giant carnivorous moose companion behind. Little Root led them not too far outside camp and then...down. The Tree Shepherd's right hand glowed to illuminate the way, but Pangolin could not understand where, or how, they were descending into the earth. He glanced back at the mole-like fae behind, but his race did not have the facial features to reveal any disposition. Pangolin did not even know if the dots on his face were real eyes or not.

"How are we doing this?" Pangolin asked Little Root.

"Magically. We are moving through an inclined tunnel. I am creating the steps to walk for your benefit, since you are the only one among the three of us who cannot fly."

"Fly? The mole-man can fly?"

"He's a sprite. Sprites can fly when they need to."

"Where are we going?"

"There. You can see it now."

Though more than a mile away, Pangolin could see the luminescent river flowing at the bottom of their tunnel.

"An underground river."

"An entire underground forest beneath the lands of the elves."

"Who occupies these lands?"

"Many travel these lands to and from their homelands—fairies, water elves, and nymphs, especially. We will ask permission from the potamides to take the river water that we need. These nymphs hold dominion over this underground river."

"Why does it glow so?" Pangolin asked.

"It is water imbued with the purest magic. It sparkles by day and glows by night."

"Humans can drink it?"

"Humans that drink it will stay younger longer, become healthier, become stronger in body and mind."

They descended from the tunnel and stepped down on the ground at the bank of the river. Pangolin could see that the river was far wider than he imagined and that it was as Little Root had said—it was an entire underground wooded world with clouds of fireflies to give an illusion of daytime.

The last time they encountered nymphs, it was dryads. Those nymphs were young, beautiful barefoot women in sheer dresses with long hair—yellow, gold, black—down to their ankles and an angelic glow. These nymphs did not come from the woods but rose from the river to float in the air and step down onto the ground.

Pangolin's magic armor protected him from their enchantment, but as their numbers grew around the three of them, he began to feel their powerful attraction. There were not dozens of them but hundreds. The nymphs paid the leshy and sprite no mind, but they were all watching him, grinning.

The mole-man waved his hands and rapidly spoke a language Pangolin did not understand. Whatever it was, the nymphs did not like it. Their faces turned to frowns, and Little Root laughed. The verbal exchange between the mole-man and the nymphs was heated, and it went on for what seemed well over an hour to Pangolin. The mole-man and one of the nymphs shook hands.

"Success?" Pangolin asked Little Root.

"We can have all the water we need, for a price."

"What price?"

"The sprite made a good bargain for us. My fellow Tree Shepherds will make the trade for the caravan. Nymphs do not care for standard money, but they can be bribed with treasure. We have the treasure they favor."

"Good. How will we take possession of the water? How will it be transported?"

"I cannot imagine living in your lands without magic. Your questions suggest such a feeble and backwards way of doing things. I do not mean to offend."

"No offense taken. I am a man partly of magic, but I will always be born of lands that have none. I am human."

"Yes. We do not have to transport the water. We will be given what you humans call a pocket-realm. Within it will be a network of wild rivers to sustain our caravan with all the water it will need to our destination and beyond."

◆◆◆

"Run!"

Nearly ten thousand men and their beasts ran through the valley of black soil and scarce brush. Fae'el was a fading light to their rear. Titan's Arch was a growing dot of light to their front. The lizard minders had drilled many times with their giant fae lizards and stayed in a tight column formation on either flank of the caravan. Traveler led the vanguard of Pangolin, the half-elves, elaphine archer-warriors, the Cut-Throats, and their pack of chamroshes. Everyone maintained a quick pace, even the six Antaean giants in their new position at the caravan's rear guard.

Elman could see the structure of Titan's Arch growing in his field of vision. Some of the elaphine archers were the first to hear a faint hiss. When the portal appeared nearly a quarter mile before them on the Trail, strange sounds that were a combination of laughter and howls erupted from it and startled them all.

"This way!" Traveler led.

He gestured to the caravan to change direction and everyone ran east. They had been running for hours, ever since emerging from the underground tunnel, but none slowed their pace.

Traveler turned his head to look at the portal and saw the first creature leap out. Gnolls were not common in the stories in the Lands of Man, but in Faë-Land they were known for their ferocity and relentlessness. They were intelligent humanoid dog-like beasts with sharp teeth and claws that always hunted and attacked in packs. Some wore scarce clothing and killed with their hands and teeth, but others wore full armor and wielded goblin-made weapons. The smallest of their kind were more akin to feral dogs. Then there were the wolf-like clans. The largest and most formidable were like giant hyenas. Traveler watched a war-pack of armored hyena gnolls charge from the portal after them. It was a war pack of a size he had never seen in all his travels. Soon their numbers surpassed the size of the caravan, with even more gnolls jumping out of the portal.

Then the army of gnolls slowed down.

"They know something is wrong," the voice of an invisible Dr'amal said.

"I want you to drive the gnolls mad. I want them so enraged they would run off a cliff to their deaths to get at you! Go!" Traveler's voice commanded.

"Spiders and snakes, snakes and spiders," the darklings yelled out in unison, cackling.

From within their moving circle Traveler watched the darklings run towards the gnoll army. They took the form of black hyena-like creatures on legs as long as giraffes. Once they crossed the circle's edge, they became visible and began howling then spat chunks of saliva at the gnolls. Several gnolls were hit in the face despite their attempt to dodge the projectiles. The gnoll army growled in unison and charged.

The cackling phookas immediately turned around to run the other way. The dark shape-shifters followed the retreating caravan—*the illusion of the caravan.*

Traveler ran faster, his dog at his side. Elman ran on one side with Dr'amal and the drows. The desert elves ran on the other, their magic falcons flying above them all. Around them was the ghostly image of the caravan.

"Fire!" Traveler commanded.

The gnolls at the front of the army moved fast. Arrows and two-blades came out of nowhere, striking dozens of them. The beasts fell to the ground. The gnoll army came at the caravan like a wave, covering the land and advancing. Their hyena laughter, grunts, and breathing echoed like thunder.

"I have never seen so many gnolls at one time," one of the drows said.

"They are almost upon us!" Dr'amal said. The drowess raised her hands, and bolts of purple light shot from her palms.

The magic javelins hit at the feet of the closest gnolls and electrified every gnoll in a ten-foot radius. More magical javelins struck. Hundreds of gnolls were stopped in their tracks, but they were mere droplets in the living tsunami of beasts closing in.

The other drows threw their two-blades. The desert elves shot their arrows. It was an explosive volley that felled many more gnolls, but the army seemed unaffected.

"We cannot outrun them," Dr'amal said, "and when they touch the illusion it will disappear."

"How far, Mr. Elman?" Traveler asked.

The half-elf's eyes were fixed on a point in the distance. "A little bit more."

"We have no time!" a desert elf yelled.

The darklings had transformed into flying hyena-creatures and flew past the caravan. Gnolls on the ground threw weapons at them, but then the phookas circled back.

"What are they doing?" Dr'amal asked.

"What they are supposed to," Traveler said. "Distracting them. Mr. Elman?"

"A little more."

"Half-elves, elves, and drows can run all day. Humans cannot," Traveler said.

"That may be true, but gnolls can run for days without rest. We cannot," a drow said.

"Mr. Elman!" Traveler yelled.

"Now!" the half-elf answered.

◆◆◆

Floating white castles hovered, and elfin riders on winged horses and winged unicorns filled the skies above Fae'el. Elfin knights, floating in the air with winged armor, also readied for battle. Outside the walls of Fae'el stood thousands of elfin warriors and archers in large formations.

At the head of the elfin ground armies, royals from different elfin races and kingdoms calmly waited for the coming onslaught. Highly ornate crowns rested on their heads, and their attire, with their armor underneath, was more colorful than their troops and extremely flamboyant.

"The fairies informed us it was a gnoll army that may number hundreds of thousands, if not more," one of the elfin attendants said to the high-elfin royals on their war unicorns.

Among the new elfin royals were Druil the high-elf wizard, and many more high elves on their war unicorns, Taylon and the desert elves on their falcon griffins, Galadaer and the woodland elves on their leopard axexs, and Staric and the moon elves on their owl griffins. There were forest elves, river elves, sub-elves, fire elves, and fairy elves.

The magical portal crackled as it took form not too far in the distance. It opened, and out came the nearly ten-thousand-strong Titan's Caravan, but when the last member's foot touched the ground—one of the Antaeans—the magical illusion faded away. The gnoll army emerged from the portal with their collective hyena laughter that echoed through the lands. The beasts saw the elves then charged them with full intensity. Elfin wizards in the sky immediately fired magical projectiles at them. The elfin land armies charged, screaming their war cries. From the floating elfin castles, arrows and projectiles of magic rained down on the gnolls.

Several portals opened behind the elfin armies as more battle elves emerged on foot and on griffin, hippogriff, unicorn, and giant eagle steeds.

CHAPTER SEVENTEEN

Sorcerers' Portal

When Traveler and his party returned from their mission, the caravan was overjoyed.

"We escaped the wrath of the gnoll army!" one of the men yelled out.

Then, väki emerged from their hidden pocket-realm.

Every man and woman, human and fae, of Titan's Caravan stood in awe, looking at the sky. The circular image of the battle between the elves and gnolls hung above them. The spell was called an "all-seeing eye" and could take many forms. One of the väki had cast the spell, and all could see what was taking place back at Fae'el.

"You looked troubled," the halfling sprite of the *tulen väki* said to Lady Aylen, who stood nearby.

She did not know how to respond and was surprised the fae even spoke to her.

"Your water elemental powers are strong," he said. "It was both your water-elemental and our fire-elemental magic that crushed the wind elf's air magic. Either of our magic would have defeated him alone, but it could have been a very long battle. He was very powerful and had more than one wizard underling with him."

"I do not think I wish to use the power again."

"You may not be ready now, but one day you will. You are an elf. You are a water-elemental. You cannot hide from it."

"She knows," Traveler said. The caravan master stood with the royals and Gwyness looking on. He looked at the princess with deep concern.

They heard gasps, and the conversation among the men increased. The numbers of the gnoll war pack seemed unending, but even so, they were no match for the numbers of elfin warriors, their weapons, and their magic. Most dark fae would have retreated, but giant hyena gnolls never did, and the caravan watched as the creatures were slaughtered.

"Those are gnolls," Quillen said at Hobbs's side.

"Those *were* gnolls," Pangolin said. "I take it that such numbers for even gnolls is unheard of?" the berserker asked the nearby elfin questing knights.

"Yes," a moon elf said. "They travel in large numbers but the size of that army would be the entire population of one of their regions. They never move in such numbers. They would destroy all the flora and fauna of the land and attract retribution from good fae."

The magical image in the sky faded.

"Thank you," Traveler said to the väki.

The väki grunted. He and his two comrades promptly marched back to the entrance of their pocket. Men around them laughed at their surly response.

"Do they truly hate even to be given thanks?" King Aereth asked.

"They do," Traveler replied.

The two fairy sisters appeared first as fireflies then took the form everyone recognized. Wildglow flew to Traveler and floated right in front of him.

"How long were you both watching?" Traveler asked.

"We wanted to see the battle," Wildglow said. "Gnolls are bad."

"What news do you have?" the caravan master asked.

"The elves thanked you for leading the gnolls to them to destroy. The gnolls would have ravaged their elfin lands. They were very happy. The elf wizard, Druil, said to tell you to take care of his men. He expects them to get to Atlantea and get lots of treasure."

"Druil and his high elves don't care about treasure, but we will get his men there along with all of us. What else?"

"The high-elfin royalty were mad that we escaped. They have all of Fae'el and the surrounding land in a circle. Their elfin magistrates wanted to hold our caravan until their tribunals were over. If we were there, we would have been trapped!" The fairies laughed. "Dumb elves. We were long gone before they arrived. They wanted to hold us, but we are too clever and powerful for them. I told them I would set my swarms on them. That scared them." The fairy sisters began to laugh again.

"Yes, yes, what else?"

"They said Titan's Caravan must have portal magic like the Xenhelmians," Wildglow said.

"They should not compare us to them," Traveler said, "especially when we did not use portal magic. That's how false rumors begin, but it is no matter."

"Yes, we simply marched away under the cover of an illusion spell. We are smarter than them!"

"What else?"

"Oh!"

"Oh, what?" Traveler asked.

"They said the goblin escaped."

"The goblin wizard king?" Traveler asked.

"Yes."

"Zem escaped?" the fae-blood of the wolf clan stood next to Traveler. "When?"

"Last night they think," Wildglow answered. "It could have been sooner."

"You do not seem surprised, Mr. Traveler," King Aereth said.

"Another informed me of the escape too," the caravan master replied.

"Mr. Traveler." It was their healer's voice. Gresham was helping the man Frog-Dor slowly move to them. Traveler walked to them.

With each step, Frog-Dor grimaced in pain. He had more mobility because of the leg braces Estus made for him, but his legs would take many months to recover. He composed himself before he spoke. "I can see the goblin wizard."

"Where?" Traveler asked.

"Was he commanding the gnoll army?" one of the fae-blood men asked.

"You seem to have a particular interest in this goblin," King Aereth said.

"Tell the king what you told me," Traveler said to the fae-bloods.

"This goblin wizard king is named Zem, a high goblin. Those of his stature travel in large caravans and larger armies," a fae-blood answered.

"Not the gnoll war pack?" Pangolin asked.

"No," the fae-blood answered. "A goblin army."

"Why do you hate these goblins so?" Lady Aylen asked. "You hate them more than elves."

"Goblins are enemies to wolves," one answered.

"They ride war wolves," a desert elf said.

"They enslave the animals," the fae-blood snapped.

"Dire wolves are enslaved by no one," another elf challenged. "They are dark creatures chosen by the dark race of goblins."

The faces of the fae-blood flushed with anger. They moved aggressively to the elves.

"We are not going to fight amongst ourselves!" Traveler said as he got between the groups.

"Say what you like, elf. Dire wolves were forced to be evil. They are not evil by nature no matter what you say."

"That is a lie," a moon elf said.

Traveler looked at Frog-Dor. "Where?"

"I can see him but not where he is," Frog-Dor answered.

Traveler returned his attention to the fairies but kept the groups of elves and fae-bloods apart. "What else?"

"Oh, there were elfin kings and queens there too. They were talking about war wizards in their lands."

"War wizards? Where?"

"Close."

Traveler looked at the perimeter of the camp to the magical circle then looked around. Everyone was within its border.

"Is something wrong, Mr. Traveler?" King Aereth asked.

"Wildglow, where did they say the war wizards were?"

"They were trying to find them, but they disappeared. That is when they were talking about the Xenhelmians and their portal magic and comparing us to them because they thought we used portal magic."

"Frog-Dor!" Traveler called out and made Wildglow cease talking. "What do you see exactly?"

Frog-Dor closed his eyes. "The vision is getting foggy."

Traveler's eyes found the drow sorceress standing nearby. "Dr'amal, can you amplify his powers like you did with Lady Aylen?" Traveler asked.

"No!" A look of fear came over Frog-Dor's face. "She cannot do that. It would put us all in danger."

"Can't the väki do another all-seeing-eye spell?" Quillen asked.

"Very good, Mr. Quillen," Traveler said. "Mr. Estus, find them."

Estus ran for the väki's pocket. By now, the camp had grown fearful.

"You believe these war wizards are close?" King Aereth asked.

"These war wizards are the ones who have been dogging us ever since Titan's Bridge. Now this goblin wizard king disappears. The gnoll army was set upon us here."

"How close do you think they are, Mr. Traveler?" Lady Aylen asked.

"We need to know, princess. And we need to know now."

"And what of this goblin army?" Pangolin asked.

Traveler looked for them. "Wait here," he said to the others.

Traveler saw the kilmoulis watching him as soon as he entered the circle.

The kilmoulis were very shy beings. They stayed together in their group and did not mingle with others, human or fae. They were a race that seemed as self-conscious about their appearance as others were disturbed by it. Traveler, however, regarded them as simply good-natured sprites.

He slipped away from the chattering of the men. As Traveler neared them, the kilmoulis kept their gaze to the ground.

"Did you want to speak with me?" he asked them.

They looked up. Traveler was not repelled by their appearance as many were. If they could hide their large noses on their face, they would. These fae not only ate through their noses, they spoke through them.

"We are not alone," one said.

Traveler asked, "Who or what?"

"Some humans, some fae, but goblins, many goblins."

"A goblin army?"

"Yes."

"How many?"

"Many more than our number."

"How far away? How long do we have until they arrive?"

"They are here now. They surround us. They hide in invisibility."

Traveler returned and walked to the man Frog-Dor. He spoke to him in whispers, and Frog-Dor nodded. Traveler walked back to his place and the conversation with the fairies.

"Wildglow, do you know this place where the war wizards and goblins hide from us?"

"We know, but we won't tell," the oldest fairy sister said in a playful huff.

Traveler turned his attention to the smaller sister. "Sunpetal, do you know the magic place I am speaking of?"

The tiny fairy sister smiled and nodded.

"If we all draw close, will you whisper the name to us, because we need to know. If you whisper the name, we will all be transported from where we stand to the very gates of Atlantea itself. This place is so powerful in its magic that even speaking its name will do that. Will you whisper it to us, Sunpetal?"

A smiling Sunpetal nodded, floating in the air next to her larger, giggling sister.

"Gather around everyone," Traveler said.

People looked at each other, but everyone did move in closer, from the leadership and warriors to the lizard minders and their giant lizards to the fae parties farthest out in the camp.

"Sunpetal, you can whisper the name of the place. What is it called?"

"Sorcerer's Gate!" she said in her high-pitched voice.

Every human and fae archer fired their bow or crossbow. Every drow threw their two-blade. Every pech thew a spear. Dr'amal threw daggers of purple magic outward from the circle. When the swarms of the fairy sisters also sped out of the circle, they heard the first scream.

All of the fae seemed to know of Traveler's deception, but the humans did not. However, everyone in the caravan reacted instinctively as the scream was revealed to be a goblin falling to the ground. Outside the circle, the entire land wavered, and the goblin army became visible to all, charging on foot or mounted on giant dire wolves.

"Archers!" Pangolin yelled.

The caravan's human archers joined in the volley attack of the elaphine archer-warriors, who were already shooting arrows, with dizzying speed. King Aereth ran to his heavy-weapons teams to take charge.

"Fire!" he yelled.

The teams launched their first volley of metal projectiles from their catapults. For the pech, they threw their metal projectiles at the attacking goblin army with their bare hands.

"Men, we must get the new magic projectiles!" Estus yelled to his own team, and led them away, running quickly.

The insect swarms of the fairy sisters kept the full force of the goblin army—nearly ten times the size of Titan's caravan—at bay while arrows, projectiles, and magic cut the goblins and their beasts down. Two of the crawling trees joined in, becoming more humanoid and smacking dozens of goblins into the air with the swing of their branches.

Unlike the gnolls, the goblins soon realized they would not breach the caravan's circle and began to retreat.

Traveler saw him. Behind it all, the goblin wizard sat on a giant bat-winged dire wolf. Their eyes made contact. Zem yelled as he pulled the mane of his flying wolf steed to make the beast jump in the air and fly off. A portal opened.

The goblin wizard flew through the magic portal like a bolt of lightning, but before it could close, Traveler flew through it himself. The caravan master was not mounted on the dog, but the dog had transformed into a humanoid flying wolf-like beast and carried Traveler in his arms.

"Not this time!" Pangolin yelled. He turned to the fae archers. "Keep that portal open so I can follow!"

Four of the elaphine archer-warriors fired special bows at the closing portal. Suddenly, the portal began opening.

"Mr. Pangolin!" King Aereth yelled. "We should remain within the circle!"

Their master-at-arms had already charged forward with a contingent of the Cut-Throats and their flying eagle-hound chamroshes. They jumped through the portal, and it closed.

◆◆◆

Zem, the goblin wizard king, had not yet exited the portal when the "dog" stretched out its arms and grabbed the flying dire wolf from under him. The goblin yelled as he fell to the earth, landing hard. The dog took the form of a larger two-headed flying dire wolf and easily crushed the neck and body of Zem's flying dire wolf.

"I will kill you all!" the goblin king yelled as he got to his feet.

The goblin king watched his dead flying dire wolf fall to the ground not far away. He turned his head with barely time to react. Traveler was upon him and brought his blade down on the goblin, but Zem caught it in his hand.

"The magic of your blade is powerful," Zem sneered, "but the magic I possess is more powerful."

"Is it?" Traveler asked.

Zem screamed as Traveler's sword erupted in transparent fire and set the goblin's hand then his entire body ablaze. The goblin wizard let the sword go and fought to save himself with all his magic from within.

"Let me help you," Traveler said. He cut the goblin in half at the waist.

Traveler flinched as Pangolin's axe-mace struck at something inches from the caravan master's face. It was a hooded human male with strange eyes—the whites were yellow, and the pupils were unusually large. Traveler had seen wizards like him before—under the Four Kings of Xenhelm. The wizard lay dead on the ground. The sound of metal on metal had been because the human wizard's arms were long, slender metallic claws. The wizard would have disemboweled him.

At that moment, Traveler realized that it wasn't that he was so focused on the goblin wizard that he failed to take note of his surroundings; he was under a spell. Another wizard, another human with strange eyes in a hooded cloak, stood nearby, laughing as he held one hand up, pointing at him. Traveler could move his head but nothing more. His magic sword floated, suspended above the ground.

In the sky, his dog was encased in a milky translucent sphere, transforming to every creature imaginable to escape but to no avail. Pangolin and the Cut-Throats were screaming as they writhed on the ground. Pangolin's magical armor protected him from most of the dark magic, but the others were transforming into animals of some kind. The chamroshes had been transformed into tiny chickens and ran away in every direction.

The full environment was clear to Traveler now. Having traveled all throughout Faë-Land, he knew where they were. The land was of dark rocky soil with a forest of tall black dead trees. Fae had many names for the place, but humans called it Necropolis.

Traveler could see eleven wizards remaining: the one holding him in a paralysis spell, another holding his dog within the magic sphere, and another transforming the men. The remaining wizards walked to him. His eyes immediately locked on the one wizard he knew was their leader. He was the only man not wearing a hood. Whether the man was human or fae, Traveler could not tell, but he had the same sickly yellowish eyes.

The war-wizard leader stepped up to Traveler. He spat in Traveler's face. Traveler slowly reopened his eyes and glared at the wizard.

"You killed many of my colleagues that day," the wizard said. His words had a magical tinge to them that physically shook Traveler's body. "The spell-talker we sent was meant for you. I do not know how you managed to escape him." The wizard looked at the dead body of the goblin wizard and pointed. "That will be the last wizard of my army you will kill, ever. There will be no Atlantea for you. There will be no life for you. We will wipe your caravan from existence, as we have done to others before. But, I will keep you alive until my master returns. King Oughtred wishes to see you again. I will remove the bones from your body and keep you in a bottle for him. Your caravan will die today, but your suffering is only just beginning."

The wizard leader looked at his men. "There is a powerful charm around his neck. Remove it!"

One of the other wizards neared Traveler and yanked for the necklace of roots and herbs from around his neck. At the end of the necklace was a small blue orb. "Where did you get this from, human?" he asked. "Was this supposed to protect you from us?"

Traveler said nothing then closed his eyes.

"Yes, human," the wizard leader said. "Prepare for the end of your men, all who you know, the end of your life." The wizard leader grabbed the blue orb from the other wizard's hand. "I will crush you like so." He crushed the orb in his sickly-pale hands.

The orb shattered but then rapidly expanded and knocked the wizards off their feet.

The wizard leader sat up. "What is—" the wizard stopped mid-sentence as his eyes began to glow. His body shook violently from the ground, and he gritted his teeth. His skin turned gray.

The other wizards screamed as they saw something. One by one, they turned to stone. The wizard leader yelled and slowly rose to his feet in defiance. His skin began to revert to its normal color.

The first arrow pierced his skull, the second his heart. The wizard leader was unshaken and continued to fight with his magic. A gorgon slithered up to him and touched his face with hers. The creature yelled. Her nostrils flared, and her eyes glowed brighter, but his glowed with greater intensity too.

The gorgon's upper female torso had green scaly skin. Her face was beautiful, but her hair was that of long hissing snakes. She grabbed the wizard's face with her clawed hands and deeply scratched down his cheeks. He remained unmoved as his skin gained more color. The gorgon wrapped her lower torso, that of a giant snake, around his legs and lower body. They were locked in a death stare.

"I—will—not—yield!" the war wizard yelled. His eyes flashed.

The gorgon screamed. She let go of his face and fell back as she slowly turned to stone herself.

The sound began slowly then grew—laughter.

"Very good, one called Traveler," the war wizard leader said. "Where did you get such a powerful charm indeed? I admire your allies. If it were any other wizard, your plan would have worked, but I am no simple dark wizard. My master did not make me the general of his war-wizard army by happenstance. I am the most powerful necromancer that you will ever encounter. How long have you had the charm around your neck? Did you expect to face us?" The wizard's skin had reverted completely to its normal pale color.

The gorgon was solid stone around his body, but with one hard strike, he shattered the creature to pieces and freed himself. He dusted himself off.

"You managed to kill more of my colleagues, so I am alone. Another small triumph for you. However, your fate is unchanged."

The wizard looked around himself. Traveler, everyone, and everything had vanished. He was not in Necropolis anymore. The barren terrain was unfamiliar.

"Where am I?" he asked himself.

He frantically looked for any familiar landmarks. All he could see was a small party approaching him from the distance. They looked human, but they were too far away to see clearly. The wizard stared at his hands.

"I cannot make...magic. What is this place?"

He looked up to see that the small party nearing him were much closer, much closer than if they were merely walking. They were men and women in simple clothing.

"Who approaches me?" he called out. "Identify yourselves!"

"Identify yourself," a male voice said. "You are the trespasser on our lands."

"What lands?"

"You are in the lands of the gorgons."

The wizard's head then body began to shake. He could not look away. The young people had reached him. They wore simple white tunics and dresses and were barefoot. However, their skin was green and scaly, and their matted hair was also green. That was not their most disturbing feature. They had empty sockets where their eyes should have been but they were not blind.

"What have you done to our queen, trespasser?" one of the male gorgon worshipers asked. "Do not fear. We will not turn you to stone. The dark magic within you is very strong."

"Yes," said a female gorgon worshiper. "We will eat you."

CHAPTER EIGHTEEN
Titan's Arch

"**M**r. Pangolin!" King Aereth had yelled. "We should remain within the circle!"

First Traveler and his dog disappeared, then Pangolin and a group of Cut-Throats followed after them with their chamroshes. The portal door closed, and they were gone. King Aereth stared on helplessly.

"They will be fine, sire," Nirgund, his guardsman, said with reassurance. Nirgund's reptile hound alphyns surrounded them both.

"I wish I were as certain of that as you are, Mr. Nirgund. We cannot even render aid should they need it."

The king turned his attention to the attack on the caravan. The goblin army was no more—goblins and dire wolves lay dead or wounded around the circle. All others had fled. King Aereth stepped to the perimeter of the circle for a better vantage point. From the swiftness of their defenses, the caravan was never in any real danger once the goblin wizard king left them.

Bragg the dwelf had a giant smile on his face. He saw the king from where he stood and said, "We will never be troubled by these goblins again, king. Word will spread of us far and wide."

"How far are these lands of the goblins?" the king asked.

"Their lands are as far away as the true lands of the elves. We are on Titan's Trail. The villages and cities we encounter here are only those that wish to do business with those traveling along it. Most fae do not." Bragg pointed. "The elfin kingdoms are that way, and the goblin kingdoms are the opposite direction. Titan's Trail literally cuts their regions in half. Though the elves say otherwise, the Trail is the unclaimed lands in between."

The swarms of the fairies returned to the crawling trees. Wildglow rattled on to her little sister as the two flying fairy sisters followed. The pech moved back to their small camps, as did all the other fae. Hobbs busily moved through the caravan, ensuring none of their giant lizards had been wounded.

King Aereth heard a heated exchange. He saw Lady Aylen moving to it with her female half-elf guards. The king followed with his guardsman.

"What is happening here?" Lady Aylen asked.

The drows, elves, and the animal-like fae berserkers had surrounded Gresham, the healer.

"This human plans to aid the very goblins who attacked us," Hax, the lionlike fae answered.

Gresham held up his hand. "That is not true. I simply asked what is the normal way of things in these lands."

"To let them die where they lay," an elf snapped back.

Lady Aylen looked out past the circle. She could see goblins and dire wolves that were still alive. "Mr. Gresham, I cannot say you have taken up a noble cause in this case. They did attack us without cause."

"Yes, princess. I asked the question. I received my answer. The matter is closed. I will return to my healing tent."

"Do that," another elf said. "You are the healer for this caravan and its allies, not our sworn enemies."

"Traveler!"

The cry of one of the male half-elves immediately turned everyone's thoughts and attention elsewhere. From where they stood, it looked like giant flapping white wings flew to them from the sky. The thing had no body at all.

"How can those half-elves see so far?" Lady Aylen asked. "I can barely see Mr. Traveler standing on the wings, and I'm a full elf—or I'm supposed to be."

King Aereth smiled. "We all have our talents, princess."

The magic of the Tree Shepherd restored the chamroshes to their normal form, but the beasts were still uneasy.

"You should separate them from their flock," the leshy said to their Cut-Throat masters. "You will know when they are ready to rejoin it. Give them plenty of food and water."

The Cut-Throat berserkers had to literally pick up their animals and carry them off to one of the pockets. The animals were too traumatized to even walk.

Pangolin sat on the ground in his camp with the giants and other Cut-Throats looking on. Hobbs had the men get him hot broth to consume.

"Here, Mr. Pangolin," Hobbs said as he handed their seated master-at-arms a large cup.

Pangolin took at it and sipped it initially.

"What was it like?" one of the giants asked.

"It was as if my body was changing into something else, but the magic of my armor was changing me back. I cannot explain it. At least I fared better than when I came across that spell-talker."

"How many of the warlocks were there?" another giant asked.

"I killed one. Mr. Traveler killed the goblin wizard king. There were, I think, a dozen more or slightly less. I am not sure."

Everyone took notice as Traveler walked to their small camp. Hobbs and the royals followed. As always, even in a caravan of its size, everyone wanted to know what had transpired.

"Your Cut-Throats are fine, Mr. I-wulf," Traveler said.

The Cut-Throat leader was relieved. "Thank you."

"When the wizard who cast the spell was killed, their spell was broken. Mr. Gresham will look after them in the healing tent until they fully recover."

"Yes, as long they need," I-wulf said.

"Mr. Pangolin, how are you progressing?"

Pangolin swallowed the last of his broth from the cup. "I was not seriously affected. Thanks to my armor. I was there, but I cannot say I know what happened. Your animal snatched me up and the others before I could see."

"You did not need to see."

"What did happen, Mr. Traveler?" Lady Aylen asked.

"Hopefully, the end. At least for now."

"The end, Mr. Traveler?" King Aereth asked.

"They were King Oughtred's war wizards, the ones who survived. What my dog and I had destroyed before were the armies. These were the general and the leadership. They were the ones responsible for all the dark deeds against us from the time we left Titan's Bridge."

"The death spell?" Gwyness asked.

"Yes," Traveler said. "And the spell-talker and all the rest. We were in King Oughtred's dark shadow of treachery, but it was his war wizards that were the instruments of his vengeance."

"These war wizards were powerful," Dr'amal, the drow sorceress, said from among them, though none could have said where she came from. "They were far more powerful than any of us in this camp." Dr'amal looked at Traveler directly. "They would have been far more powerful than you, but you live, and I know you killed them. How? What magical trick did you employ against them?"

"They are dead. That is all that matters."

"You will not share how, Master Traveler?" Dr'amal pressed. "Not that I or any of us wished for any other outcome."

"Others more powerful than them destroyed them."

Traveler realized that every human and fae had encircled him or were watching and listening closely. Even the väki, brownies, and darklings had joined.

"Mr. Traveler," Lady Aylen said. "How? Who? If we have secret magic allies who can vanquish powerful dark wizards, then we must know."

"They are not allies—not ours or anyone else's. The war wizards are now solid stone. Their leader is cursed with a fate worst than the death he planned for this entire caravan, human and fae alike."

"Stone?" Quillen asked.

"Yes, Mr. Quillen. A creature that should never be an addition to your magical book of fantastic beasts and races, as you will never be able to look upon them. They are gorgons. That is why neither I nor Mr. Pangolin, the Cut-Throats, or their animals could have seen what was done. We would have been permanent residents of the dead forest of Necropolis."

"If the portal took you there, then you too must be looked after," Mossberry, the Tree Shepherd leader, said. "You must be magically cleansed as a precaution. It is a land of such dark magic that you could be ill-affected and not know it."

"Yes," Traveler acknowledged.

"Your animal companion too," Mossberry added. "I sense him with you."

"He was encased in a magical sphere again by the wizards. Last time he was in shock. This time he is angry. I need to keep him away from everyone and calm. I will coax him out of his hiding place in the days ahead."

"I have observed your dog eats what you eat, so the magic medicine we concoct for you, will be for his consumption too," Mossberry said.

"Thank you."

"Had you been there before?" Bragg, the dwelf, asked Traveler.

"I have. Why?"

"I have as well. I was fortunate not to encounter a gorgon. I was not fortunate to escape their followers."

"If you are here with us, Mr. Bragg, then you did escape the gorgon's followers and servant creatures."

Everyone watched Traveler turn and walk out, past the perimeter, to the fallen goblins.

"What is he doing?" the drows and elves asked.

The leadership looked at each other, not knowing what to say or do.

"Mr. Traveler surely knows the way of things," King Aereth said.

Humans and fae watched their caravan master closely as he drew his magic sword and walked among the goblins still alive on the battlefield. He stopped at one goblin, and after a few moments, the goblin yelled at Traveler, but the caravan master remained still. In a shocking move, the same goblin drew a dagger and slit his own throat. Traveler simply walked past him to another severely wounded goblin.

"What is he doing, this Mr. Traveler?" one of the male fae-bloods asked. He stood with his other comrades. "If he is not going to aid them and not going kill them, then what?"

"He is doing what we should have done," Pangolin said, then punched I-wulf in his shoulder.

"What was that for?"

"Mr. Traveler is gathering information," Pangolin said.

The mood lightened among the particularly anti-goblin fae members.

"But they will not tell him anything," a drow said.

"Let us see," King Aereth said.

Traveler had to use his sword only once. A goblin tried to stab the caravan master in the back as he turned to move to another goblin. Traveler had suspected it and killed the goblin with a simple backward thrust through the goblin's chest.

Moments later, the whole camp watching, Traveler returned.

"I am surprised," Traveler said to the drows.

"Why is that?" Dr'as said.

"I did the work that drows normally have an aptitude for—gathering information, uncovering secrets."

"Is that so, Master Traveler? What drows have you encountered before us?"

"Many. The drows I encountered were thieves and bandits, and were better at gathering information through stealth—not magic—than any human or fae."

"My clan are not thieves and bandits. We are nobles."

"So were they," Traveler said with a grin.

Dr'as managed a smile back. "Though my clan concerns itself with magic, not thievery, we too are accomplished in the art of knowing and learning things. However, the real reason for our reticence is the elves. Since our elfin comrades here already regard drows as being in league with goblins, we were not about to raise any suspicions by leaving the circle and approaching fallen goblins after battle."

"Wise, but no matter. I learned what I wanted to know."

"Which is what, Mr. Traveler?"

"It is what I suspected. There are more goblins out there."

"They told you that?" an elfin knight ask.

"No, they did not. I gleaned it from what they did not say and what they tried to hide. Zem, the goblin king, traveled with his own caravan, a full goblin army, and then there was the gnoll army. The two armies have been dealt with. Where is the goblin caravan?"

Sounds of exasperation erupted from the fae especially. The Cut-Throats shook their heads and looked at each other. The elfin knights groaned.

"More?" I-wulf asked.

"Does this change our plans?" Pangolin asked.

"Not at all, Mr. Pangolin. It changes nothing. We know they are out there. But we know there are many things out there. We carry on."

"Good," their master-at-arms said with satisfaction.

"But we do not know what others may be in this goblin caravan, including if there are any other wizards among them," a high-elf knight said.

"Are you concerned?" Traveler asked. "You can return to Magica if you like."

Bragg the dwelf laughed. The elfin knights looked at him contemptuously.

The same high elf looked at Traveler. "We are unconcerned."

"Good," Traveler said. He looked at Hobbs and smiled. "Mr. Hobbs, make the preparations with the men. We set out for Titan's Arch tomorrow morning. We shall be at the edge of the Great Forest soon after."

The nightly leadership meeting was postponed for the day. Hobbs made his rounds, and I-wulf took over the duties of the sleeping Pangolin. Quillen spent the rest of the day and into the night questioning fae about gorgons for the notes in his book. He found very few fae interested in talking about them.

"You should not inquire about them," a brownie told him. "Speaking about them may draw them to you." The brownies were making their own rounds through the camp to ensure it was tidy.

"What?" Quillen had a look of fear as he followed after them. "How? Their lands are far, far away from here."

"I would be careful if I were you," the brownies said.

"And they have their dark servants too," another brownie said.

"What dark servants?"

"They are humanlike. They are cannibals and more."

"Cannibals?"

"They have the phagia. They eat skin, bone, sand, soil, stone, everything."

A look of disgust came over the lad's face.

"They walk about with empty eye sockets," the other brownie said to him.

"What? How can they see, then?"

"Magic, of course. They see and hear through magic. Maybe they hear you speaking even now."

Quillen lost all interest in gorgons after that. He returned to his campfire. When out of earshot, the brownies began to laugh.

◆◆◆

Instead of the men settling in for a quiet sleep, everyone was roused. The gossip of the day had been consumed with war wizards, goblins, and gorgons. The sight of swarms of squeaking bats across the night sky with a large full moon unnerved everyone.

The women—Lady Aylen, Gwyness, and the female half-elves—stood at their tent. Gwyness gave Lady Aylen a look.

"It is not what you think," Lady Aylen said to Gwyness.

"There are no striga or strigoi here," one of the female half-elves said. "This is still elfin land."

"We do not know these terms," Lady Aylen said. "Strigoi is what we humans—" The princess stopped and smiled.

The female half-elves smiled too. "We know what you mean, m'lady."

"Strigoi is what we call vampires," Lady Aylen continued.

"Yes, and striga is the term for evil spirits, witches, female vampires."

"The same term for all three?" Gwyness asked.

"Sometimes, they can be all three, maiden."

"I hate bats," Lady Aylen said as they continued to watch the moonlit skies as bat swarms continued across. "So many of them. None of the men will be able to sleep tonight."

"None of us either," Gwyness added.

The bat swarm migration lasted well over an hour, and the men did very little sleeping but plenty of conversing. However, Hobbs had forced himself to sleep and rose to get the entire caravan to march.

King Aereth waited in the leadership tent. Nirgund led both Traveler and Pangolin inside. Lady Aylen and Gwyness walked in afterward.

"Is it a secret meeting, sire?" the princess asked.

"I will see to the kirins, sire," Nirgund said.

"Thank you, Mr. Nirgund." King Aereth's guardsman left the tent. "Not at all, Lady Aylen. Please stay," King Aereth said. "You as well, Maiden Gwyness."

"Well, sire, what have we been summoned for?" Traveler playfully asked.

"Mr. Traveler, none here are ones to criticize, but your actions yesterday were incredibly reckless and irresponsible. So were yours, Mr. Pangolin, though that is more in keeping with your nature. Gentlemen, none of us can take such chances in the future. I do not simply refer to the fact that you, Mr. Traveler, are our sole guide to Atlantea. The loss of either of you would be a potentially fatal blow to this caravan. As Mr. Hobbs often says, we must think of the men. That means ensuring that our most important members are not killed needlessly."

"Sire, I agree," Traveler said.

"So easily, Mr. Traveler?" Lady Aylen asked. "No excuses or rebuttals."

"No, princess. The king is correct. I was reckless, and my recklessness led to Mr. Pangolin's. I had no idea where the goblin was going."

"But you suspected he might lead you to others," King Aereth said.

"I did. I saw it as a chance to rid ourselves of Oughtred's shadow. It was a dangerous gamble."

"It was successful," Lady Aylen said.

"But it could have easily gone the other way, which is the king's point. This high goblin and his elfin conspirators were killed or captured. His goblin army was being defeated by us. When I went through that portal, I expected to see his goblin caravan. Instead, he took us straight to his war wizard conspirators—Oughtred's most powerful wizards and the most powerful in these magical lands. The portal was also far more powerful than I imagined, if it could take us to Necropolis."

"You had your own magical portal," King Aereth said, "though a very dangerous one indeed."

"Once I learned that King Oughtred was still alive, I had to take precautions, sire. King Oughtred the All-Knowing. That name took on new meaning knowing his war wizards were also necromancers, and that he had become a human of undead magic. I obtained a magical charm, an orb around my neck. Two magic spells. If the orb was ever destroyed, one spell to transport a gorgon to the place of the orb's destruction. Another spell to transport the orb's destroyer to the home of the gorgon."

"Mr. Traveler, what if the necromancer had not killed the gorgon. What if it survived? What if it killed you?" Gwyness asked.

"I can defeat gorgons," Traveler said, "because I do not need to see to fight when I wield my sword. But your questions are sound. It was extremely risky. It was done to rid us of Oughtred's pursuits for good."

"Where did you get this orb from?" Pangolin asked.

"There are places where such things can be obtained for the right amount of money if you know where to go and who to see. Someone owed me a favor. I will leave it at that."

"Mr. Traveler, you must agree not to do such a thing again. You have been lucky on this journey so far, lucky for all of us. My experience has been no man can tempt their luck for too long without fatal consequences in the end."

"That has been my experience too, sire."

"I have a suggestion, sire," Pangolin said. "If Mr. Traveler is reckless again, I promise to be the adult. If the reverse, Mr. Traveler will rein me in."

"Neither of you can risk your lives, but I suppose that is the best that can be agreed on such a journey fraught with risk and dangers," King Aereth said. "Mr. Traveler, I feel we are reaching a significant milestone on our journey."

"We are, sire. To this point, we have divided up our journey by the lands we crossed. Lands of Man. The lands of the fairies, sprites, centaurs, elves. However, the most significance of those divisions is upon us. We cross from civilization into the true wild. We began at Caravan Row in the Lands of Man. Fae'el in the lands of the elves will be our last hamlet, town, city, or vast kingdom for many, many months."

"No other places of fae, Mr. Traveler?" Gwyness asked with a look of worry.

"None, Maiden Gwyness. Once we pass beyond Titan's Arch, we leave behind the third marker of Titan's Trail."

"Seven markers?" King Aereth asked.

"Yes, sire. No civilization until the last one before Atlantea."

"Will we encounter any fae?" Pangolin asked.

"We most likely will," Traveler replied. "And do not forget the goblin caravan."

"I will never forget that," Pangolin said.

"Are we well supplied for the journey, Mr. Traveler?" Lady Aylen asked.

"Thanks to the mission led by Mr. Pangolin and his party, all our water reserves have been restored and greatly increased."

"I still do not know where you sent him, Mr. Traveler," Lady Aylen said.

"Princess, there are places where such things can be obtained with the right amount of money and knowledge," Pangolin said with a grin.

"Sire, I do not wish to make light of your concerns," Traveler said. "We are all in agreement. We were fortunate yesterday, and that is not lost on us. However, Titan's Caravan will get to Atlantea and under my guidance."

Titan's Caravan marched promptly at dawn.

The night before, the men's conversations had focused on the battle with the goblin army, watching the destruction of the gnoll army, and the demise of the war wizards. They were about to leave all civilization behind them, both human and fae. Many of the humans noted that even the elfin knights were uneasy at the next long and dangerous leg of their Titan's Trail trek.

There was unease, even fear, but also exhilaration. For most, they had reached a point on the Trail that no one dreamed was possible. Some felt as if they were still dreaming. It was, after all, the lands of magic.

Hobbs had the men ready to march hours before dawn with the efficiency and grace which he always conducted himself. The steward had also gained the respect of all the fae. Everyone was in their place, standing in formation, when the leadership and vanguard moved to the front to lead the caravan.

Pangolin led the vanguard, as always. However, all six Antaean giants, not just four, joined him and two hundred of the deer-like, antlered elaphine archer-warriors. The archers were each equipped with an array of magical arrows in their quivers. Elman, the half-elf, walked along Pangolin's side. The last of them, and new to the vanguard were the fifteen male fae-bloods—the wolf clan—dressed in black attire and cloaks, ever watching with their wolf-like, yellow-tinted brown eyes.

A few yards back, Traveler led the front of the columns. When the dog appeared at dawn to join his master, they all saw for themselves what Traveler had meant. The dog was indeed angry at having faced entrapment in a magic sphere for a second time at the hands of the war wizards. Over the months, the shape-shifter had become more receptive to most of the men and even friendly to Hobbs, but today it wanted nothing to do with anyone except Traveler. It growled ferociously more than once at anyone who got too close, even the king.

"His mood will soften, sire," Traveler said. "Pay him no mind."

King Aereth, Lady Aylen, and Maiden Gwyness followed the caravan master. Nirgund and his reptilian alphyns followed behind the king; the armored female half-elves followed behind the women. The kirins did not join them, instead remaining in their pocket-realm.

Traveler told them that the dragon steeds would emerge once they crossed into the Great Forest.

Hobbs and his two guardsmen, Tyfer and Oeric, followed. After them walked the Brothers Brimm, the caravan's five musicians, and the dozen men who were the caravan's flag bearers. They bore no standards this day but would in the future. Dr'amal the drow sorceress, walked near them but apart.

On either flank were the giant fae lizards—blue, yellow, green, orange—with their lizard minders. The inside columns were the five hundred pech who pulled the carts and wagons. Then marched one of the crawling trees with the fairy sisters and their swarms in its branches and leaves. Around the base of the tree were all the other hoofed fae—more elaphine (two hundred fifty), the two hundred cervids, and the two hundred fifty rusines.

Behind them were the three hundred domestics and laborers. Estus led the next group: all the warriors of the heavy-weapons teams—one thousand men in four columns. If there was an attack, the pech ahead would set up the catapults and operate them. Behind them marched the seven hundred fifty men Estus commanded, who would go where needed, using their individual magic weapons to protect rather than fight. Gresham stationed himself with this group, along with the fae human mercenaries who were well enough to march.

I-wulf and his two thousand Cut-Throats clad in goblin armor followed. Four hundred Cut-Throats managed the group's one hundred eagle-hound chamroshes hopping and running at their masters' sides. The second crawling tree followed behind them.

The nearly one hundred drows led by Dr'as was the next major group. All the fae parties marched after them: the several dozen fae berserkers led by the lion-like Hax, the one hundred gnomes, the four hundred fauns led by the ram-horned Ammon, the three hundred rustic woodland elves led by Ethor, the fifty other gnomes and horned gnomoids, the nearly seven hundred humanoid animal men—frog men, lizard men, squirrel men, raccoon men, possum men, fox men, rabbit men, bird men, mouse men, one mole man— with their animals: giant crabs, giant turtles, giant porcupines, giant ducks and cranes, giant moose, jackalopes, and enfields.

Then there was Bragg the dwelf, his golem Glog at his side, followed by his five hundred-man party of mountain elves, forest elves, and wild elves. Several dozen managed their Diomedian Mares.

The rearguard of the caravan were the Elfin Questing Knights. One hundred fifty high elves with unicorn swords, one hundred fifty desert elf falconers with their magic birds, and one hundred fifty woodland elves with their leopard axexs. Like the brownies and darklings, the one hundred fifty moon elves slept in one of the caravan's pocket-realms until night watch.

The eighteen male half-elves moved freely throughout the caravan. The four Tree Shepherds would appear and disappear in any one of the crawling trees. Also not visible was the man called Frog-Dor.

Where was Quillen? He was supposed to walk with Hobbs, but he was near the rear of the caravan marching with Bragg.

"I have heard about you," Bragg said to the lad.

"You have?" Quillen asked.

"Yes, and I don't want to be in your magic book of fantastic beasts and races."

"But a dwelf. Why haven't humans heard of your kind before?"

"Human lad, you have to understand that humans will never know most of the races of fae. You have only encountered a very tiny number of all that exist. That will never change. You will never see us all."

"Why?"

"We remain apart from outsiders. Not just humans, all fae not our own."

"That is sad. Dwelves are half-elf, half-dwarf."

"Certainly not! We are not half-elves or half-anything. We are not dwarves. We are not elves. We are a unique race."

"Do their peoples descend from yours?"

"Maybe. Giants did descend from fairies."

"I heard that, but I don't believe it."

"It is true. But for dwarves and elves, if their races did descend from mine it was so long ago that there is no one who could say for sure anymore. My race has had very little contact with theirs."

"You do now." Quillen glanced back at his elfin comrades.

"I am unique among my kind. I am like your Mr. Traveler. I have traveled beyond my lands to form what I thought was an impressive caravan—until I learned about Titan's Caravan."

"This *is* an impressive caravan. But back to you."

Bragg laughed. "No! I will not be in your book. And I don't want you to draw me."

"But I'm a good artist. I will show you."

Quillen pulled out his magic book from the satchel on his side and randomly opened it to a page. The page was of the manticore. The lad's face darkened, and he quickly turned the page to a drawing of the other fae in the camp.

"You opened up your magic book to the very creature I have hunted for a living," Bragg said. "Some would say that was a bad omen."

◆ ◆ ◆

Traveler summoned the Brothers Brimm to the front of the columns with a gesture of his arm.

"Do you have your new instruments?" Traveler asked them.

"Yes, sir," they said.

"I want one of you here and the rest of you to equally space yourselves out to the end of the caravan. Keep your eyes and ears alert.

If you hear the sounds of any kind of bird, whether you see it our not, start playing and don't stop until either Mr. Hobbs or I tell you."

"But, sir," one of the musicians began, "we played these pan flutes, and they make no sound."

"They do make sound. We humans simply cannot hear them. Go to your places, men."

A member of the Brothers Brimm walked alongside Traveler, but when the dog bared his teeth at him, the musician moved to the other side.

"Pay no attention to him," Traveler told him. "Keep your eyes ahead and listen."

"What is happening, Mr. Traveler?" Lady Aylen asked.

"Princess, today the caravan's musicians will be its defenders."

The royals looked at the instrument in the musician's hands. The pan flute looked to be made of pure gold and had an airy glow around it.

"It is magic, then?" Lady Aylen asked.

"It is, princess."

"When will we reach this Titan's Arch, the landmark we have heard so much about?"

Traveler looked back at her. "Princess, we already have. Look up."

The caravan had been marching for a few hours. The lands surrounding Fae'el were bleak enough though the earth was soil. Plant life could grow there but did not. The farther they moved from Fae'el the more the soil became barren rock. The men thought to themselves, *At least there isn't bottomless chasms on either side of our path.*

The day sky had darkened despite nightfall being many hours away. The phenomena was unlike any they had seen before—the sky above them was a clear night with a myriad of colored stars in the distance. The humans could not see the spectacle through the cloud cover, but the fae could. Lady Aylen was a full elf, so when she looked up, there it was—Titan's Arch.

"How did I not see it before?" she asked.

"Because you did the same thing the men were doing, princess. You assumed what Titan's Arch looked like rather than simply seeing what is around you," the caravan master replied.

King Aereth and everyone else looked up too, except for the fae around them.

"I do not understand," the king said. "I see nothing."

"Sire, we are already under Titan's Arch," Lady Aylen said, looking up at the sky.

"I do not see anything," Nirgund said to himself. "There are just clouds."

The female half-elves giggled amongst themselves.

Gwyness looked at them. "Well, show us where. We do not see them."

"Titan's Arch is not under the clouds," one of the female half-elves said. "Titan's Arch is above them. The clouds are not real clouds."

"Shall we stop?" Traveler asked.

King Aereth looked at him with a grin. "Can we, Mr. Traveler? It would not be dignified if we walked into the person in front of us."

Traveler gave the signal for the vanguard to stop. An elaphine was always looking back to them. One of them called out to Pangolin, and the master-at-arms gave the signal for the vanguard to stop too. Pangolin walked back to them.

Every human looked up at the sky, but no one could see it.

"Where, princess?" Gwyness asked.

"There! See the outline," Lady Aylen said, pointing.

"We do not see anything. Clouds and blue sky. Nothing else. Wait. What's that?"

"Stare at it awhile, Gwyness. You see it?"

"I see a line."

"Where?" Quillen called out. "A line? Oh, I see it!"

Giants, elves, drows, and other fae laughed amongst themselves, watching the humans stare up at the sky.

"Blind, I say," one of the pech remarked.

"Mr. Traveler, we are under Titan's Arch now?" Pangolin asked.

"Mr. Pangolin, we've been under Titan's Arch for the last hour. We are coming out from under it. Think of the size of Titan's Bridge. Then imagine it as an arch and hundreds of feet in the sky above us."

"It is astonishing," King Aereth said. "How can such a massive structure stand?"

"It has been standing for eons, sire," Traveler answered. "Just as Titan's Bridge has and all the structures of Titan's Trail."

"What was it we heard of harpies, Mr. Traveler?" Lady Aylen asked. "One of the fae said the arch was infested with them. Harpies would perch themselves on a structure so far up?"

"Many ages ago, princess, one of the fae races that worshiped Titan's Arch made their own monuments to honor it. It is believed that they viewed the Arch as their god. Those monuments are ahead of us—a series of giant arches. This valley path funnels down into them. The people who made them are long gone, but their monuments have been home to harpies ever since then."

"Why is that, Mr. Traveler?" Nirgund asked him.

"Parties must pass under Titan's Arch to continue on the Trail."

"What if one were to take another way, bypassing Titan's Arch?" Pangolin asked.

"Think of the path through Titan's Arch as no different than crossing Titan's Bridge. Stepping off the Bridge means stepping off the side into its near-bottomless chasm. Bypassing Titan's Arch means the end of one's journey forward. There is a magical barrier that prevents crossing. One can see the Great Forest but cannot cross the barrier to it. Then there are the creatures.

"It is the reason that the harpies have remained here and prospered for so long. They have an endless food source. They devour the creatures that attempt to travel the path under Titan's Arch to get to the Great Forest. The creatures never stop coming. No need to ask me what the creatures are. You would get a different answer depending on what fae you asked. It is why fae-kind leave the harpies be. Strangely, the harpies protect this part of the Trail from the creatures, but from all others too."

"The creatures are giant insect-mammal hybrids," Dr'amal said, "larger than horses. They travel in large packs."

"Have you seen them?" Gwyness asked the drowess.

"My people have, but we must not confront them. Their bodies are also poisonous to all magic."

"We should continue on," Traveler instructed.

"How many harpies will we encounter?" Pangolin asked.

"Druil the high-elf wizard was not exaggerating. The arches are infested with them. But, have no fear. We have the most effective weapon against them," Traveler said then patted the lone Brothers Brimm musician on the back.

Again, they witnessed the change of the skies above them. Gone was the clear night sky in the middle of the day as it faded to a more normal bluish sky. Stars above were obscured, and the clear view of the true Titan's Arch disappeared. Ahead, one could have easily mistaken the series of giant arches for the landmark along Titan's Trail, if one did not know of or see the true Titan's Arch above. The Harpy Arches was what they were colloquially known as by many fae. They were not titanic, but at fifty feet high, they towered nonetheless. The path wound underneath each pockmarked, vine-covered, and cracked arch. The monuments that stood before were a dim reminder of their past splendor.

However, neither human nor fae paid any attention to the ancient arches as they neared them. Lining the top of each arch, spaced some fifty feet after one another over the path, moved black things in a collective fit of yells, caws, and clicking sounds.

Johnter was the Brothers Brimm musician who nervously walked with the vanguard. He played the golden magical pan flute with vigor but heard barely a whisper. Pangolin walked along unaffected too. However, all the fae of the vanguard winced, especially the elaphine archer-warriors and Mr. Elman.

From their position, the guardsmen Tyfer and Oeric handed Hobbs and Quillen a javelin each.

"Both of you can manage with these," Tyfer said.

"Such a small weapon, Mr. Tyfer?" Hobbs asked, looking at it.

"Mr. Hobbs, it is best you do not carry a full spear. The beasts could grab it from your hands with ease and stab you to death with it. A javelin is not so easy for their claws to grasp but solid enough for you to do your own bit of stabbing."

"Mr. Tyfer, you do not think the harpies will get that close, do you?" Quillen asked uneasily.

"Lad, I do not know. Hopefully, Mr. Traveler's plan works."

The caravan neared the first arch on the path. Suddenly, dozens—hundreds—of harpies took to the air, startling many in the caravan. Some of the caravan stopped.

"Keep moving," Traveler yelled as he looked back and gestured forward.

Hobbs watched to ensure the caravan moved forward, but he saw the look of fear in the men's faces. The steward looked up. The frenzied beasts circled them, flapping their wings wildly, both yelling like people and cawing like crows. Hobbs had to fight his own fear as some of the harpies in the flock flew closer. The harpies were much larger than the humans had thought. Fables always spoke of them as the size of a large bird, but these were the size of a full human. They were humanoid females from the waist up—matted hair, gaunt facial features, black eyes, and jagged teeth—and the legs of a bird below, with fearsome talons. Their arms were the wings of a large bird, and their human halves were covered in hair and feathers. The harpies circled them in an agitated state but did not attack.

The caravan moved to the second arch and its harpies joined the flock already in the air from the first.

"Mr. Hobbs," Traveler said when he turned.

"Yes, sir?"

"Go among the men and keep them moving and calm. Inform them that the magic flutes the Brothers Brimm play are enshrouding us in an invisible magic barrier that should keep the harpies at bay. The sky will go dark with their numbers, but we will make it through."

"Yes, sir. I will reassure them."

Hobbs moved with Tyfer at his side.

"Will this invisible barrier truly protect us from these harpies, Mr. Traveler?" Lady Aylen asked. "Or is that the hope?"

"It is the plan, princess."

"How many of these arches are there, Mr. Traveler?" King Aereth asked.

"Fifty, sire."

The royals gave him a second look.

"We will make it," Traveler said with confidence.

When they reached the fifth arch, the sky was indeed black with harpies hovering and circling above them. Their sounds also grew in intensity.

"Master Traveler," Dr'amal said, appearing as if from nowhere as always. "Should we not do something? If I were to throw a dagger spell at them—"

"You would shatter the barrier and enrage the harpies. No. Let the musicians concentrate and play their magic pan flutes. We must march without losing our nerve. Ignore the harpies. Put it in your mind that they cannot breach the barrier. We're past the fifth arch. Only forty-five to go."

"If I could make a suggestion, Mr. Traveler," Nirgund said.

"Please do, Mr. Nirgund."

"On many a dangerous trek, my warriors and I would…sing."

"Berserkers can sing?" Gwyness asked. Lady Aylen laughed.

"Ah, the singing game," King Aereth said, smiling. "Great suggestion, Mr. Nirgund. Would our singing weaken the magic of the flutes, Mr. Traveler?"

"Not at all, sire."

"What do you suggest we sing, Mr. Nirgund?"

"Well, sire, we had some very gruesome songs we sang that would not be appropriate for womenfolk or the lads."

"Thank you, Mr. Nirgund. I have very sensitive ears nowadays," Lady Aylen said.

"I am not a lad," Quillen protested. "I am a man!"

"You are a lad, Mr. Quillen," Nirgund said to him. "But do not worry. Before you know it, you will have your wish."

"Mr. Nirgund, let us make it simple so all the men can follow along. 'Forty-five Arches to Go' will be the song," Traveler said.

"Yes, sir!" Nirgund said, smiling. "I will lead it and add my own flair."

Men watched the light-hearted exchange of the leadership. How could they be so calm when above them dark flying creatures grew in number and their collective frenzy intensified?

"Forty more arches to go, our caravan marches to know..."

Nirgund led the caravan's singing with zest doing his best to keep their eyes on his performance and not on the skies above them. The harpies screamed as loud as they could, but then the men sang even louder to drown out their sounds. It became a strange competition, and Nirgund found that he was joined by dozens of the darklings, who had taken the form of smiling balls of fur with slender arms and legs to dance around him. The brownies also emerged to lend their voices to the cause. The participation of both human and fae made the Brothers Brimm musicians more confident and encouraged them to play with more vigor.

Twenty three more arches to go, Titan's Caravan marches fro.

No harpies or hags, goblins or bats, shadows or ghosts, wizards or rats

Will stop our path, frighten our wrath, sully our bath, only make us laugh

We cross the Trail below, on our fabled quest to riches so.

The sky was so thick with harpies that the creatures were crashing into each other. They did not scream anymore but cawed like birds then made their collective clicking sounds.

"What are they doing, Mr. Traveler?" Lady Aylen asked. "What do the clicking sounds mean?"

"It means they are growing frustrated and tired, princess. None of us will become their food today."

The harpy sounds stopped. Not only did the harpies circling them fly away but all the harpies perched on the arches ahead of them began to take flight. Men cheered as the flying creatures disappeared into the distance. The musicians continued to play the pan flutes, but all the arches were without a single harpy.

When they passed beneath the final harpies' arch, even Pangolin managed a smile as he looked back at the front column to Traveler.

"Your plan worked, Mr. Traveler," Lady Aylen said as she admired the caravan master.

"I have been known to have a few good plans, princess." He looked ahead at the horizon. "The Great Forest awaits us."

CHAPTER NINETEEN
Snail Run

"Can we make the Great Forest before night fall?" King Aereth asked.

"We can, sire," Traveler answered. "We travel beyond these rock plains. Then, we enter the lands of the Great Forest and can make camp there."

The caravan had been marching for a couple of hours when Mr. Elman raised his hand to signal the front columns. Traveler and the dog moved to them. Suddenly, the caravan master bolted ahead. The dog transformed its legs into those of a panther. Traveler jumped on the dog's back, and both man and beast galloped off.

Pangolin gave the signal as the vanguard stopped. King Aereth gave the signal for the rest of the caravan to halt.

"Can you see anything ahead, princess?"

Lady Aylen squinted. "No, sire. I see Mr. Traveler. He has stopped, but I do not see what he is looking at."

"Is his weapon drawn, m'lady?" Gwyness asked.

"No, but his dog is an able weapon himself. Wait. Mr. Traveler is gesturing."

They watched as Pangolin, Elman, and several of the elaphine archer-warriors ran ahead of the vanguard to their caravan master and his dog. Most of the front of the caravan stepped forward to join the rest of the vanguard.

"I hope we do not have to engage in another battle so soon," Nirgund said aloud.

"Look." One of the female half-elves pointed ahead.

Traveler and Pangolin walked casually back with the archer-warriors. Mr. Elman and the dog, now in its normal form, followed in the rear.

"What is it, Mr. Traveler?" the king asked when the men reached them.

"No danger, sire. I have both good news and not so good news."

"Please, Mr. Traveler, give us the bad news at once," Lady Aylen said.

Traveler grinned. "How did I know you would say that, princess? The bad news is not so bad. We will have to make camp here for an extended period of time."

"Extended period? How long, Mr. Traveler? Why?"

"Because we have the misfortune, or fortune depending on your point of view, of being cut off by a snail run. My personal view is that it's a good sign, and its sight will be a treat for the men."

Traveler stepped to their steward. "Mr. Hobbs, there is a slight dip in the land ahead. Set up camp all along it. The snail run is already passing."

"Yes, sir. I will see to it," Hobbs said to Traveler.

"What is this snail run, Mr. Traveler? Mr. Pangolin?" Lady Aylen asked.

The men laughed.

"Snails, princess," Traveler answered. "A fairy caravan of giant snails."

"Another caravan?" Lady Aylen asked.

"We may be moving beyond fae civilization, but that does not mean there is no one else out here. Caravans are the normal way of travel in any remote land—human or fae."

"Mr. Traveler, I thought we were beyond the lands of the fairies," Quillen said.

"We are Mr. Quillen, but fairies travel outside their lands, too, and these are insect fairies. Get your magic book. You shall have plenty to sketch today."

Quillen's face lit up with a smile.

The land beneath their feet had changed from hard gray rock to rocky soil, then to the richest soft soil that many had ever seen. Tyfer had been a farmer's son in his youth and knelt to grab some of it in his hands.

"I have never seen soil so full of vitality to the touch," he said to Oeric. "There isn't anything that could not grow in it, and anything that did would be of the largest and strongest specimens that you ever did see."

"Well, we are about to cross into the Great Forest," Oeric said.

"And we are about to see giant snails," Hobbs added.

Their steward had the men set up the full camp in moments. Nearly ten thousand lined the transition in the land from the old to the new region of the Great Forest. The forest was days away, but they could see it in the distance. More was visible to the normal human eye because the land seemed to curve upwards. For a moment, there was temporary panic as they could also see something flying in the sky that could only be a roc, but the fae reassured the humans that they could see it but not the reverse. Even if it could see them, they were nothing more than ants to it and not worth the day's flight to attack them.

Traveler and the Tree Shepherds were the only ones in the Caravan, who had seen a Snail Run before. It was a caravan of giant snails with luminescent shells twenty feet in diameter, carrying fairies unlike any they had ever seen. Though the skin of the snails glistened with a coat of transparent slime, the beasts still looked majestic with their fleshy, pulsating antennae that had eye-like bulbs at the end. The fairies they carried, some with a few, others with dozens and dozens, looked like snails themselves. They were humanoids clad in insect-exoskeleton-like armor, and their eyes were in their antennae.

The fairy sisters could not resist. They flew over to gossip with the new fairies. Both races were equally fascinated with one another. It was clear to the caravan that the fairy sisters would literally talk with every one of the snail-like fairies they could.

It was also clear why Traveler had them set up camp. There was no way for them to pass. The fairy caravan was a moving sea of hundreds of thousands.

"Probably millions of fairies," Traveler told the leadership.

"That many, Mr. Traveler?" Lady Aylen asked.

"Where are they going?" King Aereth asked.

"These fairies are called lymnaeans. They make their annual pilgrimage from their lands in the east to the fairy queendoms in the west."

"Queendoms?" Lady Aylen asked. "I like that word."

"Do not get carried away, princess. Only queens rule in fairydom, so kingdom is a word that would not make any sense."

"But why, Mr. Traveler?" King Aereth asked. "This annual pilgrimage."

Traveler looked around at the men who watched the passing fairy caravan. The Tree Shepherd Mossberry walked to them.

"Mossberry," Traveler began. "My colleagues have asked me about the lymnaean annual pilgrimage. My understanding that it is a rite of passage for its youth into adulthood. For the adults, it is about the great trade between their western and eastern regions."

The leshy gave a bellowing laugh. "Yes, Master Traveler, that would be one way to describe it. It is for males and females of the west seeking mates being brought to the east. The next year, the reverse happens. Do you not have the words in humankind?"

"Yes, Mossberry," Traveler said. "But we cannot say those words now. We have youth present who are not yet ready to hear such words."

"I heard that!" Quillen said, not looking up from sketching in his magic book. "I know exactly what you are talking about and I know all the words."

"Good, Mr. Quillen. You do not need to tell us then."

"I like these fairies," Nirgund said.

"Do not get any ideas, Mr. Nirgund, about joining one of these fairy caravans," Traveler said. "I recently had such a conversation with a fairy already, actually our fairy sisters' mother. Even a berserker like you could not handle a fairy."

"I don't know, Mr. Traveler," Nirgund said, smiling. "Ladies have never complained before."

"Mr. Nirgund, fairies have thousands of children in their lifetime, by different male fairies—not only because they are a polygamous race, but because no male fairy can handle them. If a male fairy cannot, what would you do—human male?"

"Thousands?"

Those in earshot began laughing.

"The smallest, weakest, slowest fairy would leave you dead in the bed, Mr. Nirgund."

Quillen burst out laughing, and everyone else laughed louder.

"Mr. Quillen, do not listen to the adults talking," Hobbs scolded.

Nirgund had a sick look on his face. "So, Mr. Traveler, no human-fairy sex, then?"

Pangolin dropped to the ground in laughter.

◆ ◆ ◆

A contingent of the lymnaean fairies visited Titan's Caravan. The leadership greeted several dozen of them, joined by the Tree Shepherds and several of the elfin questing knights.

"We are honored," Mossberry greeted.

Even close and within their camp, it was not clear to the humans if the fairies were male or female. They were given a tour of the caravan as they feverishly chatted amongst themselves in another language.

"They are very impressed with us," Mossberry informed the receiving group of humans and elves. "They have never seen such a group of so many different fae and humans together. They are very taken with our two fairy members too. They plan to seek an official trade agreement with their queendoms."

"Very good, Mr. Mossberry," King Aereth said. "Titan's Caravan bringing alliances together."

"How long is their journey?" Traveler asked.

"They have been traveling two months, and it will take another to arrive at their destination. Though they ride giant snails, the animals are magically capable of moving across water and gliding through the sky," Mossberry told them.

"Have they encountered any unusual dangers?" Pangolin asked.

"Nothing unusual. Their people have been making this same journey every year for thousands of years. The path is well protected, and even the lands, with their small animals, insects, and plants, welcome and expect their movement every year."

"Any rumors of things they have heard in their recent travels?" Traveler asked.

"There the answer may be of interest to us," Mossberry replied. He looked at Lady Aylen. "It concerns you and your maiden, but we can speak of it after we have entertained our lymnaean guests."

Lady Aylen and Gwyness looked at each other.

As dusk arrived, enraptured humans and fae of the caravan watched the passing lymnaean caravan. The giant snails did not leave a trail of mere slime as their tiny counterparts in the Lands of Man did but a glowing path of light. The lymnaeans that visited their caravan had rejoined the Snail Run. The men were told that it would not be until midday of the day after next that the last of the giant snails and snail fairies would pass beyond their view.

Hobbs had relaxed the night duties to allow the men to watch the fairy caravan in their small camps along the line. However, the leadership gathered for a last meeting in the outer edges of the land of elves before stepping across to the official region of the Great Forest.

Quillen had been excused to continue his book chronicling while he sat with the men. Everyone else was present with two additions.

"Please, Mossberry, do tell," Traveler said, seated on a stool.

The royals and Gwnyness were seated on one side, the king and Nirgund on the other. Pangolin, I-wulf, Estus, and Gresham sat on stools across from them to form a circle around the standing Tree Shepherd. Hobbs stood at the entrance, watching. The other guest was the dwelf, Bragg, who also stood with Hobbs at the entrance.

"The lymnaean fairies encountered other fairies—the name of their queendom is unpronounceable to humans—but these fairies had news regarding the last elfin princess of the lost water-elfin kingdom of Faylen and its academy of battle clerics and sin-seers," Mossberry began.

The words made Lady Aylen and Gwyness uneasy.

"What did these fairies want?" Lady Aylen asked.

"You, of course, and your human female aid. The fairies said that a party follows in search of Titan's Caravan—water elves and others."

"You know this term sin-seer?" Gwyness asked the Tree Shepherd.

"I do, in a fashion. As Tree Shepherds are a special clan of leshy, sin-seers are a special clan of battle clerics. They are guardians against the fiends of the night. I know no more than that. My people never met a real one." He smiled. "Until now."

"The other terms they used were necro-seers or…spectral slayer was the other."

"Yes, they have many names among fae and have through the ages. The abilities of individuals and clans have also varied through the ages to suit the enemies they faced."

"Well, you still haven't met a real one," Lady Aylen said. "I have only been an elf for less than a year, a true one, and neither one of us has mastered the powers we supposedly have or gotten a full accounting of our history. You said 'others.' What others pursue us besides water elves?"

"Faoladh," Mossberry answered.

"What are faoladh?" Gwyness asked.

"I believe your people call them lycanthropes."

"Werewolves!" Gwyness jumped up from her seat.

"Maiden, not them," Traveler said to calm her.

"I am sorry," Mossberry said. "Your human tongue is far less precise than fae. They are faoladh. They are a race of light."

"Good werewolves, Maiden Gwyness," Nirgund chimed in.

Traveler looked at the guardsman and smiled. "Mr. Nirgund, you are an expert on these legends."

"Only the ones of my lands, Mr. Traveler. Nothing compared to you though."

"Go on, Mr. Nirgund," Traveler said.

"I do not know much more other than they are from the ancient lands of Ossory and are humans who can shape-shift into wolves at will, day or night."

"Yes, that is true, or humanoid wolves," Mossberry said.

"Why would they seek us out?" Gwyness asked.

"You are a Faylen sin-seer, and your elfess is a Faylen battle cleric. The faoladh were allies. They fought at your side in wars against the fiends of the night. They served as your scouts in the lands of both fae and humans."

Gwyness sat back down.

"However, we must not make assumptions," Traveler said. "Not all water elves are allies, and not all faoladh are good. We must not forget Oughtred lives."

Mossberry nodded. "Wise approach. I agree with Master Traveler. They could seek you out to join you or to kill you."

The women were visibly upset by the words.

"Thank you, Mossberry, for sharing this critical news with us," Traveler said.

"There is one more thing. You met a white elfess in the city of Druid Keep."

"Yes," Lady Aylen replied.

"She has sent her guardian to meet us ahead. An ancient giant in black with a silver knight's helmet."

"And giant clawed hands," Gwyness added.

Mossberry smiled. "We will encounter him ahead with the information promised to you—the full accounting of Faylen's mages and warrior clerics, who are no more. He would have met us at Fae'el but, for obvious reasons, chose not to." The Tree Shepherd nodded.

"Thank you, Mossberry," Traveler said again.

The Tree Shepherd took his leave from the tent. Hobbs closed the flap and drew nearer to the group.

"We have good werewolves after us who may not be so good," Lady Aylen said.

"But we will have the information we seek too," Gwyness said.

"I will be brief since we will soon be in the Great Forest at last. Lady Aylen and Maiden Gwyness, this party of water elves and faoladh may reach us, or they may not. In either case, you must watch for them. Lady Aylen, you possess the ability to sense when another of your kind is nearby. If you ever have a notion that another water elf is nearby, you are to speak up. They could be hiding in invisibility or beneath our very feet. There are pockets of underground lakes and streams all throughout this land. Mr. Pangolin." Traveler looked at their master-at-arms.

"Goblins."

The caravan master grinned. "If we keep this up, Mr. Pangolin, the fae will begin to think there are humans who can speak in each other's minds." They heard Bragg chuckle behind them. "Yes. That goblin caravan is ahead of us. Their single purpose will be to take revenge on the party that killed their king. However, I do not believe it will be goblins and dire wolves alone. Goblins have many dark-fae allies. Their king was not just a goblin but a high goblin. Expect much more, Mr. Bragg."

The dwelf strolled from the entrance to stand before the group. "Yes, Mr. Traveler. I believe I, too, know what you will ask."

"There may be a manticore out there."

"Yes, there may, Mr. Traveler."

"I asked you this before, but I have to again. How good are you?"

"I have killed nineteen of the beasts. In my lands, I am renowned for my ability. In the lands of the dwelfs, we were plagued by the dark creatures. They killed many, including members of my own family. I learned to hunt them. I learned to kill them. I learned to make them fear me. But I hear you did not do so badly against your caravan's encounter."

"I can anticipate their actions but no more."

"It is a good thing that Mr. Quillen is not here," Estus said. "I wish I weren't either. Goblins, werewolves, and manticores."

"As you know well, fae are terrified of the beasts," Traveler said to Bragg.

"They have good reason, indeed. We should all be."

"Good. We have a greater expert than myself on the creatures within the caravan. We will remain here until the Snail Run moves on, then we'll finally set out for the Forest." Traveler looked at King Aereth. "Sire, you, too, have a burden."

"Yes, I know."

"King Oughtred threatened to kill you by the hand of your dead son. We know he is alive, and further, he is alive through the means of dark magic—necromancy."

"It means he likely could make good on such a threat."

"It is what you must guard against."

The king nodded.

"Mr. Traveler, it seems that we are only beginning the journey. Even after all that we have been through. It seems different now. More than merely leaving behind civilization," Lady Aylen said.

"It is different, princess. Titan's Caravan has all its human and fae members, at last. We know that we travel in the shadow of the kings. We know the wrath of their war wizards may still threaten us ahead. But I dare say, we are a caravan as powerful as any that have passed through Titan's Trail. I fear we will face death ahead, but I have no doubts of reaching Atlantea. We will make it to the fabled kingdom."

CHAPTER TWENTY

The Great Forest

Two full days passed before the last of the lymnaean-fairy caravan moved westward. Fortunately, there was much to occupy the time of the caravan while they waited. Hobbs kept the men on a light routine so they could still enjoy the leisure of watching the Snail Run.

"Look at this," Lady Aylen said, noticing the reappearance of the fae-blood woman, Ursi.

She looked like she had been sleeping for ages. Dr'amal joined her at a campfire and handed the fae-blood a large plate of food. The fae-blood ate as if she had never eaten before.

The royals and Gwyness watched them.

"She has been sleeping all this time?" Gwyness asked.

"Yes, Mr. Traveler said her race has to hibernate from time to time. Her specific clan is the bear clan. Those fae-blood men are the wolf-clan."

"Too many wolves on this journey, m'lady," Gwyness said.

"I would agree," Lady Aylen said.

"Ladies, it looks as if we prepare to set out," King Aereth noticed.

◆◆◆

The vanguard halted the march of the caravan. Pangolin looked at the Antaean giants. Both were equally concerned.

"Do you still see it, Mr. Elman?" Pangolin asked.

The half-elf stared into the forest, now merely a mile away. The lush, green-leaved trees towered more than one hundred feet above them with trunks of nearly fifty feet in diameter. But that was not the source of concern.

"It's watching us, but I don't think it will attack us." The half-elf jumped.

"What is it?" Pangolin asked.

Mr. Elman relaxed. "It is gone."

"Are you certain?"

"Yes. It ran away."

"How large was it?" Grakdar the giant asked.

"The chipmunk was almost fifteen feet tall on all fours, but it's gone. It did look friendly though."

The lead giant, Grakdar, scoffed. "Half-elf, no animal that large is friendly when the tallest among us is only eleven feet tall. We giants do not call this the Great Forest. We feel that name lulls one into a reckless and foolhardy sense of admiration. It is the Giant Forest and there is no pattern to the size of animals within it. You may encounter a fifteen-foot squirrel and then a swarm of twenty-foot fire ants or a thirty-foot snake."

"Are we well equipped to defend against any of those?" Pangolin asked.

"We are, human Pangolin. We have magic armor and weapons. So do you. Elman can see things before they appear, and the elaphines can move fast enough to dodge any attack while they fire their magic arrows."

"What about us?" one of the male fae-bloods asked.

"You fae-bloods probably will get eaten or crushed, whichever you prefer."

◆◆◆

Titan's Caravan had entered the Great Forest!

The trees were taller than those of the Dark Forest, but no sunlight was blocked from above. The sounds of birds and animals surrounded them, normal for any forest, whether in the Lands of Man or Faë-Land. The grass stood higher than the giants' heads, and nearby flowers stood taller still. However, they walked upon a clear dirt path free of debris or plant life.

Quillen pointed Hobbs's attention to the base of one tree. Giant twenty-foot mushrooms encircled it, white in color and spotted purple.

"I wonder if they are edible," the lad said.

"Remember what Mr. Traveler told us," Hobbs reminded. "Do not eat anything outside of our own food. You have heard the fables as many times as I. Humans eat one thing and become a giant, something else you shrink to the size of a pebble."

Quillen laughed.

◆◆◆

Lady Aylen had to put a cloth over her nose and mouth. Gwyness looked around and noticed the pollen in the air. She looked at the female half-elves, and their eyes were watery and red.

Traveler stepped back to them. "There is a nearby giant pond. The particles in the air are from it. It will pass."

Lady Aylen nodded.

◆◆◆

The caravan came out from one area of thick tree growth to a more open area. The three crawling trees spread out their branches to provide cover to the members. King Aereth smiled as he looked up.

"We have a very efficient party," the king said.

"We do indeed, sire," Lady Aylen said.

In the mind of every human and fae was what giant animal or beast they would encounter first. Everyone's eyes scanned the trees and brush around them, the branches and leaves above, the grass on their sides. They heard the sound of animal life carried on the refreshing breeze but saw not even a bird or insect above.

Traveler and the dog sprinted away from the front columns to Pangolin, who had stopped the vanguard with a raised hand. The front watched them closely. Traveler retrieved his small telescope from his cloak and peered out. He walked back to the royals.

"Sire, keep the caravan here. We are going to scout ahead."

"What has happened?" Lady Aylen asked.

"There is what remains of another caravan ahead of us. It appears they are all dead, people and animals, or it could be an illusion or trap. We will find out. Mr. Hobbs."

"Yes, sir."

"Fetch Mr. Gresham, and have him wait here." Traveler looked past them. "There you are."

They all turned to see who Traveler was looking at—the drow sorceress.

"You wish for me to accompany you?" she asked.

"I do."

Traveler and his dog ran back to the vanguard. Dr'amal followed closely and effortlessly behind them. With Pangolin and most of the archer-warriors, they dashed ahead.

One of the elaphine archer-warriors returned to the front and retrieved Gresham. The healer had his own team of lads to assist him, eager to continue their medical learning.

"Stay here," he said to the lads. "When I know it's safe, I will signal or send for you. The first rule of a healer is never to become a victim on the battlefield yourself, or there will be no one to help the fallen."

Gresham ran as quickly as he could, but the hoofed fae moved so fast they seemed to run on the air.

♦♦♦

Half an hour later, two elaphine archer-warriors returned. One went to the vanguard, the other to the front.

"The one called Gresham calls for you," the elpahine said to the three lads.

They sprinted away, each carrying a leather bag.

"Has anyone survived?" King Aereth asked.

"Only a few, but they may not survive the night," the elaphine replied.

"It is an elfin caravan?" Lady Aylen asked.

"Yes," the hoofed fae responded.

"How many elves?" Lady Aylen asked.

"About a hundred."

"Do we know who attacked them?" King Aereth asked.

"Yes. Wizards and goblins. Mr. Traveler said you should see. He said to bring you too."

King Aereth and Lady Aylen looked at each other. The royals put Hobbs in charge. They were startled when, from nowhere, their dragon steeds appeared. Gwyness smiled as she neared hers and stroked the side of its face. Two fenodyree walked to them.

"How do they know?" Gwyness asked the two hairy sprites.

"Kirins always know," one said.

King Aereth galloped on his golden kirin to the site of the fallen elfin caravan, followed by Lady Aylen on her lucent-blue cat-fish-like kirin with the unicorn horn on its head, and Gwyness followed them both on her antlered black-furred kirin. They left their guardsmen behind, as the fenodyree told them that the kirins would protect their riders.

Half a mile away was the elfin caravan. As they neared, they realized that it was not a land caravan but a flying one. The dead animals were all winged—horses and hounds, their bodies broken and bloodied. Magic winged wagons were shattered and shrewn across the ground. The Cut-Throats stacked dead bodies of elves together. The elves had markings on their garb of noble warriors, but the caravan's elfin questing knights watched quietly from afar. The royals and Gwyness trotted past the elfin questing knights and stopped where other Cut-Throats erected a temporary healing tent.

The royals and Gwyness dismounted their kirins. At the entrance, Traveler stood with Pangolin, looking on at what took place inside.

King Aereth was about to speak when Traveler handed him a piece of an orange-and-white flag. "Xenhelm," the king said angrily.

Lady Aylen touched the fabric. "Does this mean they are here in the Great Forest too?"

"None of the elves have recovered yet," Traveler said, almost in a whisper.

Inside, Gresham attended to an elf, bandaging his wounds, aided by the healing lads. There were only five other elves in the tent, all of them on the ground and covered with whatever cloth could be found to keep them warm. None of the elves were conscious.

"How many were there?" King Aereth asked.

"It was a party of a hundred, sire. They were en route to Fae'el...to meet us."

"Why?" Lady Aylen asked.

"To warn us, princess," Pangolin said. "One of the elves was conscious briefly and was very determined to keep us from continuing on to Atlantea."

"Why?" Lady Aylen asked.

"He said they were part of a larger flying caravan on their way to Atlantea," Pangolin continued. "Sire, the elf claimed they were attacked when they arrived at the gates of Atlantea."

Traveler touched the piece of Xenhelmian flag in the king's hand. "By them."

Lady Aylen shook her head. "I will not be turned back by this. We have come too far. How could they have gotten to Atlantea and back here so quickly? Impossible. I do not believe the elf's words."

"Princess, the Xenhelmians are not the only ones to use portal magic. Elves and other fae have done so for thousands of years."

"Do you believe the elf's tale, Mr. Traveler?" King Aereth asked.

"Sire, it does not matter. Here, I wholeheartedly agree with Lady Aylen and Mr. Pangolin. The words of a half-dead elf are not going to delay or stop our journey."

"Good," Lady Aylen said, relieved.

"How did these elves die then? And their animals? How were their wagons destroyed?" King Aereth asked.

"They were attacked someplace else. As they attempted to escape through a portal, they crashed from high above to their deaths. I looked at all the elves, and at least one of them I am certain was a wizard."

"They fell to their deaths?"

"Yes, princess, but this wizard was killed a different way. We had to immediately burn his body. His entire insides were a hive of maggots."

"Oh no," Gwyness said.

"That is a sign of dark magic," Traveler said.

"What should we do about the elves who survived?" King Aereth asked. "Leave them here? Take them with us to be under the care of Mr. Gresham?"

"Absolutely not, sire," Pangolin said. "If they are part of some treachery, then we cannot take the chance of having them within our caravan. We had spies before. We will not have them again."

"It is not something I would normally do, sire," Traveler answered, "but we will leave them here. We can have one of our fae cast a messenger spell and get word to Fae'el that there are elves in need. It should not take long for the spell to arrive, and with the type of powerful elves at the city now, more than a few will be able to cast their own teleportation spell to retrieve these elves."

"What is it that you are not saying?" King Aereth asked.

"As with all things, sire, we will face the danger when it comes. Remember, I lived in Atlantea."

"So you do believe the elf?" the king asked.

"I do not know what to believe, sire. What we do know is King Oughtred lives, he is out there, and he has many allies. However, we have many allies too. Titan's Caravan travels under the banner of many fae, including a lost elfin kingdom of historical note. Even without our own allies, what we have assembled here is an impressive caravan by any measure."

"No truer statement could be said, Mr. Traveler," King Aereth said.

"We may also have many more allies that we are not even aware of. We cannot concern ourselves with unknown dangers. There is only one thing for us to do now. We will help these elves as best we can and then move away from here on our fabled quest. I will even offer Mr. Gresham my healing services if need be."

"You will get no objections from us this time, Mr. Traveler," Lady Aylen said.

"We have now reached a part of the Trail that is wild, long, and more dangerous than any part we have crossed before. There is no city to go back to nor any city for us to stop at ahead. We only have ourselves to rely on out here. I am sure we all agree we want to be on our way and through the Great Forest as quickly as possible."

"Hear, hear," Pangolin declared.

"And, sire, let us take no chances with that piece of Xenhelmian banner. We are in the realm of magic. Burn it," Traveler said.

The Fabled Quest Chronicles through the Great Forest continues in
Book Four.
To Release in 2019!
Join my VIP Readers' Club at <u>www.austindragon.com</u> to be notified.

THANK YOU FOR READING!

Dear Reader,

I hope you enjoyed *Comes the War Wizards' Wrath*.

Can You Write Me a Review?

If you enjoyed *Comes the War Wizards' Wrath (Fabled Quest Chronicles, Book 3)*, I'd greatly appreciate an honest review on one or more of the following sites:

Reviews are the best way for readers to discover good books. My writer's motto is simple: "Readers Rule!" Thanks so much.

Always writing,

Austin Dragon

CONTINUE THE ADVENTURE

Get Your Next *Fabled Quest Chronicles* Books!

- ***Through Titan's Trail*** *(Fabled Quest Chronicles, Book 1)*
- ***In the Shadow of the Kings*** *(Fabled Quest Chronicles, Book 2)*
- ***Comes the War Wizards' Wrath*** *(Fabled Quest Chronicles, Book 3)*

- ***Fabled Quest Chronicles Box Set*** *(Books 1-3)*

Also by Austin Dragon

See all my books in fantasy, science fiction, and horror: http://www.austindragon.com/books

Want to know when the next Fabled Quest novels come out? Sign up to my VIP Readers' Club! Click **HERE** to get started: http://www.austindragon.com/be_a_vip

<u>Quillen's List of Races, Beasts, and Monsters of Myth and Magic</u>

<u>**Alphyn**</u> - a fae wolf-hound with black fur and a knotted tail, a ridge of knotted fur along its back, a lizard-like underbellies, and eagle-like forelimbs. Alphyns are rumored to be able to spit fire.

<u>**Animal Men**</u> (Animaloids) - human-like fae that have the features of a specific animal. In Titan's Caravan, one animal men has the features of a lion, others are cat-like, another reptile, and another boar-like.

<u>**Antaean**</u> - members of the sub-race of giants regarded as great warriors, ranging in height from eight to twelve feet. Antaeans wear shining armor and helmets. Their greatest magical power is that when they directly touch the earth in a deliberative stance, no force in the world can move or harm them.

<u>**Axex**</u> - pronounced A-Z-E-X. They were popular in the Lands of Man before the griffins. They have feline bodies and swift runners. Smaller ones are used as hunters and watch dogs; larger ones are used as steeds.

<u>**Boggart**</u> - Malevolent and mischievous fae inhabiting fields, marshes, holes in the ground, under bridges or other topographical features. They can make things to disappear, food to spoil, and animals to go lame. They also have been known to abduct children or small animals. Can become extremely uncontrollable and destructive

Many are human-like in form, ugly, hairy and often with bestial attributes, arms almost as long as tacklepoles". Other accounts give a more completely beast-like form: fearsome creature the size of a calf, with long shaggy hair and eyes like saucers.

Rumor that brownies or similar sprites could turn into malevolent boggarts if offended or ill-treated.

<u>**Brownies**</u> - halfling sprites who look like old men with short curly dark hair and wear brown pointed conical caps and clothes. These fae

are nocturnal, coming out at night to do their daily chores. They make their homes in enclosed dwellings or traveling wagons.

Bugbear - a type of hobgoblin that appears as a creepy bear and in human fables lurked in the woods to scare children. In Faë-Land, they are malevolent dark sprites who do much more than lurk, including kidnapping and devouring children.

Buggane - a humanoid shape-shifter with a mane of coarse, black hair; eyes like torches, and glittering sharp tusks. They are unable to cross water or stand on hallowed ground. They are occasionally called upon by the fairies to punish people that had offended them.

Caladrius Bird - a pure-white bird able to take a person's sickness into itself and then fly away, dispersing the sickness and healing both itself and the sick person.

Catoblepas - a beast from magical lands outside of Faë-Land that looks similar to a buffalo: small horns, matted hair hanging into its eyes, its much larger head bobbed close to the ground. It can turn a living thing into stone with a steady gaze.

Centaur - one of the major races of fae who live in patriarchal societies. They are half-man, half-horse; having the torso of a man extending where the neck of a horse should be.

<u>Sub-Races of Centaurs:</u>

<u>Cyprean centaur</u> - centaurs with large bull horns sprouting from his head.

<u>Hippogriff centaur</u> - centaurs that are part hippogriff—forelegs of a giant eagle and hind half of a horse.

<u>Stag centaur</u> - centaurs with massive antlers.

<u>Flying or winged centaur</u> - centaurs with massive eagle or angel wings capable of flying at great heights and great speed.

<u>Unicorn centaur</u> - has a dark complexion with a single ivory-like horn pointing upwards from its forehead.

<u>Cat centaur</u> - instead of a horse body, they have the giant body of a cat. There are lion centaurs, tiger centaurs, and panther centaurs.

Cervid - one of the race of deer-folk, a hoofed fae of normal human height with small horns, one above each brow. As archers, they carry short dark wooden bows.

Chamrosh - a fae hound with an eagle head and bird wings sprouting from its back. They particularly hate hippogriffs.

Cù-sìth - the name means "fairy dog" and it is as large as a small horse with a shaggy, green coat. It has pointy green ears and a long curled tail. Some have a long tail rolled up in a coil on its back. Often, it has other animals such as birds and squirrels resting on its back. Forest fae, especially leshies, have them as watch dogs or guardians.

Dark Fairy - a sub-race of evil fairies who look like other fairies but wear dark colors and prefer shadowy regions. They are practitioners of dark magic and are mortal enemies of fairies of light.

Darkling - the name given to the phooka by Traveler when he first encountered them in Faë-Land as a lad.

<u>Phooka</u> - also known as pooka, púca,phouka,phooka,phooca,puca,orpúka. They are fae shape-shifters that always take the form of some humanoid animal or animal but always black in color. The malicious ones are violent and dangerous, taking the form of frightening black animals. The benevolent ones are given to mischief and harmless pranks, not unlike fairies, but they can be quite helpful and are only dangerous to evil beasts and beings. All phookas can take the form of dogs, foxes, wolves, cats, horses, goats, rabbits, birds, and much more to frighten and shock their enemies. They are especially fond of changing into distorted versions of those animals or a combination of more than one or changing into humanoid forms with animal features.

Deer-folk or Deer People - one of the races of fae who live in patriarchal or matriarchal rustic, nomadic societies. They are a pack society who live and travel as a group at all times. They are part of the hoofed-fae races, which includes fauns, satyrs, and centaurs.

<u>Sub-Races of Deer-folk:</u>

<u>Cervid</u> - a hoofed fae of normal human height with small horns, one above each brow. As archers, cervid carry short dark wooden bows.

<u>Elaphine</u> - the largest species of deer-like fae with deer noses, ears, eyes, and huge antlers sprouting from their heads. As warriors, they wear armor and chainmail. They carry long bows as tall as they stand—over six feet and made of smooth, immaculately polished white wood. They are fae archers as gifted as elves and centaurs.

<u>Rusine</u> - are deer-like in appearance—large eyes, a black deer nose, and cloven feet. These humanoid fae are short compared to most humans, no taller than five feet in height. Most prominent is their large deer-like ears that are in constant motion.

Diomedian Mare - a carnivorous horse-beast with wolf feet rather than hooves. Elves have been domesticating them for ages for benevolent purposes.

Dire wolf - a large black wolf used as steeds by goblins.

Drow - or dark elf (not to be confused with a night elf) is a member of an elfin sub-race characterized by dark bluish skin, most often white hair—though some have black hair, and their eyes often have irises of a bright color, such as blue or purple. Drows wear only dark colors like black, dark blues, and dark purples. The original Drow sub-race had separated from high elves due to embracing dark magic. Drows abandoned the practice long ago but remain enemies to all elves, and most fae.

Dwelf - a fae who looks like an elf but have a large, brawny, wide frame and is very tall. Elves have tall sleek bodies; dwelves are bulky like that of a dwarf, but aren't halflings.

Elaphine - the largest species of deer-like fae with deer noses, ears, eyes, and huge antlers sprouting from their heads. As warriors, they wear armor and chainmail. They carry long bows as tall as they stand—over six feet and made of smooth, immaculately polished white wood. They are fae archers as gifted as elves and centaurs.

Elf - one of the major races of fae and the one most resembling humans in appearance. They are humanoids characterized by pointed ears, taller than the average human, and slim in build. They have fair to porcelain-like skin—though there are sub-races with darker skin. Their eyes can be one of many different colors, depending on their sub-race and clan. Their senses, strength, and stamina are far superior to humans. As with many fae, they can make themselves invisible through magic in their natural environment, can move at extreme speed whether running or fighting—almost seeming jump from one point to another in the eyes of humans, and are very long lived. Along with centaurs, they are known as the top archers in Faë-Land. They fight with blade weapons never bludgeoning weapons, and bows, never crossbows.

Different sub-races of elves have additional physical and magical abilities.

<u>Sub-Races of Elves:</u>

<u>Desert Elf</u> - one of the elfin sub-races of the outer desert lands of Faë-Land.

<u>Drow</u> - or dark elf (not to be confused with a night elf) is a member of an elfin sub-race characterized by dark bluish skin, most often white hair—though some have black hair, and their eyes often have irises of a bright color, such as blue or purple. Drows wear only dark colors like black, dark blues, and dark purples. The original Drow sub-race had separated from high elves due to embracing dark magic. Drows abandoned the practice long ago but remain enemies to all elves, and most fae.

<u>Forest Elf</u> - one of the elfin sub-races of the large forest lands of Faë-Land.

<u>High Elf</u> - one of the elfin sub-race of tall, regal elves, exceptionally beautiful/handsome in appearance. High elves consider themselves the most royal and highest of all elves. They dwell exclusively in highly advanced and magical cities.

<u>Mountain Elf</u> - one of the elfin sub-races who live in the mountain lands of Faë-Land.

<u>Wild or Savage Elf</u> - they have light brown hair, bigger pointed ears sprouting from the sides of their heads, fanged teeth and clawed nails on their hands. They are tall, muscular, and their eyes had the look of a wild animal.

<u>Wind Elf</u> - one of the elfin sub-races who are elves with air elemental magical abilities.

<u>Woodland Elf</u> - an elfin sub-race known as the best trackers in the forests with strong societies built around hunting. They have eyesight more powerful than eagles and magically can see the "after-presence" of prey they are tracking. There are two main divisions: Rustic—who live in wooded lands of modest hamlets, and Hunter—who fashion themselves after high elves and live in large tree cities.

Enfield - a fae animal with the head of a fox, foreleg like an eagle, and the hindquarters and tail of a wolf. Domesticated ones are primarily used for hunting.

Erymanthian Boar - a giant monstrous boar with red, white, or black eyes. Protruding from most of its body, including its head and forelegs, are bony, jagged, blood-stained tusks. It also has a sharp bony ridge along its back.

Fachans - a taller than average bald humanoid that looks like a human cut in half. However, its physical form was natural to their race—a single eye in the center of its forehead, a large and flat nose, a large mouth filled with jagged teeth and a single arm protruding from the center of its chest. They move on a single muscled leg with large throbbing veins. They wear animal skins for clothing that cover their hairy, weather-chapped skin. Their attacking weapons of choice are spears and multi-chained flail clubs.

Fae - the sentient and dominant humanoid species of the realm of magic known as Fäe-Land.

Fae-Blood - A member of a fae race rarely seen by humans who appear to be visibly indistinguishable from an average human. They wear black attire and colored stone necklaces. There are many clans named after a specific animal, such as bear, wolf, cat, chameleon, hawk, etc., and each clan has its own unique magical powers. As their name suggests, they are fae whose very blood is pure magic.

Fairy - one of the major races of fae who live in matriarchal societies governed by queens. Fairies are often insect-like, but there are also bird-like, reptile-like, amphibian-like, mollusk-like, snail-like, and plant-like races. They are shape-shifters able to take the form of other animals, such as smaller mammals, birds, or insects. Like sprites, their different sub-races and tribes have differing magical powers. Like many fae, they possess the ability of "sizing" wherein they can magically increase or shrink their size to defend themselves. Fairies live and work with animal companions, most often birds or insects.

Sub-Races of Fairies:

Lymnaean - a sub-race of fairies. These fairies look like humanoid snails clad in insect-exoskeleton-like armor, and their eyes are in their antennae. They travel on giant snails.

Faun - one of the major sub-races of hoofed-fae who live in patriarchal, rural societies governed by kings and chiefs. Fauns and satyrs are very similar, but they are not the same race. Fauns are shorter than the average human, often with a goatee, and both male and female fauns wear tops. They are peaceful, reasoned, and congenial. They often act as guides.

Sub-Races of Fauns:

<u>Common</u> - have pointed ears, goat horns sprouting just above their eyes, legs of a goat, and cloven hooves.

<u>Grand</u> - have large curving ram's horns sprouting from their head and are above average human height.

Fenodyree - also fenoderee, are hairy sprite halflings, covered from head-to-toe in thick, woolly hair. Similar to brownies, they like outdoor work and can be very helpful performing arduous tasks. They are also fond of caring for livestock and animals.

Flying Horse - a horse with the wings of a giant bird and capable of flying. They can be of any color and different kinds have differing magical properties. They are also (incorrectly) called a pegasus by humans, but Pegasus was the name of a specific legendary flying horse.

Ghoul - an undead creature but, unlike a zombie, are intelligent and calculating. They are extremely strong and only special magic or physical force that can destroy their entire physical form at once can kill them. They can also turn another into a ghoul with physical contact, such as with a scratch or bite. Ghouls serve dark masters and "live" to commit acts of evil.

Giant - one of the major races of fae who live in patriarchal societies governed by kings and chiefs. The majority of the giant races are warriors, all possessing great strength, but others have kingdoms of diverse occupations. Giants can range in height from ten to one hundred feet.

<u>Sub-Races of Giants:</u>

<u>Antaeans</u> - members of the sub-race of giants regarded as great warriors, ranging in height from eight to twelve feet. Antaeans wear shining armor and helmets. Their greatest magical power is that when they directly touch the earth in a deliberative stance, no force in the world can move or harm them.

<u>Cyclops</u> - a sub-race of giants with a single eye in the center of their forehead. There are any different clans, both civilized and savage.

Some are gifted builders, craftsmen, and merchants. Others are scholars and artisans. Rare ones are seers and oracles, able to see what cannot be seen with the normal eye or the future. There are also savage clans known for their ferocity and cannibalism.

<u>Gegenees</u> - a sub-race of six-armed, twelve-foot tall giants who wear blackish war-paint over their entire body. Their favorite weapons of choice is the double battle-axe. They are mortal enemies of the Antaeans.

Giant Animals - domesticated ones are used as steeds, guard animals, or beasts of burden. Titan's Caravan includes giant crabs, giant turtles, giant porcupines, giant ducks, giant cranes, and a giant moose.

Gnoll - a race of evil predatory humanoid canine creatures. They are known for their cunning, ferocity, and relentlessness. They have sharp teeth and claws and always hunt and attack in packs. Some kill with their hands and teeth, but others wear full armor and wield goblin-made weapons.

<u>Sub-Races:</u>

<u>Dog</u> - the smallest of their kind were more akin to feral dogs.

<u>Wolf</u> - larger than dog knolls and often hunt in smaller packs.

<u>Hyena, giant</u> - the largest and most formidable of gnolls. Their war-packs are larger than all other kinds of knolls and feared by all.

Gnome - fae halfling sprites known for their perpetual happy-go-lucky personality, amiability, and love of dancing, singing and music. They often have beards but not always. They often look older, but there are baby-faced clans. They always wear hats, though gnomes exclusively wear pointy, often red, conical hats.

Gnomoid - there are many races of sprites similar to gnomes, though not as good-natured. They also wear hats but not the pointy conical ones of gnomes.

Goblin - one of the major races of dark fae that resemble a kind of elves in appearance. Their skin is green, their frame stout and muscular, their noses flat, and their pointy ears were larger. They are the mortal enemies of elves.

Golem - a humanoid automaton made of metal, wood, or clay animated by magic. Their intelligence and abilities are based on that animating magic.

Gorgon - one of the most feared humanoid fae of dark magic in the fae realm. Their upper female torso has green scaly skin, hands ending in claws. Their lower torso is that of a giant snake. Though their faces are beautiful, but their hair is of long hissing snakes. All fear their death stare—a magical gaze that can turn any living thing of any size into stone.

Griffin - a fantastic beast with the body, tail, and hind legs of a lion and golden yellow fur. Its head and foreleg talons are that of a giant eagle. The animal is known for its echoing roar. Griffins are often used by fae as royal steeds or guardians of treasure. Like hippogriffs, they have a fondness for eating horses of the Lands of Man.

Sub-Races of Griffins:

Owl griffins - are griffins with the head of an owl.

Grunt - a sub-race of sprites with large heads, brutish arms, slightly hunched, and thinning dark hair. Their facial features are also larger: noses, mouths, and ears. Grunts are not very intelligence but are extremely loyal.

Half-Elf - humanoid with one elfin parent and one human parent. They have pointed ears but often not as pronounced as a full elf. They are far stronger than an average human and possess superior senses. Many often have the same magical abilities as their elfin lineage or to a lesser degree. They have a much longer life span than humans, and some have the ability to communicate telepathically with other half-elves, suggesting that elves, secretly, have the same ability.

Half-Goblin - one parent is goblin and the other human. They have pointed ears, green skin, and its goblin features vary: one or more horns, a large pointed noise, and a larger chin.

Haltija - a sub-race of sprites that guard, help, or protect something or somebody. Haltijas appear as frowning full-bearded halfling men with pointy hats. They are nocturnal sprites like brownies, coming out at night for their daily tasks. They are ill-tempered, rude, surly, and hate being talked to directly. They are also shape-shifters. A clan of haltijas is called a väki and there are many different clans in Faë-Land.

Sub-Races of Haltija:

Tulen Väki or väki of fire - the clan of haltijas who wear charred dark brown and orange fabric clothing. They are a race of guardians with the elemental magically ability to conjure and control fire and use warm air to heal or burn.

Väki - Besides the tulen väki or väki of fire there are also väki of specific trees, forests, mountains, water, precious metals or gems, underground lands, etc.

Harpy - an evil female creature much larger than the average human. They are humanoid females from the waist up—matted hair, gaunt facial features, black eyes, and jagged teeth—and the legs of a bird below, with fearsome talons. Their arms were the wings of a large bird, and their human halves were covered in hair and feathers. They are fiercely territorial of specific of structures or places where they live and protect together as a flock.

High Elf - one of the elfin sub-race of tall, regal elves exceptionally beautiful/handsome in appearance. They consider themselves the most royal and highest of all elves. They dwell exclusively in highly advanced and magical cities.

Hippogriff - a fantastic beast that has the hind half of a horse and the front half, including head and forelegs, of a giant eagle. It is known for its loud eagle shrieks. Like griffins, they have a fondness for eating horses of the Lands of Man.

Hobgoblin - the creature is about three feet in height. Their pointy ears are longer and thinner, sprouting from the sides of their heads. Their noses are hooked. Their teeth are long and sharp like piranha, and have beady little eyes. They wear dark clothes—tunics and trousers—and curled pointed shoes.

Humanoid Animals

Sub-Races of Humanoid Animals:

Frog men, lizard men, squirrel men, raccoon men, possums, fox men, rabbit men, bird men, and mice men.

Ichneumon - a giant weasel-like beast able to wrestle and kill beasts ten times their size. They despise any snake creature and can kill a wurm many times its size. They are impervious to fire attacks.

Imp - this dark fae is a small, gray, ugly humanoid creature, with bat-like wings, big ears, and tiny horns poking out above its eyebrows. Its skin is either stone-like or scaly. Imps are known for their destructive mischief against unsuspecting fae or humans. Their wild pranks are often a result of boredom rather than evil. When discovered or caught they are given to wild outbursts as they run or fly away. Imps can also be very territorial—bound to a specific region or love to hide in specific objects, especially magical objects. Though most of their pranks are harmless, they have been known to engage in more serious acts such as taking babies or small animals, leading people astray to their death, and starting fires. They are also shape-shifters, which they often take full advantage of in their pranks, and can turn invisible as they escape. Imps have been used as spies or agents for evil wizards.

Ipotane - a fae race of half-horse, half-humanoids. They have a man's body, hoofed feet, and the head of a horse, and they wear trousers alone. They are a semi-intelligent race similar to minotaurs and are not regarded as part of the hoofed fae races of fauns, satyrs, or centaurs.

Jackalope - a fae animal that is a rabbit with antlers. Domesticated, they are used as watch dogs and for hunting.

Kilmoulis - a race of shy but good-natured sprites with huge noses that cover most of their faces. They always stay together in their group and did not mingle with others, human or fae. They are regarded as lazy creatures by most fae, other view them as disgusting, eating by stuffing food up their noses. Magically, they can smell and distinguish animals or beings leagues away; an ability not possessed by any other fae.

Kirin - also ki-rin or quilin. A fantastic beast from the magical lands beyond Faë-Land, and is often called a dragon-horse (though there is another magical beast by that name). These intelligent animals serve as companions, guardians, and protectors. They have varying characteristics of other animals to match their environments and varying magical abilities. They can fly, whether they have wings or not, and can swim or gallop under water.

They never harm benevolent life or pure souls, but they are swift and fierce to attack if threatened or to protect a defenseless or pure person threatened by a malicious thing. They are thought to be a symbol of luck, good omens, protection, prosperity, success, and longevity. They are also rumored to see future events before they happen.

Leshy - known as guardians of the forest, they are male fae with white skin and hair and full beards of living grass and vines. They have bright green eyes and hooved feet, and some have horns and tails. They areshape-shifters known for the ability to take the form of any animal or plant. They can shrink to the size of an insect or grow to the size of the tallest tree. They can imitate the voice of any human or humanoid, make the sound of any animal, and can scream horribly to frighten enemies. They often keep animals as companions, the favorite being a cù-sìth.

There are also dark leshies given to leading travelers astray, kidnapping, or making people sick.

<u>Tree Shepherds</u> - are leshies who control any number of magical, sentient trees—walking, crawling, or flying.

Lizard, Giant Fae - or giant rainbow lizard of fae. The lizards can be blue, yellow, green, or orange. They hatch from large melon-sized, leathery eggs and grow to over twenty feet long, not including the tail. Together, giant fae lizards walk, defend, and attack as a pack. They can magically see invisible fae beings and animals during the day, must have heat during the night to sleep, and have magical regenerative powers, including the ability to grow severed limbs. As they mature, they exhibit other magical powers based on their environment and keepers.

Lunatishee - a sub-race of dark fairies. They are wingless fairies covered in sharp thorns over their entire bodies, no taller than gnomes, and look more like devilish males than fairies.

Lycanthrope - is it an evil humanoid of dark magic with the ability to shape-shift into an animal, or is it dark animal with the ability to shape-shift into a humanoid? In the Lands of Man, werewolves are the most known, feared and the most powerful of lycanthropes, werewolves are extremely rare. More common are werecats, wererats, weredogs, etc. They always fight enemies to kill but can turn survivors into a lycanthrope with a bite or scratch.

Manticore - a giant creature with the body of a bat-winged lion, human head with a massive mouth filled with razor-sharp teeth, and a scorpion-like tail that can fire spine projectiles. It is a pure evil predator feared for its stealth, cunning, and wickedness.

Merfolk or Merpeople - See Mermaid or Merman.

Mermaid - one of the major races of fae who live in matriarchal underwater cities governed by queens. They are beautiful female humanoids with a large fish tail instead of bipedal legs. Their skin is an almost luminescent light blue; they have long, flowing hair, and their eyes can either be similar to fish's or human's. The only clothing they wear are a type of brassiere—like cloth wrapped around their breast area several times.

Malevolent mermaids love storms and floods, and are present at shipwrecks and drownings. Also, like sirens they can lure and attract humans and other humanoids with their enchanted singing, often to crash sea-going vessels onto rocks. Benevolent ones can help victims of natural disasters at sea and have been known to fall in love with humans, giving up their fae life to live as a human.

Merman - Ugly male sea humanoids that look like a brown fish but with the head of a man—blue-green hair, unsightly teeth, and slits for eyes. They enjoy storms and being present at sinking ships. Despite their appearance, they can magically cure sickness and lift curses. Others are sages and oracles.

Minotaur - a race of semi-intelligent fae that are humanoid bulls. Minotaurs have sharp, pointed or jagged, dual horns protruding from their heads, large bull ears, and extremely muscular necks. They wear loincloths and sometimes use weapons such as axes, maces, and clubs.

Nisse - A sub-race of sprites who are very friendly and gregarious little people, knee-high, wearing bright green pointy hats as long as their bodies. They are never without a smile on their face. There are both men and women. The bearded men dress in standard dark tunics and trousers; the women dress in lighter colored dresses with their blond or brunette hair braided behind them. Other nisse wear red or orange hats too. They are believed to have shape-shifting abilities too.

Despite size, they have tremendous strength, like all sprites. Often they are protectors of farmlands, livestock, and animals. They are easily offended by rudeness, laziness, and the mistreatment of animals.

Nymph - one of the major races of fae who live in matriarchal societies. They are enchanting, beautiful women with long hair. They look human, but have an angelic glow. Human men are helpless to their powerful, magical attraction; fae men can also be susceptible to their enchantment.

<u>Sub-Races of Nymphs:</u>

<u>Crinaeae</u> - water nymphs of fountains

<u>Dryads</u> - nymphs of the trees

<u>Hamadryads</u> - nymphs that live in the trees themselves

<u>Hydriades</u> or ephydriades - water nymphs

<u>Limnades or Limnatides</u> - water nymphs of lakes

<u>Naiads</u> - water nymphs of fresh water

<u>Napaeae</u> - nymphs of wooded valleys

<u>Oceanids</u> - water nymphs of oceans

<u>Pegaeae</u> - water nymphs of springs

<u>Potameides</u> - water nymphs of rivers

Ogre - a carnivorous giant humanoid, often with large fanged teeth, and especially fond of human or humanoid flesh. It can be anywhere from eight to fifty feet or more. Many are deformed or misshapen with one or more heads, and oversized facial features or body parts, such as hands, arms, or heads. Its skin is often a sickly greenish or gray color. It wears animal hides or fur for clothing. The creature is a solitary hunter that roams its chosen territory. Along with trolls, ogres are not considered by fae as part of the fae race of giants.

Orthurus - a two-headed giant wolf used as attack dogs by dark fae.

Owl Faun - a fae humanoid animal that looks like a faun but with the head of an owl. Hoofed fae often have them as bodyguards or sentries.

Pech - halfling sprites with wild, bushy eyebrows—the far ends pointing up—have big noses, and even bigger forearms bulging from their tunics. They wear off-white tunics, dark trousers and boots, and dark caps. They are some of the strongest sprites in Faë-Land.

Pegasus - see Flying Horse.

Phooka - also known as pooka, púca,phouka,phooka,phooca,puca,orpúka. They are fae shape-shifters that always take the form of some humanoid animal or animal but always black in color. The malicious ones are violent and dangerous, taking the form of frightening black animals. The benevolent ones are given to mischief and harmless pranks, not unlike fairies, but they can be quite helpful and are only dangerous to evil beasts and beings. All phookas can take the form of dogs, foxes, wolves, cats, horses, goats, rabbits, birds, and much more to frighten and shock their enemies. They are especially fond of changing into distorted versions of those animals or a combination of more than one or changing into humanoid forms with animal features.

Pixy - a tiny sprite that appears as an insect-winged man with a child-like face and pointy ears, who wear a green pointed hat and a green outfit. They are prone to mischievous but harmless pranks. They like to play with animals, especially horses, music, gather in groups for dancing or horseplay, and their favorite pastime is to pester humans, which includes leading them astray and stealing children!

Puck - a sprite taller as an average human male known for their intelligence and craftiness. They have slightly hunched-over posture, skinny and elastic arms. They have bushy eyebrows like pech, long noses, and large ears. The sprites also have slim prehensile tail from their backside.

Roc - a predatory bird creature of such immense size that it looks like a black cloud in sky when it flies. Sizes of the creature have ranged from large enough to grab an elephant from the ground in its beak or talons to rare ones have been large enough to snatch up a city. The flapping of its wings can also cause hurricane-like winds.

Rusine - are deer-like in appearance—large eyes, a black deer nose, and cloven feet. These humanoid fae are short compared to most humans, no taller than five feet in height. Most prominent is their large deer-like ears that are in constant motion.

Satyr - a race of fae, cousins to the fauns and similar in appearance. Satyrs are much taller than the average man. They have a darker complexion, their eyes are more feral looking, and their build is much thicker.

<u>Sub-Races of Satyrs:</u>

<u>Giant</u> - more hulking in form, some ten to twelve feet tall. They had fanged teeth and their eyes have a look of animalistic wildness.

Spell-Talker - a rare demon that looks like a pale human male with pure black eyes. On either side of its mouth are holes—used to magically lock its mouth closed by its master. It can kill any living thing by simply speaking words of dark magic over a steady but short period of time unless stopped.

Spriggan - a sub-race of dark fae (dark sprites). They are ugly, old-looking halflings with large child-like heads. They have surly dispositions, but delight in making mischief on others. They are found of looting dwellings of possessions, stealing cattle or animals, or cause disease among livestock or animals, and can even cause small buildings to collapse. They have been known to kidnap human children, leaving ugly changelings in their place. Despite their size, like other sprites, they can change their size instantly, either increase their size to that of a giant to fight, or smaller than the eye cans see. Magically, they can also cause sudden whirlwinds to frighten and summon storms to blight crops or green fields and damage green forests. They are fond of old ruins, caves, and underground habitats. They are often used by other dark fae to guard buried treasure. Dark fairies also use them as bodyguards. They can cause storms at sea but salt water is poison to them.

Sprite - one of the major races of fae who live in patriarchal rural societies governed by kings, chiefs, or clan chiefs. Sprites are human-like halflings or smaller but like all sprites and fairies, they possess the ability of "sizing" wherein they can magically increase or shrink their size to defend themselves.

Sylphs - a powerful race of fae who live in matriarchal celestial societies in the sky governed by queens. Like nymphs, they are enchanting, beautiful humanoid women with long hair. Because of the glow of their skin and the sheer white garb they often wear, some humans have mistakenly called them angels. However, they are air elementals who possess great magical power over the air, wind, and, according to some fae, the weather itself.

Tarasque - the lionlike beasts are larger than elephants with bodies covered in rock-like turtle shells with spikes, they have six clawed legs and long ridged snakelike tails ending in spiked ball. Some have scorpion tails, others forked tails.

Tree People - A race of fae tree humanoids with bark for skin, wide eyes, and loosely foliated branches for hair. Known for their ancient wisdom and ability to speak with all fae flora and fauna.

Tree Shepherd - a special clan of leshies who control any number of magical, sentient trees—walking, crawling, or flying.

Troll - a carnivorous ugly giant humanoid fond of human or humanoid flesh. The baldish but hairy humanoids have large noses and ears, arms are longer than average, their legs a bit shorter, and both hands and feet are oversized. They are nocturnal creatures and hide underground or deep caves during the day. Direct sunlight kills them by turning to stone.

Tulen Väki or väki of fire - the clan of haltijas who wear charred brown and orange fabric clothing. They are a race of guardians with the elemental magically ability to conjure and control fire and use warm air to heal or burn.

<u>Unicorn</u> - a magical horse with a large single horn one to two feet long protruding from his forehead. They can be of any color and different kinds have differing magical properties; some are also winged and can fly. Unicorns are a favorite steed of elves and an animal companion to fairies.

<u>Väki</u> - a clan of haltijas. Besides the **tulen väki** or väki of fire there are also väki of specific trees, forests, mountains, water, precious metals or gems, underground lands, etc.

<u>Woodland Elf</u> - an elfin sub-race known as the best trackers in the forests with strong societies built around hunting. They have eyesight more powerful than eagles and magically can see the "after-presence" of prey they are tracking. There are two main divisions: Rustic—who live in wooded lands of modest hamlets, and Hunter—who fashion themselves after high elves and live in large tree cities.

ABOUT THE AUTHOR

Austin Dragon is author of the new epic fantasy adventure *Fabled Quest Chronicles*, the cyberpunk detective series, *Liquid Cool*, the *After Eden Series* (including the *After Eden: Tek-Fall* mini-series), and the *Sleepy Hollow Horrors*. He is a native New Yorker, but has called Los Angeles, California home for the last twenty years. Words to describe him, in no particular order: U.S. Army, English teacher, one-time resident of Paris, political junkie, movie buff, Fortune 500 corporate recruiter, renaissance man, dreamer.

He is currently working on new books and series in science fiction, fantasy, and classic horror!

Connect with Austin on social media at:

Website and blog: http://www.austindragon.com

Twitter: https://twitter.com/Austin_Dragon

Pinterest: http://www.pinterest.com/austindragon

Google+: https://google.com/+AustinDragonAuthor

Goodreads: https://www.goodreads.com/ADragon

<u>**Other books by Austin Dragon**</u>

See all my books at: http://www.austindragon.com/books